Swifter Wings
than Time

By the same author

Time Will Tell
Familiar Acts

Swifter Wings than Time

JUNE BARRACLOUGH

'Love hath swifter wings than Time'
Edmund Waller (1606–1687)

ROBERT HALE · LONDON

Photoset in North Wales by
Derek Doyle & Associates, Mold, Clwyd.
Printed in Great Britain by
St Edmundsbury Press Ltd, Bury St Edmunds, Suffolk.
Bound by WBC Ltd, Bridgend, Mid-Glamorgan.

Contents

Prelude

1981

'Here it is,' said the young woman. 'Uncle Jacob said I must give it to you – with his love. I'm sorry I've been so long –'

The old lady in the high armchair before the fire of real logs, real flames, turned towards her granddaughter.

'Did you look inside?' she asked in an amused tone of voice.

'No, I promised him I wouldn't. He said it was to be a surprise.'

The blue-papered package was secured with removable Sellotape so that the old lady's hands might easily strip it off. She did so, unfolded the paper and found a stiff-backed envelope inside.

'Hand me that paper-knife will you? – on the table.'

Rachel found it and gave it to her and the grandmother slowly slit open the envelope, peered inside. Something wrapped in tissue paper, but a card as well. She tipped the envelope upside down and took the card out.

'Give me my glasses, dear – I used to keep them round my neck but my husband thought it made me look too school-mistressy.'

The glasses were found, handed over, and put on. Rachel tried not to hover. The card was none of her business. But the old woman read the message slowly before putting down the card and contemplating the tissue-wrapped inner parcel. Then, suddenly she began to unwrap it, and finally sat holding two photographs.

After a pause, she said, 'He's had the old one copied to make it bigger and clearer. Look!'

Rachel advanced to the chair and looked over her

grandmother's shoulder. On her lap was a group photograph of some poor-looking children standing in three rows behind two male teachers, one of the latter with an enormous moustache. '1885' was written at the bottom in curly script.

The same photograph, but larger and no longer sepia-tinted, was being scrutinized by the older woman. Rachel took hold of the smaller one. Straightaway she recognised one of the boys. Tall and handsome, fairish-haired, with a straight nose. It could have been taken in the boyhood of the man she had just left in London, except for the clothes. Pointing to a smaller boy standing next to him, a boy with darker hair, but a nice-looking boy too, her grandmother said – 'That's my father – your great-grandfather – James Caston.'

'Who's that?' asked Rachel, pointing to the taller, fairer, boy, though she knew already who it must be.

'James Stainton.'

Now at last they might talk, thought Rachel. But how to begin?

'That was how it all began,' said Freda, still looking at the photograph.

Part 1

i   1885

There were over forty children that year, boys and girls, in Standard Three, Mr Taylor's class, at Wike Board School. Five of the boys were called William, with the variations of Bill and Billy, Will and Willie. There were three Herberts – two Berts and a Herbie, two Ernests and two Wilfreds, one of the latter a Fred. Also other Freds of the plain sort, and two Alfreds, one of whom was known as Fred and the other as Alf. But the two who were called James curiously enough never had their names shortened to Jimmy or Jim, except by their enemies.

On the class photograph of that year – an innovation, the first time the school has been photographed – James Stainton and James Caston are standing next to each other in a windswept playground, mill chimneys as backdrop. The master, Charles Taylor, sits on a too small chair in the middle of the front row next to the Headmaster, Mr Roebuck, whose moustaches are bristling with cold. If you look carefully you will see that of the boys all but the two Jameses are scowling: arms folded like puny prize-fighters they look stonily ahead. Standard Three have been well-drilled. The girls stand together on the other side of the picture, pinafores over their dark frocks, and you can see one girl's boots at the end of one row, Cissie Phillipson's. She is eight years old, as they all are except for Bill Boocock who is nine-and-a-half but has been kept down a year for stupidity.

James Stainton, a tall, handsome, neatly dressed boy, and James Caston, likewise good-looking, but smaller, were inseparable at that time, which was odd when you came to think about it, Stainton's father being an overlooker and piece taker-in at Marshall's Mill, and little Caston the son of a humble weaver in the same mill with few prospects. But earlier that year they had become friends as the result of a fight which had taken place just behind the playground featured in the photograph. Not between the two of them, no, neither liked fighting – but James Caston *was* one of the combatants. Fights swept up all the homegoing children into a tight knot of watchers, and were usually held at the edge of the school 'field', a wilderness that reached beyond the asphalt playground at one side of the school up to the mill dam. Some fights were of course spontaneous and did not gather so many spectators but this one was like an old-fashioned marriage – 'arranged' – the teachers having been, as all knew, convened by Mr Roebuck to a meeting in one of the upstairs classrooms, an unusual occurrence in itself, something to do with the last inspection.

The reason for this fight was simple. James Caston was not an unpopular boy, if not as respected as the other . James. Sometimes, however, one or two of the rougher children would jeer at him, even some of the girls, and shout 'James Caston's Mam's a fast 'un', probably because they had heard some rumour at the mill where his mother also wove. Maybe too it was because he was such a nice-looking boy. He put on no airs, but his looks disturbed them and he became a scapegoat for their frustrations. He bore all this stoically with a shrug of the shoulders. Other girls, gentler ones, liked him, though he was not yet such an object of covert admiration as was James Stainton. The latter was however seen as a bit stuck up, though this did not detract from the slight awe with which they regarded him.

The day of the fight Bill Boocock had surpassed even himself. He was a bull-like boy with big red fists and a big head, and his cuffs and blows were legion. Even girls kept out of his way. Up till now, however, James Caston had been spared his taunts and his fists, since he knew how to keep well away from bullies, unlike others who would defend themselves by trying to aim a kick in the groin or ganging up in twos or threes. But that morning Billy had bullied one of the girls. Not Cissie Phillipson, who was well able to look after herself, but a smaller, cleverer, girl, Elsie Johnson, who despised him.

The boys and girls didn't play together and were also divided in the classroom, boys on one side, girls on the other. There were two playgrounds, or rather one divided into two, with a door at each end of the school building, one for boys, the other for girls. Occasionally of course there were forays from the boys' end into the girls' territory, but on the whole the girls kept strictly to themselves, often taking a long rope into the 'field' and indulging in complicated skipping games. But this dinner-time Bill must have chased Elsie into the field. Whether she had answered some threat of his with a rude rejoinder or some taunt about his lack of brain was not clear. Something had snapped in Bill and he had held her pinned to the railings and pulled out her hair-ribbons, twisting her arm behind her back. There, James Caston had come upon her, abandoned and weeping. The bell for afternoon classes had already sounded, but Elsie's arm hung limp and her face was tear-stained, her ribbons on the ground. If he had been more perceptive he might have noticed that she looked more angry than hurt. 'What's up Elsie?' he asked. Amid fresh sobs she told him, not detailing the reason for Bill's attack but gulping out that her arm was brocken she was sure it was brocken. 'I'll pay him back! I'll get him!' said James. 'You'd best go and tidy yoursen up,' he added kindly.

It was a matter of honour that you did not grass upon your classmates though the girls did sometimes complain of the boys, which might lead to a caning. Sometimes even parents had been known to sort things out. 'I want him punished,' said Elsie. 'I'll tell Mr Taylor.'

'Nay,' said James. 'Don't now – I'll thump him!'

'Will you really, James?' She must have looked doubtful. James was now committed to an action which his common sense told him would end in disaster.

The first lesson that afternoon was handiwork for the boys, neddlework for the girls, in different rooms. The rumour was passed on behind hands that James Caston had challenged Big Bill Boocock to a fight after school because he'd picked on a lass. Big Bill sat scowling, not making more than a perfunctory effort to paste together his 'book-backs' from material given to the school by a friendly wallpaper merchant. The jackets were for hymn books and the few text books Standard Three possessed. After Standard One, slates were discontinued, and everybody was given an exercise book for sums and composition, which also needed strengthening. James Caston, a deft and nimble-fingered boy, was not so quick with his task today, already regretting his quixotic promise to Elsie, for he knew he would lose the fight. Nevertheless the others were excited. Nobody liked Bill Boocock. Not because he was stupid but because he was a bully.

James Stainton too was impressed. He was a healthy-looking boy who had been in the class only a term, having moved back from a more salubrious part of the town when his father was promoted to overlooker at a bigger mill. His hair was longer than that on the other boys' cropped pates and was of a pleasing fairness. He always looked clean. 'He'll get himself killed,' he was thinking to himself when he heard of James Caston's challenge. As he cut and snipped and folded and pasted his task, accomplishing twice as much as any other boy in half the time, he wondered what he could do to help the smaller lad. They were a daft lot here, he could not help thinking. But if Boocock had 'brayed' Elsie Johnson he could not help wishing it were himself who had found her. He needed some act to establish himself even more firmly amongst these new mates. It was rumoured that Cissie Phillipson, who was self-important, was going to tell Mr Roebuck, but he didn't believe that. Cissie didn't court unpopularity. Anyway, boys fought all the time; the whole school seemed sometimes to be fighting, though it was unusual for a big lad like Bill to fight a lass.

When he came back from ringing the handbell, his new job as class monitor, and the class was dismissed to leave early that afternoon, James Stainton went up to the other James who was surrounded by a crowd of children as they filed out of school past the handbasin and the coat pegs and through the door into the playground where there was already a group of gossiping girls. He could not see Elsie Johnson among them.

'Are you really going to fight Bill Boocock?' asked James. The other boy was looking pale, but he flushed, saying, 'I promised Elsie. He hurt her arm an' all.'

'I'll be your second then,' said James Stainton with a recollection of some duel fought in a book given him for Christmas.

James Caston felt awkward. He didn't know the other James very well although he was aware of his father's position in the mill.

'Out! Go home the lot of you. Get along with you all! We're busy,' shouted Miss Ashworth, shoving them all into the playground and shutting the door when all were away. They were the last boys to leave and somebody else was in charge of the girls' end to check there were no lingerers.

'It means I hold your jacket and summon medical aid if you're injured,' he said.

'You what?'

'A doctor. And if it's an arranged fight you have to have an ally.'

James Caston tried to look grateful but he was dreading the contest. Already he could see Bill Boocock at the far end of the playground swinging his arms. A few onlookers were already scuffling around in half combat.

'He's over by the field,' he said.

'He's big, so you'll have to punch him low down – try and trip him up,' his advisor went on. 'Do you want to practise on me?'

'Nay,' replied James Caston. 'You'd beat me too.'

Big James looked amused but he felt this was really no laughing matter. He wouldn't really want to fight Bill himself and he was nearly as tall if not so burly.

"Am bound to lose – but'a promised,' said James Caston.

'You've got guts,' said Stainton. He was going to add 'I wouldn't like to be in your boots,' but forebore, from delicacy.

The knot of spectators had already moved up around Bill at the edge of the 'field' and there was a feeling of heavy suspense in the air, a smell of blood. Fights were supposed to be forbidden in the school grounds except for the usual scuffling and horseplay, but arranged fights provided regular excitement, often leading on to other fights and to a realignment of power, or promises to 'get thee tomorra'. But unlike some schools in the town this one did not have regular gangs.

They saw the two Jameses walk up, and one girl said, 'What's Teacher's Pet doing with James?' The girls were excited but there was still no sign of Elsie.

'Are you sweet on Elsie then?' the bigger boy was asking the coming warrior as they came up.

'Nay! But he's a right bully. She'll have gone home to her Mam. Do you think her arm was broken?'

'Nay, lad,' replied Stainton in his best imitation of his father pooh-poohing some extravagant claim at home. 'Nay – she'd have yelled louder, and they'd have noticed.'

They came up to the battlefield near where the fence had fallen down into the field.

It was March, and cold. 'Rub your hands on the side of your trousers to get 'em going,' said James Stainton. 'Try and get him down – trip him up, then you can punch him when he's on the ground – that's fair, he'd do same to you.'

But Little James knew that Boocock could punch him anyway, didn't need to bother about getting him at a disadvantage. He was in a daze. But then, suddenly as he looked over at Boocock he felt unafraid. He was right to challenge him, but if he was going to be killed let it be over quick.

'Here there James Caston,' bellowed Bill Boocock. 'Want a feight?'

'Aye.'

The children crowded into a circle to protect the fight from the prying eyes of adults, and the arena was ready. Outer jackets were taken off, James Stainton solemnly taking Little James's thin grey button-up top.

Bill Boocock was punching the air and almost dancing with glee. He still had an under-jacket on; the one on the ground was stained and dirty, a large rent in the back and one sleeve thick with mud.

Alf Naylor shouted out: 'We'll start you off – I'll count three. Keep still, Boocock. Where's t'other lad?'

'Reet. Art ready?' bellowed Bill.

'Aye.' James Caston stepped into the 'ring'.

'Fists – no kickin',' shouted another boy.

Into a sudden silence, Alf intoned 'One, two –'

James Caston squared up to the larger lad who seemed like a giant to him and from whom there emanated a sour smell. If he could be nippy like, Bill being so big and slow, he might get round his back and pin one of his arms. He couldn't aim higher than the other boy's shoulders.

'Three –!' shouted Alf.

The girls' indrawn breath could be heard for a second like a sigh over the sea, but then the air filled with shouts and James Caston shouted too – 'Take that, you big bully!' and lunged sideways. Bill had taken aim with his fist at James's chin but had missed, but James was not to be spared for long. Angry, hating this great lump of a lad, he began to rain blows upon his stomach, but Bill took his flailing arms and pinned them behind him, twisting him round. James took aim with his leg and kneed Boocock once more, almost turning a somersault to do so. Then

Bill roared out a sound like 'Bugger' and stumbled, and they were both on the ground. The shouting and booing rose to a crescendo as they rolled over and over, the small boy quicker, trying to get on top, unable to because of the other's superior force. Then, with a lunge, James's nose was punched with a big raw red fist and he felt a warm sticky sensation. Enraged, he seized Boocock's ears and squeezed and squeezed. But Bill's blood was up. He pulled the hands away, took James's head, the boy trying to push him off with all his might. Bang went the head on the bare ground.

'Give in! Give in!' he shouted. The girls were shouting, 'Come on, James, come on!' But James lay motionless on the ground.

'You've killed him!' shouted Cissie.

'Stop t' fight,' shouted Alf Naylor. Bill stood up, grinning.

'Let's have a look,' said James Stainton in the sudden silence.

'Gerroff,' said Boocock then and pushed his way through the crowd. Big James knelt down at James Caston's side. 'Give us a hankie,' he said. A girl obliged.

'Eh up! There's teacher,' shouted a girl and they all, except Stainton, turned to look. But Boocock was well away over the drystone wall into the mill field.

James Stainton wiped the blood of Little James's face, which was white, his eyes closed. Cautiously, he felt the back of the boy's head. There wasn't any blood there, he'd just knocked himself out, or rather Bill Boocock had.

At that moment Little James opened his eyes. James Stainton felt an enormous relief, and registered at the same time a strange sort of attraction emanating from that pale face. 'You did right well,' he whispered.

The crowd had now all mysteriously melted away though a few girls were still standing at the far edge of the playground near the gate.

Miss Jackson was approaching, uselessly blowing a whistle.

'Can you sit up?' Caston tried, managed with the other boy's help and was promptly sick. He had guts, thought Big James. To pit himself against that great lad who had more strength than he knew what to do with and no brains.

'Have you been fighting?' She came puffing up, the teacher, with her silly question, reproving him who had nothing to do with it.

'Aye,' he replied briefly.

'Can you stand up, James Caston?'

'He's been sick, Miss.'

'But who was he fighting? Not you, James Stainton?'

'No, Miss.' But his lips were sealed to any further enquiry and she knew she would get nowhere with any more questions.

Together they hauled James up, groggy, but fortunately in one piece. He touched the back of his head gingerly. Head banging was forbidden – like biting and scratching, which the girls did when they fought. Or had he just fallen? He couldn't remember. It was over! He looked round for his vanished but not vanquished opponent.

'His nose is bleeding,' stated Miss Jackson unnecessarily. – 'Come into school and I'll mop him up.'

Leonie Jackson was relieved the damage did not seem too great. It had been her job to clear the girls' end after Miss Ashworth had gone up to the meeting, but she hadn't seen the children round the corner by the field. She wanted to go home, hadn't been asked to stay for the meeting since she was only a probationer. But she'd been tidying up her classroom for a few minutes when a faint shouting had penetrated her consciousness and alerted her to the continued presence somewhere of children. Would she be blamed if someone had got hurt? She wasn't sure. They were always having fights, these children, little savages.

'Sh!' she said and put her finger on her lips as they passed the stairs to the upper classroom where Mr Roebuck was in conclave with his acolytes. At the basin she took James's handkerchief, soaked it in cold water, mopped the other boy's face and forehead, made him stand with his head leant back, helped him put on his jacket when the bleeding seemed to have stopped. 'Hold the compress to your nose,' she advised. 'And get off home the two of you. I'm surprised at you, James Caston. I didn't think you went in for blood-baths,' she added as they turned to go. He was such a good-looking little boy. She felt she'd rather like to mother him. The other boy had not been the one he had fought, she was sure.

Little James's colour was slowly returning though the lump on the back of his head had swelled up. She made a mental note to check on him tomorrow provided he were in school.

The two boys trailed slowly out.

'You were right brave,' said Big James as they walked out of the school gate together, crossed the road and stood for a moment.

'Thanks,' said Caston. 'I lost though.'

'Nowt to that. Hope he's scared – they'll tell him you're dead, I expect.'

Afterwards James Caston could hardly believe he had fought Bill Boocock. Some unspoken common agreement kept the two henceforth apart.

The two Jameses became firm friends from that day on, the only ones allowed to call each other Jim or Jimmy. Unalike in background as they were, there was something they shared; perhaps it was a sense of justice. They admired each other, though they never declared such sentiments aloud.

Elsie Johnson had never even said thank you, only, 'You shouldn't have fought him. I'd have got my Dad.'

'That's girls for you,' said James Stainton.

Bill Boocock remained unpopular with both staff and scholars but was used more and more as time went on by Mr Roebuck when animal strength was needed for moving desks and chairs, tables and blackboards.

When James Stainton thought about that fight later he couldn't believe that Little Jim had it in him. He was such a girlish-looking lad, easy to please, kind. The girls liked him too, no doubt about it.

Eventually Big James went off to Higher Grade School at eleven but they still met in the city and went out together now and again. They both played chess, and Stainton's father sang in the Old Choral Society so got them tickets for the concerts. It was a pity, he said, that Castons didn't have the brass to educate their lad. But Little James didn't become a half-timer; at thirteen he was apprenticed to an engineer to learn the trade of engine fitter for seven years. Big Jim, after a course at the 'Tech', joined the firm in which his father was to rise from overlooker to manager, later to found his own mill, a small one to begin with. Yet throughout all their adolescence, until that day in September 1896 when at the age of nineteen Caston 'had to get wed' to a girl called Nell, Cissie Phillipson's sister, who was only seventeen, they would watch out for each other. When a daughter was born to the young couple, whom they named Freda Eileen, they drifted apart somewhat, but James Stainton never forgot his old friend. The affection was possibly more on his side, he thought, but Caston, always one for the girls as he grew up, had been 'caught' too young, a fact which his friend regretted. He didn't blame Nell Phillipson; James Caston was an attractive young man, and had good prospects.

Part 1

ii *Freda*

1919–

For a breeze of morning moves,
And the planet of Love is on high,
Beginning to faint in the light that she loves
On a bed of daffodil sky ...
Alfred, Lord Tennyson, *Maud*, xxii.2

Freda's mother Nell Caston, once Nell Phillipson, wasn't a bit like her sister Cissie. She was pliant and affectionate, and so dependent upon her husband for confirmation of her own worth that when James Caston died suddenly of the Spanish flu in the autumn of 1918 she seemed to shrink, become parched like an underwatered plant.

Cissie tried to be sympathetic to her sister. After all, to think that they'd all come through this dreadful war, her brother-in-law included – though he'd never volunteered for the front and was too old by 1917 to be called up – only for him, the breadwinner, the father, the husband, to be struck down at only forty-one.

Nell was thirty-nine and had looked even younger before that terrible afternoon when she'd held her husband's hand for the last time as she sat at his bedside in the infirmary. After that, everyone had done their best to rally round her. Freda had been very upset, and sorry too, naturally, for her mother. She had liked her father, whom she strongly resembled. But the resilience of youth, and a certain impatience and irritation she

had often felt in the past for her mother, allowed her to hold on
to her self-control in public. At the funeral she supported Nell,
whose arm was tightly held on the other side by sister Cissie, but
she was able at the same time as mourning her father to note
who had come to the church and who had not. There was a tall
man whose name she could not remember though she'd seen
him before. He was wearing an officer's greatcoat and carrying
his cap, just as though he had that morning arrived back from
France.

It was November, and peace had just been declared, but the
people were pinched, thin, grey, from four years of rationing
and hardship. Freda however did not look either grey or
pinched, but alive with the bloom of youth. She was twenty-one,
taller than her mother, and with James's straight nose and
brown eyes. But unlike the father whose death she was
mourning she had never given that impression of gentle
bewilderment which had sometimes been his. Nor was she in any
way like her mother who normally exuded a lazy content, even
sleepiness, an easygoing woman who besides worshipping her
husband had always been a little afraid of her daughter.

Like Freda, Cissie had in spite of her grief registered the
presence of Nell's husband's old friend James Stainton in his
army togs. It was years since she had seen him to speak to,
though their James said he had met him once or twice when the
latter was home on leave. But Staintons were no longer on a level
with Castons, if they ever had been.

Before the war James Stainton had built up the business that
his father had started and it had been carried on by his father
when he volunteered to fight. He'd soon be taking up the reins
again, she thought. His father, now in his late sixties, would be
wanting to retire. They said Old Stainton had been strongly
against James's volunteering. But at the same time he must have
been proud of him, and considerably relieved when he returned
safely. So many young men, especially the officers, had not. She
wondered if Nell had seen him, over at the side.

If James Caston had married at nineteen when Freda was on
the way, his old school-mate had waited for another ten years or
so before marrying Evangeline Harris, one of the daughters of a
wealthy businessman, whom he had met at the tennis club. The
Staintons had had two children, a boy, Valentine, and a
daughter, Mary, before Evangeline had had a 'nervous

breakdown'. Only later had it been revealed that the Harris family was mentally unstable, with a streak of religious melancholia. James had not looked beyond surface attractions when he courted her. His emotions towards her had never been deeply engaged, but that was a secret between him and his Maker. As he stood pretending to sing a hymn, he thought he'd done well in every department of his life but the one in which James Caston had been lucky. Women had always liked Little James but he had been faithful to his Nellie, had said so once when James asked him.

Stainton could not help feeling now a kind of subterranean grievance that a marriage begun as you might say with a shot-gun had turned out so well, even though after Freda's birth Nell had been told to have no more children. The birth had been almost a disaster for the young woman and James Stainton understood it would have been as much a one for his friend if she had died. No details had been gone into but Caston had made it clear he valued his wife more than any possible future sons. There were ways of averting pregnancy, he said, and no more children had been born to the Castons after Freda. The couple had seemed happier than any other couple he knew in town. In the past, young women might have wanted to mother Little James, but he had turned the tables and looked after his wife in the same way. He had had a steady job as fitter in the small engineering firm he'd been with since his apprenticeship finished.

James Stainton had in the past invited the little girl, Freda, to the Christmas party he gave every year at his own mill, and he remembered the composed child who looked so like her father. He glanced over at her now, could see only her profile where she looked straight at the parson, her face rising out of a high-collared coat. He ought to have gone over to see her and her mother before today, but felt some reluctance, a notion that they might think he was condescending. When the parson began to read from Corinthians he was suddenly back at school, remembering old Roebuck read from the good book ... sitting on a bench next to the boy whose adult form was now in a brown box at the front of the church. Tears prickled his eyes, but whether they were for James or himself or shed for all the pain and misery he'd seen in France, he could not have said. It occurred to him that in a strange sort of way he'd loved James

Caston, that there had been something that had lain in all their lives unfinished between them and now it was too late to do anything about it. His boyhood seemed more interesting, more important, than his present life ... Ridiculous! ... he enjoyed business, loved his children.

He wondered what Freda was doing now. When he remembered seeing her last she'd been about eleven, must be ten years back, walking along with her father on a Saturday afternoon in the big city of Woolsford. They lived in a small terrace house in Brigford, a house where he had never visited, for some reason keeping his friendship with James, such as it was, a separate thing, belonging to a drink in the town or a chat at his club, where Caston always looked uneasy. He remembered James saying that Freda was a 'clever girl' and they hoped she'd do some commercial course so that when she was older she'd be able to earn a living away from the mills. Later he'd wanted her to be a teacher, but she'd refused, said she didn't like children.

Stainton's own children, at home with their mother, seemed a thousand miles away as he stood with the rest of the mourners in the cemetery chapel. He could not help feeling relieved that he was for an hour or two away from both Lina and the two bairns, it would be time enough soon to take up the reins of home and work. This was his last leave, and demob would soon follow. Had he joined up to escape his wife and children, to have a man's life? He'd been doing well and had lifted the firm up since he'd joined it at the turn of the century, yet he'd wanted a different challenge, he supposed. It *had* been some sort of a relief too to get away, in spite of the dangers and the dirt and the battlefield, just as today he was back with his boyhood memories, away from 'ordinary' life. He looked at his watch.

Cissie, who had never married, was thinking what a handsome man he was. Especially in his uniform. What had her brother-in-law ever had in common with him? Still, he must have felt enough to come to the funeral, must have retained something from his early days after he became a rich man, he with his mill and all. They'd all have a word with him after the service was ended or when they had gone over into the cemetery.

Freda, coming out of the chapel, also noticed him again. Now she remembered who he was – that friend of Dad's who had made money and yet who had joined up, the man who years ago had given parties for the children of his operatives, to which she'd been invited. Their eyes met as he moved up to them and Cissie prepared to shake hands with him, Nell seemingly too tear-sodden to acknowledge people.

'I am sorry,' he said, and Cissie said, 'Thank you for coming, Captain Stainton –' as though she hadn't sat in the same classroom with him over thirty years before! Nell looked up then and murmured something.

'This is Freda,' said Cissie later when they had had the committal and there was still a crowd of friends and wider family and neighbours round the grave or beginning to straggle back to the cemetery gates.

They shook hands, and James said, 'Your father was a great friend of mine. If there is anything I can do?'

Freda said, 'Thank you for coming – I remember you, Mr Stainton.'

How like her father she looked, and yet so young, with an expression he could not quite give a name to. 'Please come along to the tea,' said Cissie. 'Everyone is invited.' She thought, let him see how we live, Mr High and Mighty, who lived in a big house in Eastcliff.

'Thank you – but I'm afraid I have to get back, Cissie. Don't forget, I would be glad to help.' Did he mean financially?

Nell looked up again then as he began to move away. 'Freda is a secretary,' she said inappropriately. 'James wanted her trained, Mr Stainton.'

'Yes, of course.' He shook hands again, and then with Freda looking at him he felt at last the reality of Little James's death. As though somehow, being no longer there, he was yet being carried on in some curious way in his daughter, children being the only immortality most of us ever know. But he turned away and put his cap back on. Others crowded round then and he walked down the cemetery paths and saw the waiting carriage which was to take the principal mourners to the house where old Mrs Phillipson was probably waiting with cups of tea and ham. It was bitterly cold.

Freda felt her nose freezing and her eyes stinging in the wind. What a handsome man though, Captain Stainton, and he had looked really sorry. She felt compunction then for her mother, decided to try to show her a little more affection to tide her over the next few weeks. But it was all so dreary, this benighted place, and the cold and the death and the prospect of nothing now but work, work, work. Mr Fuller, her father's employer, had promised a little pension, but it was not enough. Mam might have to work again. Cissie had been a piece weaver for years.

She saw the tall military figure turning down the road in the distance but was then recalled to her duties by her Aunt Cissie and they all moved on and out.

A few months after her father's funeral Freda was sitting, alone for once, before the kitchen fire of the small house on Rose Terrace. Nan, her maternal grandmother who now spent a lot of time with them, was visiting a neighbour a few doors down, Cissie was doing an extra shift at the mill, and her mother was lying on her bed upstairs, still heavy with a grief that would not leave her.

1919 had begun hard for them all. Freda was still looking for a better-paid office job, one for which her commercial training had well fitted her. From the middle of the war she'd worked in the office of a mill as the looms rolled out greatcoats and gaberdines, busy because of the war. At least it hadn't been a munitions factory, but it had been poorly paid. Cissie had found her that work when a factory job in munitions threatened and the office staff had been cut at the place where she'd worked from the age of sixteen. Clerical and typing work had been hard to find unless you went into the city. Her father had encouraged her to stay for the time being at home with a handy job only half a mile away. He himself had been busy with engine orders, often working long hours, and had wanted to feel that Freda would be there as companion to her mother, which would be less likely if she arrived home from Woolsford an hour later, and tired, and had to leave early in the morning to catch the train from the town centre.

Cissie hadn't been living with them then. Only since her father died had Cissie decided to move in and help out. Freda resented her presence but knew her mother needed her near. Old Nan lived a few doors down, where Cissie usually shared her home. Nan lived on the money her children managed to give her, for she had had a very large family, six sons as well as the two girls Nell and Cissie. Cissie's money was now helping to keep Nell afloat, along with Freda's own meagre earnings and the tiny pension. Freda would have preferred their taking in a lodger but that was out of the question unless Cissie moved away and lodged back with Nan. As it was, Freda was now squeezed into the tiny box-room at the top of the house and Cissie had Freda's own old room, for there were only two proper bedrooms in all. Only because they needed Cissie's financial contribution was the arrangement at all tolerable. They ought to feel grateful, for Cissie was a skilled weaver on piece work and earned good wages. Nan had said she could manage for a bit without her elder daughter, two of her sons helped her out. The truth was that she had always found her bossy – no wonder she'd never wed!

It was Saturday afternoon and Freda would soon have to rouse herself to go down the road into the town to buy some soap for Monday's washday. Cissie had asked her to, and she ruled the roost at home at present, Nell being too lethargic to think straight, so it was Freda's job to go shopping for odd items forgotten by Cissie. Nan did the food market every day, seemed to enjoy it, but even her efficiency sometimes broke down for she was getting on, and forgot things. Usually Freda liked to escape out of the house, especially if they were all in it, but was savouring half an hour to herself, hoping her mother was asleep. It was March and bitterly cold still; the fire banked up with 'slack' for long-lasting warmth was comforting. Coal was short, but they managed. Over and over again they had calculated what they could manage to live on and had so far avoided the necessity for Nell to go to work. Provided Freda could find a better paid job, they would be all right. If she did, Cissie might go back to Nan and leave them in peace and her mother rouse herself back to life.

Freda had never been sure exactly how much her father had earned. He'd known her own wage to the last penny, but men guarded information about their finances jealously, and even Nell had not seemed sure. Freda had a vague idea that it was about four pounds ten shillings, but prices had advanced so much since 1914 that anything extra he'd managed to bring in had been swallowed up. Maybe now the war was over things would get back to normal. But if prices fell, that might mean less work. She knew about such matters from her own work in the office and from listening to the boss and his brother talking in her presence.

She got up slowly when a glance at the big black clock with its

gold and white face over the mantel told her it was already four
o'clock. She might go into the market as well to see if there were
any fents that might do for clothes. She needed a new dress. One
thing Nell could do well was sew on the old treadle
sewing-machine that had stood in Nan's parlour ever since
Freda could remember, unveiled at night when housework was
done. Freda had never been able to get the hang of it, in spite of
being an engineer's daughter, but her mother was clever with
such things and used to go over to 'borrow' it. If only she would
perk up! – Perhaps a nice bit of material might encourage her to
do some sewing, and once she was back doing something she
liked she'd stop brooding?

Although the kitchen was their chief sitting-room on most
days, there was no mirror there and Freda could not be
bothered to go into the adjoining, cold 'best room' to look in the
glass. One cheek was burning from the fire, and one leg, where
she'd pulled up her long skirt, was also warm, the other freezing.
She hoped she'd not mottled her legs unpleasantly under her
wool stockings. You always paid for warmth one way or another.

As she went out into the backyard which they shared with the
rest of the terrace, it not being divided there, only at the front
where the tiny gardens were now full of vegetables, she thought
how wonderful it would be if they could all go backwards in time
a year or two. Even if the war *was* still going on she'd rather have
her father alive. People said he'd spoilt her, but that was not her
own opinion. She missed him, but as much for the sake of a
harmonious household and her mother's peace of mind as for
her own. This was not altruism but an expression of her true
feelings. When things were ordered and peaceful at home she
could concentrate without guilt upon herself, dream her
dreams, whether of a dashing suitor or a new dress or a good
meal … not that she expected anything but a new dress. Food
was still boring if not positively nauseous; the men she met, who
might be sweet on her but too tongue-tied to express themselves,
bored her too, and so she tended to concentrate her thoughts on
clothes. There was a 'gown shop' in the little town, patronized
for the most part by mill-owners' wives who could not be
bothered to go into Woolsford, and you could get ideas from
what the proprietress, 'Madam Joyce', had in her window. Then
Nan could cut it out and her mother make it for her; it was about
time she pulled herself together. How she could cheer her

mother up was beyond her. She'd tried sympathy, and mutual tears, and expressions of help and loyalty, but her mother was lost, almost zombie-like.

Freda turned down the end of the row where it fronted a large 'unadopted' field which had also been turned over to vegetables but was lying at present mostly unweeded. People were weary. She pulled her collar round her neck and crammed on her brown velvet tam o'shanter. In one hand she held her shopping bag, a coarsely woven hold-all, and needed all her strength to hold on to her cap in the sudden wind that buffeted her at the corner of the lane that led into the main road down to the town. Thoughts of the market were buoying her up a bit for she loved wandering there, though there was not usually much of interest for sale at present. She'd often gone there as a child with her father on a Saturday and they'd listened to the huckster who sold Hodson's gripe syrup and other bottles of 'home-made' bright green and shocking pink mixtures, guaranteed to cure most ills. That made her think of the uselessness of such remedies for the influenza and her face darkened as she turned on to the causeway by the trees that shaded the gardens of the houses at the side of the road. They were larger houses than those of Rose Terrace, some set back a little and backing in their turn on old cottages that had been there for hundreds of years, or so her father had once told her. But she didn't want to think of her childhood. That was now over, her father gone. Though she was twenty-one he'd treated her like a little girl.

A little further down she passed the house the Staintons had lived in after they'd left Wike and come into the town, before old Mr Stainton had moved his family into a largely squarely built 'mansion' with a driveway and a shrubbery in Eastcliff. The Staintons were not really what Nan called 'posh', for like most townsfolk who lived in such houses their money was only a generation old. But they had never been poor either, at least not in the memories of the present inhabitants. Neither had *her* parents ever been poor, as her maternal grandmother's family had once been. There was a wide gulf fixed between the really poor and the respectable skilled workers, the same gulf that was fixed between their own present position, even with money coming in, and those who like the Staintons had left the working class. Others who had not done quite so well as the Staintons but better than the Castons included people like her friend

Kathleen's family who lived in a bigger terrace house set back from the road with a garden in front and net curtains at each window.

Freda understood these distinctions. She would like to live in a larger house even if one not as grand as the Staintons' present residence. Nobody showed respect to folk just because they'd made a pile. You had to earn that in Brigford. Doctors and solicitors apart, they were mostly people possessing much the same background. The doctor's wife, 'Mrs Doctor Green' as she was always called, spoke in a different sort of voice and had a son at boarding school and her own special circle of friends, whom they would see coming out to visit in a motor car, but the doctor's own grandfather had only been a tradesman when all was said and done, even if he were now set apart. Her grandma made even finer distinctions than she did between the various gradations of poor to rich. Sometimes she thought these rigid class divides, which included the No Man's Land between the respectable working class and the middle class – Kath had told her once that *her* father was not a 'worker' – were as subtle as the imperceptible shadings of lilac bushes from palest mauve to mauve with a slight tinge of pink through to purple and then dark violet with a tinge of red. Yet an awful lot of fuss was made, with people standing on their dignity about their exact social position. Her father had not cared about such things, it was mostly women who kept these ideas going. Even Nell would say how honoured she would be if she might come upon one of the doctor's wife's old gowns at a sale at the chapel bazaar – and yet feel it was not quite her place to be seen in them. But you were always taken at your own estimate – that was one thing her father had impressed her with. Don't put on airs, but don't let yourself be trodden on either.

It *would* be pleasant not to be always worrying about money. Not Dad's fault. Business ran the town, provided the mayors and the councillors and governors of the grammar school which Freda had attended from the age of twelve to fifteen before her commercial course. She found her thoughts wandering once again to a better post; she might hear of something through the grapevine this afternoon, you never knew.

She did not really notice the grime and the soot that settled over everything from the factory chimneys, for she was used to it; did not mind walking rather than being carried along in a carriage or even a tram, though that meant you had to be careful when you crossed the road so that you didn't tread into a neat deposit of manure left by one of the many horses that pulled the carts. She crossed the road and went into the little town and on to Commercial Street, smiled as a man passed her and raised his hat. Another of Dad's old friends, she supposed.

A tram passed her at the bottom of the road on its way into town. They said there was going to be a bus service soon between the nearest town and Brigford, that went nearer Rose Terrace. She might catch the tram on its way back and walk through the Rec. Thank goodness it wasn't raining. Puddles were death to smartness when your skirt was long, though they said fashionable people were wearing them an inch or two higher this year and hers were now almost mid-calf. Her boots were dusty though.

She passed one or two citizens in bowlers and wing collars, their heavy dark coats camouflaging stout stomachs. One was twirling a cane. No women from the same class; they'd be at home toasting their feet at the fender on such a cold day. She'd better get a move on, go to the chandler's for the household items and then wander round the old market and perhaps have time to go over to Penny Benham's to look at the gewgaws. She had a weakness for jewellery, and the covered alleyway with its stalls had been a favourite haunt of her childhood. There had been farthing toys, like celluloid dolls, and paper dresses for them, a penny a book, with which she had amused herself. Often as a child she'd have gone for a walk after shopping, sometimes alone, or with other children, before going home, to watch the barges on the canal. Especially if the lock gates were opening, to watch the strong patient horses and the swarthy bargemen people said were a sort of gipsies. Not today though. Too cold, and it was muddy down there – and she was no longer a child.

Brigford had both a river and a canal and there was an 'island' in between the two where old Mr Stainton's sister's husband had started a toffee factory in a hut. Most of the early places of business were started in one-storey huts and there were many other old one-storey buildings squeezed between newer buildings in the town, where the 'tubber' sold and made his wares, or shoemakers plied their trade. The place was always busy and smelly in its valley, like several other towns of the district, none of them far from the open country, near land dotted with quarries out of which the beautiful stone of the area came from which had paved half London. The town was quiet only during Rush Week when all the operatives suddenly decamped *en masse* to the coast, usually to Blackpool, where for a week they would board in houses on little streets not so different from their own, taking their own food to be cooked by the landlady whose pride and joy was her aspidistra in the front window. Freda was remembering such holidays as she bought her soap and candles, recalled to these memories by the name Pocklington which was the same as the man's who sold ice cream on the sands. Holidays seemed not only years ago, which they were, but belonging to another era, pre-war, pre-misery, and seventy miles away.

"Allo, Freda,' said a voice at her elbow and she turned to see a friend of her mother's behind her. 'Bye it's nippy!'

'Yes.'

'How's your Mam then? Any better?'

'Not really – no worse though.'

'Aye she's tekken it hard, has Nell. Well give her my respects – I've to buy summat for my man's tea. They say potted meat's come today and Owd Jim's got tripe.'

Freda moved on, crossed the road and went into the Market Square. James Stainton noticed her bright trim figure standing out against the gloomy grey buildings. He too had been thinking of the coast. Not Blackpool but the more genteel Morecambe where he was considering buying a little villa now he was back at work. For his wife, for Lina, who was still suffering from the 'nerves' she'd had ever since Val was born, worse since the birth of their daughter Mary six years before. Holidays might just set her up, and he could afford to lay out a bit with the profits his father had made, half of which he had handed over to him. Stainton Senior had gone into the mortgage business too some years before and often lent to townsfolk, once they'd saved a deposit, on houses which he'd bought himself from time to time. What with the war reducing this type of business he'd been glad to take over the management of the mill once more, if only temporarily when James volunteered, but swore he'd retire the year of his son's return. He'd probably go to Morecambe himself, thought his son. Which would make it a good idea for Lina to stay there now and again, even for longish periods, where his father could keep an eye on her.

He looked across the street at the disappearing figure of the girl he still thought of as Little Freda, James's own appellation. He wondered if she'd found a better job yet. Since his old friend's funeral he'd been demobbed, then up to his eyebrows for weeks with work. He made a mental note to investigate further.

There was so much to do, for apart from his work at the mill he was involved in the project of establishing a British Legion branch in the town and with vague plans already afoot for a war memorial. Although the armistice had been signed, there had been no date fixed so far for the local people to celebrate the real end of the war. Not surprising, since most things were still rationed. There was a shortage of meat – even he was eating much less than he had in the army. Sugar was scarce and the ubiquitous ration tickets were needed for most things. James Stainton was not the kind of man who would use a black market. Because he had 'brass' it did not mean that he would take unfair advantage of those poorer than himself, though unlike most wives Evangeline Stainton took little interest in following up reports of what was at the butcher's.

How did folk manage financially? He feared things would get worse now the war was over. How did anyone know whether the market for textiles would be the same as before? The town had a variety of industries but textiles were its lifeblood – silk, cotton and wool, both spinning and weaving and dyeing, as well as engineering, wire-drawing, carpet-making and the sale of the stone delved from the nearby quarries.

He went back to Eastcliff on foot – the walk would do him good, he thought. People greeted him as he passed along the road at the bottom of the town with its trams to the city, and after twenty minutes walked up the steep hill to the village where less than ten years ago he'd at first rented then bought a grand house for his bride near his father's house, and called it 'Laurel Bank'. As usual now when he neared the drive that turned off an old lane at the top of the hill and swept across 'his' land to 'his' house he felt a mixture of depression and guilt. He did not think he deserved to be plagued with either. He'd thought that perhaps his absence at the war might have cured or at least alleviated his wife's depression, if that was what it was, but she seemed fixed now in a weary sort of alternation between low spirits and weariness and a hectic new-found belief in God.

He did firmly believe that she wasn't 'mad', only ill. Outwardly she was regarded by outsiders as 'quiet', unless they saw her in elevated mood; and as a rare chosen soul by the priest in Woolsford to whom she confided her insights. This would not have mattered, except that he couldn't have the children affected by her, so had engaged a middle-aged woman to help keep an eye on them and also to teach Mary. Val was at boarding school. James had decided to send him one night when he was in the front line and thought he would never get out of the mess alive. He wanted his son to have a profession. But he didn't want to think about the war. It was *over*. He shook his head involuntarily as he walked through the wrought-iron gate.

Before she died his mother had often come to Laurel Bank to help Lina who took little interest in the running of the house. For the first few years of their marriage Lina had been an active, jolly sort of person, but later, doctor after doctor had pronounced as to the existence of a 'neurasthenic' type of illness, saying time would cure it. The births of the children must have been the catalyst, a shock to her system. But why? She'd been a healthy young woman, good at tennis, reserved towards men – which he'd seen as a good thing at the time – and she'd seemed happy to marry him.

Now the doctors said she needed more activity so he intended to motor to the Dales when the petrol situation improved and take her out of herself. It was just as though she was mourning something, but he couldn't imagine what. He thought of Nell Caston's tear-blotched face – now *she* had something to cry about! But he was beginning to feel cross with Lina again – and that would not do.

He went into the house and the maid, a girl from the mining district – maids were like gold dust, preferring to work in factories – took his hat and coat reverently. He went upstairs. Lina was lying on a long sofa before a bright fire and he said cheerfully, 'I brought you some flowers from Bradley's – I thought as we've nothing much in the hothouses at present you might like a bunch.'

'Oh, thank you, James,' she said weakly. 'How kind.' She looked a caricature of the woman he'd wed ten years ago, spoke mechanically, said only what she knew he wanted to hear.

'How are you feeling?' It was one of her depressed days. He could not decide whether he liked them better than the days on which she became excitable and spoke of Providence, of making a little chapel in the grounds.

'Have the children had their tea? I wouldn't mind a cup – I walked back – sorry if I'm late,' he gabbled out of sheer nervousness.

She rang the bell and asked Joan the maid if the children had eaten.

'Yes, Mum – they're in the nursery with Mrs Petersham.'

'Bring Mr Stainton a tray of tea then,' she ordered.

Now he'd have to sit and drink it with her.

'I was thinking you might like to take a little holiday on the coast,' he began, when he'd drained a cup and poured himself out another.

'Oh, I'm quite all right here, James,' she replied.

'Well, we'll see – I had the idea of buying soon a little place for holidays – the children would like it – do them good – we could all go – stay from time to time …'

'Won't you be too busy?'

She seemed to be making an effort, so he went on. 'I could go for weekends all through the summer once the mill's working smoothly – and I believe Father's thinking about retiring there too!'

He thought, now if I could offer her the promise of a church there with a parson she could talk to. Sure to be plenty doctors there since it's full of old people.

Yet *they* were not old. Lina was only thirty-nine. Half their lives might be before them.

'I know you always want the best for me,' she said in a small voice, but without enthusiasm. He put out his hand and she allowed hers to lie for a moment in his.

'I think I'll go up to the children,' he said. 'They might like a game of Lexicon. Come up to the nursery with me, will you?'

She smiled weakly. 'Sorry, I've a bit of a headache – I'll stay here.'

He sighed. No sooner did he think he was getting somewhere than she brought up some ailment, some excuse. But he must try to be patient. She was less agitated and less depressed than in 1916 before he'd gone away. But his presence did not seem to affect her one jot either for better or for worse. Did she still resent his decision to join up?

Whilst James was playing cards with Mary and Val, rather

enjoying the childish game, Freda was still in the town, staring in the window of Madam Joyce, Mantle-maker, not at a gown but at a hat, a square-cut 'Cossack' hat, in dark brown velvet which she was coveting with all her soul.

She drew away reluctantly. It cost a third of her weekly wage, was not for the likes of her. But why not? She felt cross. It was a fact that she earned at present only thirty shillings a week, and their food bills alone came to just under two pounds for the three of them, four when Nan came round. She decided to go and see how much the tripe cost that the neighbour had mentioned. Meat was still on the ration but there was such a shortage of it that having a ticket meant nothing. Udder and tripe were off the ration, not liked by everyone. Nell however loved it. She'd buy an onion or two to make a nice meal for Sunday. Last week they'd had rabbit pie.

There was just a little left in the market so she bought a bob's worth. Passing on then to the grocer's she saw some tins of salmon and Californian fruit in the window, there only because they were too dear for most folk. If she earned a bit more she'd be able to afford a tin now and then. She was getting like an old housewife, her not even wed! Since her father's death she'd had to grow up. How grand it would be to offer her mother a salmon tea like they'd used to have now and again the three of them in the old days.

She must buy the *Gazette* and see if there was any job advertised – but she knew what the answer would be.

When the letter came signed 'James Stainton' she could not believe it, went rushing to Nell, still in bed that Tuesday morning.

'Look, Mam – it's from Captain Stainton! He says there might be a job for me in the office! He's offering thirty-seven and six a week! – So long as my shorthand is satisfactory, he says.'

'But you never wrote to him, lass?' Nell sat up and leaned on one arm, taking the letter from her daughter.

'No – but you remember he said at the funeral, was there anything he could do –'

'Do you think Cissie spoke to him?'

'She *might* have seen him, but she's said nothing.' Cissie had already left for work before the postman arrived, as her shift started at six.

'She never said owt to me. I expect he's just being kind – he and your Dad were real good pals years ago.'

'He wants me to call in tomorrow night for a "test" when I've thought it over – after work. It's seven and sixpence more than Boothroyd's pay me now. They've only got a clerk who can't type or use shorthand. So he needs a person as soon as possible –' She waited whilst her mother slowly read the rest of the letter. Nell looked less lethargic as she gave the letter back.

'Do you think you're up to it?' she asked shyly.

'Of course I am, Mother – it's what I'm already doing, but the mill's bigger – that'll be why there'll be more work.'

'Will you write to him then saying you'll go in tomorrow to see?'

'I can't now – I've got to go to work in a minute. I will tonight and ask a lad to take the letter in to him.' Neither of them thought of telephoning. Freda was not allowed to use her present office telephone for personal calls.

'How much notice will you have to give Boothroyd's, lass?'

'Well, I won't say anything till I know for certain he wants me. Then I'll ask. Mr Stainton would know, I suppose, how long to wait.'

Her mother lay quietly after Freda had gone to work taking the letter with her. The sun came into the bedroom and she thought it was a good augury. For the first time since her husband had died Nell Caston wanted to get up. She did so, washed her face in water from the ewer, brushed her hair, put on her old skirt, which was too loose round the waist since she'd lost so much weight, and went downstairs. She'd go over to Nan's and tell her the news. She felt quite wobbly as she made her way down the back of the terrace passing each freshly washed and donkey-stoned step until she got to no. 8 and went in without knocking.

The old lady was sitting by her fireside tatting.

She looked up as her daughter came in, but showed no surprise; she'd known she'd come round back to herself one day. 'You'd never guess,' Nell began, and told her mother the whole story quite animatedly. It had given her a new lease of life. Nan listened, said only – 'Well, it's about time he offered something, seeing as how he and James were so thick once. Is Freda pleased?'

'Over the moon but not counting her chickens.'

'Oh, she'll get it – she's a clever lass is Freda!'

They sat on peacefully and then Nan made a pot of tea to be ready for when Cissie came off shift. Cissie'd have something to say, no mistake.

Nell was thinking, Cissie can go back home now! Me and Freda'll be all right!

The night before her interview at Valley Mills Freda had a bath in front of the kitchen fire. The water had to be heated in the boiler, which was at one side of the kitchen range, and then poured into the tin bath that hung in the cellar and was usually brought out only on Fridays. There was no bathroom in any of the houses on Rose Terrace, and the water-closet, a name they now used instead of privy since privies had been fitted with cisterns, was out across the yard. Each house possessed its own in a little brick lean-to whose white-washed walls and stone floor were scrubbed clean every other day.

Before the bath, Cissie had opened a ceremonial tin of corned beef when she came back from work. 'We shouldn't eat it unless I get the job,' suggested Freda who felt uncomfortable. If she did get it it was almost certain that her mother would hint to Cissie that she ought to go back to live with Nan. Nell wasn't very good at asking for things but pursued a sort of sweet obstinacy when she wanted something, usually getting her own way, and Cissie was well aware of the situation but unsure whether her sister's recovery was complete. Nell had seemed to perk up almost miraculously when Freda had received the letter from Stainton.

Freda enjoyed the bath and washed her long hair at the same time, drying it before the kitchen fire. Tomorrow after work she'd take the tram to the 'New Mill' – Valley Mill – 'Stainton's' Mill, and she had decided to take her new skirt to change into after work. Nell was already talking about making her a new dress from the fent Freda had seen in the market but not been able to afford, and looked almost her old self as she made her plans to go over to Nan's sewing-machine and work there for hours in peace.

'Don't talk about it till I know for sure,' said Freda, fearful lest if the job were *not* in the end offered, her mother would relapse into lethargy. What a responsibility she was, now that her husband had died. Yet Freda would rather the responsibility were hers than her Aunt Cissie's. Cissie however was sceptical of most folk and warned her not to rely on Stainton's.

'Those who come last are first to go,' she had said lugubriously, cross that even her best week of piece work would not bring in the same amount as Freda might earn as 'secretary'. 'I hope you haven't forgot your shorthand,' she added. 'You said there'd not been much call for it at Boothroyd's!'

Freda too was a little worried about this if truth were told, but contented herself with browsing before the fire with her old Pitman's as she turned first one side then the other and then her back to the warm glow from the banked-up fire.

'You'll make her nervous,' said Nan who had come round after the bath had been emptied and stowed away down the cellar along with a few eggs in isinglass, a sledge, and the ice skates, wrapped in newspaper, that awaited a winter sufficiently cold to freeze the little lake in the valley.

'You won't be using them skates again,' Cissie said when she came back up the stairs. It had been her father with whom Freda had gone skating two Christmases ago. Why did Cissie always choose to say the things that made her most sad?

When she arrived next evening at a quarter past six at Valley Mills, a little breathless from the walk from the tram stop and worried her hair was flying all over the place in the wind that was hardly ever absent from the town, Freda suddenly stopped feeling nervous. After all, she *had* a job. It wasn't as though they could not manage unless she got another better paid one, though Cissie's presence irritated her. There was a door at the bottom of the building and she could see lights on in the big weaving room through the long windows. The door pushed open and immediately led on to a flight of stairs. She climbed them and saw three doors ahead on this landing. The stairs went on to another storey. One of the doors, a polished mahogany affair, curiously impressive after the dingy stairs and wooden outer door had a brass plate on which was written 'Mr James'. Not even his surname! In the distance she could hear the faint clatter of looms. She knocked at the door and a voice said, 'Come in.' James Stainton rose from his desk across the room by a small window. The room was cluttered with filing cabinets and tables on which were piled samples of wool and bits of stuff. On another table there were large ledgers and in the corner an antler coat and hat-stand.

'How do you do, Freda?' He didn't say 'Miss Caston'. She
supposed it was to make her feel at home. 'Do sit down.' He
pulled a chair out across from his own and went back to sit
behind the desk after taking her coat and hat.

Then he sat looking at her quietly. Was he waiting for her to
say something? 'It is very good of you to think of us,' she began,
nervously now.

'You're very like your father to look at,' was all he said. Then
he seemed to pull himself together and added briskly, 'I shall
have to try you out – have to be fair. If you're satisfactory, you're
with us on a month's probation or they'll think I'm favouring
you! What about if I dictate a letter to you now and see how you
do?'

'I'm very grateful for the chance, Mr Stainton,' said Freda,
taking out her notepad which she carried always in a large bag.
She had decided not to say 'Captain'. 'I wouldn't want to work
anywhere on false pretences.' She felt quite brave saying this and
only hoped she would find she could take down shorthand as
well as his father's old secretary.

'Let's get it over with,' he said. 'Then we'll have a cup of tea,
shall we?' He took a letter from the table before him and having
ascertained she had a pencil began: 'Further to your order on
the 10th ult we are pleased to offer as required ten bales of best
piece worsted grey herringbone at 17/6d wholesale price and
await your further instructions. Yours faithfully, Freda Caston,
pp James Stainton'. He looked at her as he said the last words
and she blushed.

But she looked up. 'I usually put the name of the manager
first, with a "pp", and then mine,' she suggested.

He smiled. Freda was determined to keep her end up, he
thought. That was quite a daring thing to say to the boss. 'Yes,
that sounds better,' he said, and laughed. 'Date at the top. Valley
Mills etc. etc. and I forgot to say it's to Sladdins Tailors, 66
George Street.'

'Yes, I left a space for that,' she replied.

'Now you can type it,' he said and motioned to a large
Remington at a table in the corner. 'We haven't a separate room
for the secretary yet,' he said. 'There's the old clerks' room next
door though and we can fit you out there at first. Florrie Brown
used to work there – the light's better.' He must have been doing
his own typing, she thought.

She took the pad and he handed her a piece of foolscap.

'You want the date under the address or in the middle?' she asked.

'Oh – under the address.'

She got to work and he pushed a bell on the desk which must have been electric for there was a tap at the door and a woman put her head round. 'Tea for two,' he said. 'On a tray, Bessie – and sugar.' She disappeared. Everything seemed easy going, thought Freda. She must not make a mistake though, and have to retype, or he would think her a fudger. It was her experience so far that however easy-going bosses were they preferred their secretaries efficient.

She typed quickly, having decided on a neat layout, and passed the letter to Mr Stainton for his signature. 'Excellent,' he said after a moment's perusal. 'No spelling mistakes either!'

She waited and he said, 'Come and sit at the table and we'll have tea. Afterwards you could type the envelope too.'

'Are you going to send it then?' she asked, surprised, thinking it had been only an exercise.

'Certainly! I don't believe in wasted effort. It will do very well. We are behindhand with the correspondence. You can even post it yourself!'

There was a tap at the door and the 'girl' Bessie, a woman of about forty, sidled in with a tray of tea, white cups, a cream jug and a sugar basin and a large brown teapot. Two biscuits on a plate.

James had hoped to goodness Freda was capable, for what would he say to her if she were not? Her father had always lauded her abilities, but that was the way of fathers. Looking at her letter he had seen immediately that she was more than competent. It looked professional. He poured out the tea, not indulging in any embarrassing byplay over 'Who shall be mother?' He seemed extremely competent himself, thought Freda, accepting the tea gratefully. He did not speak whilst she drank. She wanted to ask, make sure she had the job, but dare not, would leave it to him. He drank his own tea and offered her another cup. 'No? Then I will. I've such a thirst since France.'

She waited. He put his cup down and said, 'I can't offer you as much as the women munitions workers were paid, I'm afraid, and we don't know yet how trade will go this year and next, but what I can give you is over a pound more than my weavers – I'll pay you that from the beginning, but I can't promise a definite rise either later on. That is, if you accept and want the job for the present.'

Freda took a large gulp of air into her lungs. 'You're offering me the job definitely then?'

'Of course I am! The month on probation as I said, but I'm sure there won't be any difficulty. You'll work for me and for my father at first. He comes in now and again, but that won't be for long. My ex-partner, Mr Oswald, is leaving next month, but he's been away looking for orders and you can finish that correspondence as well. Now, what about bookkeeping?'

Freda was dreading this. She hadn't so much experience with that, as Boothroyd's had employed a part-time retired person for their accounts, but she was sure she could learn. 'I've only done a bit of ledger work,' she said. 'But they're starting a class once a week for double entry – I saw it in the library – I could learn better there if I attended it.'

'Splendid!' he said. 'I can help you with that to start with too. Arithmetic one of your strong points?'

'I was always good at it at school,' she answered. She hated this having to blow your own trumpet, but if you didn't somebody else would get the job!

She wanted to say once more, thank you for giving me the chance, but didn't want to sound too humble. He'd not read out the letter too quickly and she had not had to ask him to repeat anything; he'd be easy to work for if he was always like this!

She took the envelope and asked him if she should type it straight away. 'Please,' he said and poured out another cup for himself. He watched her as she took down the address which he repeated once more, between sips. Head bent, pad on knee, a lock of hair on her forehead. Long thin fingers, legs together primly ... dark green jacket and skirt which suited her colouring, the reddish gold tinge in her brown hair. Her father had had that tint too in his darker hair. He shook his head, unconsciously disturbed. It was all so long ago now, his own boyhood and the pre-war years, his pre-marriage days ... This morning he'd been full of business problems, having heard two contradictory rumours about the cotton markets: that in Lancashire new mills were to be built by two manufacturers whose names he knew, who were sure big new markets would now open up and who were anticipating a return to peace-time conditions; but also that orders were so low at present in Brigford that the manufacturers were going to give their operatives two weeks off at Easter, which was not far off. His mill was worsted of course and there were differences between the worsted manufacturers and the cotton manufacturers. For the present, worsteds were holding up but it was all very worrying and he foresaw lack of work once the coats and uniforms, orders from the government, ceased, no longer needed. Nothing had been cancelled, but it might soon be. Cotton was trickier and more susceptible to Far Eastern competition, but the next few years must see a build up of markets, not a contraction. The silk mills hadn't done too badly with parachutes and fine items, and the pure woollen mills had managed with blanket orders and suchlike. It all went out of his head as he watched Freda working – the problems of dyers who depended upon textiles and the problems of wire drawers who depended on orders for machinery – and not least the problems of updating his own looms. No problems with the workforce, they'd been doing much the same one way or another for over a hundred years and that was a comfort.

As she handed the envelope over to him and he signed the letter and she stuck it into its envelope he said, 'Does your mother get a pension from Fuller's?'

'A little one, but it's dependent on the old owner there.'

James knew that a very tiny old age pension existed nationally but nothing yet for widows. 'And your aunt? – Cissie Phillipson – she's still at work?'

'Oh yes – she never wed, Mr Stainton. She helps my grandmother too. At present Mother gets ten shillings a week from Mr Fuller – but he's made no promises.'

'Wouldn't you like another cup of tea before you go? You'll be able to tell your mother tonight that you've got the job. Will she be pleased?'

'Oh, yes!'

'Your father was a clever man, a good worker – made those engines all himself – fitted them out. It needs a lot of skill to do that.'

She flushed, her eyes sparkled but he could not tell whether from tears or content.

'How *is* your mother?'

'She seemed to have come round just lately. We had the doctor –'

As bad as that. His old friend had probably paid insurance through some benefit or sickness club, he thought, so the doctor would be paid. He wished he could do more for them but they'd be too proud to accept something for nothing. This was the best he could do, employ Freda, and as far as he could tell he'd get the best of the bargain there.

They finally shook hands and he told her to give in her notice. She'd need a fortnight. 'Don't forget the post,' he said and passed over to her her own handiwork. When she'd gone he remained for a few minutes in his chair looking out of the high window until he shrugged into his greatcoat and left the mill with the last shiftworkers.

They were all waiting in the kitchen for her return when Freda pushed open the house door. Nell was up, and busy mashing the tea. She looked wan, but purged, and kissed her daughter when she heard the news. 'I'm going to have a good clean up tomorrow,' she said. Never one for an excess of housework, unlike most of her friends and relations, Nell had still always washed and mangled and ironed, dusted and polished, and blackleaded the range, and scrubbed the step with donkey stone making a neat white edging to the threshhold. But since her husband's death it had all fallen to Freda when she had the time, or Cissie, with the help of Nan who did all her own housework as well. She resolved to make a big effort. James would not have believed she'd let things go even if it were grieving for him that she did so. She sat with Freda in the kitchen when Nan had gone home. Cissie was upstairs in her bedroom, tired from the day's labours. 'I'm right pleased, lass,' said Nell. 'Course even if Dad hadn't gone, you might still have tried for a job at Stainton's once Mr James came back from the war. Dad did mention it now and again to me. What's he like?'

Freda found it hard to describe her new boss. 'Friendly like – I pleased him with the work I did for him, a letter he wanted typed, but I don't know if he'll always be so easy to please. He asked after you.' She didn't say he'd enquired about the 'pension'.

'It's put a bit of heart into me,' said her mother. 'I know I've been a burden these last months.'

'Will you make me that new dress, Mam, when you've got things back to normal? I know you mustn't overdo things, but a bit of sewing would be nice – you can leave the grate – I'll do it – and all the rest.'

'Nay, your grandma's been doing all my washing and yours – I've to do my bit now. I might do a bit of tatting when I sit down – and there's the embroidery I was doing when your Dad fell ill ...' She was already making plans. Freda felt a little guilty, but was glad her mother seemed restored to life. She looked forward herself to her new work, would do her best and hope it was good enough.

Freda had been taken on in April, just before the cotton mills fell silent, and passed Mr Stainton's 'probation' in the May of 1919. She knew she was efficient and she got on all right with the other non-weaving staff who consisted only of a part-time elderly widow, Mrs Marsden, taken on by Stainton from goodness of heart, and the 'girl' Bessie, who made tea and swept and helped with the burling and mending after sorting the post. There was no office boy, which was a relief. Old Mr Stainton stopped coming into the mill by the summer but there was plenty work for her. Chiefly putting the accounts into some sort of order. The old man had been a good works manager but a bit vague over his ledgers. She supposed it had been easy to make a profit during the war, knowing nothing of old Stainton's interest in houses.

James knew she worked hard and did not regret taking her on.

Nell made her two new blouses and a dress on the machine which was still oiled and repaired if necessary by Nan. Freda looked smarter and happier than she had looked for a long time. Mr Stainton was always polite, and insisted she asked if there was anything she didn't understand. She'd fallen on her feet, she thought. He didn't talk a lot to her, which was a surprise after her initial interview, but occasionally he'd stay in her small room for a short chat after bringing in the correspondence, or remark on something when she had finished any dictation he had been giving her in his own room. She felt 'at home', a valued employee, even if she were also the daughter of an old friend. Once he said, 'Your father was an interesting person – we got friendly at school because he fought with the class bully.'

'What! – Dad?' she asked in genuine surprise.

'Yes – he was chivalrous, you know.'

'He was clever,' she said in a rush of confidence, not quite sure what 'chivalrous' meant. 'He used to know where to dig up pig-nuts in the wood for me – I never know where to find them now!'

Mr Stainton looked interested so she went on.

'They're earth nuts, you know, folk used to eat them ...' She stopped, embarrassed. Sometimes he would seem to stare at her before recalling himself.

Trade was bad though. After the cotton mills closed at Easter they reduced the work force or put people on short time.

One afternoon in late June Freda went to the town library. She was for some reason still thinking about the pig nuts. Nobody else seemed to know about them. She'd look them up in the encyclopaedia. She went up to the first floor where the reference library was, along with some pictures bequeathed to the town years ago. The room smelt both of dust and polish. It was quiet, one of the few places where you could be alone and warm. Not that she needed the warmth today since the fugitive summer had at last arrived and sunbeams were coming through the library window in speckled bands of warm light. She sat down with the encyclopaedia. She'd worked all morning; Saturday afternoon was her favourite time. Sometimes she went into Woolsford with her friend Kathleen, but Kath had a summer cold and so Freda had decided to go to the library before shopping a bit in Brigford. But once she sat down with the book she felt lazy, disinclined to get up and walk down into town. It was on such days that she had been taken by her father to dig for those pig nuts she'd mentioned to Mr Stainton. She took the heavy illustrated book and smelled the pleasant scent of old paper. 'Pignuts or earth nuts', she read: 'The edible root-tuber of CONOPODIUM FLEXUOSUM an umbelliferous plant found in woodlands, also called earth chestnut. Sometimes also ARNUT (dialect).' ... Her father sniffed them out, she always thought, and she remembered her excitement when he told her to dig and there not too far down the precious plant she thought was magic ... She looked up. She did miss her father. As much as Nell, though she had made less fuss about it. She pretended he'd be there when she arrived home and they'd go for a walk in the woods again ... Those days he'd always had time for her, though she knew he'd loved Nell best. Only right of course, his wife. But it was Freda he'd taken ice-skating, or to watch football matches. She'd have done better to be a boy, really ... it was a pity she had no brothers. She didn't much like boys though, at least not the ones she'd been to school with or even the ones who asked you to dance at town functions, like the Harrison boy. Boys were different from men, men like her father or Mr Stainton, who'd been boys together once. She supposed if one day in future her friend Kathleen died she might want to help her child as Mr Stainton wanted to help her?

Soon there was to be a big celebration for Victory. James Stainton was on the committee and had told her about it. There were to be flags and bunting and bands playing and a procession. All the women were making new summer dresses for it. Mr Stainton was on lots of committees. He said the future should be worked for and had been to meetings concerned with the establishment of what he called a League of Nations. She wasn't sure if this was his name for it or there really was such a thing. He was always mentioning his 'committees'.

Despite her vow not to think about her childhood. Freda would often find herself lost in a dream of the past. It was odd; why should she want to dream about those years 'before the war'? Was she so miserable that she must console herself with thoughts of the days when she had apparently been happy? *Was* she unhappy? Well, of course, she missed her father – but that was not quite what she felt was wrong. She liked her new work and had been accepted as a permanent 'secretary' exactly one month after being taken on by James Stainton. Cissie was still with them, which might account for her dissatisfaction, but her mother was much better. It was almost, she felt, on those days when things seemed clearer, chiefly because she had a little time to think, as if she were still preparing herself to say goodbye to something and the goodbyes were getting too protracted. Usually though she told herself that last year had all been too much of a shock to her system and she needed time to sort herself out. She was grown-up now, wasn't she? And yet she even found herself thinking about old neighbours, or games she'd played with other children. One day she was thinking about the knot grass she'd used to gather for a lady who had come to live a few years ago down the road from Rose Terrace and with whom her mother had struck up an acquaintance. Mrs Goodbody was a herbalist, and concocted endless medicines to alleviate her neighbours' ills. One of them necessitated this type of grass, which grew in abundance a mile away.

She had finished a letter for Mr James and was waiting for him to begin dictating another but for a moment she was far away, daydreaming of a summer a few years back. Mr Stainton must have noticed, for he said, 'A penny for them,' which recalled her to the present. She started guiltily, and blushed.

'Oh, I was just thinking about gathering herbs for a lady I used to know – well we still know her but I haven't helped her for years … it all seems such a long time ago.'

'You were miles away,' he said and she sensed a gentleness in his voice.

'I'm sorry, Mr Stainton – were you ready for the next letter?'

He wanted to say, yes, but it doesn't matter, I love to watch you when you are pensive. Instead he said, 'You're too young to have thoughts of the past!'

She wanted to reply, I don't think much about it really, but it was not true; she seemed to have come to a sort of full-stop in her life despite the new job, which she enjoyed. She was puzzled, and a small frown appeared on her broad forehead. But she unconsciously attempted a smile, though the frown had been unconscious too, and he said, 'What was knot grass a cure for?'

'I can't remember, I'm afraid,' and she bent down to her shorthand pad so that he had no alternative but to continue some boring letter about price increases of raw materials.

Afterwards he thought I'm beginning to feel I can't do without her. He looked forward now to going to work, whereas at first on his return from the war he had had to wrench himself back into it. He wondered if she had a steady 'boyfriend' as some Americans he knew called a young woman's young man. She was so good-looking that she must have, but perhaps on the other hand she was too refined to please the young men back from the war who were used to taking their pleasures with cruder women? Others of Freda's age or younger who had not been in the war because of medical problems might not be her type. Those even younger would be too young. She was the sort of young woman who needed a subtler, cleverer type of man … When he caught himself thinking this he recognized danger and hastily put his thoughts on another track. But they would not stay there. He'd catch himself thinking that all young men might be too tongue-tied, too immature to understand or appreciate a girl like Freda. But I don't really know her, was his next thought. I only think I know her because of the man who was her father.

He resolved to get to know her better in a purely friendly way. After all they were together for hours in the office.

Girls needed excitement, admiration, he thought, and nobody has had the right sort of excitement for a long time in this country. Deliberately he avoided thinking about 'his' war. That was something he had determined to forget. Maybe it would come back to him years later but for the present he was sick of the misunderstandings of the civilian population about what had happened over in France. You could not describe it, so he did not try to do so. He was luckier than most of the men who had been over there. Many had not returned, and of those who had, some were wounded, some psychologically stuck in their experiences. He on the other hand was stuck in another past. But he was alive, and healthy. The local paper had just published the Brigford figures of killed and wounded. Almost 500 young men had been killed, 180 missing or taken prisoner, and almost 700 wounded, not to speak of those who had returned ill from the effects of mustard gas. Out of a population of 30,000 men, women, and children, almost a tenth of the males had been affected. He would do his best to forward a better future for the survivors. He had taken time to sketch out the formation of the town branch of the British Legion and towards the establishment of the local League of Nations branch – what Freda referred to as his 'committees'.

These thoughts, and the time he spent thinking about Freda, did not in any way stop him from also seeing to the future of his business. Like most men he could compartmentalize himself, and as his reactions were quick he could switch from one mode to another without difficulty. He knew that if anyone in this benighted world could make 'brass', he could. If he did not, the reason would be that the problems of post-war trade were insuperable. But he'd have a damned good try. At first he had thought it would be easier if he had returned to a nice, keen, healthy wife. Or if he had some girl tucked away with whom he might have a simple, uncomplicated relationship as he had had once or twice with 'Mademoiselle from Armentières' or her like in Arras, but now he could not imagine that type of thing satisfying him. Unfortunately he could less easily imagine Lina's suddenly changing and becoming a real wife again. Like Freda, he occasionally seemed to be back in some past when things had been different. His present situation seemed untenable, yet it *must* hold. His military service had settled nothing for him except to prove that he could be as brave as the next man if necessary. It was not his own bravery now that worried him but an inner emptiness when action had to come from himself not from orders from his superior officers. But what action? He could look at Freda and enjoy the sight of her, and there was plenty to do in the business. And he was kind, he thought, to his wife and children. Before he married, he had always thought that love and intimacy would come together quite easily. Only after had he realized there had been something missing in his relations with Lina, and this was long before she fell ill.

France had proved that it was not the abandon of sex. A perfect love ought to be in both heart and body, he thought, and envied the young who had still time in which to find this out.

As he stared at Freda during office hours he envied her youth. He could not have said when the thought came to him that the mystery of Freda might contain what he was looking for. Prolonged acquaintance with a woman who worked for you should effectively remove inchoate yearnings. Yet he found that as time went on it did not. But he was careful to provide Freda with a small cubby-hole for her typing so that she should not feel under his scrutiny.

It was June now and the month had brought with it better weather, not always the case in their northern fastness where some folks kept a fire going in the parlour most of the year.

His thoughts were still amorphous when the day came for the town to celebrate at last the end of the war and the signing of the armistice. The date had been fixed for 19 July and he as a businessman and an ex-officer could not but be involved. They deserved their celebrations, he thought. He was however temperamentally averse to such things and detested brass bands. If only the town had a little orchestra to play something other than hymns and marches and popular songs. But he suppressed such disloyal thoughts.

Freda was wearing a new dress, once again of dark green, that colour which suited her so well. She could not help thinking though as she put it on that morning that it would look better in silk or taffeta with a sheen to it. She had never yet possessed a taffeta dress, such as the one she had seen in Madam Joyce's window, now freshly refurbished and with union jacks propped coyly next to the 'Model' in the window. But this new dress of a cotton and linen mixture, made by Nell from the pattern cut out by Nan, did look good. She was to go with her mother and Nan to join the crowds that afternoon. Cissie preferred to meet her own mates from the mill.

The whole town workforce had the day off for the celebrations and already as they walked down the road towards the centre of Brigford they could hear the various bands tuning up. The town was famous for its own brass band but today other mill bands were to join them in renderings of patriotic airs and Tommies' old favourites. Nell said, 'Your Dad would have loved the music,' as they came into the road leading to the square and saw one brass band massed on a platform, one of many, apart from the principal dais from which various speakers were to declaim in front of the town hall.

The big clock there stood at almost three and crowds were already thick in the square itself, in all the adjoining streets, and in front of the Methodist chapel. People were still moving around. Others were at the first-floor windows of the shops that lined Commercial Street to see the 'procession' of dignitaries and bandsmen, local schoolchildren, and returned soldiers and sailors pass on their way to the square.

Freda and Nell pushed on towards the square. Nan saw an old friend, Mrs Longbottom, and decided to stay put on some steps by the side of a shop. There were chairs on the big platform in front of the town hall which Nell looked at longingly.

'I've a cup of tea for you both when the band's finished,' said Nan's friend. Ethel Longbottom lived on the way out of the square down which the procession was to move after the speeches. One platform was raised at a junction between two roads and on it more brass instruments could be seen gleaming.

'I'll come along after then. Ta,' said Nell.

The children of the local schools were already waiting in various streets, accompanied by their teachers, and Freda saw another long crocodile of little girls making its way to them as she passed by with her mother. The three leading children were staggering under the weight of Union Jacks on poles. More harassed schoolteachers accompanied them. Almost all the folk, even the children, were wearing straw boaters or panamas, and Freda was glad she'd put a new band on her last year's straw boater and dyed it a dark green to match her dress.

'Oh, look at all them flags!' said her mother pointing upwards.

High across the streets there were strung lines and lines of bunting and even the pillars of the gas-lamps had red-white and blue festooned around them in stripes like Blackpool rock, culminating in a large Union Jack. Everywhere was colour and noise and pushing folk. 'Couldn't we stay here – not bother to go right into the square?' suggested Nell who still got tired when she walked very far. But Freda wanted to hear the speeches, and so they followed the children and saw more flags, more bunting and another platform of bandsmen as they finally came into the square itself. The sun was shining, and the summer dresses, many of them like Freda's donned for the first time, looked as though they belonged to some other warmer clime. Yet they were orderly, these crowds, obediently forming into lines along the streets and, once in the square, waiting more quietly now for everything to begin.

A hush came upon them all as a space was made at the far end for the procession to arrive. By the time they did, Freda had managed to find them both standing room quite near. The sound of the town band was now heard approaching from the other direction, playing 'It's a long way to Tipperary'. On arrival its members stepped up the wooden stairs to the platform without stumblings or falls, though a cheeky boy called, 'You've dropped your trumpet, Mister!'

The temporary platform was large, and up the steps at the other end there mounted the mayor and his staff, the mayoress – but no other wives – accompanying. *They* were now to be seen at the long windows of the town hall behind, waving flags. Behind the mayor, resplendent in his gold chain and red robes, came the mace bearer and the town councillors.

Special Constables lined the edge of the crowd as another party approached and ascended the stairs. These were representatives of the Services, among whom was Captain Stainton. Nell nudged her daughter, who nodded. Then representatives of the three military hospitals nearby and members of the various committees who had arranged the day, the vicars of the parish bringing up the rear. Finally they were all on the platform and the band stopped. All except the mayor sat down. His speech was to be relayed by loudspeakers all over the square and the crowd waited expectantly. 'We see better from here,' whispered Freda.

'My Lord,' (this to the Lord Lieutenant of the County who had so far escaped notice, nobody knowing what he looked like), 'The Mayor of Halifax (boos), Councillors, Ex-Servicemen, Ladies and Gentlemen – and Children. We are here to mark the ending of the worst war this country has ever known, and to celebrate our victory over Germany and her Allies.' He paused. 'First we are to give thanks to the brave men – and women – who risked their lives in the service of their country. Above all to remember those who did not return.' There was a sort of collective catch of the breath and Nell's eyes filled with tears. Her James hadn't lost his life in war but it seemed all one to her. That nasty influenza had arrived as part of it all.

'I would ask for a minute's silence whilst we remember them,' added the mayor. Complete silence followed except for a dog barking far away.

Somebody in front of Freda had managed to get hold of an official programme and she borrowed it when the next speaker got up to address the crowd. It was Alderman Baldwin, a 75-year-old Liberal whose son had died in the Boer War. 'There has been much talk of a memorial to those who died in our town,' he began. 'I am glad to be able to tell you that a committee has been formed to consider this matter and also to discuss the plan to cast bronze medals to be distributed to all returning servicemen.' Cheers. 'To this end I am pleased to start a Heroes' Fund today and your contributions will be gratefully received at the town hall during the next three months. You may have wondered what you could do practically to show your gratitude for the sacrifices made on your behalf, and this is one way. All contributions – however small – will be appreciated. On another note,' he continued, 'the Trades Council has met and will continue to meet under Councillor Asquith to find work for those returning warriors who have not yet found it.' (Cheers). He sat down, amidst clapping. They liked Councillor Baldwin, one of the Old Guard.

Freda looked up where the bunting moved faintly against the blue sky. James Stainton, sitting on the platform and wondering why he felt he had no right to be there, saw her, and his heart leapt. Was all the carnage, all the muddle, all the years spent so unpleasantly by so many less lucky than himself, arranged to this end, so that he, James Stainton, former captain in the King's Own Yorkshire Light Infantry might acknowledge on a sunny July day that some things were worth living for, and so worth dying for? His thought was mingled with regret that Lina had not seen fit to come. The children were down with Mrs Petersham somewhere in the crowd.

The Vicar of Brigford stood up and moved to the front of the platform. 'Let us pray,' he intoned. The people who attended his church were used to his Southern speech and resigned to his talk of 'Gord', so obediently bent their heads. Others looked embarrassed or suspicious and yet others looked indignantly for their minister from Bethel. 'O Gord who has guided us towards this day and towards the victory of the Right and Just, we give thanks for our deliverance from the yoke of war and pray that Thou wilt guide us and aid us in all our future travails.'

Then the Methodist minister of Bethel, the largest chapel in the town, added his own prayer in a more robust and less humble tone ending with the words, 'We shall not forget the dead, but today is for celebration and the hope that never again will the wolves of war ravage our homes and our lives.' There was a faint cheer and the mayor got up then and announced that there would now be a hymn: 'O God our help in ages past' and then a rendering of the *Dead March* from Saul by the band. Most inappropriate, felt James Stainton, on his plinth. They have not decided whether this is a wake or a gala. He had not been allowed to have any say in the music.

The hymn was however sung with gusto before the band struck up in blazing sound and later modulated from the march into a cheerful song of celebration, 'Come Lasses and Lads'. Scarce had they finished than the mayor, who had been confabulating with his councillor next to him, announced, 'By popular request – "Ilkla Moor!" ' A great roar went up from the crowd, relieved at last to know the sad part was over. The band was to stay when all the bigwigs had departed and the formal processions had wound round the square, and was to play 'Popular Items', Freda discovered when she looked once more over the neighbour's shoulder. Kathleen had caught sight of her and wriggled her way through when the band arrived at the *National Anthem*. All stood as they played and then the Lord Lieutenant rather self-consciously proposed, 'Three cheers for Brigford.' The shouts which resulted sent starlings roosting on the town hall roofs into a flurry of startled wings.

James could now see Freda quite clearly. No one else was wearing that shade of green and the sun was not in his eyes, though it cast brightness over the square as the band now began a medley and the platform shuffled off, James among them. Freda was with another young woman now; he wondered where they would go next. He himself was invited to 'partake of refreshment' along with fellow officers and businessmen in the town hall. But he lingered, unwilling to lose sight of her, though losing her meant only he could look forward to the next time. What a tumult of feeling she aroused in him – a mixture of excitement and adoration. He recollected himself. This was no way to behave. But he realized, as he followed the others down from the dais and into the black stone building behind, that the way he was feeling – a mixture of hope and agony – must be what people called falling in love. So that was it. As he took a glass of beer from a white-aproned Senior School child deputed to serve on this auspicious occasion, he knew that all his energies ought from this moment to be directed towards keeping his feelings secret, now that they were no longer secret from himself. But if only he could take her tonight to the dance at the town hall!

Freda had seen James on the platform and thought how handsome he appeared, even at a distance taller than most of the others except for the Lord Lieutenant. He had been in his uniform and that was somehow exciting, though he had grumbled to her only a few days ago that he felt under false pretences and had hoped never to don it again. 'The last time,' he had said.

But Kathleen wanted to 'see the sights' so Freda left her mother, who pushed off to Mrs Longbottom's, and wandered round the square as snatches of music from the various bands mingled in the warm air. An ice-cream vendor was doing good business on the corner as the folk passed and a lemonade man outside the butcher's was telling the folk to toast the town in 'summat better than beer'. Freda knew all the pubs and inns would soon be full. 'Let's go to the library gardens,' she suggested, after one more look up at the town hall windows where she was sure she saw Mr Stainton still looking out.

It *was* James, listening to Baldwin behind him, excited for an old man, saying that the future must now be planned and worked for.

'But my future?' thought James to himself. What will that consist of? His children yes – they *were* the future. But so was Freda!

* * *

In the days that followed 19 July James Stainton was busy organizing a day trip which would take his workforce in several charabancs to a beauty spot. This was an event that had used to take place by train before the war, but now that the town boasted a 22-seater charabanc James thought it would be a good idea to hire it as an experiment, with a view to longer journeys in later years – Llandudno perhaps, or Rhyl. He kept thinking how much better it would be if he could take just Freda in his own motor which had been laid up during the war but was now ready again for the road provided he could obtain the petrol. This had so far been impossible, and Lina hadn't yet had her fresh air.

He had had time to ponder his new feelings toward Freda when after a day's work he would return home to do a bit of gardening; Lina had formerly enjoyed planting and planning, but at present took little interest. He concluded that the uncanny intimacy he had felt with Freda right from the day he had 'interviewed' her must have been because of her relationship to his old friend Caston which connected her with his earlier days. Did Freda too associate him with her father? Possibly. He knew from what she had said that she missed him, and that when she thought of her childhood she thought of him, just as he too remembered James when he recalled his own youth. When memories of school or even his time at the Technical College surfaced it was always her father who seemed to accompany them, though after they had parted at school and gone their different ways it had been only occasionally that they had seen each other. Those days must have meant more than he had realized. He was shy of mentioning her father directly to her but did so occasionally.

'Mr Stainton talks about Dad,' Freda said to Cissie, who sniffed and said 'I should think he does – they were good friends till he made his brass and married that Evangeline Harris. We weren't good enough for *her*.'

'He never says much about his wife,' said Freda.

'I should think not! – what call would he have to talk to *you* about her?'

Cissie looked at her indignantly but curiously. She had now returned home to Nan's, but life at Rose Terrace went on much the same for Freda and Nell. Cissie and Nan were always round at their house. At least Freda now had her own bedroom back, yet this, which she had so longed for, meant that she must not be always going up to it, must talk to her mother downstairs in those long evenings when Nell might edge pillow-cases with tatting, or bring out the embroidery they were both doing on a large tablecloth. Freda found embroidery a bore, not soothing enough to let your thoughts wander, since you had to keep breaking off threads, starting on new colours. She knew her mother needed her as a companion but felt she made a poor one. What had her mother and father ever talked about together? When she was a child they had always appeared to possess some secret life from which she was excluded. Not for the first time she wished that she had had a brother or sister. I was an only child because Mam was ill having me, she thought, but having only me must have made it easier for them to save. She knew many of the large families of some of the children she'd been to school with, and knew their poverty and despair. Her father hadn't been a drinker either, so they'd saved on that item too. He'd have a glass of beer just occasionally if pressed, but always said he didn't really like ale. That had pleased Nell and Cissie – and their mother – who had suffered from an alcoholic father and husband before he fortunately died of drink. Dad had 'rescued' her mother from that household. Well, all his temperance and prudence hadn't given him a long life; it was a shame, something you couldn't understand, it made you angry. No use them at chapel telling you that these virtues had their reward in heaven; they should have their reward on earth! But she knew that 'nothing was fair'. Even if Dad had lived they'd never have been rich. Everywhere now people were finding it hard to manage. They said prices had doubled since just before the war.

She thought how kind Mr Stainton was being to her, even though sometimes she wondered if he was going to say something critical, for he often paused in mid-sentence and looked not quite at her but beyond her. He had made a small room for her out of a store-room so that she could get on with her work in peace. Sometimes he went on about his 'committees', and she tried to appear interested, since *he* was. But committees didn't seem to get anywhere – he said as much himself to her. But he would go on trying, he said. At least he didn't need 'committees' to plan the mill trip. It was to take place on August bank holiday and they were to go by popular demand to Ilkley. She wondered if he would be taking his wife, and mentioned it to Bessie. 'What, him take Mrs Stainton! You don't know her – a real misery she is. I shouldn't think so. Eh, I'm right looking forward to it, aren't you?'

Freda wasn't sure if she was looking forward to it. From her Aunt Cissie she had heard of the sort of outing where everybody palled up but on which some of the men went off for illegal booze and came back the worse for wear. Tea and buns would be nice though, and she'd only seen the moors once, years ago with her mother and father when they had all gone for a treat to celebrate her father getting a rise.

Her mill work did not bore her; she enjoyed it. It was her life at home which felt more and more tedious. She knew there was some notion hanging in the air of her finding a 'young man' and it irritated her. She was happy alone, it wasn't George Kershaw she needed, the only young man she had ever really been 'out' with during the war, who had bored her even more than her mother did. She felt a complete absence of feeling when she remembered him. He had kissed her and then said, 'I respect you too much, Freda, to go further.' Without quite knowing how to describe this behaviour she had called it 'pompous' to herself. She would certainly not have wanted George to 'go further' but would have enjoyed feeling that *he* might want to. He didn't even seem to want to; it had all been settled in his mind before he took her out: 'Freda is to be respected'. His mother had probably said those very words to him!

Though he was the same age as her father, Mr Stainton was not boring. Of course she didn't think of him as a 'man' but as a person, older and wiser and richer than anyone else she had ever known, though in some ways he seemed a lot younger than her father. She admired him for being rich, respected him because he was kind, and yet was a little mystified too, for he sometimes looked 'disappointed'. It must be that wife of his, described by Bessie – the 'Harris girl' as Cissie had described her. It must be odd coming back after a war. Perhaps he'd expected everything to be easy and lovely, and it wasn't? What sort of woman though would Mr Stainton have chosen? He could have had pretty well any woman in town, she supposed. They said his mother had been in the mill herself, came from quite an ordinary family – but that was fifty years ago! She sometimes thought he looked restless, would pace about the office in a distracted way in the middle of dictating a letter, and then wonder where he was. She was pleased he had found her a little room of her own.

'Going up in the world,' said Cissie. 'Your own room and all.'

'It's only about six feet square,' replied Freda, laughing, but she *was* pleased.

Once or twice when she went in with letters to sign or queries about the books she was copying for him he would ask her how her family was, or ask her how she spent her evenings. She told him she was hoping to save up for a piano. They had always wanted one and you could get secondhand ones quite cheap nowadays. Once she brought two teacakes for her dinner, and he said, 'Those smell good,' so she offered him one. Surprised, he took it, and told her later he hadn't tasted bread as good since leaving his mother's house. 'Nan baked it,' she said. After that she got to taking him a teacake now and then.

The day came round for the charabanc trip. On the Sunday Freda washed her hair and shone her boots and laid her green costume on the bed. It might rain so she took the gaberdine Mam had just finished making for her on the machine from stuff the mills sold on to the market if it had slight faults, nothing you could see. She'd already been fitted out with a new skirt and another summer dress but showed no inclination to sew herself. Not that Nan would have allowed her to use the precious Singer.

They all met in the town square rather than outside the mill, to avoid the long pull up the bank. There were five charabancs, three hired from the neighbouring town. The sun was out, but a slight wind made Freda, sitting squeezed between Bessie and Mrs Marsden, clutch her green boater. Everyone awaited Mr Stainton who was to give the signal to move. He arrived, spoke to the drivers and they were off. Freda had never been in a charabanc before and it was bumpier than a tram. Already there were squeals from the mill girls all sitting together. The married couples sat self-consciously apart. In the last of the vehicles was ensconced Mr Stainton in a panama, along with his father, also wearing one. Freda looked out with interest once the town was left behind. They skirted Woolsford, took an unfamiliar road, and made their way north and west. 'Fancy them getting the petrol!' said Mrs Marsden. 'The master said the council was allowing each mill just enough to take their folk out for the day,' said Bessie who, despite being a practically silent person in the office, often picked up bits of information.

'Have you been to Ilkley before?' Mrs Marsden asked Freda.

'I think when I was little – Dad took me. But it seemed a long way away then to me.'

'Nobbut fifteen mile,' said Bessie.

Freda looked across the land that now lay before them. They had passed through Shipley and skirted Yeadon, and once they'd passed through Menston she saw the moor stretch for miles on their left. 'Shall we go into the town?' she asked. But the chara was slowing down for its occupants to get off and walk round a bit before going on further on foot for refreshments. It was a different world up here, she thought. They were very high up. Clouds sailed above them and a few sheep wandered on the short grass.

'Town's over yon by the Wharfe,' said Mrs Marsden. 'But there's Cow and Calf rocks not far off and "Mucky Dicks" – I went there once with Bill.'

All the occupants of the charabancs were now walking round, breathing in the fresh cool air. 'We're to walk over to the farm,' said a young woman who had been in one of the other vehicles. 'Then we'll have an appetite for us tea.' This seemed to be the plan. Freda would have liked to stay alone for a bit to look round but obediently followed the others. Some of the men were capering about, released from labour for a day. Mr Stainton came up to her.

'Good morning, Freda – did you have a nice journey?'

'Yes thank you, Mr Stainton. Are we going into the town later?' She had been told that you could see Paris fashions in the shops here and wanted very much to see the wares of towns other than Brigford or Woolsford.

'There are hundreds of prehistoric remains,' he said. 'And plenty rocks, apart from the ones everyone visits – are you warm enough?' She felt a little self-conscious at first, having to walk along with the boss. Mr Stainton's father was still in one of the charas. 'My father gets tired walking so will meet us over at the hostelry,' said James. Most of the workers had now gone on ahead, some running, others in chattering groups. As most of them had known each other for years she felt it did not matter if she did not join them. They also preserved their distance from the office staff though she was quite willing to be friendly. A large beefy-looking man, the overlooker, seemed to be in charge. Mrs Marsden and Bessie had moved away.

'A walk will be good for us,' said James who was wondering

whether he had acted injudiciously in seeking out Freda. But he had deliberately not travelled in the same charabanc as her and would make a point of speaking to others of the workforce later, so he felt it was only natural that he should walk with his secretary.

They followed the last vanishing charabanc in the direction of the farm that dispensed tea and sandwiches and 'ham on the bone' to trippers. 'It will be nice by the river,' he said. 'And you will be able to wander round the town later.'

'It's lovely *here*,' she replied – 'you forget how dirty everything in Brigford is. But it will be nice to see the town.'

'Did you want to go shopping then?' he asked her, smiling.

For answer she smiled, took off her hat and let it swing by its elastic band. 'I came here once with Dad,' she said after a pause.

He looked at her, feeling suddenly overcome with a desire to take her in his arms and kiss her. But they were far from alone, however broad and high the sky and however distant the expanse of moor. Ten minutes would bring them in sight of the farm and ahead of them a group of older women weavers were plodding along. *They* would obviously have preferred, like his father, not to have to get down and walk. He would have to remember that next time.

'I thought we should have a breath of air – I forgot some people might be tired,' he said.

'*I'm* not tired, Mr Stainton.'

'No – but you are young – I'm not tired either – I like walking.'

She looked across at him. Like the scenery he seemed different. He was in what she supposed must be his holiday clothes, a casual linen suit and a soft collar. They made him look younger. In a sudden access of confidence, she said, 'I can race you to the wall!'

He looked at her in surprise, but then, 'Done!' he said and they both started off at the same moment winging across the springy turf.

Freda reached it first. 'You didn't try!' she said as he came up a few seconds later and stopped in front of her as she propped herself up against the dark drystone wall, panting a little.

There was a skylark singing now above. 'You can hear the curlews from here too,' he said. 'Very melancholy they always sound. People shoot grouse not far away. It's all moor really, until you get to Settle, but there's a lovely view of Wharfedale from the top.'

Yet he seemed loth to go on walking, so she said, 'Are we the last? I think the others are all gone.'

'I shall have to be sociable,' he replied, with a sharp look at her.

Freda felt liberated, a little peculiar. The way they talked together was so different from the way they spoke at work. Of course at work there were no skylarks and no larking about.

All he wanted to say was, Don't go, Freda. don't go. Let's just stay here and then go off together west, take a bed for the night in some inn, carry on walking, never go back ... But he pulled himself together. How should he behave towards her, not to give her the impression of being crass or vulgar, and yet show her he cared? It was simply impossible. He could neither follow his desires nor help showing her that he preferred to talk to her, to be with her. What did she think of him? She was not a 'forward' lass so he'd probably never know. But the way she'd looked at him before they ran towards the wall had not been entirely devoid of complicity.

They came up back on to the lane now and saw a field and a fence and long, low white-washed farmhouse with a sign 'TEAS'. Men and women were already perched on the walls, crowding in at the door. He groaned, 'I'll have to leave you here to be polite to them,' he said. 'But later, if you like, we might escape and have a cup of tea in the town? Look at the river? So long as we're all back from whatever we've been doing by five o'clock in front of the church for the charas.' He raised his hat. 'I'll join Father now – I think Bessie is over there.' And he was off along the lane to where one chara was parked.

Freda waited for a moment by the gate and then pretended she'd just seen Bessie and Mrs Marsden who were waving to her. 'Did you get lost?'

'No – I was looking for – prehistoric stones –' she said glibly. Better not to stress Mr James's walking along with her. She didn't want to be regarded as a 'favourite'.

They ate their bread and butter and ham and drank the hot, sweet, strong tea among crowds from other places, for this was a favourite spot. Then Freda walked down the hill with a score of others in search of the town and the river. They seemed friendly enough, if a little reserved, spoke of the wonders of the place and of those who'd decided to go to the Cow and Calf rocks instead of walking into the town. As it was bank holiday, all the little shops were open for trade and there was a general air of well-being and jollity. Freda, having told Bessie she would have a little walk to the church or maybe look in a few shop windows, waited first by the little bridge and looked into the brown water. She didn't like crowds, would always find herself somehow moving away, wanting to be left to her own devices. She wondered where the tea shops might be. Oh well, she'd have a look at the shops first.

Gracious me! what a price everything was! The shops looked like little temples, far grander than Madam Joyce's. Mill-owners' wives from all over came here and to Harrogate. How lovely it must be to belong here, not come just for the day, get away from the grime and work, perhaps have a little shop of your own ... She was lost in reverie after walking round the town, which was not large. The old part seemed to be up a hill where led a cobblestoned lane across the Wharfe. She turned back and decided to sit down for a bit again by the river.

James had been filled with panic shortly after he had left Freda so that she might rejoin her co-workers. He was mad to concentrate his attentions so brazenly upon his young secretary. Would his father have noticed? He made a big effort to talk to everyone, to draw one or two aside even, so that nobody might think Freda had had preferential treatment. But nobody seemed to have noticed, and he calmed down. What was more natural than that he and she, who were together for hours at work, should not spend a few minutes chatting? He was foolish, not knowing what to do and then the next moment longing to run away with the oblivious Freda. But was she *completely* oblivious? He could not decide, decided to stroll around a little and perhaps to take that promised cup of tea before they left. When he saw Freda alone by the river he stopped in delight.

He was tired of equivocation, hadn't done anything wrong ... but as he took the few steps across the road in her direction he did feel obscurely guilty. There has been enough guilt in my life, he told himself. The guilt I feel towards Lina is unnecessary, for I'm convinced her woes are not my fault, though she is my responsibility ... I can't ignore them ... I can surely be pleasant to Freda, as I try to be pleasant to so many people? ... He recognized his own deviousness, one half of his brain always contradicting the other half. The reservation uppermost in his mind however, as he approached Freda was that he might be disturbing her solitude, and he felt then a sort of shyness, that he might even become an object of ridicule to her.

He said, 'What about a cup of tea then?'

Could he go on pretending that he was just being polite? If he didn't, she might take fright. But she looked round, did not appear surprised to see him standing there and replied – was it guilelessly? – 'I'd love to – I was watching the water, how it moves – it's never the same for more than a second, is it?'

'It is the light,' he answered, looking at her eyes but trying not to gaze too long at the limpid hazel. 'Are the others there?' she asked as she got up from the ground. 'Your father?'

'Oh, he is with Ramsden the overlooker supping a pint –'

'Wouldn't you prefer beer, Mr Stainton, to a cup of tea?'

'No – not really – I'd rather have a cup of tea – with you.'

Might that not alert her to his feelings? Did he want her alerted or not? He was all at sea with himself. It would be better never to try to express his feelings, would certainly be more sensible. But then she said, and revealed both her awareness and her innocence: 'You're very kind to me – I like to talk to you, but …'

'But I am your employer and old enough to be your father.'

She coloured a little then, perhaps not sure which of the two was worse, but said after a moment as they walked along together, 'I've always liked older people best to talk to. Young people can be so *silly*.' Did she mean young men? he wondered.

'Oh, I am very silly too!' he replied, which made her laugh a little guardedly.

'Maybe I should go to look for Mrs Marsden and Bessie?' she said primly.

'It is only a cup of tea, Freda,' he said, knowing that if it were, the conversation would not have needed to take place.

'Then I accept your invitation,' she answered. Was she being pert? No. Where did that grace come from which he saw in all her movements?

He knew he had said enough – too much. More would make tomorrow at work impossible. He needed time to think, but the idea of planning a 'strategy' disgusted him. They must chat over tea about matters unconnected with themselves. He knew he must not take verbal advantage of her but could not seem to help wanting to plant a few seeds of awareness in her. He sensed that she enjoyed admiration. Her father, James Caston, had most likely admired her, once she had grown from a little girl into this lovely young woman. He did not want to think of fathers.

In the tea shop there were one or two other folk from Valley Mills and James felt both relieved and slightly awkward.

Freda certainly sensed that she was not being treated by Mr Stainton as an employee. More like a friend, she thought, and felt a little shiver of delight at his interest. But it would be just for today as it was a holiday and he felt carefree.

'Do you sometimes bring your children here?' she asked him as they sat down at a table in the back of the large tea rooms.

'Here in this teashop?'

'No – I meant to Ilkley – or on other outings – Do they ever come on the firm's outings with you?'

'They are too young – were certainly far too young the last time the firm had a trip out of Brigford – before the war.'

'Oh yes, of course.'

There was silence. 'How old are they?' she asked politely.

'Oh, Val is nine and Mary is seven now.' He knew she would not mention the children's mother and was determined not to do so himself. Sentences like 'She is a semi-invalid and never accompanies me anywhere' would fall too readily from his lips and make him feel once more guilty, though as a matter of fact it was not for want of urging that Lina did not come with him. Neither did he want Freda – or anyone – to feel sorry for him. But – 'You must meet my children,' was out before he could think. 'The boy is away at school now, but Mary is being taught at home.'

'The boy is away *now*? – isn't it the school holidays?' asked Freda who was also fairly literal-minded.

'Yes, of course – but he goes back in September.'

'I am not very good with children,' Freda said, accepting a cup of tea poured out by her employer and bethinking herself to offer him a buttered scone from the plate brought by the overworked waitress. She was enjoying herself. Whenever or wherever else was she given the chance to have tea with a gentleman who seemed to enjoy her conversation and who took it for granted that she could behave herself properly? With Mr Stainton she was no longer somebody's daughter or niece or grandchild but a grown-up woman. She liked that, and indeed felt grown-up. 'If I had been,' she added. 'My father would have wanted me to be a teacher.'

'Yes, I believe he once told me – you like your present work though, don't you?' he was emboldened to ask.

'Oh, yes – I do!' He was no longer Mr Stainton who was the

reason for that work but a friend, a tea-time companion, a *very* grown-up man.

'How is the book-keeping going? I forgot to ask you.'

'It's quite fiddly, but I expect I shall improve if I work at it. Then I shall be of more use to the firm.' She smiled, and he could not help smiling too. 'Isn't it lovely here? I never want to go back to Brigford,' she said.

He thought, she is easily pleased, has never been anywhere, but has the urge to make a better life for herself. 'No, Brigford is not a very beautiful town, is it? Yet we are so near the countryside, we are lucky in that.' He was amazed how he could manage this small talk, but it came easily.

'Eastcliff, where *you* live, Mr Stainton, is very pretty.'

'Yes.'

'We used to go for walks up there – above Eastcliff – Sholey way – and further to Moon Woods.'

By 'we' he supposed she meant herself and her father. They seemed to have been close. 'There's a rambling club they're thinking of forming,' she went on, as he appeared interested, never took his eyes off her face. 'I thought I might join.'

James cleared his throat and poured another cup of tea for her. 'I expect it's nicer for women to go about in twos and threes, in groups? – Do young men intend to join too?' he offered.

Freda felt obscurely that he was teasing her. She had certainly no intention of joining a rambling club to meet young men, he must not think that! 'Oh, some older men will join, I expect,' she replied artlessly. 'The young ones play table tennis or go swimming – not many like rambles for their own sake.'

'You find sports dull?' he asked.

'Well, I like to swim – Dad taught me – but ping-pong is so boring!'

She was chatting away, a faint pink in her alabaster cheek. At her ease now as he watched her. But how many teas would it need for her to be able to call him James instead of 'Mr Stainton'? Impossible! Yet he called her Freda, not Miss Caston.

'There is talk of new tennis courts in Eastcliff,' he said, for something to say. 'You might like to join the club there?'

She blushed, then said, 'Well – our family is not posh enough for that, Mr Stainton.'

'If you ever wanted to join, you would only have to ask me to be your referee,' he said.

'Oh, it would be too expensive,' she replied. 'And I only played for a year at school.'

He looked at his watch. Nearly time for the journey back. He must find Mrs Marsden and deliver Freda to her. He would deny himself the treat of placing himself by Freda's side on the journey back. Through the window as he paid and they made their way out he saw his father and the overlooker. Time to be off, but first there was the tedious business of rounding everyone up for the return journey. Freda had seen old Mr Stainton too.

'You will want to be with your father – I shall look for Mrs Marsden,' she said unaffectedly. He opened the door for her to go out first, could only just refrain himself from putting his arm round her as he did.

In the days after Ilkley Freda began to look at James Stainton with new eyes. He did not say much and they were very busy in the office with a rush of sudden orders which had cheered them all up, but the morning after the trip he had exclaimed: 'I did enjoy my works outing! – I hope you did too?'

'Oh it was lovely – but I didn't want to come back.'

'I hope it's not *too* bad now you are back? There are worse places than Brigford!'

She caught herself thinking of him in the intervals between typing and adding up figures. The trip would not have been so pleasant without Mr Stainton. Neither would work. When he was in the room she felt noticed.

The Wakes, or 'Rush' week, came later in August but most folk had decided to save up for next year in Blackpool, not risk their savings, if they had any, before they knew how trade was going.

James sent his wife and two children to Morecambe for two or three weeks, she did know that. He told her he hadn't the time to stay there himself, but would visit at weekends.

One balmy Saturday at the end of August Freda persuaded her friend Kathleen to walk over to Eastcliff and then to turn down to a small valley where she had often been with her father, following the stream to the north-west up to a village north of Eastcliff where woods began. Kath was not a keen 'rambler' but was usually willing to follow where Freda led. She was now walking out with Joe Harrison but he was away on the coast at present with his parents.

'How do you like Stainton then?' she asked as they sat by an old

abandoned water wheel on their way back to Eastcliff by the
rhubarb fields, from where it was only a walk of a mile or two to
the outskirts of Brigford. They might even catch a tram if they
eventually walked in one direction down the hill.

'Your new boss?' pursued Kathleen as Freda seemed lost in a
brown study. She had heard the question and found it a difficult
one to answer. She'd been five months now at Valley Mills but it
seemed like five years.

Finally – 'I like him right well,' she said. 'He's a – kind man.
Never gets angry – not with me anyway.'

'They say he's unhappily married,' said Kathleen sagely.

'Do they? Why? He doesn't talk about his wife.'

'I don't know – they say his wife's a bit – touched – you know – a
bit potty!'

'No, I believe she's an invalid,' replied Freda, somehow unwilling to discuss Mrs Stainton, but they might as well get it over. Kath
could be quite persistent. She herself didn't like gossip but
sometimes you had to pretend you did.

'Aunt Cissie says that she didn't want him to join up,' she said.
'Dad never said much about his family, it was only Mr Stainton he
knew. Mr Stainton often mentions my dad too.'

'Maybe that's why he took you on?' suggested Kathleen
tactlessly.

'He gave me a test before he did that,' answered Freda, a little
cross. 'He says I do my work well,' she could not help adding.

Kathleen worked in a boot and shoe shop, had no higher
aspirations.

'How's Joe?' Freda asked, to change the subject from herself or
her employer. She then had to listen to a long tale of Joe's
preferences, his mother's character and Kathleen's carefully laid
marriage plans. Apparently Mrs Harrison was keen on her for a
daughter-in-law. 'Has he asked you then?' Freda couldn't help
probing.

'Oh aye – but we're not engaged yet – he's saving up for the
ring,' Kath answered proudly.

Freda was silent for a while but then said, 'I'm glad then, if he's
the man you want.'

'Don't *you* want to get wed then?'

'I don't know – one day, I suppose – not for years though – I've
never met a lad I liked well enough.' It was true. And she'd like to
marry someone who would take her away from Brigford.

'The lads were always looking at you but you frightened them!' said Kath.

'How do you mean? I only went out with that George Kershaw. Anyway most of them were in France.'

'Oh, you'll meet Mr Right one day I'm sure,' said Kathleen, meaning to sound comforting. Lads didn't like girls to be too choosy and her friend Freda always looked a bit aloof. Freda tried not to feel annoyed.

Later that evening when her friend had returned home after sharing a fish and chip supper at the Castons, Freda's thoughts reverted to what she had said about 'lads'. In Brigford everyone knew everyone else's business. She would loathe being an object of speculation. Even Mam was talking about starting on her 'bottom drawer' – the objects which Freda must acquire whilst waiting for Mr Right. It didn't seem anything to do with her, that was the trouble, all that being courted and flashing a ring. Really, she supposed she'd stopped thinking about it since her father fell ill. It didn't seem important.

Later, in bed, she woke, unusually for her, at three in the morning, out of a confused dream where Mr Stainton had been sitting with her by a stream like the one she and Kath had sat by, up at Norwood. They were talking about marriage. In the dream she said, 'I'm glad *you're* not married!' and he smiled up at her and held out his hand, which she took.

When she woke later in the morning she remembered the dream that had woken her earlier with a mixture of puzzlement and shame.

Nell Caston née Phillipson was regarded by many folk as a bit of a 'slutter-bucket', the town's appellation for a woman who was easy-going, not averse to leaving her window-cleaning or her scrubbing if the sun came out. This was unfair, for she had always managed to run her home reasonably well – without worrying much what other people thought. It was true that James had helped her a good deal and had also had his own special tasks like cleaning boots and bringing in the coal and tending their patch of garden, but she had always cooked tasty dinners, though she preferred making pretty clothes on the machine. But now that James had gone and she had recovered from the worst of her grief she was at a bit of a loss. She'd kept the house for James rather than Freda, had indeed loved James more than she'd loved the daughter who was the result of that love, who had nearly cost her her life. James had doted on Freda as he had doted on his wife; Freda had always been closer to her father than to her mother. Nell often wished she'd had other children, a son in particular, for she preferred men, in spite of the excesses of her father which had led her to marry so young.

If she were not sewing or otherwise employed she would find herself with time to spare in the evenings after Freda came home from work, and for the first time in her life she wished she felt closer to her daughter. Their conversation was limited to Freda's recounting of her day unless Cissie or Mrs Phillipson came in for a time when it usually degenerated into gossip. When Freda had had her tea she was quite content to read a book from the library unless it was one of the evenings for her bookkeeping class. Nell knew that Freda like her father was 'clever' and she did not resent her long periods of silence, but she felt obliged, if Freda had nothing else to do, to urge her to go out and enjoy herself. If the girl were content to stay in the house she knew she ought not to grumble, but Freda might as well be out for all the intimacy she offered. Nell herself was not a 'reader' though Freda brought her books from the library to try to tempt her. 'Don't you want to go out?' she would ask and Freda would eventually answer: 'Perhaps I'll go to the baths on Saturday with Kath,' or 'I might go to the lectures on Sundays if the idea comes off.' She had heard of this new idea of Sunday lectures from Mr Stainton. Freda was conscious of quite deliberately banking up time so that one day her mother might be glad she was 'getting out a bit'. Though she preferred at present to read or to be alone with her daydreams she sensed that one day she might need the freedom to go out of the house on her own devices. Kathleen and the table tennis at the chapel might be an alibi later if she ever needed one, wanted to go further afield, just as the idea of joining the rambling club next spring might seem a useful thing to do. Then she would start, and ask herself: What can I be thinking of? Where should I go? Who might I want to be with in the evenings or at weekends? If that time ever came, however, Nell would be ready to be pleased. Ever since the trip to Ilkley, Freda's thoughts had centred more and more upon her employer. When she was in the office of the mill she hardly connected the man who dictated her letters, the man whom everyone looked up to and from whom they took their orders, with the man who had talked to her so pleasantly in

August. Not that he was not pleasant in the mill but he was more guarded.

In September there was a strike on the railways but it impinged little on Freda. Events in the world outside the mill and her head seemed dreamlike. There was more reality in the books she read or in her own thoughts. What *was* she dreaming of on those long autumn evenings? Love? Success in her job? Happiness? A husband worthy of her? Though James Stainton was constantly in her thoughts they were not yet fixed on him in a 'romantic' way, were rather a pleasant accompaniment to her life. She still didn't think of him primarily as a 'man', just a nicer person than anyone else who had appeared so far in her life. He was married, settled, lived in what people said was a beautiful house; was older than her: the twenty years that separated them debarred her from making an easy assumption that he 'fancied' her, an assumption which if she had received that amount of attention from any other male would have set her thinking. Mr Stainton showed her another way of living, talking, being. She disliked talk of 'fancying' anyway, but he made her dream of a future that was disconnected from him but connected to the idea of somebody like him. She knew her presence pleased him, but she'd be out of her mind to think of him in any other way! The relation was one between two people who liked to talk to each other when they were out of the mill and who worked together well in it.

All this was before the concert given in October by the new Town Orchestral Society and before Armistice Day in November, the first of its kind and celebrated on the 11th of that month.

These two events carried a disturbance with them so that later Freda was to look back upon the beginning of October that year as the last time she was her old self, content to sit reading or to look into the fire and dream a little.

Freda had never heard of the Orchestral Society and had never heard any music other than songs, hymns, the piano playing of relatives or acquaintances, the offerings of the town band and some school 'concerts'. Kathleen had learned to play the piano and there were little pieces which she played quite well; at school a mistress had played Chopin, which Freda had enjoyed, but that was the extent of her knowledge. So when Mr Stainton told her one afternoon at work that this new 'society'

was to play in the town the next Monday evening and that he
happened to have been given tickets, and had one over, and
would she like it, her first reaction was to ask him what sort of
music it would be.

'Well, they call themselves "orchestral",' said James, 'but as
there are at present only a few of them I think it will be chamber
music.' Freda wondered what on earth that could be and James,
seeing her puzzlement, went on – 'I think string quartets, or trios
for piano and stringed instruments – I used to go with your father
when we were young, you know, to concerts in Woolsford.'

'I've never been to a concert like that – only to concert parties,'
said Freda. 'I'd love to come – but is it expensive?'

'I'm offering you a spare ticket, Freda,' he said, his eyes on her
face.

'What time does it start?'

'Seven – but it's not your bookkeeping evening is it, Monday?'
He knew very well it was not.

'No, that's Wednesdays and Fridays – well, thank you, Mr
Stainton.'

She wondered whether she might have to dress up but was later
told not to, and that they were only 'amateurs' but they were said
to be good.

Why did Freda not inform her mother that the invitation was
from her boss? She did not, said only that there were some tickets
at work for a concert and she might go on the Monday, would be
back at ten. Nell was pleased. Freda was going out at last. Freda
decided to wear her green suit with an art silk jersey of a rose
colour. It was all quite exciting but she hoped nobody she knew
would be there, so she could listen to Mr Stainton who knew about
everything, even music.

The recital was to take place in the Sunday School Hall of the
largest Methodist chapel in town. It had a raised platform from
which children usually heard the Superintendent deliver his
homilies. Freda had not attended that chapel, preferred another
nearer Rose Terrace which was newer. But she had stopped
going there since she was about fifteen, having taken fright at the
implication that if she continued she must become a member.
Religion meant little to her really.

He was waiting for her at the entrance and she followed him
into the hall. About a hundred people were already seated and he
led her to two seats at the side at the back. A cyclostyled

programme was on the seat at the end of each row and James studied it. 'Schubert,' he said. Freda knew that was the name of a man who had written some of Kath's pieces and also a march which the piano-player sometimes executed at the silent cinema. However this said 'String Quartet in D minor' and James pointed to it and said, 'They are very ambitious.'

James had chosen seats so that he need not see many of his acquaintances who might wonder who his companion was, but after all there was nothing wrong in taking an employee to have her musical tastes improved! He might greet one or two friends during the interval and would behave impeccably towards Freda.

'He wrote it almost a hundred years ago,' he said and she nodded. 'It is his greatest quartet,' he whispered.

Four men came on the dais, no one she recognized, and she sat back to listen, after one surreptitious glance at Mr Stainton who was looking serious.

When they began to play, after many coughs and shuffles from the audience, she found the music at first rather strange. Sad though, she thought, and the 'tune' kept coming back and then disappearing again. It reminded her of a poem they had read at school called *The Lady of Shalott* by Alfred, Lord Tennyson. She wondered why. The last part of the music was very energetic and quick and powerful – though still sad. There was a burst of clapping when they had finished and she joined in it. But what would James Stainton ask her? She hoped that she would not say anything silly – he knew this was her first real concert.

After the interval when James returned from smoking a cigar, having bought her an ice-cream, provided by the firm who had the barrows in town and who had thoughtfully seized the opportunity to make a few sales here as well as at the cinema, one of the musicians sat down alone at the piano to play some Liszt. The programme said 'Années du Pélerinage' and it was really grand, she thought. She turned to Mr Stainton as the notes died away and found that he was looking at her with a strange expression in his eyes. As the clapping started, James, instead of adding to it, took the hand that was in her lap and for a few moments held it, lightly. She turned her face away at first, embarrassed, but he continued to hold the hand so she let it lie and looked at him once more. He was not looking at her now but as she continued to look at his profile he turned back to her again and this time he smiled, released her hand, and whispered – 'Romantic music'. Freda did not know what to think. She had liked the feel of her hand in his, the slight pressure. His hand had been warm, but not hot. The clapping continued and under its cover he whispered, 'May I walk you back home?'

She ought not to be surprised, she thought. She nodded.

They got out quickly since they were at the back of the hall. Outside, it was cold and bright with a starry darkness and the smell of burning leaves.

He did not take her hand again but walked alongside her. 'How will you get home?' she asked. 'Have you brought your carriage or your motor?'

'No – I have my bicycle!' he replied and she laughed. Mr Stainton was well known for riding his bicycle. The walk was uphill under the shelter of trees which had not yet quite shed their leaves. There was complete silence around them.

'May I take your arm?' he asked.

James was feeling overcome with the music and the nearness of the young woman, very much wanting to kiss her, but feeling that he might startle her, frighten her. Yet she had not pulled her hand away. That might be because she was his junior, his employee. How the hell could he tell her they were equals when they were not at work?

He did not kiss her but spoke a little of the music, and when he left her at the end of the lane leading to Rose Terrace he took her hand once more and said, 'Thank you, Freda –'

At work next morning he was quiet and a little subdued but she was determined not to allude to anything unless he did first. The feel of his hand mingled with the feeling of the music. She wished she could repeat both experiences, but separately. Mam had not asked with whom she had gone and she had let it appear that a few of her co-workers had accompanied her. She hoped that nobody who knew her had noticed who she was with, but she did not think they would have done, for nobody likely to have attended the concert would know *her*.

On 11 November, designated as Armistice Day, all the mills in town were to start their buzzers going at exactly eleven o'clock, after which there was to be a two minutes' silence. In bigger towns and cities cannons would be fired. James had decided that at Valley Mills the workers should stand in silence wherever they happened to find themselves, and remain standing until the buzzer started up again after two minutes. He had no intention of speaking to his workforce, many of whom had lost sons or brothers or sweethearts in the carnage in France. He wanted to forget his own war too but feared the two minutes would remind him of it, tell him he had survived when better men had not.

He had not attempted to hold Freda's hand again since that evening in October, and neither had he said anything to remind her of it. He had no idea what she thought of him. She had been her usual efficient self since that evening, always greeting him with a pleasant 'Good morning, Mr Stainton.' He ought to be ashamed of himself, and was – a little.

Freda knew that he often stared at her when he thought she would not notice. She was beginning to acknowledge to herself that James Stainton had some strange kind of feeling for her, but dare not go so far as considering what kind it might be – was it more than a merely friendly one? The hand-holding, the memory of the feel of his hand over hers had sometimes kept her awake at night, but at other times it seemed dream-like. She had not such a high opinion of herself that she assumed men might fall in love with her unless she had shown them some initial interest, and she had never considered James Stainton in this way until the trip to Ilkley. Yet she wished he would hold her hand again. Perhaps he felt guilty about that?

James, still half-ashamed, not of his feelings but that he had let them show, also rebuked himself for cowardice, for not being fair to Freda. What was the use of half-measures? He should have done nothing or have been prepared to tell her that his feelings for her were more than those of friendly affection. He was in love with her, whether he wanted to be or not. He decided that as soon as the buzzer went that morning, even if Freda were in the room at the time, he would remain silent, but take the opportunity of looking steadfastly at her. Their two silences would be a little exciting, he thought. As soon as the second buzzer went he intended to say that he regretted having acted rather foolishly but hoped she would forgive him. The plan sounded rather weakly conceived even to James and he waited for the buzzer with more than a little trepidation, scarcely thinking at all of the war and the reason for the silence, thinking only of his 'confession'. Should he make a completely clean breast of it, tell her he loved her, but promise never to mention it again? That, too, sounded like having things both ways.

In the event, nothing went according to his plan.

Freda was in his office when the clock crept towards eleven, and when the buzzer sounded his only thought was that nobody else would enter for two minutes at least. He had time to think how irrational this was, since he was often alone with her in the office and had never taken advantage of it, as the sound of the first buzzer was still echoing in their ears. He looked across at her. She had been seated, listening to his dictation, but had put her writing pad down and stood up when the buzzer started. She had gone for some reason to the window, and looked out at the cold, foggy November morning. He was suddenly reminded of matters that should have been of far more moment than the desire he had for this young woman: memories of Zeppelin raids rose – but served only to add to the strange excitement he felt in his heart. Before he knew it, he had got out of his chair and moved to be by her at the window. Freda half-turned in the silence, and James stood looking at her. Neither moved until the second buzzer sounded, when she gave a little shudder. James moved towards her then and kissed her on the cheek. Freda felt she was underwater, and in a sort of dream put her finger to her cheek. She knew she did not feel surprised, but had no ready words on her lips. He cleared his throat but continued to look at her.

'It means something to you,' she said finally and moved back to her chair. But she did not sit down at first and Stainton stayed where he was.

'I mean the war –' she said. 'You fought in it.' She had no idea why she had said that.

'It meant something, yes,' he replied. 'But you also mean something to me, Freda.' She waited; her heart was hammering. 'I've wanted to do that ever since the Victory Celebrations in July!' he added.

She looked puzzled. Had he seen her there? She had seen him. 'I will never forget this Armistice Day, Mr Stainton,' she said calmly.

'I don't want you to forget,' he said. 'I would rather think about you, Freda, than about death and war.'

'My father –' she began. She had been thinking about her father at first by the window.

'Have I upset you? I'm sorry, Freda,' he said.

He had not intended to kiss her, no he had not! But he now felt tremendously relieved.

'No,' she said. Her father and James Stainton were muddled in her mind. But one was dead and the other had just kissed her.

'It will make no difference,' he said, 'to your work – our work together – you can forget it if you want. But don't go and leave me, will you? You are the best thing in my life!' She looked at him, thoughts of her father and of death receding.

For answer she, at first timidly, then resolutely, put her hand towards the man, and he took it, and kissed it.

When Bessie came in with the tea-tray they were sitting opposite each other over the table, Freda's head once more bent over her work.

Later that day, as she was in her small room finishing typing out the letters he had dictated to her before the buzzer had sounded, he came in. Shutting the door carefully behind him. She looked up. Was he going to kiss her again? No. Instead, he said: 'Freda, I know I should apologize – and yet I don't want to!'

She waited. Was it wrong that he had kissed her cheek? She supposed it must be, or that folk would think so.

'I only wanted to say –' he cleared his throat – 'that I have – feelings for you which I know I ought not to have – and I should not have let them show – but I'm glad I did! Will you forgive me? – tell me I should not –' he paused at random.

'There is nothing to forgive, Mr Stainton. I – I like you –'

'It is that I *love* you, Freda,' he finally got out. 'I have to say the words. Now you can find another job if you feel you must! We can continue as before though, if you stay. But I had to tell you or it would not be fair. You can forget it if you want!'

Freda's heart was thumping. She got out, 'I like to be here – and if you – like me – well it will not stop me working for you, will it?' Yet she knew that he felt love; she could see it in his eyes. Love to Freda was a sort of holy grail she had always hoped to be led to one day. That it should be James Stainton who led her to it was what her dream had told her. In a flash she accepted it.

'If you accept it, I will try to behave myself,' he said. 'And when there is nobody else about, please call me James.'

The others called him 'Mr James' though!

It was to be a secret then? Yes, she supposed it must be. She felt excited, not at all apprehensive at this moment. He represented security for her, kindness. But she felt her cheeks burning. She lifted her head and stared at him full in the face. He did not look excited, but upset. 'You are married,' she finally got out, still wondering even then, whether perhaps he did not mean that sort of love.

'I know – and therefore it must not be. But you had to know.' His voice was thick. She saw incredulously that she had caused him to suffer.

'Here at the mill, it seems funny,' she said. 'But I like to be with you even for work – James.'

'We might meet elsewhere,' he went on, emboldened, but distracted, forgetting that he had told her she might forget what he had said. 'You are very young – I don't want love to be a burden – I want you to be happy!'

Yes, she could see that, and she *was* happy. 'Oh, perhaps we could go for walks together in the summer?' she suggested, burning her boats and revealing her inmost fantasies. 'But I will not tell anyone –'

'It will be a secret,' he said.

'Yes.'

He stood by her side and she felt his breath on her face, under the faded fair hairs of his moustache which had slightly tickled her hand before.

'People will say I am wicked! But it is not that I want to take unfair advantage of you – just that there is something in me I don't want to – maybe *can't* forgo.' And that I want to give you, he thought. But it is a selfish desire.

She smiled. How could he be wicked? He was a good man even though he was married and should not therefore be saying such things to her. Freda knew nothing about 'leading men on', acted perfectly naturally, but she had never paid much attention to those who spoke of Sin and the necessity for 'pure' women to refuse temptation.

'A new beginning,' he said. 'But we can carry on life as before, can't we, now things are out in the open?'

Freda said demurely, 'It will depend on you, Mr Stainton,' and spoke wiser than she knew.

Now he felt he must go, and he had his hand on the door knob, though he wanted to take her in his arms. 'Yes, I know. I wish you could depend on me for *everything*, not just a job and a wage!' He smiled, and Freda set seal on her own life when she chose to return the two kisses she had received, warmly on his cheek, with all the spontaneity and freshness of youth.

* * *

The image of her standing at the door he took into an imagination that was already full of thoughts about her: Freda – with her gold-brown hair piled up at the back of her head, a few wisps escaping down her neck in soft tendrils … Freda with her heart-shaped face and her bright, hazel eyes and the full lips which so tantalized him. Not by any gesture or remark or a stray absent-mindedness did he let any of this enter into his life at Eastcliff with that wife who was a different species from Freda, or with the children whom he loved so dearly. Freda might have been their elder sister, he thought. Thank God she was not. He appeared quite normal at the mill on 12 November, a Wednesday, and they worked together in a companionship he hoped he might hold onto. 'Now you must go to your class,' he said at six o'clock when the buzzer went.

Freda, who had been more excited during the intervening hours than she had ever imagined she could be, was nevertheless also schooled in patience. Now she knew what his feelings were she was in no hurry to push things any further. She had decided on her way home that, yes, he must 'fancy' her. That had given her a feeling of delight mixed with trepidation but she was as used to hiding her true feelings at home as James was. So now she just said 'Good Night', and he smiled at her and told her he was pleased she was taking the trouble to improve her knowledge. It was true, he *was*. He admired women who got on with things, and knew she must have occupations other than those of which he was part or to which he was privy. He savoured all the part of her life he did not know about; it all added to the mystery of Freda. He should be able to keep his idea of her set apart from the gross promptings of the flesh. Did he have to be like other men, always moving in to take what they did not yet possess?

He had a lot to think over, liked to recall that sight of her in the crowd in July; the way she had listened to the Schubert in the Sunday School hall, music that he found heart-wrenching; the stillness of the room after the buzzer had finished sounding the day before, all his thoughts about war and death fading away and changing into his new mental landscape of Freda, overcoming all his own war weariness, the last years in France, and even before, at home, when he had become so tired doing what he had conceived of as his duty. He thought of the trip to Ilkley, Freda by the swift flowing river ... Why should a man be made to feel that such thoughts and memories were a sort of disloyalty to his wife when that wife was no longer one to him in anything but name? Yet as he walked back home up the hill, after Freda had gone to her bookkeeping, greeted by so many who knew him in this small place, he could not help acknowledging that if Lina were hale and hearty and if they were a real couple he would not be able to exonerate himself. But then he might not feel as he did, and that was disloyal on the other hand to this new love which he refused to see only as the object of his parched physical self that needed fresh woods and pastures new. If he were true and loyal and faithful to Lina he was not true to himself, and if he were true to his inmost feelings he was disloyal to his long ago promises. He had once thought that marriage to a seemingly pleasant woman and a shared domestic life was all that life was to offer him, though he had been a romantic youth. His children did not enter into the equation at all. I just want Freda there near me, he thought again and again. If she took fright and decided to leave the mill what should I do? There would then be nothing to look forward to, nothing at all! He pondered such things in his heart, aware all the time of the fragility of mortals, the passing of time and the precious quality of Freda's youth. There was no reason why Freda should feel anything for him remotely resembling what he felt for her. She knew that her father and himself had been close years ago, and that probably made him more accept-able. If only he were a disembodied creature, a spirit who might commune with Freda's own spirit ... but he knew that love always wanted ever more closeness. He wanted to be closer to her than anyone had ever been since her infancy, wanted in other words to possess her even while hating the idea of this 'possession' when looked at in the light of reason. But then most things looked at in that light lost their excitement. His wife had once told him long ago that he was a 'a very rational kind of person'! What would she think of him now? But it had not even been true then. Did he want Freda to possess *him* too? All unknowingly she already did, in all the ways that mattered, he supposed. The beloved, Freda, was the possessor of the lover – himself. How could he ever become the object of *her* love; would he want that? Yes, he would; the intensity of his emotion seemed to require it.

But if he won Freda, 'had' Freda, made her what in the district they called a fancy woman – he'd even heard the old word 'leman' used – would his love eventually melt away? There was only one way of finding out: to possess her. He shrank from it at the same time as longing for it. Why could men not stay for ever, as he had been for some months now, in this blessed and enthralling dream of infatuation? Was it a return to youth, now that he was over forty, settled, respectable?

He *loved* Freda, might love her more in sensual bliss, but that was not finally what he wanted from Freda Caston, though he might want to introduce her to it. He had no idea whether she would want that from him. Talking of walks together was Freda's way of showing him she had put him into her own personal landscape, he supposed, didn't mean that she was casting herself before him for him to do what he wanted. Only because he was that wretched creature, a man, did his love lead naturally to desire; it seemed the best way of losing the self to find it in another. Was he *so* tired of himself?

James had not often been a prey to such introspection of self-doubts and it had the effect of upsetting all his estimates of himself. Or Freda had upset them! And yet ... he would not want her to be 'lost' even if she might one day love him back, even if it already gave him pain to think of her with any other man. Wretched jealousy was already on the scene before anything was ventured! Holding her hand and kissing her cheek had so far been enough, and he shivered at the memory of those two silent minutes when they had stood together by the window as if the future were set out before them compressed into time's silence and stretching away in space into infinity, not into the mill yard below and in front of them. Oh, no doubt that sex was selfish and a destroyer of love! *Love* was not supposed to be selfish. Was that a valid distinction?

Such thoughts would recur as he shaved in the morning with his 'cut-throat' razor. For a time after his return from the battle-front he'd grown a beard but had shaved it off after James Caston's funeral because he decided it made him look older than his years. In an affair of passion, love and sex were the same, or at least not separable – that was what most *women* thought. But an affair could be accomplished much more easily and with less effect on others' lives if love were extracted from the sum. Was that all he 'really' wanted from Freda? He laid down his razor aghast at the thought. He had been in love before, years ago, before his marriage, and not with Lina Harris, but it had surely not engulfed him like this? Adultery was a nasty word and he had always striven to be an honourable man. The episodes in France had not touched his spirit though perhaps they should have done. If he wanted Freda it was because he loved her. It was as simple as that. Then a little worm of doubt would niggle itself into his thoughts! 'Do you not love her because you want her?' Why should one be more ashamed of the one than the other? The religion in which he had been brought up said one should be. But his feelings were 'pure', he was sure – bright and strong and tender.

He struggled with such thoughts as the days went on. They did not destroy his feelings for Freda though he trembled before what might destroy that, or change it, aware of the power of compulsive passion, what a book he had read in France called 'obsessional lust'. If he were given a choice in the matter and the Almighty offered him a lifelong mutual sexless adoration between Freda and himself, would he not accept it, and reject an expression of love which had less to do with the hidden recesses of his imagination and all to do with physical compulsion, more powerful because of his love for its object? He went on struggling with himself, unable to speak to anyone of such things, least of all to Freda. There was a magic in his thoughts about her that came into his mind when he could not sleep and thought of her pale face and her sudden blush, and her quiet voice and the swell of her breasts under the high-necked blouse she wore for work. All the mystery of a human being. The delight he took in her real presence was different. It left him dry-mouthed, and yet it was not a 'merely sensual' delight. Seeing her, studying her, listening to her every word, was a different sort of entrancement. Alone once more he would puzzle over what it had been and why.

All these convoluted thoughts were not stopping him working and fulfilling his obligations; indeed he appeared to have been given a new access of energy. He might be poring over an order or a project for new machinery or even having a drink in Woolsford with an old friend, betraying nothing of his inner thoughts, but as soon as he had a moment to himself his feelings for Freda would return. Wanting to serve her ... to sacrifice himself for her ... to protect her ... desires almost as powerful as when, back at the mill, he might unexpectedly catch sight of her, the silhouette of her shoulders against the square-windowed glass in the door of the old storeroom. He would notice the days when she was paler and there were faint circles under her eyes, and would want to take her hand in his again and cover it with kisses, stroke the soft skin of her inner wrist. He wanted nothing to change, to stay for ever in this dream of love, himself and herself together for always in an eternal moment.

But he hardly ever considered divorce, though Lina might even grant him one if he did not mind the obloquy of being a 'guilty partner'. It would have to be Lina who asked for it though, and he was sure she never would. In any case he recoiled in horror before the idea of being unfaithful to his children who were also his responsibility until they were grown.

There was undoubtedly an affinity between the two of them, thought James, but he was chary of stressing to her his great affection for her father and was uncertain whether Freda felt the same affinity. The realization might come to her one day that she might do what she wanted with her father's old friend; he was sure she had no idea of the extent of her power. Because she was young she would be so far uncorrupted by ideas of sexual power, or 'feminine' qualities of coyness and sentiment. He felt she had no other men in her past with whom she might compare him, though why was a mystery, since other men must have found her attractive. Most young men however did not want to deliver their souls over to young women; in that respect Freda was lucky to find him. Then he thought, but I do not really know her! – maybe I've made her up to be what I want, the woman I can love? That thought made him fearful when he was absent from her, made him fear revealing the depth of his passion for her. It was an indecent, terrible, strange passion that might be dangerous to him as well as to her ... she might laugh at him, mock him. Those who declared themselves in the drama of love, usually men, who had to take the initiative, were very vulnerable. But he would take that risk, imagined he could convince her this was no sordid seduction. She might misunderstand? But what was there to misunderstand? She had certainly, he guessed, been surprised.

At other times, when all these thoughts wearied him, he would think that he had not just suddenly become young again but filled with the conviction that he had never known a woman before. He thought of the progression from hand-holding to cheek and hand-kissing and from that to one day kissing Freda on that mouth of hers, those full lips, and he felt as if he were seventeen, and might court a rebuff if he tried to go a little further in some furtive embrace, though that was nonsense, and his embraces would be furtive only because of the circumstances.

These cold worm-like feelings and fears did not stay long with him and he resolved to banish them. He was longing for the opportunity to show her what he felt for her, how he adored her.

Yet although his fears did not succeed for long in banishing his love, he did also wake from time to time in the nights that followed 11 November with the curious conviction that James Caston beyond the grave might in some way know of his own feelings for Freda. He did not believe in an after-life, nor in messages from the dead, and recognized his apprehension for a sign of guilt. What might James have thought of him if he knew? But, for some reason he could not fathom, he knew that if James had not died he would never have fallen in love with the man's daughter. He would have missed what he felt were the most intense emotions of his whole life. If Freda became his lover would she too think of her father and be filled with guilt?

No, he felt sure that Freda would think it was nothing to do with her father! Perhaps one day she might even reassure him. When it came down to it women were more practical than men, accepted love with less fuss, were, if they were given the chance, less conventionally moral, even if they were censorious of those feelings in others. He argued this way with himself as he tried to fall asleep again. Even if he could sometimes imagine Freda talking to him and convincing him that he had done no wrong in loving her, did his very responsibility for her rule out any further physical intimacy?

If he abandoned himself, in the midst of whatever practical difficulties to these good, strong – even reasonable – emotions they might alter for ever the life of a young woman whom he knew would then become even more dear to him. If he did not, and left Freda alone, his love might fester, turn sour and defeat him, leave him ready perhaps to die in the spirit, remaining alive only to look after his family, try to do his best – as he had always done – for his wife. Wryly, he thought he ought to be a Mohammedan who would be allowed another younger wife. Why was conscience always on the side of conventional wisdom?

Naturally he said nothing of any of this to Freda and saw that she, from an initial incredulity, had quickly grown to accept the fact of his affection even if she had no idea of the extent of his worship of her. He could tell this because she acted towards him with a certain confidence though never with an easy assumption of intimacy.

Before Christmas that year they were very busy: it might be a false dawn for the industry and he could not yet relax his efforts to find new markets. Life at Valley Mills went on therefore just as usual and if anyone noticed their owner's new mixture of energy and occasional preoccupation, nobody remarked upon it. They were only just getting back to normal after the war.

Freda knew she must carry on just as before; she was a good worker, and the memory of the kiss, and now the frequent smiles from James in her direction, made her happy and even carefree. She sensed that one day this situation must change but was content to wait. She was a young woman who had always kept her feelings to herself, except with her father, and one who hated embarrassments. James's impulse had not made her at all embarrassed and that, she felt, was strange. Her knowledge of what some young men did to young women had embarrassed and even mortified her but had touched nothing essential in her being. She would leave it to Mr Stainton – James – as she now thought of him when she was alone. He would explain further, or let matters rest. In the meantime she would be cautious. If he kissed her again though, she would be ready!

James, in spite of these bouts of introspection when he was stricken with guilt, lay low, biding his time, but continued to take a simple pleasure in having Freda around. Things went on like this until Christmas which was during a damply cold and misty week. The employees were to have two days off. Christmas Day was a Thursday and the orders were not large enough to make opening the mill worthwhile on the following Friday and Saturday morning. Boxing Day was not usually a free day for the firm but many mills were still working half time and had the Friday off in any case, so the Valley weavers and burlers and menders joined them for one-and-a-half days' unpaid holiday.

Freda spent Christmas Day with her mother and grandmother and aunt as usual. Nell was beginning a heavy cold but insisted on cooking a meal of roast pork, to which Cissie and Nan were invited. Presents consisted of things made at home: a new blouse for Freda and a pair of stockings from Freda to Nell. Cissie and Mrs Caston never bothered much with Christmas boxes, early financial struggles had made both concerned about waste and they neither expected nor received much more than cards. Freda however had bought each a pair of gloves from the market and was glad that she was now well enough off to be generous. It was not the first Christmas without James Caston; that had been last year when they had hardly noticed the festival at all. Nell had intended to go to the grave on Boxing Day but Freda offered to go on the Sunday instead if Nell's cold were not better and to take the little holly wreath they had made to place on the grave, which now bore a simple flat stone with 'James Caston 1877–1918' cut into the plain grey slab. On the Saturday, Nell's cold had not improved though her nose had stopped streaming, so on Sunday morning Freda insisted she would take the wreath and give her mother an afternoon in bed. The dread was always that a cold would 'go on the chest', and Nell hated illness. She agreed therefore, and on the Sunday when they had finished the cold pork, with some cabbage and potatoes cooked by Freda and taken up to Nell in bed, the former departed, holding the wreath in a paper bag. She knew the grave was tidy, but had been there only a few times since the funeral, her mother always taking a weekly walk alone in that direction on Sundays. Freda held the small parcel in her gloved hand. It was misty and cold and she did not expect that the cemetery would be much visited that day since folk would have gone on the Friday or Saturday.

It was not a long walk; up the road and across the park and then down another road a little uphill, the old Turnpike that led finally to Eastcliff. The 'new' cemetery was about fifty years old and had impressive gates. A gravel path, with grass stretching away on each side in what had once been a meadow, arrived at a stone arch spanning two small chapels, one on one side for the Church of England, another for the Free Churches. Even in death they were divided: her father had once pointed this out to her and said he could not understand folk. It was the same God, and the same fate attended the worshippers – why should people lay such impor-tance on their temporary differences? James's own grave was on the far side of the Free Churches' chapel, where the newer grass stretched right up to a dry stone wall, over which was conti-nuation of the meadow land near the older lane, older than the Turnpike, that also led to Eastcliff.

She passed the monuments erected by wealthier residents of Brigford to their dead: a white angel in flowing draperies was the one she liked best. There were many headstones and many wreaths, and flowers in jars standing on the graves, the wreaths sometimes atop the headstones, but today she could see only about ten yards ahead and it was an eerie feeling. She had never been frightened by the cemetery but was glad when she came to the central arch, beyond which were the graves of mostly poorer folk. The doors of both chapels were locked, though a faint smell of incense lingered near one, probably from the morning service held here once a month by a popish parson.

She went under the arch and out into the half-filled cemetery beyond. Her father's grave was to the left, at the end of the second pathway, next to the grave of a small child who had died of pneumonia the same week. Nell had drawn her attention to it: 'Our dear little Florrie lies here where once she played so gaily'. Nell had thought these words beautiful but Freda had secretly doubted that Florrie had ever played here in the cemetery. But perhaps she had been brought to put flowers on a summer grave and had danced around childishly, unaware of the reason for the place?

Freda remembered the direction and soon arrived at her father's stone. Here the mist had partially dispersed but it was cold and she did not wish to linger. At least it was not windy, as it had been at the funeral over a year ago. She remembered seeing James Stainton that day and paused for a moment in her placing of the small wreath at the foot of the slab under the figures of James Caston's dates of birth and death. There ought to be a rose tree for the summer planted at the side of the grave. It was only a yard or so away from the slab on the other side, some woman called Mabel Althorpe who had died that autumn. Behind it however there was a larger space and she resolved to enquire about a small shrub. The grass edges were neatly clipped, and in summer the grass had been regularly cut – the workers here did their job efficiently. For a moment she stood looking down at the words of her father's name, trying to believe that underneath in a coffin were the remains of the father she had loved, but the effort was a vain one. On the one hand she knew it was so; on the other it did not seem possible, seemed to have no connection with the person she remembered, and she could not believe it. She rubbed her hands to get them warm and folded the paperbag, putting it neatly in her pocket. In the distance she could hear the voices of women, come also on a post-Christmas pilgrimage, but they faded away as she walked back towards the archway. As she was passing under it and just about to go out on to the path and back to the road, a figure loomed suddenly under the arch on his way to the plots at the other side. She stopped, for it was James Stainton. He stopped too, in disbelief. He was carrying a larger wreath than her own and was dressed in a heavy grey overcoat and gauntlet gloves, a grey scarf flung over one shoulder and a soft Homburg hat on his head.

James said questioningly: 'Freda?'

'Mr Stainton!' she exclaimed in her surprise, changing it to – 'James?'

'Freda!' he repeated, with joy in his voice. He put his wreath down on the flags and advanced, arms outstretched. His overcoat was pearled with moisture and his breath sketched an arabesque in the cold air. 'What are you doing here? I thought the place deserted.'

'No – there were some women,' she said. 'I came to put a wreath on father's grave.'

'And I on my mother's,' he said. 'Will you come with me whilst I do that? You must show me your father's grave – it was over the other side, wasn't it?'

'Yes – further back – I'll show you.'

They walked along together. Mrs Stainton's grave was on the left before the arch, an urn topping a plinth. 'It's hideous,' James said. – 'But my father wanted it like that.'

Freda read 'In loving memory of Alice Stainton born on the 28th of December 1850 died on the eleventh of June 1917'. He put the wreath on the grave that looked like a bed.

'She died when you were in France?'

'Yes – I could not come back for the funeral – she'd not been ill long.' He stood for a moment, silently.

Freda took his hand in her own gloved one, for he looked sad. They stood together for another minute in silence then James put his arm round her. 'You feel solid enough,' he said. 'I thought you were a ghostly vision – I was thinking about you.' Freda had not been thinking about him since the moment when she had remembered his presence at her father's funeral, but now she leaned against him. 'You are cold?' She pulled her cap down further over her ears in answer. 'Show me James's grave and put your hand in my pocket. Nobody will see us!' She put her left hand in his pocket, slipping the glove off first, and encountered his own hand that was cold but now also gloveless and together they walked back under the arch and to the Caston grave.

Perhaps it is a 'sign' thought James. Here together, laying the ghosts of the past. When he saw the small wreath placed on his old friend's grave he stopped and drew her closer to him. He was trembling. 'What a place for a tryst,' he said lightly. And then he bent down to Freda's cold face and kissed her lips. They were not cold, though her nose was, and he brushed his lips over the whole of her face. Freda opened her eyes which she had automatically shut and saw his own blue ones regarding her. He buried his face then in the little cap on her head and they stood entwined for what seemed a long time before he released her, murmuring: 'Oh, Freda – I do so love you! All through Christmas I've been thinking about you. Did you think of me at all?'

'I did on Christmas Eve and in the evening of Christmas Day. I was wishing I could give you a present!' she answered honestly. There did not seem to be any connection between this tall, handsome, overcoated man whose cold hand she had held inside his pocket, whose lips had wandered all over her face, and the man whose orders she took daily from across a table, whose letters only four days ago she had indeed been typing. Vaguely she recalled her thoughts about them both, as though the reality of the two was nothing to do with their presence, but only with the place one had held and the other had begun to hold in her heart.

'And tomorrow,' James was saying – 'Tomorrow it will be "Mr Stainton" again – I wanted to invite you round yesterday – but how could I without inviting your mother? – It would be living a lie?'

'Mother has a bad cold,' Freda said. 'Did your children have a nice Christmas?'

'I believe so – in a few moments I have to go back to them. My wife is abed – I slipped out because I needed the exercise, and my father is laid up too. He usually comes here on Christmas Sunday.'

'Both of us doing something for someone else,' replied Freda. 'It's my mother who comes, generally.'

'Oh, Freda,' he said. 'I wish we could run away – now – to somewhere nice and warm and have tea in some hotel where nobody knows us.' There was a catch in his breath and she saw he might be thinking of more than tea. She looked round again. The mist was lifting slightly. 'You know how fond I was of your father,' he said as they walked slowly back to the archway.

'I expect he was of you, too,' Freda replied. 'But it is all past.'

'Do you think the past has reverberations?' he asked her, stopping suddenly.

'My father's past, do you mean? *I* am too young to have a past,' she said lightly.

'We both loved him,' James said sorrowfully. 'But there *is* something of him in you.'

Freda had not thought of it quite like that before and it made her feel a little uneasy. 'You look sad,' she said.

'But I'm not sad when *you* are with me – I want to kiss you again!'

For answer Freda gave him a kiss on his mouth and put her arms round him. To James she made life seem full of promise.

'Promise me you won't kiss anyone else,' he said, foolish for a moment.

'Well, I might kiss Mother,' she said playfully. James had a manner that belied his feelings, she thought. He could half-joke about what was serious to him and it accorded with the slightly ironic attitude people had sometimes reproached her with too.

'We can't stay here in the cemetery, but I don't want to leave you here,' he said.

'We could walk down the road together,' said Freda. 'Except I suppose you will be going home in the opposite direction?' After all, she thought, we met by chance, both doing perfectly innocent things and why should I not walk with him?

He sensed a small rebellion. 'What I meant was I'd like to take you to a tea-shop – if not an hotel – and talk to you where nobody knows anything about us.' And then take you to bed, he thought.

'They are all closed, since it is Sunday,' she said. 'It would be nice to go to Woolsford on a Saturday though – there is a lovely shop there with cakes and scones!'

He laughed. Then Freda looked sober again. 'We shall see each other tomorrow – as you said.' He was now, she felt, The Man, the one with whom she wanted to spend not only her working hours but her few leisure hours too. Why should she not?

'We can always go to the mill,' he said slowly – 'not today, because it is too late. But nobody goes there till midnight to stoke up the boilers, and we could be together without anyone's being the wiser. Do you go to church? Chapel?'

'No.'

'Then we could meet whilst the good folk are at prayer,' he said. She was silent so he said, 'I don't mean to sound bitter – it is just that it is all so difficult.'

Freda was thinking how she admired him and how strange it was to have been kissed by those lips that were now talking to her. But she said: 'I'd like to be able to see you – I think of you a good deal – but I understand you – we – have to be careful. People gossip – they do nothing else!'

It was his turn to admire her. 'I just feel I never want to be parted when I am with you. I know I have to manage – *you* have to as well.' He was far from believing that it was as difficult for Freda alone as it was for him; her body was not yet awakened whilst his had begun to torment him.

'You make me feel – different –' she said. 'When you are there, I mean – as though I didn't exist – or, you know, the person I *was* didn't exist. But I know it will all be the same when I go home – that's life, I suppose.'

He smiled at the unsophisticated end of her sentence – but knew that underneath there was also a dormant sophistication that only a few weeks with him would bring out. The mature Freda could be and do great things, he thought, moved by her mystery. He both wanted and did not want her to be in thrall to him as he was to her. 'I have to turn here,' he said drawing her to him. There was no one about; opposite was the yard of the monumental mason where half-hewn slabs and gravestones and figures loomed out of the mist. She did not want him to go, he could tell. But she swallowed and said, 'You make everything different – but I was quite content before, I think.'

'I'm sorry,' he said, and was.

Freda thought, I'd like to go back with him and not worry about his family and all that. It is not part of the man I know. We could just be together, and happy. The idea that he might have power over her to make her want something she had never wanted before had insinuated itself and as she grasped the half-formed thought, he said: 'You have power over me, Freda – I don't know why, but you have. So you will have to be strong for both of us if we are to try to love each other. It's because I love you that you have that power!' They stopped by the far wall of the mason's and embraced once more, this time drawing their bodies closer.

'I love you, James,' she said. 'But I will take care not to be seen with you for your sake!'

'And yours too, Freda my darling,' he said and she thrilled at the unexpected words. Nobody had ever called her that before. Her father had said 'Love' to her and 'dear' but never 'darling'. It sounded exotic.

'Also, you see, for my wife's sake,' he said taking the plunge so that she would realize the difficulties. Freda thought, she need never know. 'I hate having to say that,' he said. 'And really it is the children …'

But nothing has happened! he thought to himself. There is still time to draw back.

'It could be fun to pretend, I suppose,' Freda said. 'I mean at the office.'

'I wish we need not pretend anything,' James said. 'It's undignified and not the way I want to think of you.' He kissed her hand before turning back towards Eastcliff Road.

Oh, he was so nice and so thoughtful – and so attractive. Freda mused over his words as she walked back home in a dream. Though she was cold she was excited, had to walk twice round the park to become normal once more.

Sunday lectures were what James suggested for their meetings for the time being. They were to take place in the New Year and they could both go, and then be together afterwards – or pretend they were attending in order to go somewhere else. The lectures were only every fortnight but, as James said as he held her hand and kissed it at work late one evening of the following week – 'It will be something until the better weather comes.' As he had walked back in the dusk that Sunday he had felt like an escapee from prison or a young boy forbidden to see a friend. Freda said, 'Oh, then I shall be able to use my alibi,' and laughed, and so they planned for the first time a clandestine meeting.

The first Sunday lecture was on the solar system and had an audience of about one hundred. Freda understood very little of it but decided that James would explain it if necessary. He was sitting at the back and she was in the middle row with nobody she knew. The lecture would be over long before the time Freda had intimated to Nell, so that she might see James afterwards, if only for a cup of tea in the church hall. 'We can see each other for about an hour afterwards this time,' James had said, 'And we can think about each other during the lecture!' Freda found this idea rather exciting although it turned out that the first lecture went on longer than they had expected. There was scarcely time to drink a cup of tea before she had to return home.

'Did you understand it at all?' he asked her, appearing at her shoulder as she tried to negotiate tea, her handbag and the programme.

'Not really,' she confessed.

'Somehow I feel that we might give the next one a slip,' murmured James.

The existence of that fortnightly lecture had however been enough to give Freda the liberty to be out on Sunday nights in future.

The next lecture was to be at the beginning of February, but before then Freda had had more time to think about James Stainton and their meetings. Standing next to James in a crowd of people had its own peculiar pleasure, but she longed to be alone with him. It was very pleasant to chat in the office with him even though people were for ever in and out of the place. The difficulty of being together and alone away from the mill made time at work precious.

When, one week at the end of January, James had to go away on business to London she found the office a desert. It was during those few days that Bessie asked her how she was liking working for 'the master'. His absence seemed to have unlocked her tongue.

'Oh, I'm very happy here,' Freda said.

'Aye, he's a good boss. Doesn't tek liberties, like some I could mention!' the older woman said. Freda waited for elucidation but as none appeared to be forthcoming she asked what Bessie meant. 'Why – you know – some on 'em are right wick – think a lass is there just for their bit of fun!'

'Who is like that?' asked Freda, pretending to look down at her work as Bessie stood with the tea-tray obviously ready for a gossip.

'Mr Greenhalgh for one, at Marshall's – haven't you heard about *him*?'

'No,' replied Freda faintly. 'What does he get up to then?'

Bessie smiled conspiratorially. 'Wick, like I told thee.'

'But what does *that* mean?'

'Lass, don't tell me your Mam's never used that word!'

'No – she hasn't. Does it mean wicked then?'

Bessie burst out laughing. 'Nay, lass, wick, *you* know – lively, ready to be lit and all!' She lowered her voice. 'Hasn't tha' nivver heard on "dipping his wick"?'

Freda blushed. So that was what it meant! Bessie was surprisingly crude. But she rallied and said, 'I suppose it might mean "woken up"?'

'Aye, it does an' all – woken up! Aye!' and the woman went out chuckling.

'I thought Freda Caston a bit stuck up,' she said to her sister that night. 'But she's not – a bit young for her age, I reckon, but she knows what's what.'

Freda pondered the insinuation later, at home. She now remembered Cissie using the same word once to her mother; they had lowered their voices when she came into the room. Freda was well-acquainted with the facts of life. She might be a virgin but from an early age she had heard the ruder boys describe those proceedings which she at first thought too distasteful to be possible, but on later reflection decided must actually happen. She thought about this now. What had been presented to her as an invasion, a disgustingly sordid and dirty going-on was suddenly invested with excitement. When James had kissed her she had felt something melt inside her, hadn't really thought about it then directly, but realized later that she had desired him, as it was obvious he had her. But the talk of men being 'wick' and using female employees for their own pleasure was not an agreeable one. James was not like that! He might want her, he was only human, but she knew that he loved her and that such acts, when committed on account of love – in the way she was sure her own parents had committed them – looked quite different. It made her realize she was truly a part of the whole world of women now. But she also knew that if even a suspicion of such acts arose, it became the cause of great gossip. The men couldn't have cared – not that many men she had met acted so shamelessly – but the women had their 'reputations' to think of. What was regarded as natural for men to get, if they could, even if it were the cause of much ribaldry later, was still seen as 'shame' upon the woman.

The Friday before the next lecture James was back from London and said, as she was leaving that evening, knowing he would not be in the office in the morning though she would have to be, 'Freda – meet me at the mill on Sunday instead of the Sunday School? Will you? I'm being driven insane missing you – what with work and – everything! Just to talk. Freda?' His voice was low. She must have looked uncertain, for he went on, 'The lecture's to be on the internal combustion engine – I don't think that will interest you, will it!'

'Everyone knows everyone else's business,' she said. 'I don't want to be remarked on, James.'

'Why, what's the matter, what has happened? – has somebody been saying something?'

'No – it was just Bessie talking about Mr Greenhalgh at Low Mills being "wick"!'

'Oh, for God's sake, Freda! – he's an old lecher – you can't think –?'

'Of course not. No, I don't – but that's what "they" will say if we are seen together!'

'I know – but I love you.'

She touched his hand that was on the desk over the letter he'd been signing. 'James – I wish we could go away!'

She felt rash, angry that such subterfuges as a lecture society had to be used in order just to meet a person of the opposite sex in the town. Of course it was his being married that made all the difference ...

'Let's talk at the mill,' he said again. 'I'll be there at seven and if you want to go straight on to the lecture, then we will.'

'No – I want to talk to *you*,' she said. But she meant kiss you, let you kiss me and hold me in your arms – whether folk think it's wrong or not.

Valley Mills on a grey February Sunday. Freda came up the stairs at five past seven having seen that the light was on in the upstairs office. If the watchman challenged her she'd say she'd forgotten her pay packet. But James would have seen to that. She was excited, yet upset. What was the use of being loved when these things were forbidden? She forgot all this when James opened the door at the top of the stairs and, having closed it, took her into his arms with a long sigh. They remained entwined, not kissing, just holding each other for a long time until James took off her brown cap and she shook her hair out that was never kept very tidy, pins always falling down her neck.

'What is it to be?' he murmured. 'The lecture or a game of ping-pong at the club? Or a Sunday swim?' She laughed, pulled free and saw he was looking at her with a mixture of what she thought was 'devilment' and shyness. He had lit only the gas globe on the wall so that their shadows till he drew the curtains were enormous.

'Just here with you,' she said. 'But can I make some tea? Let's pretend we have all the time in the world, and then we can talk.'

'I'll help you,' he said, and together they located the gas ring, the kettle, two cups, and Bessie's tray and sugar.

'No milk,' said Freda.

'Never mind.'

She felt perfectly happy and perfectly safe with James but when finally they were seated side by side at the familiar table, sipping their tea, he said, 'People will say all the wrong things about us if ever they find out – the fact that I adore you, Freda, won't make any difference. "That's what all men are like", they'll say. And I can't blame you if you believe them. I sometimes wonder myself.'

She looked at him earnestly. 'Oh, you are not like that,' she said. 'I *don't* believe them – How can other people ever know?'

'You see, Freda,' he said slowly, and took her hand, but looked away. 'If we – if you – became closer to me – in the way men and women can be – which is what I can't help hoping will happen one day – nobody would stick up for you whereas they'd just say a few rude words about me.'

She knew he desired her and she *wanted* him to be closer in that way.

'What good are words?' he said then and he put his cup down and kissed her neck and her lips and her eyes, kisses which were returned with fervour by Freda. 'I've to talk to you,' he said again. 'About my marriage – if it were a good one I suppose I would not risk what people call an "adventure" – but really I have no business to make excuses. I know I'd love you in any case! – The fact is, my wife no longer cares for me – nor I for her, though we are not enemies. We grew apart when she was ill – after the children were born. I felt it was my fault, but that it would pass. It never did, and she began to be depressed and sluggish, then full sometimes of a sort of peculiar glee – in love with God, I suppose – a sort of religious mania worse than her neglecting herself, neglecting everything, even the children. I tried my best – it's gone on for nine years now. It was worse after the little girl was born – a child she said she wanted, I did not force myself upon her – but I cannot leave her, for she has no one else but me. So you see, Freda, I've been very unhappy and I can't see that it has been my fault ... if it were, I'd know, I think. It was all a terrible mistake and now we are both caught ... We were never right for each other and *that* was my fault. I didn't know myself, you see – I thought it was enough to be kind and have a family and look after a wife, love our children. I knew that I wasn't in love with her at first as I had been, oh, once or twice before I married. But I thought it was better to settle down to be a good citizen. And in spite of everything there are still ties between us – you see – or do I sound completely selfish? I did not plan to fall in love with you, Freda – I never expected anything more out of life. And I feel so bad about it – that if you accept me I shall ruin *your* life too ...' He did not look at her as he finished this long speech.

Freda was listening to him carefully. 'I am sorry,' she said finally. 'I mean about your marriage – your wife – I suppose most people marry for the same reasons you did?' She was thinking, Oh, I wish *we* could be married!

'My being married doesn't stop the way I feel about you – but I suppose it could spoil it. Yet, Freda, it's the purest thing I've ever felt! Can you understand that? Though I dream of your being my wife – that's what I should like, oh yes –' He had tears in his eyes.

'If we ever could, you know – go away together, I would – with you,' Freda said.

'You'd be taking such a risk,' he said. 'I too – but it would hurt you, not me – Oh, Freda, my darling girl – I couldn't bear to have you sullied by a hole and corner thing, but what can we do? Must I court you for seven years like Jacob did Rachel and have you leave me then?'

But we could not marry like they did in the Bible, Freda thought. His wife will always be there and he is too honourable to abandon her. His children too ...

Freda had always taken time for her emotions to be aroused but once they were they burned steadily. She had never desired any man before; now that James loved her – and she believed in his love – she was ready to respond. That had nothing to do with the sordid details of what they called 'seduction'. she felt a new power in her – to 'seduce' James Stainton? – and also a curious need for self-annihilation.

He looked up. 'Now I've said what I had to say – let's forget it and be happy even if it's only for an hour or so!' He made no move to embrace her but put his hand over hers that was lying on the table next to the sugar basin.

Freda seemed to see a sort of big green gate in her imagination;

it was shut, but she had the key, and beyond it was a garden of pleasures and sun and happiness. She sighed. But she got up, went over to him, put her arms round him as he sat there and pulled his head to her breast.

They stayed for an hour together at the mill that evening, talking, holding hands, occasionally kissing. James wanted no more than this just then, content to feel she was for once close to him; he stroked the soft skin of her face, gazed on her, drank her in as if she were a magic potion that would alas too soon be snatched away. Freda, having felt the weight of his head against her breast in that first gesture she had instinctively made, was also content. It *was* strange to be so close to a person of the opposite sex – yet it was still to James Stainton, Mr Stainton, as well as to that still unfamiliar human body to which she felt herself attracted. When he said, 'We shall have to go soon, darling,' and pulled her gently on to his knee, she shut her eyes and put her arms round his neck. The only man on whose knee she had sat had been her father years ago when she was young enough to be considered a child still, and the memory was a little strange.

'Does your little girl – Mary – sit on your knee?' she asked him, rousing him from a lapse into drowsy contentment before they must force themselves apart.

James looked into her eyes and saw they were a little troubled and there was a slight frown on the smooth forehead. 'I suppose she must do occasionally,' he replied. 'Though she is not a demonstrative child – I suppose it's my fault that I've never felt near her – I was away when she was a baby. Mrs Petersham is the person she cuddles – not my wife.'

'It's nice to be close like this, even though *I* am not a baby!' Freda said. His answer, honest as it had been, had reassured her. She did not say to him, 'When I was little my father used to let me sit and play with his watch chain on Sundays'. Fathers and lovers were two different species and must not be confused. But being close to a person was a bit like being a child again. It felt comfortable.

James however knew that affection would inevitably be displaced by desire and half-dreaded that. He was not sure whether Freda was *completely* innocent; he would like her to be so, but that would also make him feel even more guilty and responsible. In answer perhaps to his unspoken thoughts, Freda said again, 'I am no longer a child,' and kissed him on the mouth. She felt a compulsion to lay herself emotionally open to him, to allow him to take what he wanted from her, though she was still unsure what exactly she wanted herself, apart from this need to be wanted. James kissed her in return, gently, softly, and she knew that it would not be today, but that it would be soon when their kisses changed their nature.

For a time after this Sunday, James found he was able to live on quite contentedly in a haze of unsatisfied desire. If only he could manage to consider Freda as a close and intimate beloved person who would sustain him in the matter of 'ordinary' life, not feel he would in the natural course of events possess her body ... He put off thinking about that. Meetings were difficult to arrange and he could not bear the idea of a fortnightly tryst in his office which might degenerate into a sort of regular bout of adultery, making Freda nothing but the object of a middle-aged lust. He wrestled with his conscience. Would the fulfilment of his desire make life easier or harder for him, for her, for them both? Where would it, could it, all lead? He did not want to feel 'compelled', was glad that so far he had managed a passionate affection, but longed when he was at home – where he felt more lonely than at work – to have more than that. If he had had an ordinarily dutiful wife used to matrimonial embraces it might have been easier; he might have been able to imagine Freda whilst making love to Lina, but that was impossible, had been impossible now for years, since Mary's birth. *Was* he affectionate enough to his children? He pondered this, thinking of Freda's question, and decided he was probably a remote figure to Mary, if not to Valentine. In the middle of a night when he could not sleep, he wandered into Mary's bedroom and contemplated the round fair face on the pillow and pondered whether Freda's becoming his might alleviate, or release, his obsession with her, so that he might do his duty by *this* child and contain his life within the conventional elements of family. He was both intelligent and honest enough to know that no man is compelled to act out his desires – and was in any case used to suppressing them. He wanted to be happy but also wanted to be released from this long unease that was his life at home.

When one dark Sunday evening in March he did contrive another meeting with Freda at Valley Mills, he wept. 'Nobody but you,' he whispered and felt himself to be in a trance as he embraced her. But he was determined that whenever he and Freda did become lovers it would not be sordidly on an office carpet or over some work table, in some dark cupboard. Freda deserved better.

Just to think of such things aroused him and he moved away from her. Freda pulled him back. He cleared his throat. 'If we could manage to get away one weekend?' he began. 'There may be an opportunity in Harrogate in June when there is a meeting of textile manufacturers to discuss trade. I could take my "secretary".' He looked at her, searching her face to see her reaction. Perhaps she would be shocked. She said nothing at first, so he went on – 'We could stay in a different hotel from the others – nobody need know, in Harrogate – but at home you could say you were wanted for taking notes –'

'Oh, James, do you think we could? – I do want to be with you away from this town,' she said.

'You know what it would mean?'

'Yes,' she said, and smiled. Then everything would be all right, she thought.

But he said, 'Love can become a drug – I want you, Freda, but I know I should not.'

'Oh, what do I care for all that? – what the neighbours say, the way they all carry on here,' she burst out passionately. He was surprised, had not thought she was really an unconventional young woman, though he knew she was not ordinary.

'Don't look so miserable, James – you mean it could be a drug for *me* too, don't you?'

'No – I don't think you are that sort of woman,' he replied. 'If you were you would have been with Tom, Dick and Harry already!'

'Tom, Dick and Harry never interested me,' she said.

It was dark outside but he had drawn the blinds and now peeped out at the darkness, at all that world outside which seemed to mean nothing, not even exist when he was with Freda.

'I am glad about that,' he said. 'But I am older than you, dear girl, and I have to warn you!' Freda was feeling an overpowering desire to be taken in his arms and for the talk to stop. She still enjoyed being adored but was beginning to feel she wanted a more active part. 'I wish I were young like you,' he said. 'But then I should not dare to love you, I don't suppose.'

'Come here, James,' was her reply and he lowered the blind, came to stand near her again. She was sitting on the old table where so often they had their cups of tea and where she rested her notebooks and he his files and samples.

'I want to be with you for a whole night,' she said. 'It isn't much to ask, is it?'

'It's everything,' he said and took her in his arms again.

I am his whenever he wants me, she thought. 'I belong to you,' she said and for answer he buried his face in her hair and groaned.

'You know it will make all the difference,' he murmured.

Yes, Freda knew, but somehow she did not care, was tired of acting carefully, of seeing him sad and worried and guilty.

'We have to be careful,' he said in contradiction to her thought, 'But we will see what we can do.'

It was as a matter of fact not in Harrogate – though that was to come later – that Freda Caston lost her virginity to James Stainton, but in the woods at Sholey in May where they had gone rambling. James was supposed to be in Woolsford that Saturday and Freda had arranged to be out, muttering to Nell something about a walk with the club.

It was a warm afternoon with the sun coming through in little chinks of light through the trees that grew down both sides of a steep ravine. There was nobody to disturb their lovemaking, for ramblers kept to the top paths, and they lay hidden, near the bed of a dried-up stream. They had walked through the bluebells, which in their thousands had made Freda gasp with joy, had kissed under a canopy of green, birdsong all around them, and the sky when they looked up *so* far away above the trees. James had laid his gaberdine on the dried leaves and Freda had stretched out on it sighing with happiness. She was not frightened, felt lazy and dreamlike and powerless to start any kind of conversation. She left everything to him now, awaited whatever he wanted to do to her or with her in a mood of swimmy languor.

He was an experienced lover but had gone so long without satisfaction that he disappointed himself, although Freda did not seem disappointed. 'It will be better next time,' he murmured. 'I know I hurt you – a little.'

'No – it was nothing,' she said and her eyes were bright, her lips red, the underlip swollen with his kisses. After the initial shock it had been pleasant, almost like being rocked in a cradle. They had not taken off all their clothes in case they were interrupted but his jacket and her camisole were on the ground by them. James felt he could stay for ever in this romantic place, had forgotten how love makes any place romantic for a time.

'It will be better in Harrogate – it is in only three weeks' time –' he murmured in her ear. 'Then we can have all night and need not hurry.'

'I liked it when you hurried!' she answered.

He was amazed at her passion and her words made him lose himself once more in an access of desire. He uncovered her breasts this time and kissed them and she sighed with pleasure. It was a new world he had opened up to her.

'I'm yours whenever you want,' she whispered. 'I love you, James.'

Truly his cup ran over. For their love to be mutual was beyond his expectations and even his hopes. 'Oh you are so lovely!' he said. 'And I could make love to you for hours and hours – if you let me doze a little in between!'

'Doze now then,' she said.

'No – I don't think I feel like dozing just this minute. I want it to be as good for you as it is for me, Freda.'

But as he entered her body once more, this time more slowly and savouring the look in her eyes, he felt, how long, oh how long, can it last? how long can we be happy together before the world comes back?

The world did not come back for an hour or two. Freda was not thinking of the world at all but of the weight of his body on hers that did not crush but seemed all the time to hold her in a tightly enfolded expectation of bliss. 'Don't let me drown,' James said as he was carried away again on those long little death throes into a bliss that seemed only half his because it was of Freda he was thinking and Freda he was loving and Freda to whom he clung even as he melted away. He cried out, 'Freda! Freda! Freda! Freda!'

When he lay breathless beside her, one arm flung across her breast, she said, 'I didn't let you drown – I saved you, you see!' – and she held on to him and would not let him go as if he were her own life-raft.

After that afternoon of course everything did change. Freda however was a good dissimulator and even enjoyed acting the part of respectful amanuensis. It was James who felt he might give himself away. The rest of the world was so dull, so pointless, whilst his hours in the woods with Freda had been each instant so full of meaning and happiness. He was grateful; knew such loving was not easily found, and resolved to make the most of it. So long as Freda loved him! They would be together in Harrogate on a Saturday in June.

Freda looked round the enormous bedroom where James had left her for an hour or two whilst he ascertained the time of his meeting the next day. The group of businessmen to which he belonged was a loose one, drawn together more because of common problems than from any particular liking for each other. Three of the others were in their sixties but holding on to their family businesses until better times should come again or until they could persuade their sons to follow them in the firm. There was nobody from Brigford, the others coming principally from Woolsford, so James and Freda would have an evening and night together at least. Freda had already been window-shopping in Harrogate, a place where no one knew her and where she would not be seen by his friends who were staying at the enormous Hydro Hotel. James had booked them a double room in this much more pleasant, older, hotel.

Freda, whose first visit to *any* hotel it was, wore the thin gold ring which James had given her before they left Woolsford after a lunch at the Sphinx Coffee House. They met no one either knew but were prepared to mention that she was with James to take notes at a meeting if anyone asked. Nell had been unsuspicious and Freda was not thinking about her nor about Brigford, or about anything but herself and James and the prospect of their lovemaking.

The room had a large double bed with a vast gold bedspread and gold eiderdown, a large dressing table, an Edwardian mahogany chest of drawers and a wardrobe just as imposing. Heavy gold curtains hung over the wide window. Freda had inspected everything. Now that James was out of the room they existed in their solid heaviness as though they were a part of him. She sat down in one of the large armchairs, having looked at herself in the long pier glass next to the dressing table. James had suggested she open the window, get some fresh air in, and it was true the room felt slightly airless, but she was reluctant to do this. Whilst she was here, the door locked, she felt suspended, safe, no longer Freda Caston but a princess in a tower. She laughed at her silly fancies and got up again, brushed her hair and then looked

out of the window from behind the curtain at the side. There was
a gravel path underneath the building that led to a little wood.
There had been a view from the landing window round the side
of the hotel of the part of the town that lay down the hill, a town
whose grey streets and wide prospects she had liked when she had
walked there for an hour or two, looking at the dress shops.
Although it was June, Freda had felt chilly, and even now inside
four walls it was not exactly warm. They always said that
Harrogate was the coldest place in England.

She waited for her lover to return, wishing now that she had
accepted his suggestion and gone down to the foyer where she
could have had a cup of tea and read the paper. That was the kind
of thing ladies did in hotels, she supposed. But what did it matter
how she passed her time since that time existed here only for her
to receive warmth and love from James and to return it? Once
together where nobody knew them and there was nobody to ask
questions, for a night and a day they could pretend that this was
only twenty-four hours out of a whole tapestry of days spent in
each other's company.

She looked at the large bed, whose covers a servant would come
in to remove and whose sheets would be turned down, unless she
and James were already lying there, in which case a notice, now
hanging on the doorknob, inscribed *DO NOT DISTURB* would be
put in action and hung on the other side of the door. She wished
he would come back soon; she felt odd in the room by herself. She
wanted him to be happy, oh she did, more than any satisfaction
for herself. This sort of place was sacred to his own desire for her;
she was almost a part of him he had brought with him from
Brigford. That afternoon on the way there, he had said, 'I'd like
to take you one day to the East Coast, motor there, spend a few
days exploring – I'm sorry this is all I can manage for the present.'
But Freda had been quite overcome by the grandeur of the hotel
grounds, the whole place, and not wished for more. Yet now as
she sat there waiting for him, she thought, I could go all over
England with him and spend all my life waiting for him
everywhere. Life would be quite different for ever then. This
place might be only the first of many, though how she might
explain her future absences to Nell would be a problem. But it was
a problem which for the present she need not think about.
Married people had this sort of holiday all the time – rich married
people anyway. She tried to separate the feeling of luxury and

excitement from her feelings for the man who had offered them
to her, but whilst he was away it was too difficult. James was part
of it all. Just as *she* had offered *him* the wood at Sholey – which to
tell the truth she preferred for a tryst to this great expanse of
bedroom – he had offered her this treat and she would extract
all she could from it. He had said only yesterday, when for a
moment they were alone after work, finishing some late
accounts, 'I love you too much, Freda,' and then he had looked
down and she had remained silent till he had looked up again
and said, 'All I can give you is excitement when I want to give
you bliss.' She had pondered those words later, not
understanding what he had meant. She might ask him when he
returned.

James, returning through the Valley Gardens full of a lover's
anticipation as he moved back towards the beloved, who was the
only real person in all the town through which he strode,
remembered his words and that they had been wrung out of him
by the recognition that the afternoon in the woods, the physical
possession of Freda, had still left over all the love. A love too
great seemingly to be expressed only through the body. At least
that was what he had thought afterwards. Now as every step
took him nearer her, a repossession of Freda awaiting him in the
old-fashioned hotel, with Freda as its captive princess, he knew
that however many hotels he took her to, however many times
he might make love to her through all the gradations of desire
and all the years that might follow, there would always be
something left over – a 'remainder' as it was called in arithmetic.
Sex was wonderful, and sex with Freda more wonderful than it
had been with anyone else in his life, but it was also a sort of
agony. He could not express all he wanted. Did everyone feel
like that? Perhaps it was always the case with a much beloved
person. He knew she was happy, for she had told him that she
had always sensed he was, unlike herself, a little sad, and that she
had wondered why. She was happy because she was young, that
was it! He would be glad for Freda even to question his love if it
meant he might remain forever recreating it. But she was
neither selfish nor greedy and thought she received more than
she gave, which was not true. But there was no other way of
showing that, since he was a man and she a woman and until she
had learned the various ploys of desire they would remain

unequal, he the desirer and she the desired.

James was soon to discover most of Freda's instinctive capacity for passion. She looked such a composed young woman. It frightened him a little at first, wondering what he had unleashed, since he was her first lover. When he returned that afternoon they had, rather stiffly and ceremoniously, hung the *DO NOT DISTURB* notice on the other side of the door, before finding themselves immediately transported to a place where time had no meaning. He had imagined she would want to talk, since women usually did, but Freda stopped his mouth with her hand when he began a sentence with, 'I felt as I walked along that I might be nothing but a man exploiting your youth, Freda, had no right to be with you. Tell me it isn't like that!'

She closed his lips with a, 'You need not feel guilty, James – perhaps they'd say *I* was exploiting *you*!' She was thinking, but I am not, even though it is so pleasant to be in such a nice place with him, and looked after ...

After that he abandoned speech for a considerable time, surfacing only to say, 'Thank you for loving me, Freda,' before falling asleep in her arms. He dreamed, curiously enough, of his childhood. Her father was there somewhere in the dream but could not hear what was being said to him.

At eight o'clock they went down to dinner, Freda in the pink blouse and a new skirt, but neither was particularly hungry. James had the strangest conviction that he had 'come home', felt nothing like a seducer of young women, more like a happy child. He knew that this feeling would not remain with him but it was rare for him to live in the present.

When they had returned to their room Freda said: 'Isn't it funny how love makes you want more love – !'

'Lovemaking you mean!' said James.

He could scarcely keep his hands off her – they were made for each other, the two of them, he felt. 'However shall I be able to treat you as Miss Caston when we go back to work?' he said. He had almost said 'back to the world'.

'Oh, you will,' Freda replied – 'I shall be cold as a statue. Anyway you've always called me Freda!'

'You will make me behave myself?'

'You have always behaved yourself,' Freda replied, laughing. 'Except just when we are by ourselves, and that is not often. I suppose because it isn't allowed it makes it better when it is,' she added, willing now to talk.

'Oh, Freda, do you wish I were not so overseen with you?' He used the dialect word. She considered this. They had come a long way since the first kiss, it seemed years ago. 'It would be easier for you if you just – wanted – that?' she said gesturing with her head to the bed which they had tried to straighten out a little before going down for dinner but which an assiduous housemaid had since remade.

'Yes,' he said. 'That's true – but you know that splendid as "that" can be, it is not the reason I love you!'

'Is there a reason?'

'No – I suppose not – but I *do* love you – even if we were not allowed to enjoy ourselves I still would! More and more.'

Freda was brushing her hair. It felt strange to have a man watching her do that. Somehow brushing your hair was a private thing you only did in your bedroom at home, or perhaps in front of a female relative, and it made her feel shy. Making love was so different from anything else, you had no time to be shy. You hadn't done such things before in front of anyone. She was also thinking of his words. James loved her and so James wanted to make love to her. She had thought it a sort of addiction, a way of showing feelings, but it was not that really, it was something quite separate. She could imagine women – and men of course – who did that not out of love or affection but just out of a physical need, out of 'passion', and had startled herself thinking, now James means *that* to me more than anything else! Will it push other things out and away so that when I say I love him it will always be what I mean?

'You are looking thoughtful, darling Freda?' He came up to the dressing table and took her heavy hair in one hand as though he were weighing a fleece. 'Women are so beautiful,' he said. 'And you the most.'

For that night his guilt fled, his feelings of disloyalty to Lina, to his children, which had been bred in him by the stern Puritan morality of the place and the people amongst whom he had been brought up. It was all nonsense – guilt – he thought – the 'older man', the 'mill owner'. He was only a poor forked creature, a man, and he did not feel guilty about the woman in whose arms he lay. It seemed that with every breath they took together he received some life force, some fresh access of energy and youth from her. 'Elixir of Freda,' he murmured, but she was asleep.

Later he woke at dawn and heard birds singing in the gardens and woods, though no light filtered through the heavy brocade curtains. I have only one life, he thought sleepily, and then – Freda too had only one life. How long can that be with me? But he cast off the gloom which his thought had brought with it and turned to Freda who was immediately awake, like a child, and who entwined herself once more around him so that he felt his heart would burst with tenderness.

It was as Freda had promised. She came into work on the Monday, having returned home on the Sunday afternoon, as though butter wouldn't melt in her mouth. Indeed James felt that if he were injudicious enough to do so much as hold her hand, behind a closed door with no one but the two of them present, she would be very fierce with him. But once or twice he caught her looking at him with a tiny glint – of amusement? of roguishness?

The very discretion with which they imbued their working lives now meant that when they could be together in the woods again – for it was a lovely summer – they needed to express their feelings with more urgency. James was uneasy. How could it ever end? He did not want it ever to end, but how long could they go on playing this game of employer and employee? He thought everyone must have noticed, and even contemplated discussing with Freda a move to another place of work so that they would always be safe. He had not the heart to do it, though he knew she would understand.

Freda too had contrived to present an appearance of innocence at home and even the sharp eyes of Cissie seemed to have detected nothing untoward. As far as either of them knew, nobody had ever seen them together, apart from a farmer in Delf who did not know them, and Freda was always discreet in her references to 'Mr Stainton' to Kathleen, to her mother, and at work. She did not care, on her own account, she told herself, even if they were discovered, had a vague idea of going away one day to work in another town where James would visit her at weekends, even at night, and the only thing that worried her – because it was out of her control – was his own family life. She both wanted and did not want to know more of it, sometimes took a walk alone in the direction of Eastcliff but never had the courage to arrive on his doorstep with an invented letter for him to sign or something he had forgotten to do at work.

She had been amazed at the power she had over him, a power which in spite of everything he did not have over her in quite the same way. She desired him and was his match, but she began to want, not more passion, but a life with him, a future, and she knew it could never be. He had told her many times that love did not always need a living together, was sometimes the better for an element of separateness in lives. One day, she said: 'Promise me you'll never have anyone else, James – I mean apart from your wife – don't take anyone else to be your lover, will you?'

He promised, and she knew he would keep that promise. Did he wish to ask her the same? At first she had thought of him as 'James' and then as The 'Man', *her* 'man', and little by little she began to think of him as a person whom she would never lose, never forget, whatever happened to them both. Something would last, she felt sure, because James was James, something that was not just lovemaking or passion. She knew now what it was to be wanted, but also what it was to be needed, and that sometimes frightened her a little. Once when they were sitting on a stile after coming out of Moon Woods, he said, 'I'm no longer disappointed in life, Freda – I know I've had the best of it!' He had tears in his eyes. 'I don't need anything more.' But could *she* ever do with less? she wondered. James was always telling her how young she was, and, when he was depressed, that she could not be his for ever.

But he went on, 'I know *you* could do with more – you will want to be somebody's wife!'

She turned in surprise, for truth to tell up till now the idea of 'marriage' had hardly ever seemed an attraction to her. But now she had begun to imagine living with *him* and was not sure. 'Nobody will ever love me as you do,' she said with sincerity, and went back to him and touched his hand. He brushed a wisp of bracken from her collar.

'But you will love someone else, Freda – you are a passionate girl.'

Am I? She wondered. But what is that to do with love?

For James they were the same thing, but now she could distinguish two Jameses. As perhaps he distinguised two Fredas? No, she knew he did not.

But she did not let the thought go on troubling her. There

were some things you could not express. She had thought him at first far above her but now she knew they were equal.

Later that summer there was the excitement of an aeroplane landing in Eastcliff. Everyone had gone to watch, so it was natural for the two of them to see each other in the field next to the golf links, along with hundreds of others. With James was his son Val whose photograph she had seen, but never the real boy, and she noticed how the child looked happy to be with his father. Then for the first time she thought – that child ought to be ours – and surprised herself. Lina Stainton was not present, nor the child Mary.

She had never made a direct connection between their love-making and the possibility of a real child, and wondered why. There would be, she thought, years and years stretching away for her to have a daughter of her own, for she'd always thought of a child as a daughter. James had always told her to trust him in the matter of babies, and she had, though the idea of always having to be 'careful' had somehow annoyed her. The glimpse of Valentine Stainton had created some strange new element in their rela-tionship, though she said nothing to James. People needed years and years together, she decided, before they embarked upon having children. Her own parents had never had those years, though as far as she knew they had been happy. Of course Mam had been even younger than her own present age when she had had her. This was a startling thought. Her friend Kathleen was going to be married at Christmas and often mused aloud over her future offspring. Was love just a trap set by Mother Nature for the continuance of the species?

Freda felt confident now, poised. She had passed the book-keeping examination with a good mark and this, allied with the confidence James's own love had given her, made her more ambitious. She was twenty-two, good-looking – at least the family and James thought so – and she was not looking for a husband, since she already had a lover.

James talked sometimes in the office, when work was slack, of his interest in science, in what he called the life of the mind, and Freda listened. He talked too of the Treaty of Versailles and his unease about the 'economic settlement'. About business he was just as uneasy. 'If I hadn't inherited this firm I'd have liked to be an inventor,' he would say. He had a quick mind; that she could see and respect. It was odd that minds and bodies seemed to run on a parallel but never quite the same track. The man who talked to her about aeroplanes or mathematics or politics was the same man who seemed to need her for bodily peace, which led then to peace of mind, he said.

At the end of August it had been three weeks since their last 'ramble' in the woods and James told her his wife had been ill again; he said he had sent her to the coast with the children to stay with his father, who had now bought a large house in Bare. Freda might even visit his house in Eastcliff one afternoon, since the servants would also be away. But Freda drew the line at allowing him to make love to her in his own home. 'Let's go for a little walk,' she suggested. 'And then you can take me somewhere to tea, and if anybody sees us we can always say I've had to bring a file from the office.' James admired her caution but he longed to have Freda in the way they had been close in Harrogate, to spend the night together, which was naturally out of the question in Eastcliff. Freda could not stay away from home on a Saturday night without questions being asked, unless it were planned as part of her 'work'.

They met down by the stream of a small valley, a stream which a mile or two to the north was the same beck that rushed through the steep valley of Moon Woods. It was a hot sticky afternoon. Freda had worried it might rain and she would have to confect some other excuse to go out; she could hardly go 'rambling' in a downpour. Above the valley was the high viaduct that had carried the train from Woolsford over westwards since mid-Victorian times, and they followed the stream under the arches knowing that no one in their senses would walk that way.

It was a strange afternoon, the threat of thunder always in the air. Although his family were now away James looked strained, almost desperate. 'It's not good enough,' he kept murmuring and Freda thought he meant his physical loving until they actually lay on the grass by the stream, hidden by undergrowth, the vast stone arches above them, when he abandoned himself to her in a way she had never experienced before. He was fierce, uncontrolled, avid, made her feel something strange, never before felt, and afterwards she had the impression he had been annihiliating something. But then he begged her forgiveness, clutched her as though he could save himself from drowning only by holding on to her.

That afternoon she loved him more than she had ever loved him and that afternoon was to seal her future for many years.

It was in October that Freda realised she might be pregnant. James had always promised to be 'careful', she had trusted him. She had suspected that she would find it hard to conceive a child. The danger her own mother had been in when she gave birth had perhaps encouraged her to feel doubtful about her own normality, although the 'idea' of that daughter of her own was there in her imagination as a distant prospect. Terror and disbelief now fought it out in her head.

There had been an element of unreality when they had made love under the viaduct that hot August afternoon, something 'different', though she was not sure what. When in September her period was one week, two weeks, late, though it had never been more than a day late previously, Freda had to admit that something might have 'happened'. She thought of telling James immediately and then decided to give it a little longer. He would insist upon her visiting a doctor, she was sure, and then if the medical diagnosis was positive she would be plunged into an unwelcome certitude. Her mother's reaction to such an eventuality, and, worse, Aunt Cissie's and Nan's, were less important than the plain fact that eventually she would have to stop work, and the even plainer fact that they could not manage very well without her wage. But, worse of all, the truth of her love affair would come to light. She had kept it pressed secretly to her heart for James's sake as much as her own, did not want it to become public knowledge in the small town. His wife, his family ... her own powerlessness, a new terrible uncertain future, all collided in a jumble of anxiety and insane optimism, then a fearful pessimism.

Freda knew that there were women who got rid of unborn babies, 'wicked' women who conspired sometimes with even more wicked doctors whose commitment to prison featured occasionally in the newspapers. They must do these shameful things quite early on, she supposed. You could hardly kill an almost full size baby, which would be quite a different matter. But folk also said that procedures to put young women out of their misery also ran the risk of killing them, or at least making them incapable of bearing children in future. She had heard such things discussed; it was even possible that Nan might know of someone who had endured such a procedure, for Nan knew everything that went on in the town. How could she find out for herself? Kathleen, and one or two of the other girl friends, were not the sort of people likely to know of abortionists, since they were such respectable women. Bessie at the mill might, but then she was positively the last person whom Freda would wish to tell. There was nobody else in whom Freda could confide even had she wanted to. Cissie would say as she often did of men that they were 'wick' and woman should be warned against them, Freda should have had more self respect and common sense. *And they would all blame James*. It was absolutely essential that his name was not linked with her plight. Why she felt so convinced about this she could not have said, for she knew that such a thing might make James wish to divorce his wife and eventually marry her. But when she thought about that she shuddered away from it, felt repugnance towards a 'forced' marriage with a man whose own marriage she would have ruined. At some point though she would have to tell James and she would have to do whatever he suggested, she supposed.

She wept when alone at night for if the possibility turned into a certainty she felt in her bones that it would spoil everything – her life, James's life. She did not want a baby; though she loved James and was still caught up in the dream of him she did not want a baby, not yet. One day when she was older and richer and freer she might have a child. Not now! James might even stop loving her if she became a mother rather than a lover. Freda was under no illusions as to what babies did to women – the evidence was all around her. Especially to a woman without means, except for what she herself could earn. Yet, when she thought about it honestly she knew that a child was the right true end to lovemaking and was in a way only to be expected. But it seemed unreal and could certainly have been avoided, she thought, for even her own parents had had only the one child – so there must have been foolproof ways and means of avoiding an unwanted one?

But what was she to do? She could hardly think of the practical steps, so powerful was the strangeness of this dream baby. She would tell him in November if nothing 'happened' before then.

She was unlucky, she decided; their love was doomed. She gave not a thought to the future reality of a person made by them both. A baby might have everything to do with their love – but also nothing.

She went to the library and read up on pregnancy and birth but there was no mention of procuring a miscarriage. She wondered about consulting her mother's friend the herbalist woman, but *she* would tell Nell, and she or James must be the people to tell her mother, however much they shrank from it. The thought had come to her that James could tell her. They might then keep the birth secret; she could go away. Her mother loved small babies and she was not a censorious woman. There had been times when others had gossipped about the shame brought upon families by an illegitimate child but Nell had refused to castigate the mothers. Cissie was different and would be furious.

After waiting two more weeks she decided she would tell James on Saturday 20 November. She would ask him to be in the office at the end of the morning for she would be there in any case on a Saturday morning, though he would be there only if there were some good reason. They had not been able to go on one of their walks since early September, for autumn had come in early and it was too cold to lie outside in the woods. The Sunday lectures had not started up again either. James had in fact been impatient, had said they would meet on a Sunday again soon at the mill. He'd been away in Manchester on business and had then taken his wife to London to see a doctor so that for almost two months they had had to postpone their meetings and made do with a few kisses, desperate ones on James's part, a little despairing on hers.

On the Friday before that Saturday she said to him as she prepared to leave work, 'Can we meet tomorrow after work – will you come in? I have something to tell you, I must speak with you.'

'Oh Freda? what is it? Are you ill?' he exclaimed, immediately concentrating his attention upon her.

'No, no! – but I want to ask you something – it's all been so much of a rush these last few weeks –'

'I know – it's driving me mad, Freda – I'm sorry if I've neglected you – it hasn't been much fun for the last month or two. It's been wretched for you – I'm sorry – but I thought we might meet Sunday week. Couldn't we do that?'

'No – tomorrow instead,' she replied. 'I can't come that Sunday – Mother needs me at home – we have relatives coming to tea,' she improvised. She could not bear for them to be together in the old way at the same time as having to announce her fears to him. She wanted to remember the last time, in September, their last walk to Moon Woods, not mix up a love tryst with the shock she knew it would be for him to hear what she had to say.

'I'll come in then tomorrow morning. If it's fine we might even walk down by the lock?' he said. 'I don't have to be home in the afternoon – but why can't you tell me now?' There was a knock at the door – it was one of the warehousemen, so the conversation had to finish. James let Mr Hodgson in and said to Freda, 'Tomorrow morning then. I'll be here to go through accounts,' and Freda nodded and was off. She wished she'd had the courage to tell him then and there, but they were always being interrupted, so it was better to fix an hour when the workforce would certainly have departed for its free Saturday afternoon.

Everything was quiet. The buzzer had gone half an hour before for the workers to leave, and Freda had washed her face, combed her hair and rehearsed what she was going to say many times. She was waiting in the office for James to come up from the 'postroom' where the bales of woven stuff awaited the lorry from Woolsford, and she suddenly felt terrified, wanted to escape. Would he be angry with her? He came in, shut the door, sat down and said, 'At last! – alone together, darling – what a life,' and put out his hand to her.

She came up to him, took his hand and said, 'Please tell me what to do.'

He held on to her hand, pulled her on to his knee and said in a frightened voice, 'What is the matter, Freda? Tell me.' But he had guessed already, for she looked so frightened. It was therefore no surprise to him when she said, her face buried in his collar, 'I think I'm going to have a baby.' In a quiet voice then she repeated the dates, did not weep or dramatize herself, stated only the facts and ended by saying, 'You must tell me what to do. I think there are people who – who can get rid of babies if it is early enough.' She looked up at him and waited.

For an answer he held her tightly stroking her hair. 'Is that what you want?'

'I don't know, James. How could I manage? – you know Mother has not much money – and I would have to stop work – and I don't care about disgrace but I don't want to wreck your life – nobody else knows yet.'

He asked her more questions: No, she hadn't yet been to the doctor; Yes, she was a bit angry – but not with him. (Yet I trusted you, she thought.) 'It is my fault, Freda – absolutely, entirely my fault,' said James.

– 'But what are we going to do? – I felt my life had just begun and now I feel it will end,' she said, giving way at last to a few tears.

'I was sure it was all right,' he said. 'But nature has been too strong for us.' He was thinking furiously. 'You have said nothing yet to your mother?'

'No, I wanted to wait and tell you first.'

James regarded her earnestly. He felt sick, furious with himself, fearful of the future – but practical proposals must be considered.

'What am I to do?' she repeated.

'Listen. *I* shall tell your mother – tell her I love you, ask her forgiveness – yes, I'll do all that. I have enough money, Freda – you are not to worry about that. But I must think it all over. Unless you decide to find someone to do – what you said.'

'Do you want me to have it?' she whispered.

'I've no right to tell you what to do – I want what you want,' he replied. – 'But yes, Freda – in spite of everything,' he went on after a long pause, 'I'd like us to have a child. I thought of it for one day in the future when we'd known each other for years.' ... He did not say, I fantasized Lina's death and you coming to be my second wife ...

'I wouldn't want to stay here in Brigford,' said Freda. 'I mean, if I am to have a baby, I think I ought to go away – I could not be married. People would be unkind to Mam. I don't want to bring disgrace upon them – though I know Mam will be on my side.'

The enormity of the state of affairs was just beginning to dawn upon James. He had been so intent upon comforting Freda, telling her everything could be managed that he had discounted the effect it would have upon himself, and upon his own family too if the facts were known. His own father for one would be very angry. 'Give me the weekend to think it over,' he said. 'Say nothing yet to anyone – you haven't been sick, have you?'

'No – not at all – I feel well!' she said.

'Good, then trust me. When I've thought about how we could manage it, I'll ask to see your mother. I don't think we should wait any longer if what you say is accurate.' He cleared his throat. 'I'm sorry, little love, really I am very sorry – but we must not let it spoil anything – we still have each other even if it will no longer be a secret – it might even be easier to see each other in future ...' he went on at random.

She wanted to say, No, it is all spoilt, but she did not. She got up from his knee. Whatever James said, it was she who would bear this child, she who would have to lose her job, she who had had such bright plans for the future ... and yet she still wanted him. Maybe if he made love to her now something might happen to dislodge the baby. What did girls do – fall downstairs? drink gin? have hot baths?

'Freda, I take responsibility for what has happened. I can't blame you if this – alters – things, but promise me you won't do anything foolish to hurt the child. I suppose I *could* arrange an abortion – people do these things, you know – doctors, if you pay them enough – in London – but I love you, Freda. I don't want that.'

She looked at him doubtfully. Already there was a new something between them, a spectre of the unknown future, nothing wonderful and happy as their love had been, in spite of everything. 'No – I will have the child,' she replied quietly. 'But I want still to be Freda, still at work, be young – Mother will help me.'

He kissed her, and she promised to wait until he had made a 'plan', and went out of the office before he did, and then home, where for the time being she resolved to say nothing.

James Stainton shut himself up in his study at Eastcliff that weekend with the pretext of a load of work problems he must sort out. Lina was at the beginning of one of her moods of religious excitement which made the situation unbearable for him. She had gone off in the motor with the new chauffeur who occasionally took her to Woolsford, and Mary was out for a walk with Mrs Petersham. He locked the door and sat down in his old armchair with a pipe. First things first. Money settled upon Freda? What about finding Nell a small shop to run in a village a few miles away where she could help Freda bring up the child? It would help against the loss of Freda's earnings, and Nell might consent later to look after the child, as so many mothers did, so the daughter could return to work ... The more he thought of this idea the more attractive it seemed. But would Freda want him to publicly acknowledge paternity, make it a matter of common knowledge? If so it would reach Lina's ears, might tip her over again ... But did he *want* Lina to recover? Of course he did, if not at the expense of the girl he loved ... It was his fault, the whole fiasco, his fault alone. He'd told her to trust him ... that time by the stream under the viaduct he knew he'd not been careful enough. Horrible. Now Freda would be a mother without a husband, her life possibly ruined. Men in these parts did not take kindly to young women with bastards. What am I thinking of? My son – or daughter – a bastard? Or Freda marrying to give it a name? She'd never marry now, perhaps – was that what he wanted for her? He'd been selfish. All he could do now was try to repair the damage, deny himself what he wanted most in the world in exchange for another child. Yes, Freda would have to accept financial help, or her mother would, that was the only way. He would go to see Nell Caston, ask her to forgive him, make arrangements for them to move away, buy them a little shop – give Freda back her dignity and her work. She was a clever young woman who would want to be independent one day, he was sure. But it was all spoilt, all spoilt … Alone in the house he began to weep knowing what he was going to lose. Whatever Freda wanted, this child would be, in his or her very beginning, the end of something. Already he was looking at his love in a new light.

These practical ideas that came to James in his great distress, aware that they must act before it was too late and Freda was disgraced in the eyes of others, if not her own or his, were formulated more clearly in his mind over the next few days. By Friday Freda had still had no indication that she had been wrong to imagine she was pregnant and he had made enquiries in Delf and Owram and Kingsbury about buying a small tobacconists' and sweet shop. He took her to a doctor in Leeds on pretext of work. Their fears were confirmed.

Before he went to see Nell Caston he told Freda what they must do. She acquiesced in a numb sort of way, wanting her mother to know the truth now. By Christmas she would be almost four months pregnant, but by then James was determined her future would be mapped out for her in as generous a manner as he could afford. Nature though had won this trick.

Did James wish he had never possessed Freda? No, he could never quite say that. But if *he* had been less selfish and kept her in his imagination for the rest of his life as a sort of icon to console him, *she* might in the end have been happier. Freda had been aroused in her reciprocal passion for him and all she would say was that she could never love a baby as she loved him! He might not have ruined her life, he thought, but he had ruined the possibility of future passion between the two of them. Quickly or slowly it would now be inevitable that their love would change, once reality had broken in on it. He had changed the course of

Freda's life for ever. He wished he could change his own as much. He was not helpless; he was still comparatively young, successful, but filled now with confusion, dismay, emotions which he tried not to let appear to Freda on the few occasions they could speak freely before he confronted Mrs Caston. More than anything he felt guilty, but also angry that genuine feelings were not going to lead to happiness. In spite of everything he was excited about the coming child, though he knew that if he had denied himself a year ago, he would have been able to remember Freda more joyfully and be more content with himself for being capable of disinterested love. Yet he had to confess that he knew, and knew that Freda also knew, that sexual passion was a separate thing, separate from romantic adoration, muddying up a dream ... Why were humans fated to express themselves in such a way, why was there a gulf between love and passion, a gulf that grew wider when passion assumed command? Why was it more moral to remain unsatisfied, unrequited, self-sacrificing, than give a young woman a natural burden? He knew that Freda had not been meant to be a lifelong fantasy figure for him, unless he were to remain an adolescent in a man's body. Never before had he reached that joy with any other woman, and had not thought it possible, had thought it had bypassed him. What should he have done? And the baby, the natural result of love ... his thoughts went round and round.

There were no satisfactory answers to his questions and so he let them bide. He wished that he were not married, wished that the needs of two young children had not to come before – or at least equal – the needs of a third as yet unborn. He needed to share a home, a life, children, but with Freda not Lina, even though Freda might then inevitably be transformed by maternity into a new person. She had never once asked him to marry her. She had known he could never abandon his first family.

All he could do was to set some practical wheels turning. With determination but a heavy heart he turned them.

It was just before Christmas 1920 when James Stainton confessed the truth to Nell Caston. Nell was flabbergasted, incredulous at first. Her innate respect for Mr Stainton meant that she could hardly present him with angry accusations, whatever she thought. He had invited her out in his motor to Halifax, where he then took her to the Black Swan, bought her a brandy, and, once the shock was over, waited for Freda, with whom he had arranged this rendezvous. When Freda arrived, Nell kissed her a little timidly and kept staring at her, with tears in her eyes. But they had to discuss practicalities.

Freda and James had only a few more afternoons alone together away from the mill office. James took her in his motor to Ogden Moor after Christmas to talk. He could not stop feeling that their love was already, for them both, a nostalgic memory. He was restless; his thoughts would not settle. Above all he must not take anything out on his family, especially not on his children. 'I'd like to run away from everything!' he said.

Freda, her face averted, replied, 'If you can't, then I – in a way – must go away from you when the baby is born. Of course you can see the baby, and visit – but –'

'But not be as we were,' he finished her sentence for her, took her hand to his lips.

She looked at him, kissed him gently on the lips. 'Let us just wait and see how we feel,' she said.

Thus it was that a plan was made for both their lives, a plan that was to take effect in February 1921 when Freda left the mill, and Nell and Freda left Brigford, Freda parting from her work and from Valley Mills with great regret. They were to live in Delf where nobody knew them and where a little shop was to be bought by James and put in Nell's name and Freda's. Should Freda wish to go back to secretarial work in another town once the child was established, Nell would be there to look after the baby. James's heart was heavy. Freda seemed remote. Kind but remote. Still, they had pulled it off. Nobody in Brigford knew the truth, he was sure, except for Cissie and Nan. At the mill they were told that Freda's mother had come into some money and was buying a little shop. Which was true. Perhaps, though, Bessie had guessed.

Cissie had been angry. 'We struggled not to go down – and now, this! We may be poor, but we were respectable – wait till He hears the edge of my tongue –'

'No, Auntie – no!'

Freda's eyes were blazing – 'You're to say nothing to anyone – this is between me and James.'

Cissie flinched at Freda's using his Christian name.

'We'll keep ourselves with the shop – we'll return the loan one day, won't we Mam?' Freda went on more quietly. Nell was silent; she had always been overborne by her elder sister.

'Oh you've thought it all out!' Cissie went on.

'We loved each other' – interrupted Freda.

'If he loved you he wouldn't have put you in this position.'

'Be quiet, Cis,' Nell finally got out.

Cissie subsided, and Nan made her promise to say nothing to anyone, least of all Mr Stainton. But she refused to speak to Freda before she left for Delf.

Nell continued to stick by her daughter, and could not help being delighted, her worries over, when in the middle of May 1921 Freda was delivered of a fine son. From the moment he was born it was Nell who was to take on a new lease of life. She was only forty-two, though her husband's death had for a time made her appear older and more careworn, and the arrival of the child gave her a mission, especially since Freda seemed for some weeks to be in a state of shock. James came to see the child but his thoughts were for Freda. He loved her, but could see that something in her had changed. His own love too now seemed to consist of a stoical despair.

'You ought to bring him up as your own boy,' said sister Cissie to Nell on her first visit to the three of them, thus strengthening in Nell's mind the idea that had already occurred to her. Freda, who had imagined at first that once she was over the birth, and once the shop was established in the neighbourhood, she might see James again occasionally, found herself thinking differently. But as time went on she found that the baby preferred a bottle to her own rather uncertain milk supply and that Nell was happy to take over many of the feeds. This might have made her feel her old self again, but paradoxically she felt less and less anxious to take up her passionate affair with the baby's father, or even see him.

The birth had been long and painful – though this was apparently normal – but she had not felt the love for the small scrap of humanity that she had expected to feel, and this terrified her. The baby seemed so small, too small to have made all that fuss about being born. His skin was bright pink and his little head at first pointed like an elf. He had fat little knees, though, and soon the head looked normal again. His hair was brown and he did not open his eyes very much at first, seemed perfectly happy to drift off to sleep. In short, a 'good' baby, who sucked more vigorously on the teat of the bottle Nell had prepared for him than on Freda's rosy nipples. To Freda he seemed a changeling, a funny little creature whom she regarded with a sort of impersonal benevolence whilst Nell looked at him with devotion. The name Jacob had suddenly come to Freda after James's first visit. It sounded a little like James – but then James was her father's name too! She was quite proud of the baby, eventually recovered her equanimity, but felt strangely detached, and certainly a different person after it all. If James could not live with her, what was the use? She was tired of clandestine meetings, determined to fulfil her part of the bargain so that the child's birth should be for ever a secret. The only friend who knew she had had a child was the shocked Kathleen, and Kath was too caught up with her wedding and honeymoon and then her days of early married life to be too involved. Neither did she know the name of Jacob's father.

It was not therefore a decision taken on a sudden whim, nor a thought-out policy that led little by little to Jacob Caston's becoming in practice the son of his own grandmother. He was photographed once in Freda's arms and the photograph sent to James at the mill, where he placed it in a safe nobody but he ever opened. What James really felt Freda did not know, and could not bear to ask.

As time went on and still Freda was not besotted with the child, Nell naturally enough took him on more and more, whilst Freda served behind the counter of the small sweet shop and tobacconists in Delf just off the main road, on a lane where many folk passed on their way to work. But there soon came a day when Freda suggested she might look for proper work, this time in Woolsford, for there was a trolley bus from Delf that went into a suburb of Woolsford where there were many mills and offices. The shop was doing quite well but she wanted to earn as she had done before, be more independent. James could not be expected to pay anything further, and she did not like the feeling of being dependent upon him financially, even if Jacob was. Yet she did not mind being dependent upon Nell for help with Jacob – for Nell was happy.

In 1922 there came a trade depression, so Freda had to wait a little longer. She felt strong by then, capable of finding a good post, and quite detached from her past. For the sake of Lina Stainton and the children, no word of the baby's father would ever pass her lips. In time this became a fixed article of faith with her.

When she did finally find a good post, the child played around his grandmother in the shop, spent most of his time with her. Nell had begged her to let Jacob call her 'Mam', not 'Nan', and for a time he had called them both an infant version of the former. Later, hearing one mam call the other 'Freda', and Freda call Nell 'Mam', he drew his own conclusions and Freda hadn't the heart to make a stand. Only two-and-a-half years separated the death of Nell's husband and the birth of Freda's son, and these years could be slid over in conversation; it could be implied to strangers that Nell was pregnant when her husband died.

Why did Freda do it? Was it shame, or a reluctance to be seen as a victim, or a falling off in her passion for James? Or truly, as she herself so believed, that she might never be blamed for breaking up a family – and because Nell begged her to?

After 1922 there was a drop of almost a third in prices and therefore also a drop in wages, and less work everywhere. Freda heard the Valley Mills were often on short time. She was lucky to have the job in Woolsford. Time could not be rolled back. Would things ever get better? She knew how people had to struggle not to fall ill, how they lost money and began to 'go down', and was truly grateful for James's help. But the money was for Jacob – and for Nell to look after him. For herself she wanted something that was not just money. The shop's takings varied according to the circumstances of the villagers. They knew most of the regular customers by now, though they had still not been quite accepted as villagers themselves, having come from 'over Brigford Way', almost 'outcomers'.

Reluctantly James accepted the new order of things with Freda. He often thought with anguish of the 'little lad', but knew it was best not to be a frequent visitor there and had sensed from the very first time he saw her after the birth that Freda would not wish to take up their affair. He knew it was wise, all things considered, but he knew also that he would never have another woman now, would put all his energy into work. Nell had become far more assured away from her mother and sister; at least one person had gained from the disaster. Freda has suffered far more than he himself. She seemed to have become a different young woman. Matters were left to rest as the child grew up. What else could he do?

Part Two

i Julia

1948–

The present is the funeral of the past
And man the living sepulchre of life.

John Clare, *The Past*

At seventeen Julia Osborn knew that people thought her pretty
and lively. Prettiness was all very well, but she would rather be
beautiful, or even 'striking'. She was neither high cheekboned
nor tall, and certainly not mysterious. Being mysterious was the
quality men were said to like. Along with 'Oomph-', or 'It' –
meaning sex-appeal.

Julia doubted her sex-appeal in real life. Where she scored
was in her ability to act out on a stage those qualities she did not
possess, by pretending to be somebody else. So far the only stage
on which she had shone was that of the High School. Then, even
her mother had been impressed, and it took a lot to impress her.
Later this evening she was to take a big part in the new school
play and Uncle Jacob would be in the audience! The idea was
making her feel so excited that she might almost forget to act. It
had been ten years since he had gone away to work in Brigford,
and then the war had come and he had been engaged on 'secret'
work. But long before that, when she was only a little girl, he had
lived with them for three or four years after Granny Caston had
died. She could not remember when he had first come, but by
the time he went to live away she was eight, and missed him so
much. Now he was back again after all these years on a visit to
Yorkshire! He wouldn't be staying with them; he was only in

Leeds on a flying visit. Mother said he'd written from there, having heard from some Woolsford friend that Julia was in a play, and could he come and see her in it?

'Do you think he'll like Shakespeare?' she asked her father. 'I mean, *The Tempest*, isn't the sort of play everybody likes, is it?'

Father offered, 'Well, I expect he's coming to see us not the play' and Mother said 'Really, Robert – he could have come to see us all when the war was over – he's taken his time!' Father had looked at her in a critical sort of way, Julia thought.

Julia had decided that Uncle Jacob really wanted to see *her*, and it made her feel a bit worried. She'd been such a little girl when he'd left and now here she was, seventeen, and he might not recognize her. Uncle Jacob had always been a special person, the nicest person she's ever known. Even when she was little he'd talked to her as if she were grown up and shown her the funny sums he was doing. He'd been awfully clever even then, before he'd gone to work for Mr Stainton in Brigford, before the war. Perhaps he'd been a sort of spy in the war?

She remembered a medium-tall young man – well, he'd been about twenty, she supposed, not much more than her own present age, when she'd *last* seen him, in Woolsford and she'd thought of him then as quite grown up. It was strange he'd never visited them in the war, but it had taken him far away from Yorkshire.

Jacob was connected with her very first real memories. He'd taken her out for walks in the park when she must have been about five. She had asked him what it meant when people died. She knew later that it was just after his mother had died, her Granny Caston who had kept a shop a few miles away, that he had come to stay with them in Woolsford with Father and Mother, and Marcus her baby brother. Marcus had been an awfully whiney baby and taken up a lot of her mother's time so Jacob had amused Julia and helped Mother round the house, though she remembered that Mother had said it wasn't necessary since they had two servants they paid to do the garden and polish the shoes and light the fires. But Jacob had said he liked doing things like that, and she had often helped him, and it had been fun. She remembered being out with Jacob the day they began to dig trenches in the park when they thought there was going to be a war, and the day – it must have been the same year? – when the gasmasks were collected and everybody tried them on, and Marcus had a baby one. You could hardly breathe when you'd put the mask on and she hadn't liked the idea at all but Jacob had put his on and made it into a game. The war hadn't come straight away after that. It must have been just before he went to work in Brigford that he'd taken her to see *Snow White* and said, 'If you are frightened of the witch, you can shut your eyes.' But she hadn't been frightened of the witch at all. He'd drawn a picture for her too in her first autograph album and signed it 'Jacob Caston'. She still had it. It was a picture of a ship and it was terribly good, better than anything anybody else had put in her album.

When he'd gone away she'd been really miserable. She'd kept on asking, When is he coming back? But they'd got tired of her question and told her he had other things to do now, was learning how to make money. She'd seen him just that once in the city before he went into the Air Force, walking along with Mr Stainton's son, Valentine. She'd been with Father that time and Jacob had seemed a bit shy but he had smiled at her when they said goodbye after Father had chatted a bit to him.

She remembered, in the war when there'd been an air raid – nothing much because they'd only dropped a few incendiaries that time – Mother had said, as they were sitting in the shelter Father had built in the garden, 'I wonder where Jacob is now – do you think he's dropping bombs on the Germans?' And Father had replied, 'No, he'll be more use to them doing something technical, I expect.'

Father and Mother had always been very different sorts of people. Perhaps that was why Julia sometimes felt she was many people rolled into one and not sure which was the real person. Like when you took different parts in different plays. Yesterday she'd looked for her old autograph album to look at Jacob's painting and found it in a cupboard among old photo albums of people she'd never known. Or else the people who'd been young when they were photographed had changed a lot since? It was her mother's old albums that were the most interesting. Father had never bothered with taking photographs though there were plenty of *him* in some of them. There were pictures of Mother and her office friends before she was married, when she was a secretary, and some of her in enormous hats like buckets over her head, that covered half her face, and other, later, ones of perchy hats with veils. Mother had once modelled hats to make a little money for herself before she was married. Not in Woolsford but in Harrogate. Father had met her there and found they had friends in common in Woolsford.

Mother had once said 'I had all my hair cut off in 1925. They called it the shingle. Of course I couldn't have modelled hats with all that weight of hair I used to have behind my neck or on top or at the sides.'

Julia couldn't imagine Mother with long hair. She'd still got long hair herself though it was not really in fashion. The reason was her hair was heavy and thick without much wave and she couldn't be bothered to have it curled or permed. Maybe if she ever did go on the stage she'd have to have it cut as Mother had done for the hat-modelling?

'I don't know where she gets this acting idea from,' Mother had said to Father long ago. Julia had heard them discussing her and lingered to hear the rest.

'Well she's got a trace of your looks, Freda,' Father said.

'*I* never wanted to be an actress though!'

Mother had worked for umpteen years as a secretary before she'd met Father, whom she had married in 1929. That Julia did know. There were pictures of people dancing strange dances in the photo album, amongst the photographs that were taken before Mother married. The wedding photographs were in a special album. People had danced something called The Black Bottom, a name that had always made Julia giggle and feel embarrassed when she was little. Such a rude word for a dance! But the wedding album was full of solemn pictures, nobody smiling, mother in a long white dress and carrying a large bunch of what looked like lilies and Father looking smart with a carnation in his buttonhole. Grandma Caston was on some of them, sitting on a chair in front. On the other side were Granny Osborn and Grandpa Osborn, who were rather piggy-faced, Julia thought. The best man was a friend of Father's, Jim Wood, and Auntie Lily, Father's sister, was on the other side. No Jacob. He should have been there, though he'd only have been a little boy, she supposed, at the time. He was twenty years younger than Mother and had been born after Grandpa Caston died of influenza after the first war.

She looked in the later albums for pictures of Jacob but could find only one. He was standing with Granny Caston, who had her arm round him, in front of the shop she had kept. How old would he have been when he'd come to stay with them after she'd died? About sixteen, she supposed, though she'd thought he was grown up. He'd gone off to school every day, to the Grammar School in the city, but in the holidays he'd always been there. Marcus hadn't played with him so much, nor she with Marcus. And now Jacob was back! Not working in Brigford any more but on a visit from London. He'd be at least twenty-nine now, she thought, properly grown-up. Seventeen was grown-up in her opinion, if not her parents'.

Now she was looking forward to the performance. She'd give it all she'd got! Miranda was a dream of a part, though you had to appear so innocent and good. She enjoyed the words in the heroine's mouth: 'O Brave New World' – like that book of Aldous Huxley's. She was a voracious reader.

She was due at the school at five o'clock and would go there on the bus. The audience would not arrive until seven and the dress rehearsal had finished that morning to give the actors a rest before the first night. Then she had come home to relax. She drank a glass of milk and pushed all thoughts of the audience away as she thought now about the play. Thank goodness Marcus was not coming! He'd be sure to make some cynical remark. He was on holiday for half-term from boarding school, said he'd no interest in Shakespeare and they must go and cheer Julia on without him.

As she sat on the bus, Julia Osborn, Freda's daughter, smiled to herself. If she were good enough tonight it might make Mother agree to allow her to go to the classes they held on Saturday at the Playhouse, and then if that worked well they'd surely let her go to RADA when she was eighteen?

Jacob Caston, who had been so much in Julia's mind as she prepared for the first play in which she would play the principal female role, was at that moment sitting in his room at the Queen's Hotel feeling nervous.

He had discovered his real parentage only in 1939 when he had needed his birth certificate for the Forces. The fact that the person he had always considered his elder sister was in reality his mother had amazed him. It had embarrassed rather than embittered him at that time, for he had been loved by his grandmother. It was the lack of a father that had always given him a feeling of sadness. That his father was not only alive but

was James Stainton, for whom he had worked before joining the
Air Force in 1940, had delivered far more of a body blow. James
had said nothing to him at the time, though now when his son
looked back upon it he realized that he had been treated more
like a son than an employee. He had had it out with the old man
when he was on leave in 1942, but he had never said anything to
Freda, his mother, had not dared to visit her since the war.

James had been emotional, relieved, had asked him to say
nothing to his mother until the war was over. Now the old man
was not well, but tonight he would see his mother again! He still
thought of her as Freda. He had been told a little of the
background to his birth by James Stainton, who had insisted that
it was not *his* idea for his grandmother Caston to give him the
impression she was his mother. It must have been Freda's? Now
he had to come to terms with another fact, one that he had not
assimilated during the war, which he had spent, as Robert
Osborn has surmised, in secret cypher work as a technician
working with the new machines. This new fact was that his little
'niece', Julia Osborn, was his half-sister! He was sure she would
have no inkling of the fact, and he was not going to tell her. But
his mother must soon be apprised somehow of his own
knowledge. You could not conceal that sort of knowledge for
ever.

How he was going to do it was another matter. It might be
better to write after he had seen her? He wondered how many
men had ever found themselves in such strange a position
before. Yet she had taken him in when Nell Caston had died,
had always been kind to him, though she had never shown the
slightest inclination towards any attitude of maternal affection.
Did her husband know? Surely he must? But he doubted they'd
ever told Julia.

Little Julia had been the best thing about living in Woolsford
after Nell died. She'd only been a tiny child when he'd first
arrived – he'd met her before of course, though not often. Nell
had always pestered him to visit the Osborns and it was only
much later that he realized why. It seemed incredible that his
grandmother had never disclosed anything; he supposed that it
must have been because she really did consider him as hers. But
Julia had grown by 1939 into a lively eight-year-old girl with
whom he had always been able to talk easily, and Julia it was
whom he wanted most to see tonight. He would never tell her

unless he got to know her better and if they had things in common. Perhaps he'd wait until she was of age – four more years to go till then. He'd been so fond of her as a child, but she'd probably changed a lot, must have done.

Jacob Caston was a clever young man and very ambitious. On demob from the RAF he had decided not to return to Brigford or Woolsford but to use his knowledge of the new world of electronics to try to start a firm of his own after working a year or two in that field.

He'd never been to university but had an innate ability for mathematics. James Stainton had noticed. After that painful wartime interview when Jacob had confronted his father, James had offered to send him to Cambridge after the war, but Jacob had not decided at that time what he wanted to be and do. He'd learned enough now, he reckoned, to start something up, and his father's capital would be better employed in helping him to found a firm than in sending him for three years to further his theoretical knowledge of the application of mathematics to the new wonder machinery. He was to see his father on the morrow.

Jacob had had no high opinion of his other siblings, Valentine and Mary. Val was a square peg in a round hole at Stainton's and now at thirty-seven had apparently decided to study architecture, after his own war that had been spent in the Far East. Val did not know of the relationship; James had asked him not to divulge it. Val's mother Lina had been for some time in the Retreat at York and Val was very fond of her. That James was obviously afraid Val might blame him for her mental state was what Jacob surmised. Mary Stainton had been in the Wrens. He'd only seen her once or twice when he was working for her father and she'd been standoffish, a cold sort of woman. Had she perhaps known of the relationship? That did not seem possible, though his aunt Cissie, whom he supposed he must now consider his great aunt, had not liked her either. Cissie was still alive, living on an old age pension in Brigford. He hoped she was managing all right – she'd once told him she would never accept a penny from the Osborns. Cissie hardly ever saw Freda, he did know that, for he'd kept in touch with the former all through the war. She was his closest link with his past life with Nell. Why Cissie should take against Freda's husband was a mystery. She suspected everyone 'with brass', he supposed.

They all seemed strange now, those innocent years after his

grandmother's death, when he'd gone to live with the Osborns. He must have been an extraordinarily impercipient lad not to have twigged, but it wasn't the sort of thing you expected to discover. Once or twice he'd caught his 'sister' Freda looking at him thoughtfully but had assumed she was taking a sisterly interest in him. Her husband was a silent man, good at his job, they said, and proud of his beautiful wife, for there was no doubt that Freda had been beautiful. Jacob had throughout the war put his mind away from the subject, had not allowed himself to dwell on the affair there must have been between her and James Stainton. You didn't enjoy thinking about your parents being in love, especially if it was a forbidden love and you were the result. It was all water under the bridge now; he had his own life to get on with. But first he must see little Julia again! What he would say to her mother, or when, or how, he left to fate.

James Stainton knew that his youngest child was in the North for Jacob had telephoned him only the day before. They would meet at his club. It was more sensible doubtless to think of him as an old employee, which he had been, than as a lost son, but James, now over seventy, was proud of Jacob. The hurt and the secrecy surrounding his birth, and most of all Freda's decision to break off relations, though she had accepted money for the boy until she married and been surprised that he wanted to continue paying Nell for his upkeep after that, now belonged to a time 'before the war'. The war had made people unbend a bit, judge others less harshly. His great triumph had been to get her to allow Jacob to work for him at Valley Mills when he was seventeen or so, so long as nothing was said to the boy about the relationship. That had been the hardest thing, and it had relieved and even delighted him when three years later the boy had challenged him. He remembered Jacob asking to see him when he was on leave on a hot June day in 1942, and showing him his birth certificate. There was no father's name on it and Jacob had asked him if he knew who his father might be. Had he no inkling then?

'I believe you know my father,' he had begun.

'James Caston was my best friend when we were lads,' James had cautiously replied, for the time being content to continue with the lie.

Jacob had taken a deep breath. 'If Nell Caston was not my mother!' he said quietly, 'and my mother is her daughter Freda –

Mrs Osborn – I still can't be Robert Osborn's, can I?'

James had told him to sit down. Jacob had regarded him steadily with those grey eyes of his with a look that reminded the older man so much of the boy's grandfather.

'I thought I could ask *you*, Mr Stainton, since you were a friend of my father, or at least – I mean – my mother's father – it's all so peculiar!'

'Is there nobody else you can ask? Why not your mother?'

'We've never been close – I mean she was kind to me as a grown-up sister would be, but I can't think of her as my *mother*! I can't imagine asking her – how could I?'

James had known then that he must tell him and he felt shoddy, guilty, though he'd always done his best for the boy, who was no longer a boy now but a young man.

He had cleared his throat. How to begin? This was the child he'd first seen as a baby and whose photograph was still in his safe. That might be the best way to go about it. There was nobody else working in the mill that Saturday afternoon. Jacob had asked to see him alone. He got up and unlocked the safe, took out the sepia photograph still wrapped in tissue paper, and showed it to Jacob.

'Mam – I mean, my gran, had that picture!' Jacob exclaimed. 'Then why? – You?'

'I'm your father' said James and sat down suddenly, his knees weak. He wanted to cry, but must not, so he sat looking at the young man who was looking from the photograph to him and back again.

'I'm not surprised if you're bewildered,' James said. 'But – since you ask – you are my son!' He saw from the expression of amazement that this had never occurred to Jacob. 'We kept it secret,' James said lamely, 'I couldn't marry Freda – your mother – I loved her – yes, I loved her – though that may seem a low excuse to you –'

'No. She loved *you*, then?' The lad was determined to get to the bottom of things now, though he hadn't bargained for this.

'I believe so. Yes, she did – but we could not marry. My wife –' he stopped.

'Should I tell Freda I know?'

'You'll have to speak to her one day – she might not know you had to get your birth certificate when you joined up. She'll know one day that you know who she is. Whether she'll like it actually *said*, I don't know.'

'I'm not going to see her. I'm due back in London tonight – no, I couldn't go there – one day perhaps –'

'My own family has no idea,' James said. 'I can't stop you telling my children – they are after all your half-sister and brother – but I'd rather you did not.'

(Not after all the trouble we went to. Not after all these years.)

'I have no right to tell anyone,' said Jacob bitterly.

'Wait till my wife ... She's ill again – then you can tell them all.'

'I don't know that I want to,' Jacob said, trying to sound cool.

'Come here, Jacob – shake hands.' The older man, the father, was moved. Jacob saw it and his own voice was thick. If there'd never been a war, would he ever have discovered the truth? He'd always admired Mr Stainton, more than any man really.

'Wait till after the war – then tell her. I can't deny it if you talk about me too. Your Aunt Cissie knows. Nobody else – as far as I know ...'

Things had been left like this. Before Jacob went off for his train James embraced him, 'I hope you return as safely as I did from the last one,' he said. 'But I hope you won't make the same mess of your life as I did!'

'I'm not married, nor ever likely to be,' replied Jacob. But he shook hands and went away pensively.

When James thought back now to that scene of six years before, he was filled with new desire to make amends. The boy had a right to a father. It would all come out one day. A will was lodged with his solicitor in Woolsford leaving a child's portion to him, the same sum of money he was leaving to the other two. Pray God he would outlive Lina, for if not she would be sure to discover the truth. Wills could not be kept secret. The only other way was to cancel the bequest, give him money now, even if trade, as usual, was not good. He was tired of the struggle to keep the firm afloat. Val had no interest in it and new machinery was needed to modernize and to meet Far Eastern competition. He wanted to retire before he died, not die in harness.   He sat on, waiting for Jacob to telephone him, thinking of Freda and the days that sometimes seemed to have happened only a year or so ago. He was looking forward to seeing his son again. The young man had been capable and hard-working, far more a chip off the old block than Val, and with such a look of his grandfather James Caston! He was set to rise and be successful. James had been sure of that ever since the first day Jacob had come to work for him. But not in textiles. No. In something the little town could not offer him. He wanted to hear all about that, for in his letter Jacob had mentioned the possibility of starting up soon with his own electronics firm and even that he had contacts left over from the war, with Switzerland, and the States, where the capital was. 'Robots' they were already called by the Americans, he gathered, those machines that had once been named 'electronic brains'.

Julia looked for him in the audience. She'd seen Mother and Father near the front and heard them clapping. It had gone awfully well; she'd never acted with such confidence. That tricky long scene with Ferdinand when she had to declare her love for him had left her feeling quite full of of admiration for herself the 'admired Miranda', even though the boy who played Ferdinand, from the Boys' Grammar, was far from her ideal young man, or to be considered at all in that light. It was Jacob she'd found herself thinking of when she'd said, 'I would not wish any companion in the world but you'. The thought had just slipped into the head as she spoke the words; she'd been a passionate child, had once adored him.

Just as the curtain was going down at the end for the third time, she saw him standing at the back. She was sure it was him, but had to wait until they were all backstage again in order then to run round the 'secret' way through the old quad and on to the corridor to search amongst the people coming out. Many of the cast did that, though it was supposed to be forbidden whilst you were still in your acting clothes. 'Julia!' a mistress shouted after her – 'Back in five minutes for the photograph, mind!'

Mother and Father would not be waiting to see her unless they'd already found Jacob. They weren't the sort of parents who made a fuss of their daughter, unlike some, but they would have arrived early before her young uncle.

She was in time! He was standing just inside the main entrance to the school, by the porch, smoking a cigarette, chatting to another man, possibly the 'friend' who had told him about the play. Oh goody! Then suddenly she felt nervous. But what use was it being an actress if you couldn't conquer your nerves? She didn't want to spoil things; she was no longer an adoring little girl. But she wanted to make a good impression on him.

He looked up as she came towards the porch. 'Julia!' he cried and in a trice they were hugging each other. He didn't look much different from what she remembered, a bit fatter, she supposed. 'I'd never have recognized you', he said, 'except, when I listen to you. It's funny, you still have something of the same voice! This is my niece,' he said, turning towards the friend, who smiled and shook hands and congratulated her on her performance.

'Was I OK?' she asked Jacob, and it was as if the years had rolled away and she was eight and he was a solemn youth with brilliantined hair who told her about his homework.

'Lovely,' he said.

'I have to get back for photos,' she said. 'Mother and Father will be somewhere, I suppose – you'll want to see them –' The friend had melted away.

People from the audience were milling all down the corridors that led on one side to the assembly hall, which had become a stage for two nights, and on the other to classrooms and the side doors.

'Oh, yes, I suppose so,' said Jacob vaguely.

'Well, they know you're coming – Mother said you wrote to her,' said Julia.

Jacob had decided he must see Freda and had written to her a week ago in a sudden excess of confidence, his friend John Freeman having told him of the coming play when he was down visiting Jacob in London. But now he was no longer feeling so confident. This evening was *not* going to be the one when he alerted Freda to his new – or rather, six-year-old knowledge.

'You haven't been to see us for *so* long – I expect you're busy working?' Julia said. Julia had no inhibitions at least, he thought, but then the poor girl had no idea of the truth either. 'There they are!' she cried. 'I'm sorry, I must go – are you coming over to us for coffee or something afterwards? When are you going back to London?'

Jacob saw Freda and her husband in the crowd. 'I've to return on Sunday – what about meeting me tomorrow in Woolsford – can you –? or have you exams or something?'

'They're over,' said Julia with satisfaction – 'Shall we meet for tea at Betty's? Four o' clock?'

Jacob was amused at her swift decision-making. He hoped Freda would have no objections to his taking his 'niece' out to tea. Julia, full of adrenalin, sorry she could not stay a minute longer to talk to him but she must not miss the photograph and the cast supper, sped off light-heartedly. Thank goodness they were to have a good talk together at last. She so wanted to get to know him again. She often went into the city on Saturday afternoons, shopping or browsing.

She waved to her parents, pointing to Jacob in the mêlée, and then disappeared in the crowd, so that when Freda eventually came up to her son, Robert hovering behind her like a tug, Jacob had had time to compose himself. He was as good an actor as Julia, he thought, though his powers were not often called upon. 'Freda – and Robert – I'm so glad to have made it,' he began, 'Julia *was* good, wasn't she! How are you? – I'm sorry it's been so long – I did mean to come up north earlier but –'

Robert cut short any further explanations with an airy 'Jacob – long time no see?' and the danger seemed to be over.

'Thank you for your letter,' Freda said, looking him over. Obviously at his ease, she thought. He couldn't know then? She had dreaded this moment ever since the end of the war which she had spent worrying about him, though nobody had known that. Maternal feelings aroused by her two younger children must have caught up with *her* at last in the war. But once the war was over and he hadn't written much, she had put off inviting him to stay at Holm Royd.

Jacob decided to be fairly brutal. 'I was over anyway to see one or two people up here in Leeds. I heard that my old boss was ill.'

Freda said quickly, almost too quickly – 'You mean Mr Stainton? Yes, I hear he's been ill – getting better, they said.' But there was a catch in her voice as she spoke.

Robert, who had only half-heard this conversation from behind, as they were now pushing through the corridor at the side, said, 'Why not come over for a cup of coffee now, Jacob?' He thought, he's grown away from Brigford, you can see that. Freda has nothing to worry about.

'Oh, another time?' replied Jacob. 'I don't want to inconvenience you – it's late and you'll want to get to bed. Wasn't Julia splendid!'

Robert agreed that his daughter had indeed been a success.

'I'm glad you wrote,' said Freda, essaying a slight probe. 'I suppose you're going back soon though?'

'Tomorrow I'm taking your daughter out to tea,' said Jacob.

'I expect she invited herself?' said Robert. 'She wasn't sure if you'd recognize her after all these years!'

Freda thought, I *wish* he knew. I wish that we could make it up now, start again. Even though it might mean seeing James – and I have denied myself the sight of James Stainton for many years. Robert had always been gentlemanly about her youthful lapse, though they had never talked about it much, after her initial confession, even when the tangible result had lived with them for the last years of his boyhood, completely unconscious of his true relationship to her.

'What about meeting for a drink tomorrow then? Come round to the office?' Robert suggested.

'Well – thanks –' Her husband was obviously determined to be generous.

'Julia missed you after you'd gone,' Robert added, as for a moment Freda stopped to receive congratulations from some other pupil's mother. He didn't say *Freda* had missed him! It was rum, thought Jacob. Robert did not know he knew, but he knew that Robert must know; one day he would have to cut through the whole pretence. It might be better to start with Freda's husband. It was clear that they hadn't really expected him to stay with them now or visit them earlier. He supposed there were lots of sisters who didn't see all that much of their brothers once they were grown-up and had moved away.

'How's little Marcus?' Jacob asked Freda as he came up again and they were at last out of the building. Robert went off to bring his car round to the front of the school. They were to give Jacob a lift to the station.

'Not so little,' replied Freda. 'Only thirteen and already taller than me. He takes after Robert's mother. Awfully lazy!'

'See you tomorrow then, Jacob,' they said, as he prepared to get out of the car down near the station.

'It was lovely seeing you all,' Jacob replied. 'I'm looking forward to a long talk with Julia.' Freda looked a little sharply at him, but his face, as far as she could see in the gloomy light of a street lamp, was bland, innocent. 'Bye then, Freda. Bye, Bob.' He had always called Freda's husband that. Freda seemed to want to say something more, and he waited. But she said nothing, only held out her cheek a little clumsily to be kissed. 'I'll tell you all the news on the work-front tomorrow!' he added, not kissing her.

When he had got out of the car and her husband had started it up again to drive to their house in the southern suburbs of the city Freda said nothing for some time.

Then, 'You don't think he knows, do you?' she asked her husband.

'I don't know – but I think he *ought* to now he's grown-up, Freda. Is it true Mr Stainton is unwell?' He always called his wife's old paramour 'Mr Stainton' as befitted another generation. He'd never known him, seen him once at a meeting, but knew his upstanding reputation and had no fears from that quarter. Freda had been independent for seven years when she'd swum into his own circle of friends, and he had always been able to afford to be generous. He had not spent much time worrying about her past and it had only been after her mother died that he had realized they'd have to take Jacob, whom he'd met only at Granny Caston's, where he was regarded as her son. It had cost him nothing to have the lad with them. He'd done his duty by his wife. And the boy was a good boy.

'Yes, they say he had a slight heart attack some months ago. I wonder how Jacob knew?' Robert Osborn did not point out that quite apart from the unacknowledged relationship, Jacob Caston had probably made himself invaluable to the old man before the war, a relief from that son of his who wasn't cut out for business but had abandoned accountancy studies before he was called up.

As they got out of the car at the end of the drive to their square stone-built house outside the city on a slight rise, Freda said, 'It's too late for *me* to tell him! And I expect his father won't. I certainly don't want Julia to know.' I couldn't face it, she thought, as she put cold cream on her face prior to retiring.

Julia arrived home later in an exalted frame of mind, and Freda called out from the bedroom to congratulate her on her performance. She waited for her daughter to mention Jacob, which of course she did immediately. 'He's just as I remember him. Aren't you pleased to see your little brother, Mother, after so long? I bet he's making pots of money, don't you? He's taking me out to tea tomorrow, isn't that nice ...'

'That's kind of him,' said Freda, but she did now wish that these two children of hers – not to speak of Marcus, who was a bit of a worry – would keep away from each other. What it would do to Julia to discover she had another brother would be unsettling at the very least, at most a criticism of herself, and she was beginning now to criticize herself. Robert would have to deal with it, she supposed. Ought she to go to see James Stainton? It had been years since she'd spoken to him, but if he were going to die ought she to try to see him again? It wasn't as though she'd married a tyrant, just that sometimes she could not believe that she had ever been James's lover, could not believe that Jacob Caston really was her son, and wished she could understand why the thought of the whole thing depressed her.

Julia had another side to her that was not immediately apparent and indeed never guessed at by most of the people who knew her. Because she was talkative, expressed herself in a decided fashion, it was thought she was an amusing extrovert, full of self-confidence, impetuous. Underneath, however, she disliked this side of herself which she recognized as superficial, another reason for her wish to be an actress so that all 'that side' of her could come out without affecting her 'real' self. That self was uncertain, idealistic, forever longing for a deeper relationship than those she had so far come across. Jacob, in her childhood a quietly competent boy, had once she thought now, seen into her 'real' self. She had forgotten a lot about her earlier years but when recently she had begun to read Thomas Hardy she had immediately seen the old Jacob in Hardy's virtuous, gentle, young men – Giles Winterbourne, Diggory Venn, Gabriel Oak. It happened that about the same time she was feeling the lack of someone at home with whom she could discuss life, reveal her deeper self. Some platonic elder 'brother' began to hover round the edge of her consciousness, some young man to whom one did not have to explain oneself or cover up feeling with frivolity ...

The next morning she rose late and once dressed began to anticipate the meeting in the teashop at four o' clock with mixed emotions. She was wondering whether on closer acquaintance Jacob would prove himself to be that older wiser kinder person whom she had so yearned to meet.

She knew she tended to idealize people. She told herself however that she did not need to pretend anything with Jacob, once she had got to know him again. He was nice-looking, though that should not matter for a soulmate. He had his father's good looks, she thought, remembering a photograph of her dead grandfather, James Caston, that was in her mother's old album. Perhaps he also resembled her mother a little.

When she arrived at the teashop she did not linger as she usually did to scan the cakes in the window – she was perpetually hungry – but went straight in. He was there already, sitting at the back of the room that led from the shop. He seemed to be reading a book. When he looked up and saw her, he waved, and she said to herself, I shall be 'myself' now with him and shall get to know him better. He can know me as the person I am and not the little girl he left. Once she had loved 'Uncle' Jacob; now she could really be friends with a young man. He might be her uncle but it was more to the point that he had come to see her act, obviously wanted to renew acquaintance with her. Last night had been something different, among all that crowd. Now she must begin to get to know him again, properly. She advanced towards him smiling, full of this thought, and was unconscious of the brightness and eagerness of her face and bearing and that Jacob Caston, already wishing he could tell the girl he was her brother, was immediately captivated by a person he had never known. Children 'die' when they grow up, he thought, but something must remain, I suppose. Julia is still the same person, as well as somebody else.

He put down his book, stood up politely. 'You must be tired,' he said, as they sat down, 'after all your efforts last night!'

'Oh I had a good night's sleep,' she said. 'Did you see Mother and Father? They were out of the house before I woke this morning!'

'Only your father,' he said, looking down at the tea cakes 'menu', which did not seem to have changed much since he last ate here in 1939. Freda had finally sent a message via her husband that she had a pressing engagement to visit her friend Kathleen who was ill. He had not been surprised.

'I expect Mother would like you to herself,' she replied. 'Why didn't you come to see us before?'

'I was busy,' he replied shortly. 'And your mother knew I was safe once the war was ended. We did exchange letters occasionally.'

'It must be lovely to have an older sister,' Julia sighed, now giving half her attention to the lists of cakes. 'Nothing like they have in France!' she sighed.

'You were in France then? When?'

'Oh, last year with my penfriend. In Burgundy. It was marvellous – I didn't want to return to boring old England.'

Then she thought that sounded a bit like the Julia she did not want to be, so she continued more seriously, taking up the conversation before the menu had intervened, 'I'd love not to have been the elder – Marcus gets away with a lot more than I ever did. I suppose the gap between you and Mother was too big for you to be a nuisance?'

Jacob felt highly uncomfortable. If only he could tell her the truth. 'In France,' Julia went on, recalled now to food by the waitress hovering at their elbow, 'they have *wonderful* cakes, even though they're not supposed to live on carbohydrates like we do.'

'A pot of tea for two,' Jacob said. 'And what do you want to eat, Julia?'

'Buttered scones and an éclair,' she said promptly.

'That's scones – jam? – for two, then, and bring a plate of éclairs will you?' he said to the waitress politely.

'I'm always hungry,' Julia went on. 'But I never put weight on, you know.'

'I expect you burn it all up. You liked France?'

' "Liked", no. "Loved", rather,' she replied.

'Yes, I like "abroad" too,' said Jacob. 'In fact I'm thinking of starting some work up in Europe – a little electronics business.'

'In France?'

'No, the exchange regulations are too difficult. I'm hoping rather to be in Switzerland, with American contacts.'

'But don't you have to have an awful lot of money to do that in Switzerland? The Swiss weren't in the war so they'll be so much better off than us or the French.'

Jacob thought, I wish I could say that my father is lending me the money to start up this firm because he feels guilty about me and because I never became a proper member of Freda Osborn's household. Aloud, he said, 'Oh, I shall borrow some – if people have faith in me.'

'I'm sure they'll trust you, Jacob,' Julia said. 'You look entirely trustworthy to me – You must tell me more about the business.'

'I promise I will when it's finalized. But it'll mean I shall be working abroad. – What about you? When do you leave school?'

Julia felt, he's just reappeared in my little life and now he'll go away again.

'When will you go?' she asked him as the tea arrived in a dull pewter pot and Jacob, after one look at her, began to pour out.

'When I get all the capital finalized. I'm on to what some people call "electronic brains" – have you heard of them?'

'I think so – but I'm hopeless at science. I shall leave school next year. I'm hoping they'll let me go to RADA – that is if they'll take me there, or at the Central School –'

'You really want to be an actress?'

'Don't you think I'd be good enough? You must tell me if you think that,' she said seriously.

'My dear Julia, I'm sure you'd be "good enough" – but it's a very chancey profession isn't it?'

'Yes.'

'It must be odd to want to pretend to be other people all the time. Don't you think so?' he offered. He thought, what an irony.

'You know, when I was little, I used to pretend you were my brother and not Mother's,' she replied in a sudden burst of confidence. He almost dropped the plate of scones but recovered himself sufficiently to ask her whether she wanted jam. The jam looked rather like coloured glue.

Julia took a scone and buttered it generously. She was so young, he thought. Still not old enough to be thinking about anyone but herself. But perhaps that was not fair.

'Jacob, have you read any of Thomas Hardy's novels?' she began seriously after the first scone had been demolished. It tasted a little doughy, a little sour.

'*Tess of the D'Urbervilles*,' he replied promptly. 'At school.'

'You must read others – I don't like Tess so much – she's such a victim!'

'I don't read many novels,' he said. 'I remember your mother used to read a lot didn't she?'

'Did she? I'd forgotten. She mostly reads gardening books now and her *Vogue*. I *hate* fashion!'

She looked very fierce. 'I thought actresses would be interested in things like fashion and clothes?' he said.

'Well, *I'm* not. I suppose if I thought I could be a writer I'd rather be that than an actress – pretending to be other people, as you said. But if you can't make up your own characters you have to use what writers have made up already for you. I'd like to play a "good" character. I'm sorry, am I boring you? Have another scone.' Jacob laughed.

'You must try your luck then – I intend to make my mark too, though not in the acting line. I shall have to teach you about the higher mathematics.'

Julia made a face. Jacob was a most unactorish kind of person. Solid and, she was sure, highly intelligent.

Then 'Let's both be famous,', she said. 'You in brain machines or whatever they are, and me on the stage – but I bet you'll be successful first!'

'Well I am some years older,' Jacob replied, bearing in mind that Julia probably thought he'd been born in 1919 rather than the true date, 1921, which made him only twenty-seven.

'I wish I were grown-up,' said Julia fiercely. 'I want to leave school now.'

'Have patience.'

'That's what you used to say to me when I was angry when I was little.'

'Did I? Doesn't it seem ages ago?'

'More for me than you, I suppose,' she said. He was so nice, so kind, so much her notion of that ideal platonic brother, so unlike her real brother, Marcus. She was silent, thinking this, and he thought, she is quite unaware of her real attractions. Let's hope someone with fewer compunctions than myself will not muck up her life.

How pleasant it was to talk to him, thought Julia. Even if he were her uncle he was much nicer to be with than the sweaty-palmed boys who had so far been her fate. She'd never really liked boys, had decided she was waiting for a man. But Jacob wasn't so much that as a companion. He might not be as interested in novels or plays as she was – but had Giles Winterborne read novels and discussed the stage? She was sure not.

It was lucky for Julia that her half-brother was such a dependable sort of young man, though she could have had no inkling of the kind of thoughts that were going through his head, a little to his own discomfiture. There was still the old friendship between the girl child and the older boy that had been there from the beginning, but now that she was almost a woman, almost 'grown-up', even if her parents denied it, there was a new quality of feminine attraction. Fortunately she considered him to be her uncle. It would never occur to her that most young men spent a lot of their time feeling randy. Perhaps he did less than most. His old friend Freeman who'd been with him at the play last night (drawn there on account of another young lady, the one who'd played Ariel) had telephoned him that morning at the hotel and mentioned what a pretty girl his 'cousin' was.

'She's my niece,' Jacob had replied.

'Oh, I know she's beyond the pale, old boy – I only meant to pass an impartial judgement.'

To think that a man like Freeman would have every right to 'court' Julia, who might ascribe chivalry to his motives, made Jacob feel as protective towards her as he had always felt – but also meant that in the space of watching her in a play one evening and this teatime conversation he had stopped thinking of her purely as a 'relation'. He'd never yet been 'in love', and his life plan, if he were honest, did not make a lot of space for such feelings, but Julia, licking her fingers across from him now, would have been just the sort of girl he'd have fancied. He recalled himself with a start, as she looked up and said 'Don't let's lose touch. I *missed* you before – even Father noticed. Won't you come north just now and then?'

'Can't promise,' said Jacob more abruptly than he had intended.

'Could I write to you? Like I did at first in the war?' She was remembering the pencilled letters she'd sent to him when he'd first joined up. Nobody else had seen fit to write to him, she thought.

'Do. I'd like to keep up our old friendship,' he said with a smile.

She thought, how refreshing and restful not to have to flirt or pretend, even if he was a young man! They stayed on chatting for another hour. He had to leave Woolsford next morning and she went home on the bus feeling both elated and yet heavy-hearted. Just when you'd found your ideal man, or at least your ideal friend, he went away. Was it to be the story of her life?

Before he returned to London next day Jacob Caston did go to see his father. He found him older and weaker but still eager to lend him the money he had promised. Jacob outlined, in more detail than Julia would have understood, his plans for starting up a small factory on the outskirts of Geneva, to build a prototype machine based on the ones he had serviced in the war.

There was a lot to do before this could happen but James Stainton said he had confidence in him.

'I think your mother ought to know now that you know about us,' he said, just before his son left. He was still a tall, upright figure. Jacob wondered if the old man wanted some sort of reconciliation with Freda. It would be awkward, unimaginable – they'd never existed as a family. And what did her husband think about it all? 'Has she never said *anything* to you since the end of the war?'

'I've only just seen them again. Before, it was just letters. Bob Osborn was kind to give me a home in the thirties, I suppose. Last night she saw me as a brother, I'm sure!'

'Maybe by dint of pretending, she has really come to believe it,' said James. 'She must have changed a good deal.'

Jacob saw that his father would like to have unburdened himself of more details of his old love affair but he felt shy of hearing them.

'You must do as you feel right – but you have my permission to tell her I know you know,' the old man went on.

'It's not my mother I worry about. More my sister Julia,' said Jacob.

'What's she like then? Look like Freda?'

'Haven't you ever seen her?'

'No – I've always been careful to keep out of the family's way. You used to talk about her when you first came here, I remember.'

'She's a pretty girl – she doesn't look much like her mother – more as I remember my grandmother was. Why don't you write to them yourself, Father? Just as an old friend? Surely it wouldn't matter now? Why not meet again?' His using that word – Father – moved James more than he wanted to reveal, but the idea of meeting Freda after all these years, as a 'friend', frightened him.

'Oh but it would matter! It's a small town and even if your mother now lives in Woolsford, things get round. Osborn wouldn't like it either'.

'I'd like to tell Julia – I think she'd keep it to herself,' said his son.

'You must do as you think fit,' James said once more. After giving news of his wife ('Much the same') and children ('Mary's going in for teaching of all things'), he said hesitantly, 'I've to change my will again, as you'll have had the money in advance.'

'I was going to mention it,' said Jacob. 'But what you're giving me now is a *loan* I shall repay to Valley Mills one day. There'll be no call to give me anything else in future.'

James looked at him over his spectacles. 'As you wish,' he said and Jacob thought he was relieved that in this way there would be no embarrassing revelations over a will. 'You're feeling better?' he asked. The man's age manifested itself only in a slight trembling of the hands. 'I'm seventy-one. Enough said. By the way, your great-aunt Cissie was asking after you – she's still spry! I see her sometimes if I go down to the market. Do write to her.'

'I will.'

'And don't forget – you're to find a way of letting Freda know – maybe not immediately, but sooner rather than later. You might find it easier to write. You must forgive her, Jacob, she did what she thought was best.'

'It will be a shock.' He didn't know whether he 'forgave' her or not. The whole deception would have worked if he'd never discovered it he supposed.

'Oh, I don't doubt it will bring it all back. She was the loveliest girl in the world.' He stopped, cleared his throat, but when Jacob left shortly afterwards he hugged him with deep affection.

Julia Osborn spent her last year at school reading novels, dreaming of the stage, and writing long letters to Jacob Caston. Jacob replied from Switzerland in not quite such long letters. Freda Osborn was uneasy: why did her daughter want to keep up a sort of childish fiction that Jacob was her protector and guardian angel?

She was even more uneasy when almost a year later there arrived a letter from Jacob, this time addressed to her, the envelope typed, with 'private' in the corner. One arrived for Julia from him the same morning, but Freda being down for breakfast first was able to remove her own correspondence in good time. She took the letter up to her bedroom to read.

LES AIGLONS,
Genève.

27 July 1949

Dear Freda,
There isn't any easy way to write this letter. I have to tell you that I've known you were my mother since 1942. I asked James

Stainton about the information that I found quite unexpectedly on the birth certificate I applied for in London, because I knew you had worked for him before you were married.

It was less of a shock to know who my father was than to know that you were my mother. I'd never had a father, having always assumed he was James Caston, who was dead, but I did have – I thought – a mother. Doubtless you and your mother had your own reasons for the deception, though my real father doesn't understand them. Now I come to think about it I don't think my grandmother ever actually said that James Caston was my father, just that he was her husband, leaving me to draw my own natural conclusions. I always called her 'Mam' though, as far back as I can remember. After she died I can imagine that you wouldn't want others to know, though I presume your husband knew the truth? Even now I don't suppose you will tell Julia or Marcus?

I expect it was easier for you to let your mother look after me, since you had your living to earn, and I suppose that what may have begun as an unintentional assumption became a lie as I grew up? I ought to blame your mother as much as you. But I am resolved not to 'blame' anybody and to get on with my life. I may have lifted a burden from your shoulders. It must have been hard to go on pretending? But I don't think I shall ever be able to understand why, as soon as you knew I was out of the RAF, you didn't write and tell me.

When I was a little boy, Mr Stainton used to visit now and again, and my grandmother always said he was a great friend of my father's, so I never thought more of it. I was proud to have such a pretty and successful sister, and when you and your husband took me in after your mother died I was grateful, though I suppose gratitude is no longer really an appropriate emotion?

I shall not mention this to anyone else. I think it would be better for Robert to know I know. My father, James Stainton, has lent me enough capital to begin over here with a small firm I have founded, so you need have no worries on that score. He writes to me occasionally and always treats me as a son when I see him alone. Last time I thought he looked much older, and not well. Could you not see him now? – I know he never loved anyone as much as he once loved you. He told me so, and I believe him.

This is a curious letter to write and one even more strange for a woman to receive, I suppose. Forgive me if I don't sound very filial. I can't start thinking about you in a different way even now. I ought to have told you when I was up north last year, but could not face it. I regret not knowing for years that Julia was my half-sister, but once I knew, I realized that the affection I felt for her when I stayed with you was precisely that of an older brother for a little sister. If I had my way I'd tell her now.

I would appreciate it if you would let me know you have received this letter so that *my* mind may be put at rest. I shan't ever act any differently towards you if I see you with your family, but one day I wish you would tell me just a little about the circumstances of my coming to the world. You must have had a hard decision to make but I'm glad I was born and that I have such a fine old man for a father.

I hope you will be happy, Mother (it sounds so odd to say that) and that you will somehow make it up with Mr Stainton, my father, before he dies.

I suppose Julia would see all this as a rather romantic sort of mystery but, believe me I am old enough to know otherwise and to imagine just a little of the heartache that must have led to your decision, even though that decision may have been, as I said, more in the nature of an omission than a commission.

If you do tell Julia and Marcus, please let me know. Otherwise I shall remain discreet – unless circumstances force me to reveal to one of them the existence of a brother.

I won't write again. You will know that I write occasionally to Julia and she to me. I want to keep something alive from my earlier days.

Kind regards to Bob, whom I suppose I should now regard as a sort of stepfather? – Jacob.

Freda put the letter down. Her breath was still coming unevenly as it had begun to do once she began to read it. She sat on the pink quilted bed in the large 'Master Bedroom' of her comfortable Woolsford house, and considered. She had always both expected and dreaded this letter. Yet, now that it had come, it began to seem not too disastrous. The Freda to whom Jacob referred as having been in love with Mr Stainton was a remote figure to her conscious mind, the figure's very remoteness created through her long ago decision. The decision to let her mother bring Jacob up had not been taken with anguish, but had removed any anguish her predicament had brought about in her. A new life had then stretched ahead of her at twenty-five. She had little time then to mourn the old Freda. Everything had turned out for the best once she had found the strength to give up James. But not enough strength to reveal herself to his son. She had always suspected that James had visited Jacob as a child more often than her mother had ever admitted. She'd been working away, first in Woolsford, later in Harrogate, and then back again to Woolsford, and the child had been well-looked after. She had done her share. Except that for some deep unexamined reason she had never wanted him to consider her as his mother. Whatever it was that had 'ailed' her,

her mother had colluded in it. Nell had blossomed as she fulfilled all those maternal duties in her own forties which she had not wished to assume or not been able to assume herself. She had had to earn her own living, had been determined that even if James Stainton helped with money for the shop, and for his son, *she* must be independent, must make a new life for herself before it was too late. And she did! She had done well in both the city office of Holdsworths in Woolsford and the accountant's office in Harrogate before she returned to Kingsbury with a 'fiancé'.

She'd told Robert the truth once it seemed he was serious about her, had not held anything back when it would have been quite easy to do so. But he had not suggested that Jacob made his home at that time with them. She did not owe James Stainton anything, had let him go back to his ailing wife, a woman who had never known of his affair and, if she knew James aright, never would. She had even wondered whether her past experience had added to her attractions as far as Robert Osborn had been concerned, since Stainton was a respected figure

She put her spectacles back on. She was fifty-two now and print seemed to get smaller year by year.

Had she never loved Jacob as she ought? Even if she had not, he seemed not to be demanding anything from her at this date. In '35, just after Marcus had been born, when Nell died, she ought, she supposed, to have told the fourteen-year-old Jacob the truth, for she had immediately taken him in after her mother's death. But she had a difficult baby, Marcus, to look after and the time never seemed right. How on earth could you begin to tell a boy such a thing when he was mourning the only mother he had known?

Robert too had thought it best to leave matters as they were. She had been exhausted, almost forty, with a new baby.

The nanny they had employed for Marcus had been dishonest and they'd had to sack her; and then Robert had been worried about his business, dependent as it was on the fluctuations of the trade most of his clients followed. It had been a difficult time. Jacob and Julia had got on well from the start. She remembered having felt a little jealous of her daughter's affection for him.

How *could* she have acted any differently? They'd given Jacob a home for three years, after all, a good home! There had never been any question of his being taken to live in his father's house.

Since she had not been his 'mother' when he was growing up in Kingsbury, she couldn't start feeling like his mother later. She had had to rely on her own wits and strength of will to survive those earlier years in order to improve her position, and reasoned that one day must Jacob do the same. Why hadn't his father told him earlier, privately, before the war – at least of his own relationship to him? But no, it was always 'poor Lina' and 'what will happen to Lina? ...' He'd been forced to it in the end by Jacob confronting him with a piece of paper. But James had never told her about the meeting.

She remembered that it was the year before the war when James had written that short note offering to give Jacob work at Valley Mills, where 'a job could surely be found for him.' She'd told the boy he was an old friend of his father's and left it at that, Jacob had been pleased to find work, since he wanted to be independent.

She'd even said to Jacob, as a good elder sister would, 'You've got to begin to rely on yourself now, stand on your own feet, and this is a good opportunity.' She didn't remember telling him that she had once worked for James Stainton. Maybe she'd given him the impression then that she didn't expect him to keep coming over to Woolsford for a visit once he was working in Brigford? Anyway, he hadn't come over, had said he wanted to make his way now, and had taken digs in Brigford. She did know that Cissie had seen him occasionally because in a letter or two he'd mentioned her. For a time she'd wondered if Cissie would have given her away, but apparently she had not.

Had she been hard on the child? Certainly harder than she'd been on Marcus with whom it might have been better to lay down the law a little earlier. But she'd been hard on herself too.

Freda lit a Craven A. Julia was the problem. How would she react to the news if it ever came her way? She was gifted and wilful, if serious-minded at heart. Life would not treat Julia with kid gloves, thought her mother. But when did it ever treat women so? She was fond of her daughter but determined she would not make the same mistakes as herself. And now the girl wanted to leave them all to go to RADA, live in London. Julia talked a lot of nonsense about Free Love and Experience. Where she got it from Freda had no idea. She certainly hadn't had such ideas at Julia's age even if her actions might have led folk to think she had! Julia would judge her harshly, she was sure, and

Julia would also say 'Well, Mother, *you* did what you wanted, so don't think you can stop *me!*'

Julia was only a few years younger than she had been when James Stainton had claimed her, and the idea of Julia ruining her life in that way was not to be thought of. If only Robert were a little less censorious of his daughter. He was always finding fault with her, making her come home at 10.30 when her friends were allowed out till midnight, and he certainly didn't give her much pocket money. Perhaps he feared her being taken advantage of by a man?

With an effort she brought her mind back from Julia and Marcus to her first son. Strange even to herself to think of him now as that. Did she not love him? Well, of course she did, even if she'd not been able to show it. She'd always been fair to him when he lived with them. Robert had said she'd done well by him. But she'd never felt that passionate devotion to him she'd felt for Marcus, and Julia when she was small. If you weren't there when a child fell over and scraped his knee, weren't the person who got up in the night if he felt sick, weren't the one waiting at home for the first grubby picture painted at school you didn't feel the same. She'd been just too young then to appreciate babies.

But Jacob was also James's child. James, the man whose adoration she had enjoyed, the man who'd 'brought her out of herself'. Not for many years had she thought about their time together, of how she must have behaved ... And now he was old and – she looked at Jacob's letter once more – 'not well'. When James died, would she go to his funeral? Did she want to? Would he have expected her to? She'd been a one-time employee of his, had every right! She would even see that wife of his there, Evangeline. And the children ... It was the children who had made her feel jealous all those years ago. Val, and – what was the girl's name? – Mary.

Would James have told them they had a half-brother? The idea had never occurred to her before – Jacob had missed two other siblings. Well, she'd been an only child too, like him. If James had helped Jacob with some cash for the business he must have faith in him, for he was too good a businessman to waste money on ne'er do wells. Their son Jacob was certainly no ne'er do well; he was a clever young man, probably as clever as his father. He looked so like her own father though, which had perhaps made it seem more natural for Nell to imagine he really was her own son.

She got up from the bed, straightened out the pink counterpane, went over to her dressing table, and looked in the mirror. 'Unnatural woman' she said aloud. The face that looked back was heavier than the one she remembered. Even now it was a shock to see that older face when for so many years people had said, 'Freda still looks so young for her age.' Age was catching up with her now ... Did she feel guilty? She asked herself. Yes, but more – sorry. Jacob had not had a hard life and was old enough now to bear this blow. James, though – he must have felt guilty. Had his guilt and his love for her turned into love for their son? It must have done. She wondered how often they saw each other. He had given him money ... She wondered how much. Well, *she* would have given it to him if he had asked her! She still had her own building society account, though all the household expenses were paid by Robert; had shares too, had always been good with money. They were hers, not her husband's. Any of his she had earned, by running his household for him. Her marriage had placed her beyond the pale of gossip, had given her a niche, if it had not given her the passion, the excitement, she had once found with James Stainton. Robert had made life easier for her. They rubbed along quite well together, though he worried too much about his work, in her opinion.

'You are middle-aged,' Freda said to her reflection who regarded her sombrely in the shining glass. The years had passed so quickly since her wedding twenty years ago. In five years they'd be having a Silver Wedding celebration. Robert had promised to take her abroad next summer too. Julia had returned from France so enthusiastic, so overcome by her time there, had wanted them to go too, to see, as she put it, that 'Life can be lived in a different way.' Julia was critical of them both, she thought. They'd decided to let her go to the Saturday drama school in the city and she always returned just as shining-eyed as from 'abroad', so they had agreed to allow her to apply for RADA. The audition had not gone too badly, Julia said, and now she was waiting to hear whether they would take her. It was time she stretched her wings. Young people nowadays expected that. What could she teach her daughter, pass on to her, that she had not already done in unspoken ways since she was a baby? Julia wouldn't think her mother knew much about life, and the only way she could show her that was not true was unfortunately a way that might disillusion her about maternal advice. But things had changed, even in Woolsford. There had even been several divorces since the war, whereas before it was practically unheard of to divorce.

'What do *you* know about love?' Freda's reflection interrogated her as she powdered her nose, pursed her lips to even out her lipstick and pressed the hair on her brow into a more becoming wave. 'I did once,' she answered, but the face looked stern.

She would reply to Jacob, acknowledge his letter, leave it at that. As to James, he was only seventy-two, might be good for many years.

After his second stroke, James Stainton was nursed by his daughter Mary. His wife recovered sufficiently at the time to leave her nursing home and come to see him. As he lay slowly recovering the use of his left arm, at home, on the narrow bachelor bed that had been his for the last fifteen years, he was annoyed to discover that he had no control of the memories that poured into his head from some part of his brain not under conscious control. There was nothing he had left undone, he thought. Williams, his solicitor, had been apprised of the need to send for a certain Jacob Caston in Geneva should another stroke finish him off, and he had asked Cissie Phillipson only that spring when he had come across her in the Old Market to let Freda know, should he die suddenly. Cissie had looked at him sardonically, he thought. 'You won't want our Freda at your funeral, Captain Stainton, not after all these years, and your family there an' all!' But he had insisted she tell her, trusting Cissie to be among the first to know of any demises, births or shotgun weddings. In the end she had promised. He thought that Cissie in old age seemed gentler. She probably resented less the gulf between rich man and poor worker. Growing old, you were all in the same boat, and he was always pleased to see her if he came across her now and then. She brought back his own schooldays, was of his own generation.

'You'll have heard our Jacob's doing well?' she said.

'I'm glad to hear it,' he answered gravely. Cissie knew that he'd helped Jacob to start up and she knew he knew she knew, but she would not have thought it a matter for discussion.

He was remembering Cissie at school now as his mind flitted

here and there, with great gaps when he fell asleep, to wake a few hours later, feeling dreadful. Other memories assaulted him, but in a piecemeal way so that he wondered if he was losing his mind. He knew what had happened to him but was not sure whether his family assumed he didn't. The mill often came into his mind but usually as a background to the figures on a table of unemployment statistics which he'd once read and seemingly remembered. He struggled to fit them to dates. Peak unemployment had come shortly after Freda had married Osborn, but by then she'd had Julia, whom he had never seen. The old king died a year or two after that, after his Jubilee, which he himself had helped to arrange in Brigford just as he had helped with the celebrations after the 'Great' War. He'd got on with his work with the British Legion and the local branch of the League of Nations. His 'committees', Freda had called them. *Two* kings had followed shortly on the heels of the Jubilee and he'd distributed Coronation mugs to schoolchildren not once but twice!

By then there'd been more work in the town, young folk with a bit to spend, and one of his fellow businessmen, Alderman Sutcliffe, had founded the town's first 'Milk Bar'. Such was progress, though why he should want to remember the milk bar was a mystery! He would try to shift his thoughts into another gear but would fall asleep thinking, I must think about Freda. Sometimes Val would visit his sick-bed and he was glad to have the excuse of imperfect speech so that he need not talk to his eldest child, for he had never been close to him, though he had tried. He could have been close to Jacob if Jacob had been there. Jacob was much more like him than were his other children. Did Jacob even know he was ill? Of course – Cissie must have told him. She'd know.

How he'd suffered in the war, worrying about both his sons, though it turned out the one he worried about most was to be non-operational and the one about whom he ought to have worried was out of touch. He'd sometimes dreaded a judge asking him, 'Which one do you want to come back safely? – Come on, choose!' and had silenced his own imagination …

… Jacob had missed having a father; it had always been too late to make it up to him, he realized as he lay 'recovering'. And the image of that son who would surely make his mark on the world chased him this time into sleep … His speech came back a little and he was terrified he would say the name aloud, for it seemed to resound in his head. Jacob, Jacob ... But Jacob sometimes got mixed up with his boyhood friend James Caston. What a grand little lad *he'd* been! He tried to hear the music they'd gone to listen to together and managed to say 'Music', so that Mary brought in his radiogram and they fixed it so that he could hear it in the bedroom.

'Schubert,' he muttered later that week, and by trial and error Mary put on *Death and the Maiden*. The tears rolled down his cheeks.

'It seems to upset him,' Mary said to old Dr Green who called daily.

'A good thing he's reacting,' was all Green said. 'Let him have what he wants.'

After another stroke in the spring of 1950 James Stainton died.

> Queens Hotel, Leeds. 12 May 1950
> Dear Julia, Just to let you know I am in England for a short time. My old employer, Mr Stainton, has died and I am here to attend his funeral. I thought maybe I could see you in London on Tuesday the 16th as I shall have that evening free before I have to fly back the next day. I shall come round to your digs on the Tuesday evening and we can go out for a meal unless there is a message here before Monday night to advise me not to. In haste, Love, Jacob.

Julia wondered vaguely why Jacob should bother to come back all the way from Geneva to attend the funeral of a man he'd once worked for, but did not bother looking for a reason. Jacob was a law unto himself. His letters always cheered her when she was feeling low. The course was hard work and she didn't think she was doing too badly but she missed the comforts of home, though she would not have confessed that to anyone, least of all her parents. Home at present for Julia was a bedsitting room with a shared gas ring in a then unfashionable insalubrious part of north London.

There had already been several young men who had wanted to go to bed with her in the past year but she had not been in love with them, and it had been a bore. The one or two others with whom she'd imagined she was in love had not been interested in her and she had suffered the delicious pangs of unrequited passion. She knew she was possessive, probably frightened them away, whilst the other young men who pursued her with different ends in sight discounted her finer feelings. Anyway, young men – all young men – the go-getters as well as her unrequited passions, really wanted sex, unless there was something wrong with them. The nicest man, Tristan Carmichael, turned out to prefer to have it with young men. But with him she could at least have proper conversations.

Proper conversations were what she had with her young Uncle Jacob, by letter, sometimes, she had to admit, a little one-sidedly. She received this short letter from Jacob in Leeds with a great feeling of relief. He might even advise her about men. An 'uncle' was a bit like a queer, after all, without designs on you but interested in you as a *person*.

The funeral was a strange affair. Jacob had arrived at the parish church to find it practically full of workers from the Valley Mills, and just about everyone in Eastcliff and Brigford who 'was anybody'. The family was already sitting at the front and it included his father's wife Evangeline supported by a son and daughter and a woman who was Val's wife. No sign of Freda, but there was still time.

The under-manager who had been works manager when Jacob had worked for Stainton had seen him, and come up. 'Good of you to come,' he murmured. 'He was a fine man was Mr Stainton.' He ushered Jacob to a pew at the back as the organ began to be played.

Jacob wondered what the son and daughter would say if he pushed his way to the front of the church and suddenly shouted, 'He was my father too, you know!'

He dreaded seeing Freda, having had only the one letter from her a year ago, acknowledging his.

As the pall-bearers came up with the hearse, which he could see when he turned to look through the open door, he saw his mother and her husband come in. They were late. But she had come. Even with her husband, she had come. He bent his head in assumed prayer as the coffin was carried to the front of the church. When he looked up he saw that his Aunt Cissie had come in behind Freda, all three now sitting on the other side of the church. He had been invited to go on to Cissie's afterwards, had come on only this morning from his Leeds hotel and on the phone last night she'd been annoyed he hadn't chosen to stay in her little house overnight. He'd had not a word from Freda.

Should he feel sad? Yes, he did feel sad, but he could not weep for James. As the service began and the old words were read and responded to, he occupied himself wondering what his mother was really feeling. How would he ever know? He would have to see her in about twenty minutes, the first time since she had known that he knew of their relationship. Her letter had been short and to the point, acknowledging the truth, saying she did not feel there was anything useful to add and asking him in particular not to tell Julia. He'd see Julia tomorrow. At least that would be one good thing to come out of this visit.

How tall Valentine Stainton was, towering over the congregation so that even he at the back of the church could see him! Would he have to go up to him with his condolences? What a farce! As for Mary Stainton, he'd hardly ever met her when he worked for James but knew she was now teaching in Woolsford, had never married. How much recovered was the wife? More to the point, how ill had she ever been? Would this death finally conquer her reason? The family was to go over to Woolsford later to the vast Victorian cemetery which was regarded as the best place for successful businessmen, rather than the smaller town cemetery. So much he had been told when he telephoned the mills yesterday.

The sad thing was that he could not feel too much for James. His thoughts were all on those living, principally on his mother. How would she take this final goodbye? At least she had Bob Osborn with her. Would they go along to the cemetery? Probably not; it would be just the official 'family'. Families, he thought! He was lucky not to be caught up in one now; it suited him better to have made a virtue out of necessity, to be alone. There would not be any more money coming to him, so nobody would ever know about his existence unless Freda spilled the beans or Val questioned his father's solicitor or banker, and he was sure that James and the solicitor together earlier last year would have seen that things were well covered up. He'd wanted to begin to repay the loan but James had refused. It had been just before his first stroke.

The only person he could think of as his 'family' was Julia, he thought, and she was not here. He had come because of the past, and because he had liked and admired James and long ago forgiven him. He turned to the hymn, which he realized was being sung extremely well, the choral tradition of these parts bringing forth powerful voices. His father had loved music, he remembered from his time working for him, when for some reason the man had spoken of concerts. The organist was good; Jacob gave himself up to the hymn and then to the prayers.

Freda was finding there was no connection between the coffin and the man she had once known so well and who had loved her. Love was always powerless in the end; it was death that won. She had not been to many funerals, only to those of her parents long ago, and she was startled to find herself thinking now of this funeral as one of a sort of parent, had to remind herself he had been her lover, had known her in many ways better than anyone. How many times at first in the years after her son's birth had she wished she could go to him, ask him to take her away, to leave them all, all that family of his who were now standing sorrowfully at the front of the church! But they would never know; that was her triumph. Any mourning would be done by her in private, not here. Yet she had felt she must come. At the door one of the mourners who knew her by sight had whispered: 'A Mr Caston is here – shall I put you next to him? Of course he once worked for Mr Stainton, didn't he?' But Robert had replied 'No – we'll see him afterwards as we're a bit late,' and they had taken a pew on the other side with Aunt Cissie. The church was full. Afterwards the local paper would describe it all, she thought, would detail all the representatives of the various 'committees' James had headed or advised. They said he had died very quickly after the last stroke, according to Cissie. She did not want to think about that.

He could so easily have been killed in the first war. What would her life have been like if he had? Freda, who had been so determined to show no emotion, to come to this church only as an employee, found she was trembling, her body giving her away. But she took a deep breath and managed to control it. Robert had not noticed. She was not going to cry. More important would be the confrontation with her son Jacob, but she did not think he would make a scene, would not expect a private conversation with her. A husband had his uses, she supposed, and Robert was looking in charge of himself as usual.

James did not have a Christian faith, she thought, as the parson finished reading from the 15th chapter of Corinthians and the organist began to play another hymn. They ought to have chosen the sort of music James had liked. She remembered that he had liked Psalm 90. Had those words 'Thou has set our misdeeds before Thee and our secret sins in the light of Thy countenance' any meaning for his widow who stood there between his legitimate children?

The family were to go to the Undercliffe Cemetery in Woolsford and were to follow the hearse in a long black car. She would go one day to stand by his grave. Not now. She followed her husband out of the church to join those who were already in the churchyard as the hearse left, having only caught a glimpse of the heavily veiled figure of Evangeline Stainton, supported by her children, the tall Valentine and the grim-faced Mary as they passed up the aisle, the organ still sounding. It was a warmish day with a blue sky, the sort of day they had gone 'rambling' up to Moon Woods. She must not think of that today! Then she saw Jacob coming out of the church with a small stumpy old woman she recognized as Bessie. How did he know *her*? Oh, he must have met her when he worked at Valley Mills. All those years kept running together. Bessie came up, must be over seventy now. Robert moved forward and shook his stepson's hand discreetly.

'A sad day, Freda,' said Bessie with a sharp look at her, which told Freda Bessie might always have known, but would never say. Freda inclined her head, speechless for the moment.

'Hello Freda,' said Jacob casually. She kissed him on the cheek.

'Will you come back with us?' she asked him. Somehow his faint air of foreignness, his solidity, were comforting.

'I'm sorry, I have to get back to Leeds,' he said. 'Unless we are invited anywhere else?' He meant the Staintons, she supposed, and this was his way of ascertaining that nothing had been said to them or by them.

'No – they will be on their way to the cemetery,' she said calmly.

Was he thinking of going there himself?

They stood apart from the knots of Brigfordians for a moment. Robert had gone over to speak to an acquaintance of his own. On purpose, she realized, to allow mother and son a moment together. 'I'm sorry, Mother,' Jacob whispered. It was the first time he had ever called her that. But he looked preoccupied rather than sad, she thought. It was perhaps himself he was feeling sorry for. Why not? He had just lost his father. But Freda felt herself trembling again.

'Jacob –' she said as they stood now by the corner of the church, apart from the others – 'Don't tell Julia, will you – not yet –'

'Not yet,' he echoed. He thought, she looks pale, but that is not surprising. For a moment he felt angry that the conventions did not allow them both to be there with the coffin to see James Stainton at last laid in his grave. He had somehow assumed, ever since he had known the truth, that Freda must have long ago metaphorically interred him. Now he wondered, but it was neither the time nor the place to enquire. I'm the last of the Castons, he thought. Not a Stainton, a Caston. Not one of those riding down the High Street in the black Daimler to bury the head of the tribe.

'Caston's,' he said aloud.

'What?' Freda looked wary.

'I've just decided the name of my new enterprise. He took her hand in his now much bigger one. 'Long live the Castons,' he said.

Cissie Phillipson came up just in time to hear this.

Freda kissed her crumpled old face. Her nose was as red as her cheeks, the whole laced with tiny red veins and her hair under her best black hat a yellowish white.

'He comes after all this time,' she said to Freda, 'and won't even have a cup of tea with his old auntie.'

Robert rejoined them at that point. 'Why don't you *both* come over to us?' he said pleasantly.

Cissie looked as if she was about to agree but Jacob said hurriedly, 'Well, I've time just for a cup I suppose, Auntie Cissie – I've a lot of telephoning to do this afternoon from the hotel.' Cissie did not then invite her niece and her husband.

Robert glanced at his wife's face and did not pursue his own invitation. He turned, and a young man with a notebook and pencil was seen to be hovering around them 'The list of mourners,' he said, 'I'm from the *Gazette*.'

Freda took herself in hand. If Jacob didn't want a tête-à-tête, let him go and gossip at Cissie's.

'Mr and Mrs Robert Osborn,' said Robert, 'And Mr Jacob Caston.'

'And Miss Cissie Phillipson,' said Jacob.

All Freda wanted now was to go, but Jacob said, 'I'm to see Julia on my way back – I'll give her your love.' Robert looked surprised but recollected himself. 'See she has a good meal then, will you?' he said with an attempt at joviality.

'How's your little girl then?' Cissie asked Freda as at last they walked out of the churchyard, the reporter still interrupting other mourners who looked quite pleased they were to figure in print in the town's annals.

'Oh, she's in her element,' replied Freda. 'Goodbye Bessie,' this to the old woman who stood at the gate.

'Goodbye, Freda love. Nice to have seen you!'

Jacob looked so handsome in the sunlight, Freda thought. She wished that he was not to go away, that he did not work abroad, that they could all go home together. But it was too late for those kinds of thoughts. It was a long time since she had felt so unhappy. It was all she could do not to cry when he went off with Cissie. The tears were not only for his father but for him and all she had lost.

When Jacob Caston rang the bell of the dingy tall house in Kentish Town, he had his sister Julia's last letter in his pocket. Once, in a letter, he had teasingly called her 'Miranda' as befitted a budding actress whose first success he had witnessed, and the name stuck. 'With love from Miranda,' the letter said at the end of seven pages of her musings over what young men were like. Well, at nearly twenty, he supposed she had had plenty of time to discover.

The talk at Cissie's had been deliberately impersonal on his part. The old woman had been too pleased he had gone to her rather than to Freda to notice that his mind was not on her. Then he had had a series of tedious conversations with New York on the telephone from the hotel before taking an early train to London the next morning. In London he had consulted his city bank and then wandered into the Tate Gallery where the paintings of the Pre-Raphaelites had reminded him a little of his mother. He ought to have accepted her husband's invitation, he supposed, but could not help thinking that Freda might have been relieved he had not, though she had looked at him so sadly. Any conversation they ever had on more intimate matters should not have her husband officiating, nor should it follow on a funeral, even if the tradition was that 'family' matters always did. And he could not take it upon himself to comfort her for her loss.

He waited now for Julia/Miranda to run down the four flights of stairs and for an instant did not recognize the girl who opened the door to him. Or he had in the past two years forgotten how very pretty she was? Fresh from the North, where the rawness of feelings had been iced over only with politeness, he felt he could move immediately into warmer waters with Julia. She was wearing a mauve jumper with a scarf tied round her neck and long earrings, also of a purplish tinge. But he kissed her in the Continental way. 'How foreign you look, Jacob!' was her first remark. Then, 'I've opened a bottle of Madeira – I hope you like it.' They toiled up the stairs. 'Everyone drinks Madeira in London now,' she said as she poured him out a generous measure from a sherry glass.

'Do they? Well, Miranda – Cheers!'

'Isn't it rather expensive?' he could not resist adding.

'Terribly – but I bought this with some money Father sent me – they think I don't eat enough!'

It was true, she was rather thin.

As soon as she had seen him standing there on the doorstep looking neat and 'foreign', Julia knew two things. That she could have fallen in love with him if she had not been his niece, and that he was the same Jacob in spite of the well-cut clothes and differently styled hair. His arrival also told her that she would not be accepting the invitation of one Benedict who was the latest candidate for her attentions and that Jacob was a hundred times more attractive than any man she'd met in London. For one thing he was so easy to talk to. You could be light-hearted or serious, he didn't mind. He was better in the flesh than in letter-form, she thought.

'I hope you don't mind my writing to you, such a lot?' she said as they drank the rich brown stuff and she lit a Player's Medium, 'But if I don't write things down I find I can't understand them – and it's adolescent to write a diary!'

Jacob decided to keep things light-hearted. 'Oh, I enjoy your letters,' he replied, 'perhaps I shall collect them and then one day they will be published as the correspondence of the famous actress, Miranda.'

'It's nice when you reply,' she said a little wistfully.

'Before I forget, your parents sent their love – and your father said I must give you a good meal.'

'Oh, you went to that funeral – were they there too then?'

'Yes – your mother once worked for Mr Stainton,' Jacob replied. She could at least know that.

'Oh, yes – he was a friend of Grandpa Caston's – your father's friend, I believe – Was it very gloomy then?'

'No – it was interesting – haven't you ever been to a funeral?'

'No – and I've never seen anyone dead! I was too little to go when my other grandfather died. Have another drink?'

'No, thanks – where shall we eat?'

'I thought – there's quite a nice Italian restaurant near here – I eat a lot of spaghetti these days. Anyway I'd rather talk to you than eat.'

He thought, well, spaghetti hasn't fattened her up.

She smoked another cigarette and they went down the steep stairs and out into the evening. The restaurant, Jacob was pleased to discover, was quite genuinely Italian. London might be beginning to improve, though the wine cost far too much.

Julia had decided not to bore him with talk of other men. In any case they seemed unimportant when she was with Jacob. They drank two glasses of wine each from a carafe. She noticed that, unlike the other men she knew, he was not a great drinker. The wine uncovered her feelings and she found herself thinking again, as they waited for their dessert, what a pity it was that he was her uncle. He was such a lot younger than her mother. Perhaps Grandma Caston had adopted him as a baby, taken him in from the gypsies? Except he did not look like a gypsy. My ideal man, she found herself thinking, he really is!

Jacob found as he looked at her over the red-checked tablecloth that he was physically attracted to her in spite of everything. Cissie had said, 'Oh, Castons and Staintons always knew each other. It started with your grandfather, Freda's father. He and Captain Stainton were right close at one time.' He wondered whether there was some chemistry to explain the attraction, the affinity. Had his father felt the same for Freda, and that she was a chip off the old block? Freda and James had not been blood relations though; it was only that her father had been Stainton's friend. He and Julia were very closely related! as he kept wanting to forget. And attraction of that sort must be immediately suppressed, and for ever.

As they talked, he felt, I don't really know her. She is the same person as the little girl I was fond of, and the girl I talked to two years ago but yet *not* the same now that she is a young woman. He wondered if she were still a virgin. She certainly possessed all the attractions of young womanhood but also had an untouched air about her. He would not be the one to encourage her to lose that air. If only he could tell her she was his sister, and then they could have a different sort of relationship. An 'uncle' was just too ambiguous!

'I think you are my touchstone, Jacob,' Julia was saying, the wine having loosened her tongue as well as her emotions. At least she'd dropped the appellation of 'uncle', thank goodness.

'Nonsense,' he said, 'I know nothing about the stage – you'd be very bored with my sort of work.' She thought, he can't ever love me, what a pity.

'Tell me about your work – I'm interested,' she said.

All right, he would. This was one way out. She must know him a little better to find out how unromantic he was.

'I mean what are these machines you make and why do we need them?'

Jacob took a deep breath, but then hesitated.

'I can't even understand electricity,' Julia said. 'I'm not proud of it – I found science impossible at school – I just learnt it all off by heart to pass the exams.'

He laughed. 'Machines might even help you one day to understand science,' he said.

'You mean they are kinds of non-human brains?'

'Well, you see, Julia,' he began as the coffee arrived, 'you know that our brains are the reason for our being able to build machines to do things for us?'

'Yes – even I can understand that!' she answered ironically.

She thought, he looks young now, enthusiastic.

'Machines are the children of our brains,' he went on. 'They can carry things too heavy for us to carry alone. Microscopes can enable us to see things we couldn't see otherwise. Ships keep us afloat, aeroplanes keep us up in the sky –'

'Yes,' murmured Julia, 'I've never understood how they do that – I've only been in an aeroplane once and was nervous all the time!'

He smiled. 'The way I look at it is that only our brains can create order for us out of chaos – and we all want that, the world being so chaotic. The inventions of our brains might even impose a new order!'

'They are surely only a means to an end?' she interjected. But Jacob was well away.

'Our new knowledge – the application of our brains will give us power to control the whole world –'

'And be like gods then?' she asked.

Surprisingly, he was silent for a moment, gathering his forces perhaps, so she went on. – 'Machines – science – they can't tell us about the *truth* of anything, can they? – What to think. What to believe? –'

'No, no – scientists know they can't discover what they call Absolute Truth – good and evil, right and wrong. And anyway the theory of relativity tells us that 'truth' depends on our point of view –'

'Does it really? – but that's awful!' she cried.

'No, not awful, *true* –' said Jacob. 'The position of the observer alters what is observed.'

'So there is no knowledge that is the same everywhere and for ever for everyone?' she asked him, feeling upset and at sea.

'Well, there is *knowledge*, but I suppose you'd have to study philosophy to understand the difference between truth and knowledge …'

'Have you?'

'What?'

'Studied philosophy?'

'A bit – but I haven't as much time now for reading. I'm more interested in physics.'

'But, Jacob – even if you make machines that can push forward our knowledge it's still only human beings who are making the machines! How can a machine take over a person or understand anything not put there somehow in the first place by a person?'

'Well, there are machines that began to be invented in the war – I had a bit to do with them in a very junior capacity – one was built by some Post Office engineers, but never mind that, a great mathematician was behind it all – well, I hope to produce this type of machine. I'm not exactly an inventor myself, more a manufacturer, but this machine will be able to think more quickly in certain ways than we can –'

'But can it be *creative*? as creative as the human beings who invented them? I don't believe that.'

'I think so – I believe so. Not yet – there's a long way to go. We're just at the beginning of it all.'

'I don't like the sound of it. Though I can't believe that anything *you* invent will be bad.'

'You mean – "evil"?'

'I'm not sure that I believe in "evil" but it frightens me a bit when I hear talk about things I don't understand – I'll try and understand anything *you* tell me though!'

'The machines I'm thinking of all work on logical principles – we used some of them in our anti-aircraft systems in the war. But it's my belief they will eventually be adapted for hundreds of peace-time uses – things like television, and setting the instruments in aircraft –'

'If, like with the atom bomb, discoveries were found to cause *bad* things – wouldn't people stop making them?'

'I think that once people discover things they are bound to carry on with them somehow. Human beings are curious. You might say that's why they were given minds – to go beyond them.' He looked excited.

She was silent, so he went on – 'Look at all the things like aspirins – as well as atom bombs – that have altered our world for ever.'

'Our lives may have been altered by your "Science",' she said, 'but there are still things – like love – and death – that nobody can "invent" or abolish –'

'Oh, "love" might be the application of certain chemicals to the human brain,' he ventured, but with a smile.

'I don't like that idea – it takes away my freedom', she replied seriously.

'Don't worry. The feelings are still real.'

'Jacob – are you an atheist?'

'I suppose so.'

'I am too, as far as my reason is concerned. But my emotions are still attached to a Creator – something bigger than ourselves,' she said.

He smiled. 'There are scientists who are Christians,' he said, 'I mean religiously minded, not just Christian, but with a religious attitude to life –'

She thought, I don't meet people who talk about these things.

I suppose I don't want to push my thoughts to the edge either.

'Science doesn't make human beings less wonderful,' he said, thinking how charming she was and how he liked to observe how her brow puckered with the effort of thinking. That thought seemed condescending though.

'Tell me more about your machines.'

'Well, there was a problem of wiring them. The first one was tube-driven, but we've got things now called transistors and I have the feeling that one day they will be used everywhere in these calculating machines, though they are mostly still using vacuum tubes.' She looked puzzled, so he changed track. 'Things can happen now in a thousandth of a second, though nothing can travel faster than light. The moment a particle of matter reaches the speed of light, it turns into light,' he said – 'All these things are connected.'

'You can't have anything travelling quicker than light and the minute it does it becomes light?' Julia repeated slowly. 'I like that!' She was uncertain what a 'particle' was and what it looked like. She supposed some of her former schoolmates knew all about this sort of thing. Not just the boys, but some of the girls who had done physics – she'd never been especially friendly with them.

'That's what happens in the cosmos as far as Einstein understood it – The speed of light is just a background to what I'm doing, what they are hoping to invent now, depends on this new way of understanding everything.'

'Sometimes I think everything is in our minds,' she said uneasily.

'Then you are a solipsist, or at least an idealist! – Don't worry, all I hope to do is to make the machines which when applied will make life easier, not more difficult. I'm only an engineer, not a real scientist. I shall work towards making these new machines commercially available.' He didn't tell her then of his dream, which he shared with others, that his machines would not just be used for scientific calculations but would extend into all commercial life.

She thought, well, I'd rather someone like Jacob was doing this sort of thing than nastier people. But he still hasn't explained exactly what he hopes his machines, his brain children, will *do*!

'I'll tell you more in a year or two when things have advanced,' he said.

'Doesn't it need a lot of money to start up the kind of – workshop – you want?' she asked him.

'Yes, it does, but to begin with I've borrowed some, and I'm confident I'll be able to pay it back within a few years. I'm only one of many people doing this sort of thing. It's happening all over the world. The British were among the first to have the idea of electronic brains but our government doesn't always give enough money to British entrepreneurs, so people like me go where they can find a workforce and space to develop. In Switzerland there are a lot of precision workers – like watch-makers – they're the kind of people we need to begin with. But I suppose in the end our whole project might be taken over by the Yanks. Most of these machines are already mostly made there. Some people call them "robots".'

She thought, it has all been most interesting, even if it shakes me to know of all I do not understand and perhaps don't want to understand.

He changed the subject eventually and they left the restaurant talking about her own work and what she wanted to do with her life. He was not quite the 'Giles Winterborne' she had envisaged, but a clever man, one with a quick brain and a belief in himself which made him even more attractive to her. She wished he were not going away the next morning. It was no use constructing a Dream Jacob for he obviously considered her as a rather ignorant little niece.

When they said goodbye, before he disappeared into the depths of the Northern Line, he said, 'If you're ever in any sort of trouble – you will let me know, won't you? I'm always there to help – I don't mean financially. – I mean – well, I've no right to pry – but it strikes me that you'll have a good many young men after you, Julia.'

For a minute she felt rebellious, then a little flattered. 'Oh, I can deal with *them*,' she said. But he still looked solemn, and his farewell kiss was, though affectionate, in a curious way unsettling. She could not have said: I've never met anybody who intrigued me as much as you, or he might have thought she was trying to flirt with him. Which was ridiculous. But then why should he talk as if he were responsible for her? He is my very best man friend, she decided, and determined one day to visit him in Geneva and discover more about the way his mind worked.

'I'll write,' she shouted to his departing figure.

'Yes – do.'

He waved, and then he was gone.

Jacob felt glad then that he had seen her, glad that they had each in their own way tried to understand the other, but also uneasy. He ought to reconsider what he felt about her. Not that Julia would change his mind about anything, but it was strange to find a bright person with such a deep suspicion of what he took for granted. Other feelings he pushed back for the time being.

As time went on though, he was often to think of her, to find himself imagining her vivid face and sympathetic voice. That was not good. She was his sister, and he must remain, if not an unknown brother, at least an 'uncle' – which had to remove him from her knowledge of him as a sensual man, and put her out of his range into another orbit. Yet he knew that in another world, another life perhaps, she would have been the woman for him. He dismissed such thoughts most of the time and applied himself to his work, which was far more complicated and more exciting than he could ever have conveyed to her. Women did not bother him much. He tried not to think of his mother or of his dead father and put all his energies into his new life.

The man with whom Julia Osborn was having an affair two years later whilst she was in her last year at RADA – Rupert Dee – turned out to be less interested in her than himself. In this he resembled the man with whom she had lost her despised virginity, a certain Sean O'Sullivan. But Sean had never pretended to want anything but a pleasant companion in bed when he was not busy doing something else, and had not touched anything essential in Julia. Rupert, she had thought, was less of a friend and more of a lover, though he was a worse actor than Sean. She saw that the next few years might very well be spent with more of the same sort of young men and managed for six whole months to concentrate on her work.

The year after this she spent as stage manager in a repertory company that toured every small town in the Midlands and she was too exhausted to think of anything *but* work. She was lucky to have a job at all. She also knew she was quite a decent actress, if not an outstanding one. How long would it take for her to be given a decent part in a decent play? All her women friends were in the same boat. She considered concentrating on trying to find wireless work if that could be found, for it might be less draining than the stage work that left you physically so exhausted. Then for the first time since she was eighteen, she wondered whether it was all worth it. It was in a mood of depression that she met Martin Maynard who seemed at first to be the answer to her problems. She thought that he looked a bit like Jacob, with whom she still corresponded, having sent him postcards of all the benighted towns in which the company had found itself. But the more she concentrated on her work, the less time she had to massage the ego of Mr Maynard who was clearly going to go far. She discovered that there seemed to be little spilling over into his ordinary feelings for her, or into their companionship, of the passions expended by him when he made love. What was wrong with him, she wondered? Or was it wrong with her? She found that she was much readier to assume she was 'in love' with someone than was any man with whom she had been intimate. At these times she imagined what it might be like to unleash passion in Jacob Caston.

In spite of knowing full well that Martin had no intention of committing himself to a lasting relationship with her, Julia found it hard to let go of him. He often left her in some dingy boarding house along with the rest of the company when a better offer seemed about to be made to him, but always returned to find her, after three months or so, in some other windswept seaside town. Always, that is, until the autumn of 1956, when she received, instead of his casual if passionate attentions, a letter from him saying he had 'met somebody else'.

It was two years since she had seen Jacob and the last time had been only a quick dinner when he was over in England in '54. Suddenly she longed to see him again. He was still in Geneva. Reading between the lines of his letters she guessed that his hard work was beginning to pay dividends. He had begun to manufacture some of his 'machines', had written of a prototype produced in the States – where he had contacts – which could now understand patterns, possess memory and store knowledge electronically, 'accomplishing twenty thousand mathematical operations a second'. But on the whole he did not go into details about his work just as she was careful to edit her escapades when she wrote to him. After all, he was 'family', and she liked to keep her love affairs secret from prying familial eyes.

But a week or two after she had received the goodbye letter from Martin Maynard, who was now working in the bright lights of London, and in the midst of gloom over her professional prospects, she discovered she might be pregnant. At first she could not believe it; it had never happened before, and they had been careful. Whatever could she do? She was twenty-five, almost penniless – from choice, since her mother and father would certainly have advanced her some cash if she had asked them, but she didn't want to ask them; without a job for the first time for years – and now, this. Should she tell Martin Maynard? She felt too deeply embarrassed to do so for he was not well-off and might think that she was trying to bring him back into her life. Actually, she was fed up with him and rather relieved at his decision, which she ought to have made for herself long before. *And* he had this new girl. Julia hated more than anything else to see herself as a victim – either of men, biology, or lack of talent. She could not possibly burden her parents with her physical state and yet she shrank from having an abortion, which was in any case illegal and dangerous. *If* Martin had still been with her, *if* Martin had handed over the eighty pounds which seemed to be the going rate, according to her friends, many of whom had had their pregnancies terminated – she would have had an abortion and then gone home for a rest. But why should she be forced to give up a baby when everyone said that it was better to have babies when you were young, before getting on with the rest of your life? Yet she ought to give Martin the opportunity of an opinion, should she not? But then on the other hand he might not reply, or might do the opposite and sacrifice himself on the altar of marriage for the sake of the unborn child. That would certainly make him hate her, she thought. He would not be faithful anyway; it was not his nature. And she had decided that she was not in love with him any more, if she ever had been. It was all most unfortunate.

Jacob would tell her what to do, she decided. He would give her impartial advice. There was still time to follow either course, and they said that Switzerland was the place for safe abortions so long as you had the money to pay for a private clinic. But she was half-ashamed of herself, of her dependence on someone who had enough money to be able to offer the right sort of advice. When she began to think of Jacob she found herself wishing *he* were the father of this infant, not her fickle lover.

Jacob would never be fickle, she was absolutely convinced. And, judging by his letters to her, Jacob was a little bit in love with her. He might not know it, but there was something between the two of them that had been planted long before and which the letters had watered and kept alive. She would have to write and tell him what had happened. He'd said, that evening when he had gone away in 1951, that she must always go to him if she were in trouble, and now she realized that what he might have feared had come to pass.

Mother would be pleased if she took a little holiday, she thought. They were always nagging her to take a break. But her dread of failure had kept her away from her parents unless she had good news of a part or a job. The stage had failed her, or she had failed it, but she was not alone in that. Better realize it now than wait any longer. Perhaps the pregnancy was a 'sign'.

She must first of all write to Jacob, could not spring the news upon him without warning.

She wrote:

> You told me to ask you if I ever needed help and I think this is the moment. I need a holiday anyway so could I come and see you? Please don't be cross with me but I'm pregnant. I've decided not to tell the father, whichever way I decide, because it would annoy him and embarrass him and make him feel guilty. It's my fault just as much as his. I can come any time – I wanted to come over this next summer in any case so I hope this is not impossible for you. Let me know just that I can stay near you. I am ready to travel any time. With love, Julia.

Jacob Caston was a workaholic. His solid grey-suited figure, often covered by the green overall which he wore at work, was well-known in the district just over the border with France where he had set up his first enterprise and where for the last two years he had begun to make money, not only from sales of his prototype but from consultancies. He was part of the new world of electronics and had begun to float new companies for the manufacture of terminals and machine parts. He sensed things were still only just in embryonic form, but they *were* moving and he was in time to catch the ideas as they burgeoned all over the world, especially in the States. He had just organized a big meeting to discuss a merger, to be held in a disused aircraft hangar a few miles from his chalet up in the mountains where he retired to think.

Julia's letter put him into a turmoil of conflicting feelings. On the one hand he wanted her there straight away before she did anything rash, but he also longed to see her on his own account. He would send her the money to fly over to Switzerland and would organize his driver to meet her and bring her over to the chalet on the Friday night. Then he could do his deals Saturday as he had arranged and drive back with Julia to talk on the Sunday. His life was always like this now; sometimes he amazed himself. True to his promise to his mother he had never revealed to Julia his real relationship. But the idea of an abortion was abhorrent to him. He could not at first give himself cogent reasons for this. As he had once told her, he was an avowed atheist, but then suddenly he realized that as an illegitimate child himself he felt for the child she said she was carrying, at however embryonic a stage, as if it were for himself or his own child. He saw also quite clearly that he must acquaint her with the facts about his own birth. She was old enough to know. The pretence was ridiculous. He wondered at his mother's never having had the courage to inform her. Then he felt with a stab that Freda's daughter was in the same position as Freda thirty-five years before, but that this time there must be no confabulating. She must tell the wretched man, whatever his reaction might be. He had enough money to help her. She must also tell her mother. She could have the child in Switzerland, and he was sure that, unless the chap came over to make an honest woman of her, he himself would be able to find her work. Her French was good, he knew, and it was about time that she took stock of her talents. But if she refused his advice he would still help her.

Julia's face and voice had sometimes come to Jacob in dreams. Not that he dreamt much, for usually he was too exhausted to do anything but fall into bed and immediately into sleep, but when he did dream it was often of Julia.

He was nervous though. Would she think him too interfering? Well, he was, perhaps. But she had asked his advice!

He sent a telegram: 'Money follows. Arrange to come BEA Friday 7 Dec. Geneva Arr.1700h. Car will meet you driven by Friedrich Grässl. Love, Jacob.'

Julia packed in one suitcase all she possessed, except for her books, waited for the money, and when it came went straight to London from Colchester where she had been stranded since

September. He would be angry with her, she supposed, but he would tell her what to do. His factory, or whatever it was, must be doing well. She reread his October letter with its talk of 'office automation', but was not much wiser. Perhaps he'd have a girlfriend and they'd scold her and then send her back? But she was young enough to be excited at this sudden journey and at going abroad. She told nobody of her plans. Marcus was at Leeds College of Commerce, but they communicated seldom.

At the airport she looked at herself in the mirror in the ladies' cloakroom and put on more make up. She was too thin. Well, that would soon be remedied! She almost giggled to herself. Or it would not. She still had – just – her old passport with its photo of herself at sixteen. How innocent she looked. But quite pretty. She felt a bit nervous before the flight but had a drink at the bar and soon began to enjoy the freedom of feeling she was now cut off from everyone she knew in England. Going at last to Jacob. She had time during the flight to wonder what she was going to say to her uncle. She should have visited him years ago but there had always been her 'career'. Well, that was over, she knew in her heart. Nobody would miss her.

The skies outside the plane were blue though they had been grey in London and were to be greyish when she landed. She wondered idly whether one of Jacob's 'machines' had been guiding the aeroplane. Luggage once reclaimed and Customs over, she went up to the end of the arrivals hall and looked around.

She felt her purse nervously in case she would have to take a taxi, for she hadn't much money with her. The ticket had been a single one too. What if Jacob had slipped up and there was nobody to meet her? But then a figure, wearing a duffel coat but topped by an incongruous peaked cap, detached itself from the waiting crowd. 'Miss Osborn?' he enquired. 'I am from Herr Caston, Friedrich Grässl.'

He took her case and she followed him to his car – or Jacob's – a long black one with gleaming paintwork. 'You are thirsty? I bring Thermos?' he said when she had settled herself in the back.

'I'd love a drink,' she said. Her mouth was quite dry with excitement. Still, so far so good. He handed her over a silver cup and an open thermos from which there wafted a delicious smell of coffee. Julia had not so far felt any pregnancy sickness and hoped that this state of affairs would continue. She drank the strong, aromatic, but creamy coffee with pleasure. 'Is it far?' she asked Herr Grässl in French.

'About fifty miles to the chalet – it will soon be dark. There is snow higher up.' She lay back as dusk indeed fell. Down below she could see a lake – the lake of Geneva, she supposed – before they began to climb further. It seemed they were climbing towards the stars for they were already out, glittering in the dark grey skies when she looked out of the window. This is Switzerland and it is dark, she said to herself, and Jacob is somewhere up here in these mountains. The thought excited and cheered her. For the first time for weeks, her worries and apprehension fell away. You have a chauffeur, a large car, and a cup of coffee, and you are going to meet the person you liked – *loved*, she thought suddenly – more than anyone else in the world.

'You work full-time for Mr Caston?' she asked the driver politely when she had drunk the coffee.

'Oh yes – I am usually taking the parcels to the airport,' he said enigmatically.

'He is my uncle,' she replied.

'Ah oui –' he answered but sounded as though he did not believe her.

They began to ascend more steeply now, the road twisting and turning and at one time going through a long tunnel cut into the side of the mountain.

'Far down there the lights of the lake,' said Monsieur – or should it be Herr? – Grässl – 'Over here, mountains?'

'Do you prefer to speak German?' she asked him. 'Ach, ja,' and he began to talk in a queer dialect she assumed to be Schweitzerdeutsch of which she understood not a word. There was snow now lying on the fields they passed and she was just wondering if they would ever get there, it seemed a lot more than fifty miles, when she saw they had turned down a lane. The moon was now shining. The car drew up on a flat piece of land with fir trees on each side, ahead the outline of a house of chalet-like construction, a lamp on at the side. She got out when the car stopped and the silence struck her as though she had been in some noisy dodgem race and was suddenly in a vast hall of mirrors. The sky was lit by the moon and the stars shone more silky bright than she had ever seen them. There was no wind, but a scented tingling coldness. She drew in a big breath and stood still for a moment whilst her case was taken out of the boot.

'He will be back now,' said Herr Grässl. 'I take your case to the side – go round the front. He will be there.' She obeyed and trod a gravel-strewn path that had received a light peppering of snow for it crunched firmly under her feet. She thought she could hear water somewhere. It must be a mountain stream! Arrival in starlight, she thought. Where is he then?

He was standing in the porch round at the front of the house. When he saw her he moved out under the stars so that even when she came up to him she saw his face only faintly. He drew her on to the threshold. 'Welcome, Julia,' he said.

The short walk across from the car had made her cheeks cold, so that his warm face, as he kissed her, immediately made her think of fire and cheer. He seemed taller too than the last time she had seen him, certainly a little bulkier in the light from the porch that now haloed his face. He had been quite slim before. 'There are forests below – and mountains above,' he said before drawing her into a wood-panelled hall that smelt of cigars.

'And snow and stars,' she said. Something that had been frozen in her seemed to melt. She caught her breath when she followed him into the sitting-room for there was a log fire and a dog lying by it, who got to his feet.

'Huñdchen,' said Jacob. 'Once he was small so that was his name. Now he's full-grown.' The dog sniffed her ankles, gave a short growl, but subsided again before the fire.

Here he was, thought Julia, the man she had always loved! Not Martin Maynard or any of those other young men who were suddenly bodiless chimeras left far away, but Jacob Caston who knew her better than anyone. 'Your case will be upstairs. Will you have a drink? Sit down, Julia – I've only been home an hour – sorry I couldn't meet you – everything go all right?'

She sensed he was nervous so she said, 'Thank you for the money. Everything went fine. I enjoyed the flight. I wish I'd come before.' If I had, she thought, I wouldn't be in this mess now!

'I have a press conference tomorrow,' he said as he poured her a whisky and took it to her. She knelt down by the fire. The big dog took no further notice of her.

'Do you live here always?' she asked him.

'No – only at weekends and when I have time off – which is not often now. But I like the quiet and the peace.'

'It's lovely,' she said and sipped her whisky.

He sat down in the armchair near her and looked at her. 'You look well,' he said, after a pause.

'Considering,' she replied.

'Don't let's talk about anything yet. There's a meal ready for us. Mrs Grässl came in to make it. I'm afraid I'm no cook.'

She felt, I am in his way, he's busy.

'It's lovely to see you here,' he said, so she knew then it was all right and he didn't think she was in the way. She looked up at him. The log fire made deep shadows, like those from candles.

'Can I come to your press conference?' she asked him, thinking, I've never seen him at work.

'If you like. It won't interest you, I'm afraid!'

There was a silence. Then, 'You look quite grown up now,' he said. It was true, she did. Still pretty, though there were little half-circles under her eyes. He'd leave any probing till after the meal, had been uncertain what he was going to say to her. But she had almost taken his breath away as she had stood there before him in her long English coat looking overcome and a little shy. 'I only bought the chalet last year,' he said. She had looked down in her lap after his remark about her looks. Perhaps she'd thought he was going to say something like 'Why didn't you act your age and take precautions?' Or 'Now you're grown-up you should be ashamed of yourself.' Neither of these thoughts were anywhere near his real feelings.

'How is your mother?' he asked her when they were sitting at a small table in the room next to the sitting-room where the housekeeper had lit candles and brought in a steaming cauldron of soup and Jacob had uncorked a bottle of red wine.

'Oh, very well – I saw her in the summer, not since then. They wanted me to leave the stage. "Whilst there was still time", was what they said. I suppose they were right – I've been wasting my time –'

'But you enjoyed it?'

'Less so recently. I didn't do *too* badly – got more work than some – but it wasn't leading anywhere. They say if you haven't made your mark by twenty-two you should go – the women that is. In the end, I just felt I could be doing something else better – I thought of the wireless and had an interview, but they haven't written yet –'

'How's your French?' he interrupted her.

'Oh, not bad – I still enjoy speaking it, you know –'

'I thought there might be some work for you here – with letters – translation – up at the office –'

'Oh!'

'We'd have to see,' said Jacob. 'It's rather technical.'

When they had eaten their veal and rice and then a delicious tart made with bottled plums and fresh cream, Jacob said, 'Let's go back by the fire with our coffee.' When she came downstairs again after freshening herself up a bit and inspecting the vast woodpanelled bedroom with a white lace bedspread and cherry wood furniture, she could not resist a, 'You seem to be doing well, Jacob!'

'Not bad,' he agreed – 'Still a long way to go though!'

'With the "machines"?' she asked.

'Yes, the "machines". There's a new name for them now – computers. They haven't quite caught on everywhere yet, but I think they will.'

'Because they compute?'

'Oh they will do a lot more than that!'

She thought, I wonder if Jacob runs away from his feelings or has done so in the past? I have a feeling – perhaps it's just the wine – that there's something he's not saying, something he's frightened of. Aloud, she said, 'I think I shall get rid of the baby, Jacob. What's the point? It would only upset everybody – especially the father.' He observed her quietly as she told him the whole story. She ended with, 'You always said you'd help me and I've always known you would. But I am grateful you've let me come here. I suppose I ought not to decide anything until I hear what *you* think.'

'Is my opinion important to you, Julia?'

'Yes – yes it is. I've always trusted your judgment.'

'Babies need fathers,' he said. 'If you go ahead and have this child there won't, I gather, be a father in evidence –'

'Unless he comes back to me – and I don't really want him, you see.'

'But babies should have fathers,' he said again. 'I expect you'll marry someone one day, Julia.'

'I suppose *you* missed having one?' she said.

'Yes – but I did have one in the end!' He thought, she'd better know. Now's the time!'

'You mean my dad – he was a father to you? When you came to live with us?'

'Oh, he was very kind but, no, not your father.' She looked puzzled.

'I thought your father was dead? – my grandpa – James Caston?'

'He wasn't my father,' said Jacob.

'You mean Gran – had a *lover*!'

'No, Julia.' He leaned forwards and took her hand. 'Do you feel strong enough to hear something about your family? It also affects you?' He sounded very dramatic, almost melodramatic, quite unlike the Jacob she knew.

'Yes – of course – what is it?'

'When I said I'd always help you,' he began, 'it was because you are my sister.'

Her mouth dropped open in shock. 'I should say half-sister, I suppose. Don't worry – you are who you think you are, Freda and Bob's daughter. But I am Freda's son.'

'How do you mean?' she stumbled over the words. She had time to think that it wasn't a bit like acting a shock on a stage.

'Your mother – my mother too – had me when she was very young. I was the child of her employer James Stainton.'

'The Mr Stainton you worked for?'

'Yes.'

'Then why didn't Mother ever tell us? You were my uncle. Gran had you – I mean – she brought you up?'

'Your mother must have had a terrible shock, I suppose. They loved each other, she and Stainton – I got to know him and the truth some years before he died. But I've never spoken to your mother – to my mother – about it, only written to her when I knew the truth – or rather some time afterwards when Stainton told me I ought to.'

'But then – didn't she tell you why –? acknowledge you? – see you? – was that why you went abroad?'

'I wrote to her and she replied and I saw her once more after that – you were away – at my father's funeral – what was there to say?'

'Did Dad know?'

'Oh, yes.'

'Why didn't they tell *me*?' Julia got up and began to prowl round the room. Her mother! Who was always so tight-lipped about sex!

'Sit down, Julia. She never wanted you to know. Didn't want me to tell you either. But I thought it was time you knew –'

'I should think *so*,' Julia still sounded angry.

'I'm not angry with her – she did what she thought was right. And when they took me in after our grandma died, I was only fourteen. How could she have suddenly told me? I might not have even have believed her.'

'It makes me feel I've never known her properly,' Julia said, coming to rest before him and sinking down to the floor once more near the fire.

'Can I have another drink of coffee?'

'Have a brandy to celebrate our new relationship!'

She thought, I always wanted an older brother. And here he is! But I thought of him, as a *man* too, my ideal man ... that's impossible ... does he think of me as a sister then – how long has he thought of me like that?

'Any child you have will be my nephew or niece,' he said, 'but I think it will hit your mother hard.'

'You mean that I've done what she did?'

'Exactly.'

'I do feel angry with her – as though she'd robbed me of something. But, Jacob, when I thought you were my uncle – when you thought I was your niece, when I was little – we liked each other, didn't we? I mean, I did *like* you – I felt we were a bit alike. I suppose we aren't, you being an engineer and all that and me a failed actress – yes I am! – but it makes everything different doesn't it?' Like a snow scene, she thought, with the whirling flakes that settle differently every time you shake it, so that no scene is really the same.

He put his hand out and touched her hair. 'I'm very fond of you, Julia,' he said. 'You can always rely on me, you know. But when I say babies should have fathers it's because I never had one till I was grown-up and then it was too late. He ought to have told me earlier when he gave me a job before the war, but he was too guilty, I think, and had that old-fashioned sense of honour towards his wife. 'She was the one who was a bit off-beam wasn't she?' Julia vaguely remembered something being said about Lina Stainton by a school friend. After a pause, she said, 'Mother must have loved that Mr Stainton.'

'Did *you* – love – this Martin man?'

'Oh – well I thought I did – or that he did me – but not now – not after his going away like that. As though I didn't matter, I suppose. He thought I was tough.'

'I did resent Freda later,' Jacob said slowly. 'But I missed a father more. I had Grandma, whom I thought was my mother – I suppose it was really *her* idea and Freda just went along with it. A lot of people used to do that. There was such a stigma attached to – bastards.'

'She *must* have been in love with him, and he with her,' Julia said.

'It wasn't like now – it would be much harder and they lived in a little town.'

'I wonder if anyone else knows apart from Dad.'

'There's still a stigma,' Jacob said. And then, in answer, – 'Your great aunt Cissie does, but she won't be spreading it around. She's nearly eighty. She writes to me sometimes.'

'And doesn't Mother write to you?'

'No – only at Christmas. I think she feels I'm angry with her. I haven't been man enough yet to go and see her and make it up properly.'

'I shall tell her I know!' Julia said. 'And about the baby too. If the baby has to have a father, well, I could bring him up here, couldn't I? And you'd be his uncle! – and so he'd have a man around. Not like you without one.'

'It's your decision, Julia,' he said. 'I'll help you whatever you decide.'

'But I want to be independent too, earn my living!' she wailed – 'How can I if I have a baby?'

'People manage,' he said. 'There are crèches and nursery schools – or I have the money for a nurse. But the child must not grow up thinking *I* am its father! – There must be no more deception.' She was silent.

'Money talks,' Jacob said. 'People don't ask questions in a big city. And, as I said, you're bound to marry one day.'

'It's all too complicated, Jacob,' she said. 'I need time to let all this sink in.'

Had she considered, would she consider, he wondered, that the attraction there must have been once between their mother and Stainton existed in a shadowy form now between the two of them? He had his father in him, and Julia her mother. He did love her, he thought, as she sat by the glowing fire and the dog stirred slightly in his sleep. He would never marry. Marriage was for those who could make it their first consideration above their work, their love affairs. Not that he might ever have the latter either. But he would be rich. He would help Julia and this child if she decided to have it. It was such a temptation to act as a surrogate father. He changed the subject – 'I'm like my grandfather – and yours – James Caston,' he said. 'An engineer. Who knows, *he* might have become rich like his friend Stainton if his talents had ever been given a chance.'

Julia said, 'I believe Gran once told me that Grandpa once had a great friend called James Stainton. I'd been left with her for the day, I think. You weren't there – probably you were at school. I was only about four but I do remember the *way* she said that. As though she were somehow proud of the connection. The boys knew each other at school, she said, and I remember thinking how much *I* wanted to go to school so I could have a friend of my own. We didn't live near enough to anyone else for me to go out to play with other children. I was four when Marcus was born.'

'Cissie too, our great aunt – she knew both my father and our grandfather Caston long before her sister married one of them,' said Jacob.

Julia looked over at him but now he was staring into the fire.

'You haven't anything of the Staintons in you,' he said, after a pause, not looking up.

'The Osborns are an uninspiring a lot,' she replied.

'So what we have in common must be from the Caston side,' he said.

'Or the Phillipsons – Grandma and Cissie?'

'I never thought Nell, as she was called, was over-bright,' he said. 'I called her Mam and I loved her. She wasn't a bit like her daughter. Freda must have got her brains from her father.'

'Do you think Mother is intelligent, then?'

'Yes, very. If she'd been a boy she'd have made a good businessman.'

'Well, that's not like me,' said Julia cheerfully. 'She must have given *you* all her brains!' They smiled at each other. Things were back on an even keel for the time being.

'I'd like to go with you tomorrow to your meeting,' said Julia. 'What time do you have to be off?'

'About half-past six – the meeting is at eight before the press conference. They start early here. Not like England.'

'I'd better go to bed and try to sleep then. Wake me when I should get up.'

Jacob thought, she'll easily fall asleep. She'll be tired with the journey and then these revelations, but she's young.

'Thank you for telling me,' she said. 'I'll go up to bed now.'

'Good night, Miranda,' he said, and got up and put his arms around her lightly, and kissed her cheek. When she had gone he sat for a moment with Hündchen by the almost burnt-through logs. He would look after her. They ought however to write to Freda once Julia had decided what to do. She'd be furious over her daughter's predicament and almost as furious that she hadn't been the first person in whom her daughter had confided.

Whatever she decided, Julia could stay on with him, might even work for Castons Computers one day? There was plenty to do, including translations, now that an American firm was planning to give him contract work. That was partly what tomorrow's meeting was about. He was to float a new company and hoped to attract some German capital over from Frankfurt. He had the feeling that within a few years the Germans would be once more economically the strongest nation in Western Europe, despite having lost the war. He wished his own countrymen would wake up. But perhaps he wanted them also mild and amateurish? His father hadn't been that though!

If it were possible for one to marry one's half-sister, he'd marry Julia, he thought. Not that he could ever have married her – the Prayer Book forbade uncles and nieces from marrying too. He wished they were not related, but also wished that somehow Castons and Staintons could get together again.

He loved Julia. But he knew that he must never hold her too closely to him in his loneliness. He had learned to do without one sort of love. Yet he could not bring himself to advise her to have an abortion.

In later years Julia was to look back on the time she spent at her brother Jacob's, both in Geneva and at weekends and holidays in the mountains, as the happiest of her life. Despite the pregnancy? Or was it because of it? She often wondered. It had been a 'time out of time' and had started the day after her brother had enlightened her about their relationship. She had accompanied him to his 'conference' where there had been, at first, some meetings behind closed doors. She had lurked in the gardens of the villa, where all the parties to the agreement had met, enjoying the snow and the views across the miles of white, punctuated by mountain peaks over as far as Mont Blanc, which seemed deceptively near. Then they had all driven across more snow to a sort of plateau where there was an incongruously large, bare, building filled with journalists from the newspapers of Europe who spent a whole hour questioning Jacob and his various partners about the prospects for a sort of new federation of European companies. So much she had understood, though the fine points escaped her when German was spoken. There had been many Americans with neat turned down collars and crew cuts, all bearing expensive leather briefcases, some Germans, who were trying to look as American as possible, as well as some Frenchmen and a few Swiss and Italians. No British. When it was over she had gone down the valley in the car with Jacob to a small town just within the Swiss border where the others were waiting or arriving and where they had all gone to eat lunch in a gilded restaurant that looked like a remnant of Napoleonic glory. Jacob seemed to be able to manage a conversation in most of the languages that were being spoken, though the Americans were tongue-tied in any language but their own, relying on their interpreters, who spoke so slowly they almost sent themselves to sleep. She wished she were part of it all, and could understand what was going on. Fortunately she sat next to a Frenchman to whom she explained that she was *la soeur de Monsieur Caston*. It gave her a queer thrill to do this. What did it matter? Nobody knew her here or knew her parents or anyone else from boring old England! But it was the first time she had said those words, and they seemed to sound right.

She was to enjoy many more such lunches within the next few months. She wrote to Martin Maynard, before saying anything to her parents, and a letter eventually arrived from him, telling her of his marriage. So that seemed to be that. She had delayed doing anything about an abortion until she heard from him, for it was morally right that a possible baby's father was informed of the situation. Later she wondered whether he'd married his new girlfriend *after* her revelation. 'Do as you think best,' was all he wrote. Nothing about his responsibilities. Jacob was shocked.

By then though it was rather late for an abortion and she realized that she had let things happen this way because she wanted to have the baby. It would have been quite different if she'd not had Jacob to rely on. Without his presence and help she doubted that she would have had the courage to go through with it.

Her parents' reactions were what she had expected: shock, horror, fear, anxiety and anger. She could not blame them. She had decided however not to disclose to them that she now knew who Jacob's mother was. Her father wrote a week or two after their first reply to say he would come out to see them both, but another letter from Freda cancelled this. What was going on? Julia wrote to them again saying she understood their feelings, didn't want to quarrel with them, but would stay away at least until the baby was born. Jacob had a letter then from their mother which he would not show her at first. But she persuaded him and was horrified to discover that Freda apparently thought it was *his* fault leading her into a way of life the Osborns disapproved of. But she must have repented, for another letter followed, written to them both, in which she excused herself by implying she'd had a lot of worries over Marcus and had perhaps written too hastily. She hoped that 'once things were settled' Julia would come home. They could not pretend they were overjoyed, but would make the best of it.

'In her other letter she *was* blaming you – who had nothing to do with it!' she cried.

'Our mother has always been a little jealous of me, I think,' was his reply. Julia was puzzled. 'Only human nature,' he said. 'She lost me to her own mother and now she thinks she's lost another of her children to me.'

It was Julia's turn to be shocked. 'Marcus was always Ma's favourite,' she said.

'It will all work out when you've had the baby,' he comforted her.

But those months of 1957 she lived through before her child was born were to remain as a blissful time in Julia's memory. She knew she could not stay always with Jacob, must strike out for herself when she was stronger, but put off for the time being any meeting with her parents. If they cared they could fly out to her, she thought. Meanwhile, they would have to come round to the idea that she was her own woman and at twenty-six was old enough to accept the consequences of her actions. Jacob booked her into a Swiss clinic and meanwhile she grew contented and fat on Mrs Grässl's delicious meals, not forgetting however to take long walks at weekends and to attend French classes for foreigners in Geneva where she was pleased to find she had still a good grasp of the language. Good old High School that had given her enough grammar to build upon! She learned to type, and helped Jacob occasionally in the evenings when he would dictate the correspondence he had not been able to keep up with during his busy day. Her English, he said, was better than that of his secretary, Mademoiselle Mounier. He had such energy, always busy with some new idea, some technical procedure he must test out. She understood hardly more of his actual 'machines' than she ever had, but that did not matter as far as the letters were concerned.

Occasionally her brother would look at her speculatively. Julia was not his secretary and he knew the 'honeymoon' would not last. She would be occupied with another kind of work very soon.

Rachel Miranda Osborn was born one July morning in the Rougier Clinic in Geneva.

Apparently it had been an easy birth, Julia was told afterwards. She was patted on the shoulder and told she'd 'done very well'. The baby herself seemed to have very little to do with the feelings she had had right up to the moment of birth when she had felt like a heroine of grand opera who must suffer to be triumphant. But once the child slithered out and – quickly – cried; once the doctor and the nurse had cleaned the baby up before turning their attention to the opera coda – the delivery of the afterbirth; once the child had been weighed and pronounced 3 kilos; once Julia also had been washed and told to have a good rest and the baby placed in a crib beside her nice clean new bed far from the delivery suite, she felt in a curious way bereft. No longer 'expectant' but 'delivered'. She did not feel in the least sleepy. A little thirsty for a good cup of English tea, actually, and, by the time Rachel Miranda was an hour old, longing to see her brother who she knew had been hovering nervously around the clinic corridors. The story was that Madame's husband was away in England and that Madame's brother was seeing to all the practical arrangements.

Jacob was eventually ushered in with smiles. He was bearing a large bunch of pink roses. 'How was it?' he asked.

'Have a look – there she is. Do you think I ought to begin to feed her? They didn't say.'

Jacob looked down at the bright red baby who seemed to be asleep. Brown hair, a tiny fist visible, and a little ear. A pink sheet covered the rest of her up to the chin.

'Ring the bell and tell them I want to hold her again,' Julia said, sniffing the roses. 'I can't believe it, you know, that here she now is.'

He came up to her, took her hand and kissed it. 'Did it hurt a lot?'

'It hurt, but just about bearably. I didn't scream or anything – actually it was more surprising and interesting than anything!'

They brought the child up to her eventually, who opened her eyes and yawned. Julia thought, I've no idea what to do with babies, but I expect I shall learn.

'Isn't she small? I've never seen such a small human being except your brother when he was about six weeks old –' Jacob said.

'Will you send a telegram to Mother and Father? Just say, "All well. Rachel arrived," with the date. You can send my love. If they want to come and see, they're welcome.'

Then when he had left and she had had the nurse place the baby once more back in the bassinet where they seemed to expect her to be, Julia was brought a light meal and a glass of wine.

One part of her still seemed to be the Julia she had known up till now, the other was divided between a new self in the bed and the small creature lying near who still seemed to be part of the old Julia, not the new. Some time in the night, throughout which she dozed, and woke to watch a nurse giving the baby a bottle of sweetened water, the two Julias met and merged, and when she next held her daughter she felt herself to be one person again but one who would never be completely whole unless the child was near her. When she held her the next morning, and during the week she stayed in the clinic, being thoroughly spoilt, the idea of the child's father surfaced in her mind only to sink back again and again, then definitely for ever. This child was hers now and nothing to do with Martin Maynard, or her parents, or even Jacob who was paying for the clinic sojourn and all the fuss.

She felt an enormous gratitude to him for helping her through the last months and the weeks surrounding the birth, but her love affair with her daughter had begun. From now on Rachel would be the most important person in her life. However could her mother have abandoned the baby Jacob to her own mother? Julia wondered, as full of maternal solicitude as her breasts were full of nourishment. I shall never understand that, she thought.

They would see their granddaughter when Julia consented to come back home. Her father was 'naturally pleased' that all had gone well, but did not feel it as entirely a 'matter for rejoicing'. That was the gist of the letter Julia was to receive from England. In the meantime, if a photograph could be sent? Julia knew that it was with Jacob too that Freda felt angry. 'I think we must tell her I know about you,' she said to him one day, when she had finished feeding Rachel and was sitting down to a meal with her brother. The house in Geneva was big enough for her to have a sitting-room and bedroom of her own with dividing doors on the first floor. Why ever Jacob had rented such a large house in the first place was a mystery but rented it he had, and for the time being she was glad she had a roof over her head. She did not intend to stay with him for ever. She was already helping him again with his correspondence, and once the child was weaned she intended to find some more translation work or English teaching and then to leave. It was the only way, short of returning to England. 'It's odd that Mother would imagine I might be looked after by an "uncle" whereas if I say my *brother* is caring for me ...'

'I leave it to you,' he said. 'But *you* can deal with any subsequent correspondence!'

Freda had written to her separately to say she would buy her a small flat in Harrogate if she would return. 'Your father is upset!' she wrote. 'Please try to understand.'

But Julia had no wish to return home to live out a half-clandestine existence twenty miles away from her parents. Instead she wrote to both her parents together, enclosing a photograph of the infant, now a month old and already smiling. 'I asked Jacob about his past,' she wrote, not entirely truthfully. 'And he has told me the whole story. I'm only grateful that my brother has helped me so much. I truly did not wish to burden you with it all. But that's all past now. Rachel is here to stay and I shall find work here or in France where Jacob has many contacts. He has been so very kind but I've no intention of taking him for granted. You'll be glad to know however that his firm is doing most awfully well. Whenever you would like to come over and see us and Rachel you will be made welcome.'

Jacob smiled a little over this fulsome though curt missive.

'It's true – I shall look for work. I can't sponge on you for ever, Jacob.'

'What's yours is mine,' he said.

In the event Freda and Robert did not come over immediately to see their daughter and granddaughter. Julia thought she might find herself a job over in Savoy eventually, but Jacob insisted he kept her for the time being and she could hardly refuse. She had helped him in those little things like correspondence and never expected payment. And she knew that he liked having her around. But she also knew that she must not stay, that she must make a life for herself that did not in the end include her brother.

At the beginning of 1958 a part-time job translating for a light engineering firm over the French border turned up, which, combined with another part-time teaching post in a small private school, would enable her to rent a flat in the centre of the old town of Annecy with the help of Jacob's Swiss francs and the presence nearby of a state-run crèche. As she was not French by nationality this too had to be paid for. Jacob was sceptical, but realized sadly that though he might give her money (which he could well afford to do) he must not continue to act as adopted father to Rachel Miranda. In that position he was too close to being regarded as virtual husband to the sister whom he loved so dearly.

By the time Rachel was a year old Julia's new life had begun, and by the time the child was four she had met Monsieur Duruy, a French teacher of English in the same town, who found an English girlfriend a great help in escaping the attentions of a colleague of whom he had tired.

Julia, who had had no intention of marrying, decided that the sudden proposal of Philippe Duruy might be taken seriously if it gave Rachel a future papa. She knew that her love for the child was so intense she might drown in it. So it was that in the Christmas season of 1961, after earning a sort of living for herself for three years, Julia married the forty-year-old Duruy. It was the occasion of a patching up of the relations between herself and her own family and Jacob, a fragile patching up but at least an attempt to make bygones be bygones. A new era had begun. Jacob Caston, returning alone to Geneva from the long luncheon and the attendant family tensions, wept not from relief but from immense sorrow that his lovely Julia had now been claimed by a stranger, as for the last three years or so his own 'Miranda' had been claimed by another, younger, version.

Part Two

ii *Rachel*

1981–

Si on me presse de dire pourquoi je l'aimais, je sens
que cela ne peut s'exprimer, qu'en répondant: 'Parce
que c'était lui; parce que c'était moi?

(If I am urged to explain why I loved him, I feel I can
reply only: 'Because it was him; because it was me.')
                                   Montaigne, *Essais*, I, xxviii

They had gone away from the party together whilst others were
getting down to serious drinking. The party noise stopped
suddenly as they closed the front door of the tall old house, and
all was quiet on the tree-lined road. It had been raining; the
pavement was only dampish now but there was a smell of wet
earth as they walked down the garden path. The river was not
far away, and fleecy moonlit clouds were passing slowly over the
sky in that direction.

They stood for a moment and then she turned her face to his.
He put his hands on her shoulders, and then his arms round the
whole of her. She came up to his chin so that when they
embraced, swaying together a little, he smelt the pleasant scent
of her hair. She detached herself, looked up at him. He kissed
her and she returned his kiss. Tender exploratory kisses to
begin with, and then longer ones. Their bodies fitted together
comfortably even when the kisses became more passionate.

She had aroused his interest as much as his desire and he felt
quite in charge of himself. *She* was feeling not exactly surprised

at his kisses, but a little astonished that he was actually doing what she had wanted him to do from the moment they had met that evening for the first time. She had thought that when people talked about two glances meeting across a crowded room it was old stuff, passé – but it had happened. And she hadn't needed to do anything at all to attract him, had even averted her face from his before he moved across the room to her, and smiled, and began to talk. Which he did easily but not, she thought, with the practised aim of a seducer, more as if he were renewing acquaintance with her, as if he knew that she'd expected him to walk across the room to find her.

He was tall, but not a giant, had very blue eyes, light-brown floppy hair, a straight nose and a generous mouth, and he was dressed in an open-necked blue shirt and a pale blue cotton jacket, and jeans of the same shade. She had wondered what he did for a living and guessed, perhaps an architect. Not an accountant or a barrister, certainly. Might be an academic, but moved too loosely for that. He looked rather like one of those firm-faced men featured in old knitting patterns that she had used to look at at her grandmother's in England. Firm-faced he might be, but not twinkly, for there was something else indefinable as well. Is it reassurance I need? she asked herself. He's very 'English'.

He saw a young woman of medium height with her hair cut in a straight brown fringe. About twenty-four, he guessed. Ten years younger than himself. Intelligent, determined face; lovely grey eyes; and an uncertain little smile. Very well-dressed too. He noticed such things. Well-cut dark blue silk shirt, straight navy blue skirt, shoes with small heels. Nice legs, too and a trim waist. Some small earrings were visible when he looked up at her face again. Not an 'arty' girl at all. She had English colouring, but without being exactly fashionable or foreign-looking there was something about the way she stood, gestured, talked, that was not English ...

They liked each other, found each other's company stimulating. Later that evening at his own place he made love to her, and then they made love together and it was all very satisfying and satisfactory. Was he going to fall in love? He hoped not. But even as the thought occurred to him his body took him over again – and took her over – and when he woke up he felt a bit dazed, carried out of himself as he hadn't been for ages. But he smiled back at the face on the pillow, thinking, I deserve a bit of luck, a bit of a break, and probably she does too. Leave all the bits of 'living' in abeyance for a time? See how things go.

It wasn't as if she hadn't soon guessed who he might be, because after they'd talked and he'd said in answer to her enquiry that he came from a little place in Yorkshire she'd never have heard of, a place called Brigford, a bell had definitely started ringing ...

He was called Paul, but she hadn't caught his surname when they'd been introduced. One of the penalties of having spent your childhood in another country was that you weren't so quick to hear some muttered introduction. If it had been 'Dufour' or 'Thibault' or 'Segond' she'd have caught it immediately, but she was not conversant with the range of English surnames. She thought it had been Tenterden, or Sugden, and it was not until they'd left the party, neither really tipsy but pleasantly relaxed, and walked along Chelsea Embankment; and when she'd gone to his studio for coffee and studied his very beautiful face and felt that spark of chemistry, or sexual desire, whatever it was you called it, and known that the attraction was mutual, that she'd seen the signature on one of his drawings. *STAINTON*, it had said, and the drawing was of a dry-stone wall.

But it might be a quite common English name, mightn't it? Why should he be from the same family as Uncle Jacob Caston's father?

The story of Jacob's birth had come to her piecemeal in her childhood from her mother, and it hadn't interested her at the time because it was nothing to do with the mystery of her own father, about whom her mother had always been less than forthcoming. The tale of her grandmother's first son had interested her only on account of her grandmother, that old lady whom she remembered seeing first on her mother's wedding day. There had been little contact afterwards between her mother and her grandmother until at fourteen she had gone with her mother on that long holiday to England.

But then in Chelsea, which he said was no longer really a place for painters, and after she had very willingly entered upon what she'd thought of quite consciously as a one-night stand with the handsome Paul, she had suddenly known that it wasn't going to be that. He seemed as besotted with her as she was with him. It was time to ask him for more details of his family history.

He said his grandfather had been called James Stainton and had died when he, Paul, was about three so he had never known him, only heard from his father what a splendid old boy he was. 'Not that I trusted my father's judgment,' he added. It appeared that Paul was the Black Sheep of the family. Having refused to go to university he'd travelled all over the world, opted for a free-lance artist's life, left Brigford as soon as he decently could. 'Father was – eventually – an architect and my brother Adrian followed him in that. There was an old family firm till the fifties, but then Japanese competition became too intense and there was nothing to do but sell up. My brother still lives up there.' They were lying in bed on their first Saturday morning when he told her this.

Rachel was not too sure of all the details of James Stainton's affair with her grandmother, and as Paul obviously knew nothing of it she decided that discretion was best. She had not yet visited her grandmother, being only a few months settled in London, working for Jacob Caston's outfit. She kept putting off a visit north. Meeting Paul Stainton put it off even further. She found she was madly, passionately, in love with him, more deeply than she had been with any of the young Frenchmen she had known as a student. All she said to him later during that momentous week, was that there was some vague connection between her grandmother and the Staintons. No mention of her uncle Jacob Caston, who might be Paul Stainton's uncle too.

She wondered whether to mention that she had met Paul Stainton in her next letter to her uncle Jacob, but decided against it. She might be wrong about the mutual feelings though she hoped she was not. As time went on she felt no more inclined to write to her uncle Jacob about Paul.

Paul appeared not very interested in his own family, never mind hers, for he seemed to live for his work. It brought him little money but he lived partly, she discovered, on money from a family trust which had come down to him from his grandfather.

Rachel Duruy, who had anglicized her name to Drury for convenience now she was in London, had found working in the English capital a disillusioning experience. Her uncle had found her the job when she had decided to work in England. It was a good job and paid enough for her to rent a tiny one-bedroomed flat in Fulham – 'Worlds End' – but it gave her a busy life without giving her a very interesting one. Perhaps it's my fault, she thought. I don't belong in London any more than I felt I belonged in France. She had been tempted once or twice to throw in the sponge, go back to Savoy, or to Switzerland, and train to teach English in a lycée over there as her stepfather had done. But she hated the idea that Jacob Caston might despise her for not sticking it out and making something of it. Since she was bilingual he had found her a job in the export sales department of the West London based branch of Castons Computers, one which many women graduates would have given their eye teeth for. But there was something absent from her life. She had told herself that it must be that she was not yet over mourning her mother, whom she still missed terribly. Julia had died of breast cancer when Rachel was in her last year of a three-year *licence d'anglais* at the university of Lyon. Uncle Jacob had come when her mother died and had supported her, as she knew he had always supported her mother.

It had not been financially that he had supported her, but emotionally. Papa had not liked his wife's brother.

Her first memory of Jacob had been when she was about four years old when he had come to Annecy for what she later realized must have been her mother's wedding to Philippe Duruy. She had stayed one morning with Uncle Jacob at the flat where she and her mother lived, until at one o'clock she had been taken by him to a party in a big restaurant. It must have been after the ceremony at the town hall. She had only a hazy memory of that day in 1961, but remembered Jacob better from a visit he had made to the town two years later when she was seven.

She had come in from school still wearing her *tablier* with her name *DURUY R.M.* embroidered on the pocket in curly writing, and she'd shouted 'I'm hungry – can I have a pain au chocolat?', as soon as she had pushed open the door of their apartment, which was on the first floor of an old building not far from her Ecole Primaire. Mummy had come into the hall from the kitchen and there was a man standing behind her, who smiled.

'You remember Uncle Jacob?' her mother asked her in English.

Rachel had not been sure at first, but when he said he had

brought her a bag of bonbons she did remember that day long ago when he had taken her to the lovely restaurant and Mummy had been there with Papa and there had been her grandmother and grandfather too whom she did not recall ever having seen before.

'Hello,' she said to the man now, and he said, 'She was only four, Julia!' He looked nice, had brown hair beginning to go silver at the sides and horn-rimmed glasses.

'Oh, I remember,' she said and as she said it she *did* remember.

'You had a lovely gold watch.'

'There, you see,' said her mother.

'I have an even nicer one now,' said this Uncle Jacob. 'Look, it tells you what day it is, and the date – and the time all over the world. I suppose you can read?'

'Of course I can read,' she said indignantly. She went up to him and looked at it carefully. His wrist was thicker than Papa's, with no black hairs.

'Do you speak French?' she asked him.

'Not as well as you, I bet.'

'Don't flatter her,' said her mother.

'I am bilingue,' said Rachel proudly.

'Here's your bread and chocolate, and a drink of milk,' said her mother, and they all sat down together at the table in the kitchen where she usually had her goûter when she came home from school.

'Do you know my papa?' she asked the man.

'A little,' said this Uncle Jacob.

'He is not my real father,' Rachel continued. Her mother had looked up, distressed.

'I know,' said this uncle.

'Do you know *him* then?' she asked.

'No – and your French papa looks after you now,' he said, rather sternly, she thought.

Rachel wondered what her mother was thinking about as she looked from one to the other of them.

'Rachel always comes out with things,' she said. 'She is too precocious.'

And he said something like, children like to know who their fathers are, and Mother got up and made some coffee for them.

'Why didn't you come and see us before?' Rachel asked their visitor.

'He's busy,' said Mother, and the man said, 'I ring your mother up sometimes.'

Then she knew that this uncle must be the one who always telephoned on Thursday afternoons when Papa went to his meeting and she was not at school either because the others went to their Catholic lesson with the priest and she had the afternoon off with her mother.

Much later, Rachel was to remember the conversation, but it was only when she was grown up that she had realized that Uncle Jacob didn't want to interfere in their lives and that was why he rationed his visits and phone calls. She'd had a feeling that Papa didn't approve of her mother's brother but hadn't thought of it the other way round. 'Jacob thought nobody was good enough for me,' her mother said, years later. But that time when she was seven her uncle had given her a big English kiss when he had left. Her papa must have come in afterwards for she remembered he had been cross that she hadn't finished her *devoirs*, which you had in France right from the beginning of school attendance.

She always spoke French to Papa, and of course to her school friends. All the lessons at school were in French so it was only with her mother that she spoke English until, when she was eleven, she passed into the Sixième at the Lycée and they all began to learn English. She was obviously always the best at English. When she thought of that uncle it was chiefly to remember that he spoke English, and *was* English, like Mother. At Christmas, Uncle Jacob had always sent her a present though he did not send Mother or Papa one. When she was eight it had been a tiny radio that you could listen to English programmes on, and another Christmas a boat that went on batteries which you could sail on one of the little canals in the town. When she was nine or ten, there had been a beautiful bicycle with gears. Papa had been cross that time and argued with her mother. Papa sometimes chose to talk English – after all he was a teacher of English at another school – and she heard him say, 'You'd think that he was the child's father to send her such a present!' Had he wanted her to overhear? The thing was that mother's brother was rich, and Rachel thought that perhaps the bike was too expensive.

When she went on to the green with it the first time near the lake, she said to Papa, when they were sitting down for a minute,

'Maman says that Uncle Jacob is rich – I'm sure he would send *you* a bike like mine if you asked him!'

'I know he's rich,' Papa said.

Later, she wondered if there was a mystery about her birth and that Jacob was her real father, but Mother had always explained that her real father was in England and had married another lady, though she didn't tell her his name at first.

The Christmas after that, there arrived an English typewriter, which Papa borrowed when he wrote letters to English people or when he wrote exercises for his pupils, so that was all right.

The summer she left the little school, Papa went off by himself on a holiday and she was pleased to be alone with her mother. But she wished that she had a brother or a sister. None ever came and she asked her mother why. Perhaps Papa did not really like children, she thought. Or he had enough of them at school?

That summer, Mother's other brother, Marcus, came on a visit, and after he'd gone Mother said, 'It's about time I took you to England to see your grandmother.' Rachel remembered her grandmother from the day in the restaurant. She had liked Granny Osborn straight away. She had smelt nice and didn't ask questions like, what are you going to be when you grow up? Rachel had hardly been aware then that she talked English because both languages came to her quite naturally. The crèche and the Nursery School and the people in shops spoke in French and her mother spoke English. Grandpa Osborn was another who spoke English. He was gruff, but he gave her a doll and some English biscuits he'd brought with him.

The promised visit to her grandparents did not happen straight away after that summer when Papa went on holiday alone. Before Papa came back however Uncle Jacob visited them again. By this time she must have been about twelve and read an Agatha Christie whilst her mother and he talked in low voices in the salon. But when they emerged, he said 'Come on – I'm going to take both you and your mother out for a treat. Let's go to the Salon de Thé.'

So they all went in Uncle Jacob's car into the centre of the town to the best tea shop, one which they seldom visited because it was so expensive. Rachel knew she was greedy and hardly ever had the chance to indulge her sweet tooth. What a cornucopia there was to feast the eyes upon! – puits d'amour and éclairs and sablés and tartes aux fruits and Japonais, which had an almondy taste, and macaroons and florentines and Chantilly creams, and millefeuilles – which Mother said were called vanilla slices in England – and others with names she couldn't translate because they didn't exist in English: 'Le Délice', mousserons, ambassadeurs, opéras, succès, and palmiers and chaussons and ramequins and Babas. She feasted her eyes before feasting her stomach and Mother said, '*My* mother always said "Your eyes are too big for your tummy" when I wanted to eat sweet things.' She couldn't decide between a 'noyer' stuffed with butter cream that she knew had a coffee taste, and a 'friand' filled with cream and chocolate.

'Well, these are better than teacakes and Yorkshire jam puffs,' said Uncle Jacob. He and Mother laughed a lot that afternoon and Rachel felt happy. It was before they began to change the town by doing up all the ancient buildings of the Old Town, and the canals were sometimes a bit smelly. They walked along, the three of them, under the Arcades on the cobblestones where it was cooler and then they walked by the Old Prison on the canal island and Rachel saw one or two of her classmates who saluted her. They drove back home by the Pont des Amours where the swans were gliding under the arch and, as well as feeling replete, Rachel felt happy and peaceful.

'It's a pretty town,' Jacob said.

'I wish you lived here,' she said, emboldened by the feeling of satisfaction. 'You could take me fishing – Papa won't.'

'He hasn't the time, darling,' her mother said quickly – 'And neither would your uncle have – since he works pretty well day and night!'

'Do you really?' Rachel thought, if you could be rich it was probably worth it.

The lake was still, and the mountains in the far distance clear that day; the rowing boats lay still on the waters and the little steamer was just setting off from the landing stage to start its voyage round the lake, stopping at the villages or landing stages on each side.

'There are four churches and they are all Catholic,' she said as they turned down the street to their flat. 'We did the Counter Reformation at school last term.'

'At least she is getting a good education,' said Jacob.

They finally went to England for a long summer holiday in

1971 when Rachel was fourteen. Mother had persuaded Papa to accompany them during the first week, spent in London. After all, he taught English. Rachel was surprised and a bit disconcerted to find that he had rather a strong accent when he did speak in that language. She enjoyed London, saw Carnaby Street and bought the Beatles record, 'Let it be', which you couldn't buy easily at home. Then Papa went off to some university course and she and her mother had two weeks in Woolsford after that with Grandmother Osborn, but it was a bit sad because Grandpa Osborn was not well. Mother said she felt like a stranger there, a foreigner, as all her own old friends had gone away, left the place years ago as she had done herself. But Rachel enjoyed getting on buses to the moors and going for the day in Uncle Marcus's car to the coast where she saw the North Sea for the first time. She noticed that her mother and grandmother got on quite well when other people were there, but that once or twice Grandma seemed upset. 'Is Uncle Jacob Grandma's son or Grandpa's?' she asked her mother. 'He is Grandma's – I'll tell you all about it one day,' her mother said.

One afternoon, when she was alone with her grandmother, she was asked whether they saw much of Jacob Caston. 'Now and again,' she said. 'He is so nice – and Mother says he's very rich.'

'I don't doubt that,' said Freda Osborn and changed the subject. 'Your mother works too hard,' she said.

'She has two jobs,' explained Rachel proudly. 'At the translation bureau and at the Ecole des Sapins.'

'Wouldn't you like to live in England one day?' her grandmother asked her. Rachel thought about it. Annecy was home at present but she liked England in spite of the rain. They said that the summer was a good one but to her the weather was chilly. Yet she liked the landscape, the hills, smaller than the French mountains but bleak when you got on the tops.

'Couldn't your father come and teach French here one day?' Granny Osborn asked her another time.

'Oh, he belongs in France,' Rachel replied. And then she thought, I'd like to come here one day by myself, so she answered the earlier question. 'I think I'd like to live here,' and then added, 'but Papa couldn't earn as much money, I don't suppose, in England.' Her grandma never mentioned the fact that Papa was not her real papa, so Rachel, sensing difficult territory, said nothing either. It was a good holiday and afterwards when she got back she read *Jane Eyre* in English, and *Wuthering Heights*. They had visited Haworth and seen the Parsonage and it had been terribly interesting and a bit sad. She thought, when she had read the books, that there was nothing she liked as much in the French novels that came her way.

By 1974 when she was in the Première at the lycée doing the Bac, they were beginning to change the town. Mother was still working, though she had been ill the year before, but Papa went away again by himself and she discovered he had what they called a *petite amie*. Then her mother fell ill again, an illness that lasted on and off till 1978, when she died. Jacob Caston came to the funeral and wept. She had never seen a man cry before. But all those years between her visit to England and her mother's death at the age of forty-seven were muddled up in her mind. It was only after the death of her mother that she really got to know Uncle Jacob, and by then Papa's *petite amie* Anais Martin had become the second Madame Duruy.

She had spent two years in Lyon following a course at the Faculté de Lettres, having decided to do a *licence* in English. It was possibly a lazy way out, but she was fired with a need to learn more of English literature which had always been her favourite subject at the lycée. The course had been interrupted for a year by her mother's illness when she had returned home to keep her company but she had managed to finish the degree the year after her mother's death. Then she had decided to get advice from Jacob Caston about going to live and work in England. Her stay in Switzerland, and later in Italy at Jacob's villa on Lake Como, made her resolve to be independent, as her mother had wanted her to be, and her decision was made the easier by Papa Duruy making it quite plain he did not expect her to go on living with him and his new wife. She supposed she had been lonely then, and without Jacob's help would quite easily have accepted the proposal of one of her university friends that she marry him and live in Lyon. But although she was fond of him she knew that she didn't love Luc, and so she had torn herself away from him and from the prospect of security he held out. Security was, she was sure, somewhere in England. Grandmother Osborn had not come to the funeral in Annecy but had sent Uncle Marcus instead, who was not a bit like either her mother or Jacob and was chiefly interested at that time in racing cars and playing the

Stock Exchange. Yet she supposed that Jacob must be interested in money too or why did he devote his life to its acquisition?

She remembered the last time she had seen Papa and said goodbye and he had looked very guilty, though her mother's illness had not been his fault.

Who was she really? Rachel Osborn, because her mother hadn't been married when she was born? Or Rachel Duruy, because Papa had given her his name in France, and it was what everyone there knew her as? Or even Rachel Maynard, which was the name of her real father, her mother had told her? She had never seen him. The one name she had never had was Caston and she began to wonder again whether Mother had told a lie and Jacob *was* her father and perhaps not really her mother's brother. But Mother had said he was Freda Osborn's son. She knew without it ever being said that he had loved her mother and was the person to whom she must address herself if Mother died. But if he was not Grandpa Osborn's son, then who had his father been? It was at this juncture that a conversation with Uncle Jacob on one of his weekend visits to his Como villa, where she was staying trying to gather her wits, as well as mourn her mother, made a little clearing in the forest of her ignorance. She had been on the balcony that looked over the lake and it was a beautiful June evening. She'd walked that afternoon in the vast gardens behind the house, that stretched up the slope of the hill, and she had felt the beginnings of a sort of peace and acceptance of her mother's death which before had eluded her. Jacob had joined her on the balcony and somehow they had begun to talk of her mother and how Rachel herself had been born in Geneva and how the man she knew as Uncle Jacob had looked after his sister and seen her through that time.

'Uncle Jacob,' she said, 'Mother never properly explained. Who was your father?'

He had looked at her quizzically and replied, 'It's a wise child ...'

'Yes, I know. But why is Grandma so peculiar about you?'

'Is she?'

'Well, of course she is! You don't visit her, do you? And she never said anything about you much, except to ask me – that time we were in England – whether we saw much of you.'

'And what did you say?'

'I said what Mother told me to say – that we saw you now and then. Why was Papa so jealous of you?'

'I imagine he thought your mother was too fond of me,' Jacob answered simply. – 'I was certainly very fond of her.'

'But who are you really? Did my grandma have a first husband who died?'

'No – she was only married the once. She had an affair with a man she worked for called Stainton.'

'So you are really Jacob Stainton?'

'No. Why? She wasn't *married* to him – he was married to somebody else.'

'Like mother.'

'How do you mean?'

'Well *my* father was married to somebody else, you see.'

'I hadn't really thought of it quite like that,' he said. 'My mother's love affair ended when I was born. But, Rachel, your own mother didn't love a Stainton. She had a student affair with your father, and you were the result – that was why your grandma was distant with her – and why she stayed away. I expect my mother was relieved, when your mother married Philippe. She always wanted her to settle down.'

'I always wondered why she did. I'm sure she never loved him!'

'No – we've no right to say that. She made a new life for herself – and for you.'

'But why don't you see your mother – my grandmother – more often? I like her –'

'Too much happened when I was small. It doesn't concern you, Rachel.' Now he sounded distant.

'I wish you were friendly with her and could go back and live in England.'

'No – it's too late for that. I like it where I am.'

He poured her a drink from a frosty jug brought by his noiseless manservant.

'You are determined to go over there then?' he asked.

'Yes – I think I must. I want to see my own father, you see – and Grandma –'

She was thinking, I wish I could make those two, Jacob and Grandma, friends again. Why didn't Mother ever try?'

'I think you will be disappointed if you find him,' Jacob said. 'She cut herself completely off from him before you were born. But I understand why you feel you must meet him – just as I wanted to know my own father.'

'And did you?'

'Yes, but the circumstances were rather different.'

He did not appear to want to say any more so they talked of other things and when the sun went down behind one side of the lake she went in and ate a light supper with him before Jacob went off as usual to his office to make telephone calls and dictate letters to the secretary who always accompanied him to whichever house he chose to live in for the summer.

Pondering all these things as she lay by the side of another Stainton, Rachel Osborn – Rachel Drury – turned her thoughts to that evening a few weeks before she'd met Paul Stainton, when she had finally plucked up courage to see her own father, Martin Maynard, on the stage in a Sheridan revival.

'What are you thinking about, beautiful Rachel?' asked Paul Stainton who had previously fallen asleep by her side. It was *two* weeks after meeting each other at the party during which they had seen each other every evening to spend their time making love in his flat, or talking, talking.

'I was just wondering whether the Staintons *I* heard of were the same family as yours,' she answered.

They lay sideways, each looking at the other with nothing between them, flesh on flesh. 'Why?'

'Oh, I had an uncle who was connected with a person of your name.'

'With a woman?'

'No – he knew a man called James Stainton, I think,' she said cautiously.

'My grandfather was called James,' he said.

'Yes, you told me. What was *your* father called then?'

'Valentine – what a name! –'

'Is he still alive?'

'Yes – he's seventy or so – he retired last year. Went to live in Bournemouth.'

That must be Jacob's half-brother then, she thought.

'Had your grandfather any other sons?' she asked innocently.

'No, there was only my father and my aunt Mary. She's a tartar. My grandma was a bit peculiar, to put it mildly – she died a few years ago. She was wacky about religion – spent a lot of time in a genteel home for well-off weirdos – you know. Let's stop thinking about my family! You can tell me about yours when I've made love to you again.' Rachel gave in. He was insatiable. So it seemed was she. She gave herself up to the present, to a living man, a tender man, not to thoughts of the old or the dead. But when he looked most vulnerable, when her heartstrings were plucked by the terrible need he had to possess her, the thought of Jacob Caston hovered around the edges of her consciousness until she banished it as inappropriate.

Something kept muttering away in Rachel Drury's head that would not stop however much she tried to ignore it. She had known Paul Stainton now for two months, most of which time she had spent with him when she was not at work in Chiswick. She had managed to arrive on time at work every morning as usual though she was sure that everyone in the office must have guessed what she had just been doing. Paul got back to his own work once she had left the studio and did not appear disrupted in his routine. It was different if you were your own boss.

But she must reclaim her own territory, have time to think, which she found impossible when he was close to her. For two months she had been Someone Else, a Rachel fashioned anew by her lover, but she was uneasy. The muttering in her head might be the result of fatigue but it was also the voice of common sense.

Yet the minute she saw him again, at the end of each working day, she would feel paralysed by desire, want only to be in his arms again.

The only thing to do was to telephone him from work, tell him she needed time to think about what had happened to her. Then she could go back to her own little room, pick up the threads of herself, think what she was doing.

It was 1981 after all! Everyone was free to make love, to choose the life they wanted to lead, to fall in love – or not. To leave, too. But she felt imprisoned by this new lust which was not just lust, as though it were a raging infection, a fever, and she were some woman from long ago who had no desires of her own other than to give and receive passion. It was disturbing. She must go away by herself for a little time, ask him to let her be, though she was aware that she might have made him a prisoner too. But if she went away, would she lose him? No, she did not think so. The attraction was mutual, their actions initiated by them both. This wasn't an unrequited infatuation or a crush. Yet she did wish she knew him better, in spite of feeling she already knew him better than anyone else ever had. What was it about her that made him so passionate? For he seemed to have made something new from his idea of her that was already altering her own idea of herself. And it might be a complete fabrication! She'd wake up one day to find it had all disappeared in a cloud of enchanter's smoke.

She would go north. She was due a week's holiday. All this turbulence might be the result of her having felt so adrift for so long after her mother's death, and Philippe Duruy's dereliction. Only Jacob might help, but she dreaded Jacob finding out. Why, she was not sure, but had an idea he subscribed to the notion of a compulsive attraction between Staintons and Castons, though he belonged to them both. The last straw had been her seeing her 'real' father at last, prancing across the stage. A handsome man, with a weak mouth, and an affected manner of speaking; a rich baritone voice. Did he never think, had he never thought, of his daughter? It appeared not. She did not know what to do about him.

'They say I look like my grandfather,' Paul had said when she had teased him about being too good-looking. He must have had scores of women, though he denied it, said there was something special about her. She realized that the moment she'd seen that signature of his it had added a sort of glamour to her first impression of him, and was immediately part of her love for him. It was uncannily connected with her own family's past, and she had always wanted to belong to a family, not just to Mother, or even to Jacob.

She made the phone call from work, though her heart was beating like a drum, assured him she would be back in a week, and booked a room for the first night in a Woolsford hotel she found in the directory. She'd go to see Freda and 'have it out' with her, though quite what she meant by that she was unsure.

Her grandmother had always been a mysterious person in her eyes; it was probably the way her mother had spoken of her. Not that she had said much about Freda's earlier life, or what must have led to the conception of Uncle Jacob. Perhaps she hadn't known very much about that herself? ... A composed sort of woman, capable, rather conventional, with a prosperous husband, domestic duties and worries, and, in her mother's childhood, the dominant partner, under a deceptive appearance

of agreeing with her husband about everything – that was how
her mother summed her up:

> ... I think she thought my father a bit old-fashioned in his
> attitude to me, and Father *was* quite strict. He admired Mother,
> though I expect he had a business life of his own into which she
> didn't pry. Father was pleasant to Jacob too when he came to live
> with us – but not effusive. I suppose some men would not have
> welcomed him to their home ...
> ... I can't remember her ever smiling very much ... She looked
> preoccupied, busy, as though she'd left something behind her
> and didn't want to think about it, thank you very much ... Only
> later did I find out what it was and what had happened to her.
> But she never mentioned it. Not even after I was married when
> she knew I knew that Jacob was not my uncle ... I don't think she
> was ashamed. Just shy. And a bit scared of Jacob, I don't know
> why. If Father had been a really strong character I think she'd
> have felt happier, but I suppose she felt grateful to him for
> having married her and made her settled and respectable ... She
> used to look at me in a strange way that time we all went to
> England, and I never knew what she was thinking. She was very
> polite to Papa when he came on to Yorkshire after that Oxford
> summer school ... I know that I treated her badly and that she
> would have been on my side when I knew I was expecting you.
> But I didn't see it that way then, never saw her as a woman, only
> as 'my mother' ... and I was angry that she hadn't always kept
> Jacob with her, and allowed him to think that her own mother was
> his too ...

Such scraps of conversation Rachel remembered from the times
she had sat with her mother Julia Duruy during her long last
illness. She hadn't paid enough attention to them and now she
was going to the widow Freda Osborn, her grandmother, to try
to get to know her, and somehow to make things right, though
whether for herself or for the old lady she wasn't sure.

She had the packet in her case which Jacob had handed over
to her when she left for London six months before. She'd
promised to give it personally to her grandmother, though he
wouldn't say what it contained.

If Grandma was a mystery, perhaps her own mother, Julia,
had been a bit of one too, both to her and to Freda. Why had
Granny Osborn not come to the funeral in Annecy? Well,
she had been eighty when Julia died, and nobody had really
expected her to. Now she lived on in Holm Dene with a daily
companion to help put her to bed and get her up in the

morning. The same house on the outskirts of Woolsford where Julia and Marcus had been born. And where Uncle Jacob had lived for a time …

As the train from Wakefield branched towards that city, Rachel felt London and even Paul Stainton slip away from her. They would both be there when she returned but now she must brace herself for quite a different sort of place and quite a different sort of relationship.

Freda had insisted she come to stay at Holm Dene after her night in Woolsford and she had given her the packet from Jacob, which had turned out to be photographs of James Stainton and James Caston with their classmates of almost a hundred years ago.

'That was how it all began,' said Freda.

Rachel waited. Freda seemed to be looking out of the window into the distance so she sat down on the other side of the fireplace, the smaller photograph still in her hand.

'I ought to have told your mother about it, I expect, when she grew up, but I never knew how to begin.' She looked agitated, unusual for her grandmother. Though she was eighty-four years old she never looked less than chic and composed.

'Don't fret about it,' said Rachel.

'Oh, I know that sort of thing is quite commonplace nowadays! The world has changed. How much did your mother tell you about – my elder son's father?'

Rachel felt she must be discreet. The old lady might still not want to tell her the whole story even now. 'Was James Stainton very good-looking? He appears so on the photograph?' She answered the question with another, to show she knew the answer to the first.

'I suppose so. But that wasn't the main thing about him. He loved me, you see.'

'Mother said you couldn't marry because Mr Stainton was already married. She only knew about it from my Uncle Jacob –'

'Yes – my son eventually contacted his father. But James never told *me* that!'

'Have you not kept up with the other Staintons at all? Did they never know?'

'No, they never knew – as far as *I* know.'

Rachel, who knew from Paul that this was indeed the case, remained silent. Freda went on – 'His wife – Evangeline – was ill, you see – in her mind. Not all the time. But he felt the responsibility, and was guilty about her.'

She thought, Grandma can talk to me quite easily! Is it because she's so old now? Or does she like me specially? I hope she does. For some reason she wanted to be liked by Freda Osborn. She liked her. But she didn't quite know what to ask next, after hearing about Stainton's guilty conscience.

'Why did you say that was where it all began?' she asked, pointing to the photograph.

'Because I think – people never spoke of such things in my time – I think there was an attraction between those two boys as they grew up. I don't mean they were what they now call "Gay", but there was something. I loved my father, and he was a good husband to my mother. If he hadn't caught that terrible influenza I'd never have fallen in love with James Stainton – oh we might just have met eventually. But we moved in different circles … I was quite ambitious when I was young. My father encouraged me to be so. He'd have been terribly shocked if he'd known what happened – but then, if he'd lived, it wouldn't have.'

'Can I get you a drink of tea? You mustn't tire yourself out talking.' Rachel got up.

'That would be nice, Rachel. I don't want to bore you – I know old people are said to spend all their time reminiscing –' Rachel was far from bored, enthralled rather.

'You never told anyone else at all about it?'

'Well, my husband knew – about my son – and he was very kind. But Robert *was* kind. I didn't want to think about the past when I married him. I had a new life. It's when you are old that you go over things. I suppose it's better than forgetting.'

Rachel paused at the door. Freda went on, 'Mrs Forsyth won't be coming in today – it's her day off – but young Doctor Green will come round about five on his way to the surgery. He comes every Wednesday – very kind of him. I always tell him I've nothing wrong with me but old age. I'm quite strong, you know. I went through a bad patch about the time your mother died. I'm sorry I didn't come then. But it was before I got my new hip – and I couldn't walk very well. I was booked into hospital just the day after the funeral.' Now she looked distressed.

'Don't upset yourself, Grandma –'

'No – it wouldn't have made any difference to Julia. But before – she should have told me she had cancer … I wouldn't

ever have expected her to die before me. I had a friend –
Kathleen – who had the same thing wrong with her and she
lived for fifteen years after they'd diagnosed it ... Never mind –
go and fetch us a tray of tea. There are some biscuits Mrs
Forsyth left yesterday for us – on the table in a red tin.'

Rachel went off wondering how she might find out what her
grandmother knew of Paul Stainton. But she wanted first of all
to hear more about the old days – if Freda wanted to go on
talking. When she returned and they sat drinking their tea, a
small table between them, Freda said, 'I feel I have to apologize
to somebody and it's too late to tell Jacob.'

'Oh no, Grandma, it's never too late – I'm sure he wants to see
you and be friends.'

'He's half a Stainton himself – I follow what he does, you know
– he's sometimes in the *Financial Times* – Doctor Green brings it
for me.'

Rachel said, thinking it a good opportunity, 'Do you never see
his brother around, then? Valentine isn't it?'

'Fancy your knowing the name! – no we don't know each
other. Anyway he retired down south. He didn't do very well,
I'm afraid, as an architect – put up some terrible buildings in
Woolsford in the sixties. They pulled a lot of lovely old offices
down – where I used to work. A great pity.'

'Perhaps he was more like his mother?'

'I don't know. I never knew her. All I heard about *her* was
from James. He was such a devoted husband.' Since Freda
appeared eager now to go on talking about her old lover, Rachel
decided to wait to ask about Val's children when there might be
an auspicious moment.

'There was such feeling between the two of them, your
great-grandfather and Jacob's father, and I think James liked
me because I was the man's daughter. Mind you, I never
thought at first of the difference in our ages. My father died
comparatively young and he was a very clever engineer – that's
where Jacob gets his sort of brains from! ... Oh I know now I was
wrong to give him to Mam to bring up, but I was set on proving I
could manage, and determined Lina Stainton would never
know. She never did. It wasn't our love that was wrong – it was
the circumstances that were.'

Rachel thought how when she said 'Mam', she seemed
younger, with a sort of tenderness in her face. She must have

been a beauty once and still had good cheekbones. Unlike so many people of her age her mind did not wander and she didn't repeat herself. Rachel could tell that she'd never been one to unburden herself.

'Tell me about it – I really want to know – do you think there was a sort of – curse? – upon the two families then?'

'There was something that bound us. But we're in charge of our own destiny. I was foolish, I suppose. It's hard to remember what you felt when you were young – and there was no help available from older people. You just had to behave yourself, and if you didn't, you paid the price. But I know now it was my baby that paid, not me.'

'He's all right now,' Rachel said a little feebly, wondering whether that were in fact true, but Freda went on, 'I couldn't love him, you see, when he was a baby – not the way you're supposed to. Later, I did, but it was too late. My own mother was a better person to bring up a child than I was. But I should have let his father see more of him at first and later, even if it were secretly, just the two of them – let James acknowledge him as he grew up. Privately, I mean. There could never be a public acknowledgment.'

'But he came to live here, didn't he, when your mother died?'

'Oh yes, and by then I'd two more children. Your mother – and she was a handful – and Marcus, who was exhausting –'

'He didn't resent you at that time, Grandma –'

'No, not then – he didn't know. I thought it better after that, that he never knew, as I hadn't had the courage to tell him. But James told him when he asked – never told *me* he had! though, never wrote ...'

'Didn't you ever see Mr Stainton at all after you parted?'

'Oh, I saw him sometimes in the street in Woolsford, or his picture in the paper, but it had all gone, all that love! He went on loving *me*, I know he did. I wanted all the unhappiness to stop there with the birth and to make a clean break. But you never can. Even if folk think they have, it all comes back later.'

'And you did love him – I mean, at first?'

'Of course I did. In those days you didn't endanger your reputation and risk having a baby for a bit of fun – at least I didn't – though we did have fun too!'

'Was he very handsome?'

'You asked me that before, Rachel – handsomeness isn't the

thing you should be looking for. People set far too much store by looks nowadays.' Rachel felt suitably rebuked.

Would she have fallen for Paul Stainton if he were ugly? Well no.

'He was a lovely man – we were suited, really suited – I gave him up when I didn't need to have done. I can see that now. But I hadn't any money of my own – and he had a wife, and we might have had other children together. He could have bought us a "love-nest", I suppose, but we could never have married and in those days things like that disgraced a woman. I didn't want to be somebody's secret. James would have gone on, oh yes, he would! I broke his heart when I decided to break off with him.'

'He didn't break yours, though?'

'I suppose he bent it one way and if it had gone on bending it would never have got back straight and I'd never have married and been like my auntie Cissie.'

'Oh, that reminds me', Rachel said, 'Uncle Jacob asked me specially when I came up north to look at his great-aunt's grave and tidy it up if it were neglected.'

'Why, lass', said Freda in surprise, lapsing into Yorkshire, 'I've seen to that! I always do my duty. *He's* not the only one.' She was sardonic, and Rachel laughed.

'I don't know why I've been telling you all this – but it can't matter now,' said Freda.

'I like to listen to you.' Rachel went across and kissed her grandmother's old cheek which was still smooth in spite of her age.

'I think you are more like me than your mother was,' Freda said after a pause. 'I've had a good life in spite of all I've been telling you.'

'I wish you'd invite Uncle Jacob here, Grandma. He'd love to come!'

'Oh I'm not sure about that. Let bygones be bygones.' But she looked disturbed.

There still seemed to be something more that Freda wanted to tell her and over the next two days she began several times to say something but then stopped. Dr Green had called after that first teatime when so much had come out. He was a nice, capable looking young man in his early thirties, and after he'd gone Freda had said 'He's not married – he'd make a girl a good husband.' Rachel wondered if the old lady had a match in mind. She was feeling more and more uncomfortable about not mentioning the fact that she had met Valentine Stainton's son in London. But she also wanted to know more about how Freda had seen her own daughter Julia as a person, for there must be unfinished business there unless the old lady was a monster of egoism, and Rachel felt sure she was not. But Julia appeared to be the one person whom Freda avoided discussing apart from her remarks about the funeral.

Two days later though, a rainy, cold, windswept day, she came into her grandmother's sitting-room to see if she had woken from her afternoon nap, which Freda took every day between half-past two and three o'clock, and found the old lady, as she thought, still asleep. But when she turned round again to tiptoe out, she heard her say something in her half-sleep that sounded like 'Bessie'.

She waited a moment and Freda had her eyes open when she turned back at the door to check again. 'Hello, Gran – did you want something?'

'What time is it? I was dreaming.'

'Nearly three – I came in to see if you wanted anything. I'm sorry if I woke you up.'

'No, dear –' said Freda in a half-whisper. 'Just stay and keep me company.'

'Mrs Forsyth has gone to the shops. She said, would lamb chops do tonight? I told her yes – but if you don't want them I can go myself for something else.'

'So long as they are English,' said Freda in a firmer voice. 'I hate that other stuff.'

'What were you dreaming about?' asked Rachel when she had sat down and helped put her grandmother's feet comfortably on a footstool, and sat down herself opposite.

'I can't remember.'

'You said "Bessie".'

'Did I? I used to know a Bessie at Stainton's Mill.'

The photograph of the two Jameses was now in pride of place on Freda's desk. Rachel had found a silver frame in a drawer full of old photograph albums. There seemed nothing of great interest in the albums except for the childhood photographs of her own mother just before the war. No snaps appeared to have been taken during the war and there were no photographs of

Jacob Caston, only one or two Polyphotos of Julia in her late teens and one of her in a play with 'Woolsford High School 1948: The Tempest' written on the back.

'I found a picture of my mother in a school play,' she began. She wished her grandmother would open up about her. Freda had said only one thing personal about her so far, that if you told Julia not to do something she'd go ahead and do it. They had evidently been temperamentally incompatible.

'When you said the other day that you wanted the unhappiness to stop once Jacob grew up, I suppose you mean – that it didn't? – I don't think Mother was unhappy all the time with Papa. Not at first anyway.'

'I wasn't just thinking of *her*,' said Freda.

'If you mean Uncle Jacob,' Rachel said boldly, 'he's got over his childhood.' It sounded as though she might be casting a slur upon Freda's decision not to bring him up herself, and whatever she really thought about that, she didn't want to seem to criticize or she'd never get any more information about the Staintons.

Freda however changed the subject. 'Have you met your father? The man my daughter said was your father, I mean?' It was Rachel's turn to feel uneasy.

'You mean Martin Maynard? It's one of the reasons I came to London. I've seen him in a play, yes, but I haven't decided yet whether to try to see him in "real life". Mother said there'd be no point and he was a selfish bastard, but she understood I'd want at least to see him just once. He never took any interest in me, you see.'

'Perhaps he thought he wasn't your father?'

'But he *was* my father! I even look a bit like him – the parts that don't look Caston or Osborn. He's quite a good actor.' Freda was silent. She was looking down in her lap and continually flexing her fingers as Rachel had seen her do countless times. It was arthritis, she said, but it hadn't taken over completely though one little finger was bent.

'Can I say something terrible to you?' Freda said, looking up. Rachel waited. What could it be?

'I know that it sounds wicked of me, and perhaps really evil – but for years and years – the reason I could never bring myself to come over to see you more often – or to invite Jacob over here – was – because I had had the most fearful suspicions about them – about my two children – your mother and my son Jacob.

They were too fond of each other – I thought. That was fine when she was a little girl but when they saw each other again and began to write regularly to each other – and then when she went to Geneva and wrote that letter saying she was pregnant ... I never told anybody, not even your grandfather, but I once dreamed they were in love – and that you were his child.' She stopped, her voice having sunk to a whisper.

'Gran – you were wrong! But they did love each other. Jacob loved my mother all her life and Mother knew how much he loved her. He'd even have brought me up. That was why she was determined to go away and earn her living and then marry – because she knew he was – a little bit – "in love" with her. Nothing ever happened between them! Mother talked about it a bit to me when she was ill, and Uncle Jacob did too, later. Because, you see, when I was a little girl I'd had the same idea. Uncle Jacob was the nicest man I'd ever met and I liked him better than Papa and I wished he *were* my papa. But he wasn't. The Maynard man is my father. You didn't truly think that of Jacob, did you?'

'It was just a horrid feeling – that I thought might be a judgment on me. I just couldn't treat them both naturally when I had such a horrible fear. You see, I thought it was the old Caston-Stainton thing happening again! I suppose I knew it wasn't really true but it was true they loved each other – I wasn't wrong about that.'

'Well, they were very suited to each other – she admired him, and he was very protective of her. I think he only likes me because I'm Mother's daughter! But Mother never knew that Uncle Jacob wasn't her uncle till after I was on the way and my father had decided to marry someone else. Finding out she had another brother was the most awful shock. That was why she was angry with *you*. I do know that. But she was already pregnant when she sought help from Uncle Jacob.'

'I see. It is the most terrible thing to suspect your own children. You've lifted a weight from my heart. Now she is dead I can confess I was jealous of the way he loved her and she him. It was my fault for not being a mother to him. I loved my little Julia too, you see, and it preyed on my mind later that it might be a sort of retribution. But I couldn't ask her, could I? She never told me anything, you know, after she was about fifteen or so.'

'Mother need not have had me,' said Rachel gently, and took the old lady's hand. 'But she did. Uncle Jacob, persuaded her –

and helped her – and I'm glad she had me, and that he did. He's a wonderful person.'

'So am I glad, my dear – what strange conversations we have been having! I'm just too old to bother with the social do's and don'ts, I suppose. You must think me very peculiar.'

Rachel shook her head. 'It's not much use to me being Martin Maynard's daughter as I haven't any desire to be an actress!'

'Did your stepfather say much about Jacob when you were small – who he was?'

'No, not to me. Anyway, I was more interested in my own father!'

Now was the time to ask about Paul Stainton. But the words dried in her throat. Her grandmother had just confessed her awful suspicions about two other Castons and Staintons and she felt that any idea of a future alliance of an Osborn or a Drury, or whatever she was, with a Stainton would be the last thing Freda might want. What was she thinking of? She was having a fling, an affair – wasn't she – not being 'courted' by Paul?

Freda was off on another track.

'It's a pity Jacob never knew his Stainton brother and sister. Mary never married, but the boy did. I saw him when he was a child – I so wished he were mine and not that awful Evangeline's. One son still lives in Brigford though. I believe he has his father's old practice. There were two sons he and his wife Esmé had – Adrian and Paul, I think they're called, and one of them went away – Paul I think.' Oh God, she was going to say something awful. She must interrupt her, tell her she'd met one of them. Paul ...

'And one of them married and then he left his wife and little boy,' she was saying. Which one? Adrian or Paul? 'I think it was Paul, the artistic one,' Freda finished.

Even though Rachel had never had any pretention or desire to follow her mother's footsteps as an actress she surprised herself now by finding it possible to dissimulate as she said nonchalantly, 'Oh, is he an artist?'

Freda had obviously made it her job to discover all she could about her old lover's descendants. 'I believe so. He had some exhibition in Leeds and was made much of – I read about it in the paper – but then went off to seek his fortune in London.' She seemed relieved to have got off the subject of her son and daughter.

'Perhaps he wasn't married?' she offered. 'Times change as you said – and people just live together now –'

'Oh, I'm sure he was married. Anyway, it's children who seal alliances,' said Freda briskly. 'Or ought to.'

Just then there was a firm knock at the sitting-room door and Mrs Forsyth appeared with a shopping basket. 'I got your prescription Mrs Osborn, and what about a nice cup of tea?'

Rachel looked at the clock. They'd been talking for two hours. At this rate they'd be blaming her for over-stimulating the old woman who now sat with a slight flush on her cheek, but replied just as firmly, 'Thank you so much. I'd love one. Come and have your Earl Grey with us. Rachel would like that too, I'm sure.'

That night Rachel tossed and turned, unable to believe that Paul Stainton was the sort of man to 'run away' from a wife and baby. He might be 'an artist' but he was dependable and kind, wasn't he? She'd always trusted her own judgment about men. Only a few days ago she'd been in his arms. Had it been a dream? No, it hadn't. She would have to explore this seemingly fated connection. Was she going to be the fourth generation to get herself entangled with Staintons?

The next day Mrs Forsyth wanted to drive her employer and Rachel into Woolsford for a bit of shopping. But Freda decided that as it was a fine day she would like to be driven into Harrogate. 'We could have tea at Betty's cafe.' So Rachel was treated to a 'real Yorkshire tea' and had to admit that the confectionery, far from consisting of jam puffs, was as good as that baked in her French home town. She enjoyed the drive, remembering her visit ten years before and how she loved the moors and hills.

Dr Green called again when they returned. Was it her suspicious mind that made her feel Freda's regard lingering a little too long on them as they made polite conversation together? He was supposed to visit only on Wednesdays, wasn't he?

When she finally got to bed that night and lay on the comfortable mattress in her grandmother's well-appointed house with its deep carpets and velvet curtains and chintzy furniture, she could no longer avoid returning to thoughts of Paul. She had sent him a card with a picture of Wharfedale and written – 'See you soon. Doesn't this make you feel homesick?' But that was before her grandmother's revelation. She would not tell him, but would wait for him to tell her. But should she even return to him at all? It was true he had not lied to her, but he hadn't told the truth either. Then she said to herself, You've known him just over two months – are you mad?

The next afternoon found her near Brigford, having told Freda she would like to see the town where Freda herself had been brought up. She knew that Stainton's Mills were no more, but that Adrian Stainton still lived in Eastcliff and it was to Eastcliff she went on a bus from the centre of Woolsford that took her almost there after an uphill walk at the end of the journey. This was where Paul had spent his childhood and this must be near where his grandfather and her grandmother had been sixty years before. It was a pleasant place and she forgot them whilst she walked down the little roads that led to lanes and fields, with a prospect of more lanes and woods and fields in the distance. What did the past matter, her mother's or Jacob's, or even Freda's? She liked this place and she wanted to be walking there with Paul Stainton. It was ironic that he had left that village and that she had had to meet him far away. But she missed the bus that would have taken her back to Woolsford at five o'clock and, much to her grandmother's amusement, had to arrive back in a taxi. 'Mrs Forsyth would have taken you, Rachel,' Freda said. 'But I expect you wanted to do some exploring of your own.'

During the last two days of her stay Freda did not reopen the story of her past or of Julia's but said only, 'Are you going to write to Mr Maynard, Rachel?'

'I haven't made my mind up yet,' she answered, which was the truth. Did she want to get to know a man who had never shown the slightest interest in her, not even sent her a birthday card, had probably forgotten her very existence?

On her last morning, Rachel said, 'Gran – I'm going to write to Jacob. I know he wants to see you. *Will* you invite him here?'

'I suppose the invitation must come from me?' asked Freda, but she did not look angry.

'Well, yes, I think so,' replied her crafty granddaughter.

'Tell him to come at Christmas then – and come yourself! I shall miss you when you go.'

Rachel was overjoyed, ran up to her and kissed her. Freda clung for a moment to her and when she left the next day squeezed her hand. It was all Rachel needed. She would bring Jacob and his mother together. Not because she was some

Pollyanna-like heroine or judged she knew them better than they did themselves but because she had realized that they were both proud and if she did not do something about it Jacob would regret it for the rest of his life. Yes, unlike her own mother, they were proud. So was she. Freda had never said whether perhaps Paul Stainton was divorced. She would find that out for herself. In the meantime she had neglected her work, about which she hadn't said much to her grandmother because there was little to say. One week up in the wilds of the north had shown her that she was not cut out for computer export sales. Independence was what she must have, but on her own terms. The trouble with her mother's and grandmother's lives had been their financial dependence upon men. Freda had managed with the help of her own mother, she supposed, but in the end had been 'rescued' by Robert Osborn, and Julia had depended upon her half-brother. Well, she was not going to depend upon Paul Stainton! He might like to depend upon her for a change? If only she could persuade him to return to the North ... A detailed plan was being formulated in her head so that by the time the InterCity train arrived back at Kings Cross she had already begun to see a different kind of future for herself.

Paul Stainton was an intelligent man whose looks belied a character of some complexity and a lack of confidence in anything that did not have to do with his work. He missed Rachel Drury terribly after her sudden departure. Had she left him? Had something frightened her? He had given himself up to loving her, giving her pleasure, in a way of which he had no longer believed himself capable, during those intensely felt first weeks of their relationship. There had seemed no need for questions and answers and probings, but he supposed that eventually they would have to return to earth. But how he missed her! She could not feel about him the way he did about her or she would not have gone away. Then that postcard, from Woolsford of all places! His best landscapes were of the North ... Perhaps he might start a series of northern abstractions, a mixture of memory and imagination, a sort of allegory of loss. His talents were not suited to abstraction, and the work of artists younger than himself he saw as pointless – imagination squandered for lack of technical ability. At least he had learned how to draw! He was turning over some old portfolios, the weak

October sunshine drifting now and again through the afternoon window when the telephone rang.

'Paul? I'm back.'

'Rachel – thank God. Where have you been?'

'Didn't you get my card?'

'Yes – but what were you doing up there?'

'Seeing my grandmother.'

'Darling – I missed you.'

'I missed you, Paul – but, look I'm going to stay in my flat for the time being. I've a lot of work to do. Letters to write, and I've to go back to work on Tuesday.'

'You said you had ten days' leave – why can't you come round here now?'

'No. I've had a week of leave but I've decided – anyway, never mind. Come over to me for supper tomorrow, will you. Do you want to?'

'You know I do.'

'Have you been working?'

'As a matter of fact your going up north gave me an idea for some drawings – something's stirring anyway. Rachel?'

'Yes?' She sounded nervous.

'I love you.'

'I love you, Paul,' she said, and meant it.

London,
30 October 1981

Dear Uncle Jacob,

I have at last been to stay with Grandmother. Although she is very old she doesn't in a funny way seem like a grandmother and when I think of her as your mother she seems different again. We had a lot of very serious talking – she wanted to talk about the past, about you and your father and about my mother too. I like her and I think she likes me. We got on very well and she spoke to me as if I were a woman her own age, anyway old enough to listen to her and understand. The upshot of my stay in Woolsford was that she invites you to come and stay with her at Christmas. She asked me to write and ask you since she finds it a bit hard to write with the arthritis in her hands. I really think you should come, Jacob. She explained all about her reasons for neglecting you years ago. The strange thing was that she had had a terrible fear that you and Mother had an affair and that I might be the result of it! Don't be angry with her. I know you loved Mother, and she loved you. Freda didn't *truly* believe it, but as Mother never told her much, she'd imagined all sorts of things and never had the courage to ask her directly. So I told her about my 'real' father. I haven't had time to tell you either that I went to see him in a play at the Haymarket a few weeks ago. He was very good but I think the pomposity of the part probably suited his character. I don't feel disloyal about him since he's never done anything for me. I haven't decided whether to confront him or write to him or just ignore him and never let him know I'm still alive. He looks the sort of person who might enjoy 'media' attention and I can just see the headlines: 'Lost daughter for Martin Maynard'. So I don't think I shall give him that satisfaction. I feel I already have enough relations!

I want to confess that I don't think I shall ever be any good in export sales. I've worked fairly hard but I don't understand enough about your products to sound enthusiastic. I shall stay until Christmas or until they can find a replacement. I have the idea of teaching French, or perhaps doing another degree here in England – or both. I am very, very grateful for what you have done for me but in the end I must rely upon myself.

I began to understand Grandma better and as I did so, I began to wonder if I'd ever understood Mother. I think I'm more like Grandma than Mother but I'm luckier to have been born at a time when little girls could learn to be more financially independent or at least a time when they don't *expect* a man to keep them. Not that Mother did, but you know what I mean (and probably don't approve?). My mother is still a bit of a puzzle to me though I knew her so well and loved her. I think your mother was hurt that Mother never asked for help from her, and cross because you stepped in. But that's all past history, isn't it? Please *do* come at Christmas. I loved Yorkshire. There must be something in my genes, I suppose, to enjoy those hills and the weather and the moors and even the voices of the people. But I'm not a bit French, only an Englishwoman with a French icing – which is very useful in some ways. Dear Uncle Jacob, do come at Christmas. I don't see why you couldn't make yourself known to the younger Staintons too – *they* don't live in the Dark Ages.

All my love
Rachel

After posting this, Rachel had two more things to do before receiving Paul and giving him the well-cooked dinner *à la française* which she had planned. First she went to the Registrar of Births, Marriages and Deaths at St Catherine's House and looked up divorces under STAINTON. Nothing there yet, and she was disappointed. She found his marriage though, seven years before, by working forwards from the year she imagined he'd have been twenty-one. Not many men married before that age unless it was a shotgun wedding, which she fervently hoped it had not been.

She found it in 1973 when he was twenty-six. To a certain Melanie Holroyd aged thirty. That surprised her, having imagined a buxom eighteen-year-old. She went more quickly after that to the births from the year of their marriage onwards and found one in 1975. So it was not a shotgun wedding and the child was now six and was called Henry.

There was just time then to attend a session at the Marie Stopes Clinic. She did not like the pill, and it was about time she stopped relying on Paul, so she had herself fitted with a diaphragm, old-fashioned though that was. She knew she was not pregnant. She couldn't help thinking that if her mother and her mother's mother had done this – surely they had been available in 1956? – neither she nor Jacob would have been born. Which was somehow illogical. But Paul Stainton was not going to be an unwilling father even if he were already an almost-divorced one! The clinic was approving of her choice, seemed *grateful* that people wanted to take precautions. Poor Freda had had no chance. And Julia, her mother, being unmarried, had possibly been refused one?

Prepared thus, with the knowledge of Paul Stainton's past, and a guarantee as to her own future, at least for the time being, Rachel Drury cooked a delicious meal of baby carrots and asparagus, bathed in a butter sauce, and roasted two poussins from Soho, and bought a French cheese likewise, and some French bread, and a bottle of Volnay 1983, which cost a small fortune. The small flat's cooker had not been much used since her arrival but bore the strain. Then she poured herself a drink and awaited the arrival of the Last of the Staintons, though when you thought about it his son Henry ought to have that title.

'Rachel – you look different! What a delicious smell! How was Yorkshire?'

'I had my hair cut ready for Tuesday at the office. Your supper is ready – and I loved your native county. How are the drawings coming along?' She sounded very brisk, answering his questions in order.

'Not bad at all. I brought one or two for you to see. I *have* missed you –'

She managed to keep her distance whilst they drank a

vermouth and soda.

'Why did you suddenly go to Yorkshire?'

'There's no reason why someone might not suddenly feel the need to go to Yorkshire!'

'I remember you told me your family had some connection with Brigford – your – grandfather, was it? – knew a James Stainton –'

'I'm amazed you remember,' she said. 'Since we were so busy doing other things.' He saw she had softened a little but was baffled why she seemed reluctant to let him get near her.

'Don't look at me like that,' he said. 'You make me feel weak.'

She laughed. 'Drinks and meal first – and then I'll tell you about my grandmother,' she replied.

He did her supper full justice and approved the wine. 'I thought one bottle would be enough,' she said, 'along with the Vermouth. Though I know Englishmen like to drink themselves under the table.'

'This one doesn't. Are you related to me? Is that what all this is about?'

'No, I'm not actually *related* to you – not even by marriage. By – love – you might say.'

'Oh?'

'Shall I go into a long family history, or do you want it neat?'

'However you like.' He was thinking how very attractive she was and how composed and how different from the woman who had made such passionate love to him and also allowed him the freedom to do what he wanted to her, which she had also wanted him to do.

'In short then: My grandmother had an affair with your Stainton grandfather, James.'

'Good Heavens! When?'

'Just after the first war. But before that your grandfather was at school with my *great*-grandfather.'

'What was your grandmother called?'

'I don't know whether I ought to tell you that, since nobody but myself – and naturally enough my grandmother – and the person who was the result of their affair – knows about it. I might never see you again and then you'd be in possession of our family secret!'

'Rachel, stop it! You know we're going to go on "seeing" each other as you put it. – Don't you?'

He looked suddenly apprehensive.

'That depends. But we can get to that subject after if you want.'

He decided to ignore this.

'How old is your grandmother? My grandfather would be over a hundred, I'm sure – and yet you say it was just after the Great War? She must have been a lot younger than him.'

'Yes, she was. I told you – her father was a friend of your grandfather's.'

'It was when he was already married then? You said there was a "result".'

'Yes. But James Stainton was already married – had been for years – to your grandmother, who was called, I believe, Evangeline?'

'Yes, she was – I told you, she had religious mania. I remember her very well – she died when I was thirteen, in my first year at boarding school. She was very odd. My mother didn't like her at all.'

'Your mother is Esmé, I take it?'

'Yes. Have you been spending your time doing genealogy? Anyway, what's it all got to do with us? Except, I suppose it *is* a coincidence that we should meet?'

'I was walking near your father's old house only a few days ago. Grandma's lived in Woolsford ever since she married,' she said, a little dreamily. But he pursued –

'You said a result? Is that what it's all about? The result couldn't have been your mother or father, because you said we weren't related. If it had been, what would we be? – I'm no good at these family trees –'

'If my mother or my father had been the result of your grandfather and my grandmother spending too much time walking round Eastcliff whilst *your* grandmother was on her knees in prayer – then we'd be sort of half-first cousins! But as neither my mother nor my father was the result of the affair it doesn't signify. The "result" was a very famous man – famous in certain circles anyway – a very rich man –'

'So, have I got this right? Your grandmother married after the affair and had a child? – Your mother or your father?'

'My mother. Mother had a half-brother who was your grandfather's son, that is your own father's half-brother, your sort-of-uncle.'

'I *think* I've got it clear … you've aroused my curiosity. Didn't my father know about this? If so, he's never said a word.'

'I don't think he ever knew – though he may have guessed some of it since he once worked with the "result".'

'I was always told by my Dad that my grandparents were a model couple. I don't think they got on all that well though, because Father always took his mother's side – at least that's what Mother said – though she didn't explain why there were two sides at all if they were all that happy.'

'Your father was a little boy at the time. My grandmother remembers him well.'

'Aren't you going to tell me more? Why should all this be so important to you? Is it because you've met *me*? Sorry, that sounds egotistic! Because I've met you?'

'It caused a lot of unhappiness,' said Rachel, clearing away the plates.

'Let me – I'll wash up –'

'Only cheese and fruit now. If you are English you'll leave the cheese to the last. As I was brought up in France I'll have it now and the fruit salad later.'

She brought in a fresh fruit salad of kiwis and tangerines and pears and apples and grapes and some crème fraîche.

'I shall do as you do,' said Paul Stainton. 'Cheese now with some more of that lovely bread.'

When they had finished it all and Paul had insisted on washing up, which Rachel thought was further evidence that he'd once been married, they sat on at the table, and drank the strong French coffee she'd brewed. He took her hand. Then, 'Rachel?'

'Yes?'

'I do love you – I missed you so much. I thought you'd gone away for good. I want you but I don't think you want me, do you?'

'Why do you think that?' she answered. After that a second cup of coffee was abandoned. The bed was far too small but it didn't seem to matter.

Later, he said, 'Am I now to know more of this fairy story you've been telling me?'

'It isn't a fairy story, Paul. It's a true story and it makes me a bit frightened.'

'Why should it do that?'

'Because you haven't told me all about yourself.'

'You haven't told me all about *yourself* either or why you think it important that your family links up with mine?'

'Tell me more about you then.'

'I know life isn't a fairy story, Rachel. You'll despise me when you know more about me.'

'Why should I do that?'

'Because I was married seven years ago and I have a boy of six whom I love and a wife who doesn't love me any more. When the child was a year old she went off to live with someone else. But I didn't want a divorce at first. Now, after five years, I do. Last spring I applied for one. Long before I met you.' He had turned his face away.

'You could have got divorced after two years. Did you go on hoping?' He didn't answer that. She pursued – 'Why should that make me *despise* you?'

'Because I'm a failure. Couldn't even keep a wife with me.'

'*She* left *you*? Are you sure?' It sounded disloyal.

'I'm telling you the truth. At first I was angry – and jealous. She went off with a rich man – a professor of art, who was already married. He doesn't like my work, says I'm no good – too "traditional" –'

'But, Paul, you could have the little boy with you sometimes?'

'Oh, I had him with me in the North last spring. When it's all finalized I'll apply for custody, though she may fight that. I didn't think a child should be deprived of his mother however much I disapproved of her. I loved her once, and it turns out now that I had no judgment at all –'

'Love doesn't always have a lot to do with judgment. Did she think you were rich or were going to be famous?'

'She knew I wasn't a pauper – but I'm not rich. I was quite successful with my work when I was younger. When I changed track and she found the critics didn't like what I was doing she went off them and me. Now we've mucked up a child's life. Which matters more than mucking up my own.'

'It sounds like your grandfather's life in reverse.'

'Tell me why you're so concerned with my ancestors, Rachel.'

'Because – for many reasons. Because my mother loved her half-brother. Because my mother died four years ago. Because I never knew my own father and don't really want to know him. Because my grandmother paid for her affair with your grandfather by losing her first son – emotionally, I mean – her mother brought him up. Because there've been four generations now of Staintons and Castons involved with each other. My great-grandfather and your grandfather, your grandfather and my grandmother, my mother and her half-brother, who was half a Stainton. And now me – and you –'

Her last words made him sit up. 'It all sounds most confusing but also as if you *do* take me seriously.'

'Grandma did her best to interest me in a nice young doctor in Woolsford – just the right age for me to marry. They still see marriage as the best thing for women, after all they've been through! My mother married a Frenchman after I was born and it didn't work out very well. He was unfaithful. And the "result" never married at all because he was convinced that his great love would have been an incestuous one.'

'You said, Castons,' he began cautiously. 'Are you talking of the chap who founded that outfit you work for?'

'Yes – Jacob Caston. He's your father's half-brother.'

'But he's a tycoon – rolling in it! Famous!'

'Yes. Isn't it ironic? I gather your father wasn't interested in "business"? Jacob was – is.'

'So you think it's Fate that has led us to meet? Do you, Rachel?'

'I don't know. But I had to tell you before it all went wrong.'

'Why should it go wrong? I mean, apart from my miserable track record?'

'It is all so peculiar. I was attracted to you the minute I met you that evening. In a curious way. As though I'd "come home".'

'I felt the same about you. I still do. You know I do.' There was a silence. Then he kissed her again.

'That's why I just wanted to get all this stuff out of the way, you see. I'm glad you told me about your marriage. Grandma heard a rumour you'd left your wife.'

'You know, you're very old, and yet very young, for your age, love,' he said and she thrilled to the word because not only did it mean what the French called *chérie* but was also what her mother's folk called each other up north. It sounded somehow more safe than 'darling'.

'What is your wife like?' she asked him when they'd finally got up and made more coffee.

'Beautiful, I suppose. Fashionable – ruthless, I'd say. But I'm prejudiced.'

'I'd have thought you were a very – stable sort of person,' she said, stroking his hair.

'So would I! – but the famous artistic temperament, you know, it must be there somewhere? The thing about Melanie – my wife – is that you could never joke with her. Not like I do with you. But I'm not saying she "doesn't understand me", I'd have told you anyway as soon as I thought you felt a little about me – I thought I'd found security with her – as well as – you know – passion – But that had little to do with anything. When *we* make love – does it frighten you? It does me, a bit. Perhaps people talk too much nowadays about their feelings?'

'I don't think I'd ever need to *talk* to you about them,' said Rachel. Stability, not exactly security, in an insecure world, was what she realized she needed more than anything. More even than physical bliss. And she knew too that if she ever bearded her unknown father in his theatrical den it would now be only if she were accompanied by Paul Stainton.

She took nothing for granted. Paul had his past life and his work and she had to make plans for her own if it were to be spent henceforth in England. She often compared her two countries, the 'real' one, and the adopted one that had nurtured her first twenty years of life, found it an endlessly fascinating exercise. Paul Stainton was very English, but because he was a painter he had perceptions that were not commonly found among the young men she had known previously and were probably not very common amongst men in general. He introduced her to some of his friends over the next weeks and she liked them. Tell a man by his friends, she thought.

She made no effort to enquire about the progress of the divorce, knowing he would tell her when it was time, but looked forward to meeting the small Harry who seemed to spend some of his time with his paternal grandparents. What would Valentine Stainton say when he discovered who his son's new girlfriend was? 'Will you tell him?' she asked Paul.

'I shall say you are the granddaughter of one Freda Caston,' replied Paul. 'And leave him to tell me if he knows anything about her?'

'And niece of the famous Jacob?' she asked.

'If he asks –'

Paul was to return to his brother's house in Eastcliff for Christmas since his son would be there with Valentine and Esmé Stainton to be handed over to his father for two weeks. She gathered that the fashionable Melanie was to spend Christmas with the professor somewhere warm, whilst she worked upon him to leave his wife – who saw no reason to make things easy for her rival. Apparently Melanie had been a model for some years before Paul fell in love with her, but by the time he knew her she was too old for it, and was now in public relations. Rachel was dreading what Freda and Jacob might say when they discovered whom she was seeing but she was determined they would meet him over Christmas. Paul was so much easier, so less tiring, than young men she'd known in France. Her French friends had strange ideas about Englishmen. Cold; homosexual if not perverted in other ways, certainly uninterested in women, addicted to horrible puddings and pies and warm beer; the wearers, if they were old, of shapeless flannel trousers and jackets and, if they were young, dirty T-shirted tattooed slobs who drank to get pissed. But the English were as bad, finding it unmasculine to take an interest in food or perfume or the look of things. The visual aspects of life had always been important to her but she was English in her suspicion of rigid formality. She loved sun too but felt she had had enough of it for the time being. Paul said that English landscape painting would not be so wonderful without the rain that made everything green, lent mist and half-tones to trees and fields and water.

Northern France was not so different, he said. But Lyon and Annecy were not northern and he must try to paint their different lights and shades sometime.

Jacob was disappointed that she intended to leave Caston Computers. She had not yet written to him about Paul. Perhaps by Christmas something would be settled. In the meantime, both she and Paul worked hard, she at Caston's, he at his easel. Sometimes they met for a drink or a meal near Green Park. By common consent they rationed their lovemaking, but each new time it was as it had been at first, happy and exciting, but also now an extension of the growing confidence they had each in the other.

'I shall be in Woolsford for Christmas with Jacob Caston and Grandma. Shall we meet there in the town or should I invite you round to my grandmother's?'

'I want to introduce you to my parents – but I'd love to see your grandmother. Let's tell them at Christmas! The divorce will be through early next year. I'd like to meet Jacob Caston too.'

'I'll see how things go, and phone you from Holm Dene. Don't forget that if you do come over you'll be meeting one of your own relations as well.'

'You realize I'm going to ask you to marry me?'

'Yes, Paul,' she said quite meekly.

As Christmas drew closer Freda felt both nervously excited and anxious. She wanted to see her son but feared disturbing the status quo, the gulf between them that had become with time a feature of her mental landscape. She told herself not to be frightened. They would carry it off. She was an old woman and had no time for shilly-shallying. It was Rachel who had done it, who had listened to her, convinced her Jacob needed her now as much as he had ever done. He was very rich and she hoped he wouldn't take it into his head to arrive loaded with presents. Vaguely she thought of diamonds and cars and caviare, but that was stupid of her. He'd sent her that photograph, and that was the best present she could have had, had touched her more than anything. That James had given it to Jacob, asking him – as her son had said in the little note that accompanied it – to give it to Freda one day. 'With his love,' James's love.

They would arrive separately, her granddaughter and her son. The one on the train from London, the other in his private plane of all things, that could touch down, he said, at the local airport. Mrs Forsyth had cooked everything in advance except for the bird, and all the trimmings were in the freezer. If only Robert could come back now and see them all together this Christmas, see his granddaughter too, whose childhood he'd missed. And if only Marcus would come home from the States! But you could not have everything.

The hall of the large house was decked with holly and there were fires in all the downstairs rooms. She had asked her companion to unpack the old Christmas tree that had been Nell's and which she'd kept for years in the attic. They had found a box of baubles too that had been her mother's once, and she had personally ordered bottles of dry sherry and a case of single malts, and enough wine to sink a ship. She hadn't forgotten how to entertain.

Jacob Caston knew that Rachel could not get away from her work in London before the morning of Christmas Eve so he had decided to arrive at his mother's house in Yorkshire on the evening of the 23rd to give them time alone together before his niece arrived in Woolsford. He had not thought he was looking forward to the twenty-four hours alone with Freda but once he was on his way a curious kind of anticipation – mixed with apprehension – invaded him. Apart from other considerations, it was many years since he had spent Christmas in his native country: the last one he'd spent at Holm Dene had been in 1938 just before he went off to work in Brigford. He visited London only occasionally in the course of his work; London had never been home. His only vivid memories of the place had been connected with Julia in Kentish Town.

He'd turned sixty that summer, and Julia was dead. He'd go on working till he too dropped dead, that was for sure. Everyone in the business was talking of a wonderful decade ahead when as many personal computers, along with word processors and thousands of games for children, would be in the homes of the 'civilized' world as calculators already were in their schools. It seemed, and was, a long long time since those first clumsy prototypes, the 'electronic brains', and the first wartime uses for electronic hardware, which hadn't been called hardware then. This civilized world ran on them now, even the very smallest business. He delegated a good deal of his own business now, but had produced his own software for the running of his own enterprises, had enjoyed himself writing that. Sometimes, though, he wondered whether thirty years before Julia had been right in objecting to his plans. Nobody then seemed to have considered what might happen when computers were no longer a means to an end but changed the very ends. Julia had objected to 'science' too, and to his enthusiasm for change. Poor Julia, whom lasers and medical computers had still not been able to save. She should have told *him* when she found that first pea-sized lump in her breast. But Julia had once admitted that she'd no objection to the latest scientific wonders that actually saved people's lives; penicillin had been the first she'd have known about. He didn't think she would have been against procedures like experimental organ transplants either, since they alleviated human misery. But she'd never had any time for moon landings or satellites. How old-fashioned both of *them* were beginning to seem now. The moon landing had not been repeated, but strangely shaped artificial moons had begun to circle Earth. Easy to think we were all now a global village, until you actually travelled, as he had done, and saw places where people still lived in the same way as they had a thousand years ago.

Julia had feared nuclear power too; they'd had a lot of talk about that. Rachel, he thought, was different. Like the rest of her generation she took television for granted, along with tranquillizers and sleeping pills. Probably the pill, too though he had no desire to make enquiries into her sex life. And now there was, he read in his scientific journals, the possibility of the fertilization of embryos outside a mother's body. Test-tube babies. Not to mention the knowledge, now current for thirty years or so, of DNA, and the cracking of the genetic code ... Perhaps study of genes would eventually show what made people fall in love with each other ...?

The Caston gene he saw as green, like a field with a few red poppies in it; the Stainton gene yellow and grey. What nonsense ... he must be going mad!

But as he looked up at the sky on entering his private plane, which he used for hopping between New York and Geneva, Milan and Zürich, he was thinking that nobody so far had been able to alter the weather, never mind eradicate drought or flood, not to speak of poverty and misery and war and starvation. Julia had taken an almost perverse pleasure in this for she had always been aware, had told him more than once in her letters, of the dangers of *hubris* and had not really been surprised to have fallen ill. 'People say "Why Me?" she had written, 'but I always think: "Why not me?"'

And now at last he was on his way to see his mother and hers. Science had changed the world but had not so far changed human beings, though doubtless that would come. Freda had always been proud – and he did not expect to find her any different.

But he was proud too. It was emotion, human feelings, that moved that other world, the private one, the one in which for a long time he had chosen not to dwell. Feelings like resentment and anger – and even love – destroyed you if you let them. He was no longer angry with his mother, nor even hurt, nor even judged her at all. The world had been different sixty years ago. Safer contraception had changed lives more than plastics and electronics.

His thoughts returned to Julia as they so often did. Was it he who had persuaded her not to have an abortion? Did young Rachel owe her life in part to him? He had never expressed his love for his half-sister physically, and could not now remember if he had ever truly wanted to, but he *had* loved her and had saved her child for the future. How melodramatic he was becoming in his old age! He wondered whether Rachel had now attempted a meeting with the Maynard fellow. She must need to know what else had contributed to her own unique self. Duruy had been no good to her as a father. Julia ought to have waited to find a more suitable partner. But Julia had been impetuous ... There was no point in harking back. He'd been angry – though of course he had no right to say anything – when she decided to marry the Frenchman. He'd also known that Julia had once loved her mother's elder son as much as he had loved her.

Strange to think he'd be going 'home'. Home was not a place for him so much as a temporal entity, so it would go on existing for him when his dwelling place might be in many places. He supposed his first twenty-five years in England had made him what he was, though that country now took a back seat in his preoccupations. 'Home' might be where a mother lived, in his case, Freda, for he supposed that for many people, as long as their mother was alive and they had no partner or children of their own it could be wherever that mother was.

Since her mother's death Rachel might possibly find a new 'home' over where the swift engines were now heading. They were now high over Paris. As far as he was concerned he couldn't imagine living his life now anywhere but Europe, which the British in spite of their membership of the EEC persisted in calling The Continent. As though Europe was nothing to do with *them*. He was rich as Croesus, had been lucky as well as prescient and hard-working; he could live where he chose. It was true that he gave away large amounts of money to international agencies and refugee councils, devoted to the relief of the starving, the indigent, the dispossessed, so his conscience, such as it was, was clear. But he might think of buying a flat in what was now often called the 'UK', if this reunion with Freda went off reasonably well. Except that it might make her think he wanted to settle there for good, a very unlikely eventuality! She said she was well looked after, had always refused the money he'd offered her. She might, just might, want to see more of him now, but maybe he was being sentimental? He would have to wait and see how things turned out for them both.

He went back to his copy of *Scientific American* and drank an ice-cold Perrier with a slice of lemon as the plane now arrowed itself high over the English Channel, and then over the mild green fields and downs of Sussex towards those darker fields of his childhood, bounded by black drystone walls, not far from the industrial towns and cities which were now, according to report, cleaner and brighter than they had ever been.

Freda wasn't waiting open-armed at the door of Holm Dene, but then he hadn't really expected her to be. When he rang the bell he saw through the spy-hole in the door to the porch and the inner door that led on to the hall he so well remembered. A woman opened this door and he thought, that's not Mother! and, for a moment, had fears of a sudden death, a neighbour waiting to let him in. But then he recollected that this must be the 'companion' whom Freda had mentioned in her letter. The outer door was unlocked, the chain unfastened and two bolts slid out of their sockets. 'We can't be too careful nowadays,' said the lady, smiling, as he entered.

'Let me take your bag – Mrs Osborn's in her sitting-room waiting for you.'

Jacob let her take the bag, which was not heavy, but kept hold of a carrier bag, full of bottles of perfume and scarves and chocolates.

'Put this in the kitchen, will you – it's Mrs Forsyth, isn't it? How do you do?'

'You look very like your mother,' she said.

'How is she?'

'Fine, fine – excited of course. Did you come by car?'

'No – by taxi. I could have hired a car but I dislike driving.'

She pointed to the downstairs cloakroom which he remembered as a hidey-hole for galoshes and old coats, and said,'If you want to wash your hands –? I'll show you your room later,' and disappeared into the kitchens at the back.

He looked around him. There was an as yet undressed Christmas tree on a table in the large oak-panelled hall and a fire burning in the grate; on the wall a large oil-painting. Of an Osborn, he presumed. It looked vaguely nineteenth century. That hadn't been there before. It'll be strange without Bob, he thought. He always used to be here. After a hasty look in the cloakroom mirror there was nothing for it but to go and beard the lioness in her den. He knocked at the sitting-room door.

She'd be in the room that overlooked the garden at the back, for that was where she had always liked to sit, and there was a sort of loggia where she kept plants. 'Come in!' And there she was. Sitting in a high-backed chair, her feet on a footstool, every fibre in her old body betraying alertness and excitement.

'Don't get up –' He advanced towards her and kissed her cheek.

'I couldn't bear to hover,' she said. 'I heard you arrive. But I wanted to see you open that door and come towards me – and here you are!'

'Well, Mother,' he said, jocularly. 'Two old people now –' and kept hold of her hand till she said, 'Sit opposite me – there's a nice fire. Mrs F is a treasure.'

He looked round the room, which he had used to know so well, except that now the wallpaper was lighter, and a deep-piled fitted grey carpet had replaced the red Persian. But there was still the pouffe on which Julia had used to sit whilst he made her toast on the afternoons Freda was out shopping. He took his courage in both hands 'Let's get it over with, Mother,' he said – 'I should have come long ago. But here I am – at last.'

'I never before invited you at Christmas – not since the year before the war,' she said. 'So the faults are mutual – and we can forget them if you like.' She sounded quite magisterial but there was a tremble in her old voice.

'You look blooming,' he said, and meant it.

She smiled. 'I could say the same for you.'

'I saw the little tree,' he said and then realized that there was another one here in the opposite corner, a real fir tree already dressed in silver and gold.

'That one in the hall was my mother's,' she said. 'Don't you remember it?'

'Mam's tree? – why, yes – she used to have it in the shop and then move it into the house on the Eve!'

She had mentioned Nell first, which he thought a good sign.

'Forty-six years since she died,' said her daughter. 'And five since Bob died.' She seemed waiting for him to say something, so he said 'Only the year before Julia.'

They were both silent; he was seated facing her now. She was looking into the fire. Then she looked up and said, 'Rachel arrives tomorrow – isn't she a lovely girl!'

'You have to call them "Women" now at their age,' he said with a laugh. 'I still think of them as girls, but the feminists say not.'

'You keep up with all that nonsense? I suppose you must, as you go over a good deal to the States. But Rachel is a very sensible girl, don't you think?'

He thought that she must still read newspapers, or else she wouldn't have followed his allusion to "women" so quickly. She pointed to the television in the corner behind him. 'I watch documentaries,' she said. 'Mrs F and I enjoy them. I even watched an Open University maths course -- it was interesting! I'm afraid I don't understand your computers very well though. I have to draw the line somewhere.'

'All built on mathematics,' he said.

'You were so good at maths, Jacob – don't you wish you'd gone to university? We did try to persuade you.'

'I learned the hard way – but I remember doing my homework here for old Ruggles at the Grammar – I wonder if he's still alive?'

'I shouldn't think so. But I have your old homework book!'

'My maths homework book – Good heavens!'

'Yes, there were a few things of yours you left when you went to Stainton's.'

That name. At last.

He looked over at her and she met his gaze steadily. 'Thirty years since your father died,' she said softly.

'I know.'

'One of his grandsons still lives in Eastcliff. Rachel went over there for a walk – she seems interested in that family.'

Jacob shrugged his shoulders, raised his eyebrows.

'Has she seen her father yet?' she continued.

'She told you she saw him acting in a play in London?'

'Yes, but she seemed uncertain whether to follow it up with a meeting in "Real Life" as she put it.'

Mrs F came in just then with a tray on which were a sherry decanter, a whisky bottle, two cut glass tumblers two sherry glasses and a soda syphon.

'Have a drink with me now, Jacob? – and you stay, Mrs F. Then you can go and unpack. Dinner will be at seven. We keep early hours.'

He got up to pour his mother her sherry and decided to take a sherry too to show solidarity with her. He liked Scotch only with ice.

'I'll just have a wee glass of whisky,' Margaret Forsyth said.

'But I must go and see how the pheasant is going.'

He raised his glass to them both. 'Pheasant, eh?'

'And a goose on the Day. We thought, tomorrow we'd have a big Christmas tea – there's never time for tea on the 25th and all the good food only goes to fill a full stomach.'

Jacob remembered the Christmas Eve teas here with Julia and Marcus opening their Eve presents. Freda believed in rationing presents out over the whole festival so as not to have a surfeit on the Day.

'I'll be back to the kitchen,' said Mrs F, and whisked herself away.

'She really spoils me,' Freda said. 'I know I'm a lucky old woman. But I didn't want to go into a home when this place got too much for me.'

'I should think not! Is she very expensive?'

'You're not to worry about that – Bob left me very comfortably off.'

'I'm glad.' There was another silence, but quite a companionable one. Freda had sipped half her glass and put it on to a small round table at her elbow.

'I truly wish I'd come before – long ago,' he said.

'You had your work to do and your life to lead – but I agree it does seem a waste when you look back on it,' said Freda.

He still felt there was a mystery about her. When he had thought her to be his sister she hadn't been at all mysterious – at least to him.

'Rachel is very interested in *all* our pasts,' she added as he sipped his sherry, Tio Pepe, his favourite, drunk by him only when in England.

'Because Julia died, and Duruy pretty well abandoned her – not that she wanted to stay with him. She told me she wanted to be "properly" English.'

'I wonder whether she'll return to live in France?'

'I'd guess she might have other things up her sleeve,' he said. 'She isn't really cut out for computer sales.'

'She could teach French, I suppose?'

'Yes, I suppose. She's very independent.'

'A good thing too.'

'So was Julia.'

'Rebellious, rather.' They were both quiet again thinking of that daughter and sister.

'I never understood Julia,' Freda said. 'You helped her when Rachel was born, so why did she have to marry that Frenchman?'

'Didn't you like him?'

'Not much, though I tried to be polite to him when they stayed here.'

'Life is full of mysteries,' Jacob said. 'The truly important actions seem to happen for no one particular reason. Or for so many reasons that when you look back you think things could not have happened any other way – but of course they could.'

'Why Julia married him was to give Rachel a father?' she said.

'Yes – but later she knew she'd made a mistake.'

'We all make mistakes. Why did I let Mam bring you up and think you were hers is still on your mind isn't it?'

'I suppose so – but it doesn't matter now.'

'It matters to *me* – I've been trying to remember exactly how it happened. I do know that I was like Julia, wanted to be independent, wanted to earn my bread, not let James keep me even if he bought us the shop whose profits helped bring you up. But I didn't want to serve in a shop – it would have been a waste of my training.'

'People are mysteries,' he said. 'More mysterious even than what Julia used to call my "Machines". Machines *can* think, in a way, and come to decisions, but they can't suffer or feel happy.'

'They can remember though?'

'Yes.'

'Julia and I both made mistakes – but weren't they ordinary human mistakes? Should I still feel guilty, Jacob?' She took her glass up again and he saw her rings winking in the firelight.

'No. Guilt is no good. And in any case it was my *father* who should have felt that – and did feel it. He told me so.'

She sighed – 'You're not really like him,' she said. 'He was quite a simple person in many ways.'

'And I'm not?'

'No, you're not.'

'It's Rachel, you know, who desired me to come here.'

'*I* should never have insisted – but she did,' said Freda. 'I do hope she'll make a happy marriage. There's a good deal to be said for marriage, you know.'

'Sorry I've never obliged,' he said lightly.

'I was thinking of it more for women – though now we're all supposed to have equality. But what's equality without equal incomes?'

'You're a good old-fashioned woman, Mother. You still believe in happy families.'

'As an ideal to aim for. Poor James didn't have a very happy one.'

Jacob stood up. 'We can talk more about it later – I'm going to change out of these travel-stained garments.' He stooped and kissed her forehead and she held his warm hand in her bonier one for a minute. Her son had come back. She didn't deserve it but here he was. Oh, if Nell and James and Julia could see them now! Jacob left her looking into the fire, her empty glass still in her old hand. He hoped he had not been too abrupt but he still found it difficult to talk about his father.

He made an effort later when they had finished the pheasant. It was delicious, not too dry, and Freda insisted on his opening a bottle of burgundy to accompany it. He did not want to offend her, though he did not feel very much like drinking that night. He was tired; his age must be catching up with him. His mother said she always went up to bed at half-past ten to rest if not to sleep, for she lay awake some of the night listening to the World Service. At 10.15 he said, 'I don't want to spoil the Christmas festivities later, so may I ask you one thing now – so you can sleep on it? James's wife died twenty years ago – haven't you now waited long enough to tell Val – and Mary – about me?'

Freda considered. The idea did not appear to shock her. 'But – I've kept quiet for so long – why spoil my secret now? I think I should leave it to you,' she replied.

'That will not happen as far as I'm concerned, Mother. Yet somehow I feel he ought to know he has a half-brother!'

He had noticed and commented upon the photograph in its silver frame on her desk. Had she ever possessed one of James Stainton in his prime? He did not like to ask.

He had thought he might not sleep very well himself, but he did. He awoke, disorientated at first, yet refreshed. The worst was over. Let other things come out gradually in their own time. They had forgiven each other and that was what mattered.

After breakfast, and when he had walked round the garden, which he noticed still consisted principally of beds of roses, a few pale ones still in bloom left over from the summer, they sat together in her sitting-room and he lit a small cigar. Freda liked the fragrance which reminded her, she said, of past Christ-mases. She said, 'I was thinking last night about my mother, when you were a very small baby. She was so good with you, so patient! She was really happy, you know, then. Like she'd been before my father fell ill.'

'She ought to have had a big family,' he said. He had mourned Nell Caston long long ago in this very house, and his memory of her was still a good one. She had been a simple woman who had loved him unconditionally, perhaps a little too uncritically when he thought about it.

'When you were a few months old and I had to face the future,' Freda said, 'she begged me to let her bring you up. She didn't say then that she wanted you to think she was your mother, just that I should leave the practical side of things to her.' She stopped, and Jacob saw she was upset, had wanted to say this for a very long time.

'Don't upset yourself – it doesn't upset *me* any more,' he said gently.

But she went on – 'I wasn't in a state to resist help – you don't know how exhausted small babies make you – or maybe you noticed when you lived here and Marcus was a few months old?'

'I do know,' he said. 'Don't forget I looked after Julia when Rachel was a baby.'

'Yes, of course – I'd forgotten. Perhaps Julia was afraid I'd take over the way my mother did and that was why she didn't come home?'

'Perhaps that was one of the reasons,' he conceded.

'Well I wouldn't have done, you know! But Mam usually got her own way when I come to think about it. Dad spoilt her. She'd had a miserable childhood, you see, and he wanted to make it up to her. She wasn't a strong character like him but if she set her heart on anything she usually got it in the end – she was quite obstinate. My getting the job at Stainton's did help her to recover from Dad's death. At least to get up and join the living again. But your arrival gave her an aim in life, something to live for. She'd always wanted a son and they'd told her another baby would kill her.'

'My grandfather must have been a considerate man,' said Jacob, a little dryly.

'Yes, he was, and he adored her. She'd got away from her sister when she married – from Cissie – who was, you know, a bit of a bully. Her married life was really happy. I remember feeling sometimes as a child that I was rather in the way.'

'Did she need to keep on the shop?' he asked – 'She always used to ask me to do the accounts, I do remember that, when you worked away – before you married. I was in Standard Three at Delf National School and I remember telling Miss Kaye I did them. I was proud of it. I did help her quite a lot.'

'She loved that little shop,' replied Freda. 'Though it brought only just enough to keep you two. The mills weren't doing all that well in the twenties, and I suppose even James found things hard. Anyway, I wanted to go back to work and Mam wanted me to. As though I'd never had a baby! It was easier to think of it like that, though I felt bad about it. You were always happy though with her, weren't you? You didn't go without anything but my presence.'

'As I see it you gave in to her partly because you wanted to "better yourself",' Jacob said 'A very natural desire – one I share with you. And you helped keep us all.'

'Well, I suppose I wanted to be independent as well,' she said. He thought how like Julia she sounded. 'I worked hard,' she went on – 'But a woman couldn't earn much in those days even if she was the best secretary in the world. It was only my marriage that made me financially secure. Your feminists wouldn't like that.' She was looking into the fire as she spoke.

'That applied to most women and still does,' he said. 'And someone has to look after the children. I think your mother was a sort of "nanny" to me, wasn't she? Nowadays, women who have good jobs pay for nannies.' He wondered how much she had loved Bob Osborn or whether he had been a haven from the grind of work. But those were not the kind of questions you could ask your mother. The ones they had asked each other had been delicate enough.

'I only wanted to try to explain to you,' Freda said. 'I hadn't remembered for years how Mam sulked when she didn't get her own way. I suppose I took what might be called the easier option.'

'Mother,' he interjected, 'nobody on earth is blaming you now!'

'It *wasn't* the easy option though,' she went on. 'It was awful. I wasn't one thing or the other, you see. Young Miss Caston working hard and doing well. Poor Miss Caston the unmarried mother, her life ruined in the eyes of most people then, if they'd known. But I was awfully young, you know, and didn't like people to think of me as a sinner. You never suffered for it, and for that we have to thank Mam. In those days there were lots of informal adoptions ... so there you are,' she concluded, and turned her face back to his.

'It's a long long time ago,' Jacob said. 'It's really all right now.'

'I ought to have told Julia, I know. But I was too proud, I suppose. I longed for her to ask for my help when she had her baby. She never did. Was she very angry with me? We didn't talk about it when we did see each other – I didn't know how to begin. You were a good brother to her.'

'At first she was furious, but she did understand later how hard it had been for you. To find she'd done the same thing – being a "single parent" herself. But it was our being brother and sister that shocked her most. Young people find it difficult to put themselves in the place of their parents.'

'Well there's one advantage,' Freda said after a pause, 'we can talk to each other as though we were from the same generation, can't we? Like the sister and brother we're not. People can't always be honest with their parents – or parents with children. It's easier with grandchildren.'

'If we'd come from a different class of society,' he said, with an attempt at a smile, 'I'd have been brought up by the old retainer, regarded her as my mother – and met my real mother later when I reached the age of reason.'

'Yes, I know. But I did give birth to you, Jacob, however much I had to deny it!'

'You forfeited the right to discipline me, I suppose,' he said. – 'But I didn't love my "sister" just out of a sense of duty –'

'We ought to have had this talk long ago,' she said.

'Well we've had it now,' he said. They looked at each other. He took her hand and kissed it. 'It's *all over*,' he said, 'you had an ambitious bastard for a son. Who knows, I might have done nothing much with my life if I'd had an ordinary beginning.'

'I'm proud of you,' she said, 'and now we're going to have the best Christmas of our lives together.'

When Rachel, arriving with her hands full of cases and bags, looked through the hall window later that day and saw Jacob decorating the small tree on the table in the gathering dusk, with her grandmother handing him little gold and silver baubles from a box on her knee as though they had been doing this together for fifty Christmases she breathed a sigh of relief and happiness. She need not have come! But she wanted to finish their story for them when Paul made his appearance in their lives. For two days she'd be here at Holm Dene in her own family but on Boxing Day she'd tell them, and Paul would come round from Eastcliff. Those two didn't need her now for anything else, and she wasn't going to worry about what they'd think when she dropped her bombshell. She loved the 'Last of the Staintons', and he loved her, and they had every intention of making their lives together. She tapped softly at the window and they both looked up, and smiled.

The Christmas Eve 'tea' at Holm Dene was a splendid affair. 'You need to put on a bit of flesh,' her grandmother told Rachel as the latter munched her way through home-made scones and Yorkshire 'parkin', shortbread biscuits, gingersnaps, chocolates, nuts and raisins, crystallized fruits, and the *pièce de reśistance*, a Christmas cake full of brandy and cherries and topped by soft white icing piped in red, with Father Christmas on a sleigh driving across the snowy surface. They pulled crackers of a kind she'd never seen before, which opened to reveal sparkling rings and brooches.

'They were what my father saved up for,' Freda explained. 'We searched everywhere for them and Mrs Forsyth found them in an old village market in the Dales where they were selling off ancient novelties!'

Freda's companion joined in all the fun. They had all listened to the Festival of Nine Lessons and Carols on what Freda still called the wireless. After tea, Jacob surprisingly produced the video of *Doctor Zhivago*, which Rachel happened not to have seen before and which they all enjoyed. After a late supper of soup and warm bread, Wensleydale cheese and apples they staggered, replete in body and heart to bed. Freda said, 'Your mother used to lie awake waiting for Santa Claus – I hope you won't have indigestion – it was all home-made – I know it's not fashionable any more to enjoy sweet things and pastries.'

Rachel hugged her grandmother. 'I liked it all better than a French Christmas,' she said, to please her. And it was true. She wanted to go to bed now and 'wait for Christmas', not stay up late for a Christmas log and champagne. Doubtless there would be champagne tomorrow anyway. She was being spoilt.

In bed she lay awake for a time but her thoughts were for the future, for a time when perhaps she would entertain a family of her own at this season. I love you, Paul, was her last thought as she fell asleep.

On Christmas Day, after the traditional dinner, and a brisk walk in the local park with Jacob, she helped Mrs Forsyth wash up.

'You ought to have a dishwasher,' Jacob could not resist suggesting.

'We don't need that for two people!' replied Freda. She was waiting for a telephone call from Marcus in the States which came at five o'clock, after which they all opened their presents. Rachel gave Mrs Forsyth a bottle of Chanel no. 5 and then waited for Freda and her uncle Jacob to open her presents to them.

Two large flat packages were waiting under the tree, which she had suggested they open last. It was her grandmother's turn to open hers.

'Why, it's the valley near Moon Woods!' she exclaimed in surprise. 'However did you find this?' The painting was a watercolour, trees crowding the steep banks on either side with their delicate green tracery, the eye led to the centre of the picture where a whisky-coloured stream splashed between stones of all shapes and colours.

Jacob was now opening his own parcel, a picture of a town in a valley seen from a distance across fields and the roofs of nearer houses. In the valley thin chimneys rose empty of smoke, under a rolling sky. 'It's Brigford!' he exclaimed. 'There's my father's mill – Look! It reminds me of a painting I saw before the war – but then the chimneys were smoking.'

They both looked at Rachel. She had been waiting for this moment and now it had come she felt nervous. 'Look at the signature,' she said quietly, a slight wobble in her voice.

'Paul Stainton,' said Jacob. 'Yours too, Mother?'

'This is *beautiful*, Rachel – wherever did you come across it?' – Mrs Forsyth was leaning over her employer the better to see Freda's painting.

'Look there's a butterfly on the stone in the corner,' she said.

Rachel cleared her throat, 'You told me one of Mr Stainton's grandsons was an artist,' she said, addressing Freda. 'But I already knew, you see. We met in London – quite by chance.'

Now came the hard part. Freda said, 'How extraordinary.'

'It was true he was married,' Rachel went on. 'But he didn't leave his wife. She left him. Paul and I love each other. He's asked me to marry him when his divorce is through!'

Jacob was staring at her, mouth open in astonishment. Freda said, 'Valentine's son? – but how long have you known him, dear?'

'Only for three or four months – long enough to fall in love,' said Rachel and suddenly she was in her grandmother's arms and Freda was holding her tightly.

'I couldn't tell you any other way,' she whispered. 'This is my Christmas surprise. He wants to come round to see you, Gran. Tomorrow. If you'll forgive me for inviting him before I asked you?'

She looked up. Jacob had not moved, but a complicated mixture of emotions succeeded each other on his face – surprise, anxiety – and maybe a little chagrin.

Finally – 'I'd like to meet him,' he said. 'I trust your judgment.'

'Oh, darling,' said Freda, 'is it really true – he wants to marry you?'

'His divorce is through next month,' said Rachel. 'I hope to persuade him to return to the North to work. He only left because his wife was making things hard for him. Her rather ancient boyfriend is a professor but Paul doesn't think he will marry Melanie. Paul said, wait to tell you – but I couldn't, I really couldn't! Are you angry with me? I hope you're not, Uncle Jacob, I wanted to tell you too face to face, not in a letter.'

'Is your mind made up then?' This from Freda.

'Absolutely. I want to live up here. Uncle Jacob knows I'm not going to stay in Castons Computers. I intend to teach French! I've an interview in Leeds next week. They want me to start after Easter, *if* I get the job.'

Jacob said, 'I wish you all the luck in the world, my dear – but I'd like to see your young man.'

'May I tell him you invite him, Grandma?'

'Of course,' Freda said quietly. 'Ring him up – we'll give you a little party tomorrow. How soon will you marry?'

'Paul says, the day after his divorce is through!' she replied. 'I know it sounds rash – but the divorce has nothing to do with me. He's been living alone for five years. There's a little boy whom I haven't yet seen. They're all at Laurel Bank for Christmas – Paul and his brother, and his mother and father up from Bournemouth. I'm invited to meet them on the 28th.' She sat down, a little breathless.

'Laurel Bank,' said Freda. She was thinking, James's house, after sixty years still in his family, and James's grandson in love with her granddaughter.

'Paul's present to me is a picture of the house – he said it was his grandfather's house –'

'Indeed it was,' said Freda.

'I gather you've acquainted him with our story?' Jacob asked quizzically.

'Some of it – he didn't know his father had another brother. We won't say anything to his parents unless you approve.'

'Well, Jacob,' said Freda. 'It was *you* who said you wished Val knew who you were!'

'Do you know him then?' Rachel asked Jacob.

'I used to work with him – after I left here – before the war. Do you think he'll want to know us? Perhaps Mother doesn't like the idea?'

He turned towards Freda. 'He sounds an old-fashioned young man, your Paul,' she said. 'Believes in marriage even after his first one failed!' She did not answer Jacob's question.

'Oh he's no more conventional than I am,' said Rachel gaily. 'But we so miss each other when we're apart – he's a painter but not all painters are rogues – in case you're worried!'

'Perhaps it was meant then – for the Staintons finally to find one of us?' murmured Freda. 'You'll have to forgive me, dear – it's a lot to take in. But I'm happy for you if you are happy. You *look* happy!'

A tall young man arrived alone at Holm Dene at five o'clock on Boxing Day. Rachel let him in. The others stayed tactfully out of sight.

'It's all right then –? I couldn't hear you very well yesterday – Harry was pretending to be a monster and Father was growling at him. Oh, let me look at you – it seems months since I did!'

'It was only on Tuesday,' she said. 'And today's Saturday!'

'Christmas is out of time,' he said. 'Did they like the pictures?'

'Very much. And now they want to see the artist.'

'Were they surprised?'

'Taken aback – but nice about it – don't say anything about –

the past – I mean unless Grandma does first?'

'Of course not. The soul of discretion.' She took his hand and together they went into the large drawing-room where Freda and Jacob were sitting round the fire, Freda pretending to read and Jacob scribbling busily on a pad on his knee. Paul thought it looked quite an ordinary domestic scene.

There was no need for Rachel to have worried about her grandmother's reception of her lover for when Freda looked up she saw a young James Stainton, the James she had been introduced to at a children's party long before the first war. Tall and fair, solid and smiling. Jacob helped her rise from her chair.

'Gran, this is Paul,' said Rachel.

'I know,' said Freda. 'He could not be anyone else.' And she took his arm and led him into the small sitting-room and showed him the photograph of his grandfather among the other schoolboys. Jacob had followed them.

'I'm sorry – this is Jacob Caston,' said Rachel – 'Uncle Jacob, this is Paul.'

'You're really *very* like your grandfather –' said Jacob. 'I worked with your father many years ago. I'm delighted to meet you.'

'Where shall I put the champagne?' enquired Mrs Forsyth plaintively from the door.

Freda took Paul's arm, 'Come back to the drawing-room, Paul, with me and we'll toast each other,' she said. Jacob looked over at his mother and thought, she looks suddenly twenty years younger. How she must have loved his father! He felt sad, out of it for a moment, no future for himself but work.

As they talked, Paul about his little son, Rachel about Paul's paintings, Freda looking from one to the other, Jacob reflected that the irony of it was that Paul and his father and brother probably lived at least partly on the money he'd repaid Stainton's years ago when his own business began to prosper. But there need be no mention of that. The young man seemed a little in awe of him. He supposed that even painters had heard of Castons Computers.

'And soon you must bring the little boy over,' Freda was saying.

Rachel looked at them, at Paul and Freda chatting away as if they were long acquaintances and at Jacob looking meditatively at them all. She thought, if I were a bystander looking at us, I might think, why does that young woman want to marry into a family that caused havoc to two people in this room? But a bystander could not see into feelings. Events had once overtaken her grandmother and her mother whereas she was acting freely. There was no child to think of, except Harry; no little Jacob or small Rachel. Harry might already have suffered, but she would do her best to make his life happy. She had not been under any compulsion to fall in love with the man who was even now laughing, possibly even flirting a little, with her handsome old grandmother. She had fallen in love with him at that party before she even knew his name, didn't want to 'escape' from anyone, only to run towards Paul. He could rely on her; she was an ordinary person who didn't want switchbacks and heights, would be content with a peaceful life in the English provinces because her earlier inner life had already been turbulent enough.

She said in a small voice – 'I do wish Mother were alive – to see us.' They all looked at her.

'My daughter,' Freda said gently with her hand on Paul's sleeve, 'She would have been happy, I think, to know that Rachel was going to stay in England – and had found someone to love her.'

'That's the plan,' said Paul. Rachel was thinking about weddings, remembering that early memory of her mother, married in a French town hall, respectable at last ... before she had discovered how irritable her French bridegroom was, though Philippe must have loved her enough to marry her? Would she and Paul ever quarrel? She couldn't imagine that. And she wasn't 'grateful' to Paul either for falling in love with her.

The child is going to be luckier than her mother, thought Freda. Poor Julia, she was not very lucky with men. Probably nobody was ever faithful to her for long ... except Jacob who is now looking at Julia's daughter as if he'd never seen her before. Sometimes she does look like her mother ...

Jacob thought, there's a glow about her when her young man is in the room – she is another person then. Is it only when we are in love that we feel we really know another person? When we wake from that dream of love do we revise our opinions, reject our old knowledge – or blame ourselves for our previous misapprehensions? Rachel has got the Stainton she wanted, unlike the others.

'Your fiancée is the granddaughter of a Caston,' he said aloud. 'You saw Rachel's great-grandfather on that photograph? I expect you know he was my grandfather, and that I am your father's half-brother?'

'Yes, indeed,' said Paul, looking a little apprehensive. What a mystery was erotic attraction, he'd been thinking. He could feel in the old lady some vestige of what had made his grandfather want her. He was not being fanciful.

'Let's drink to your professional success,' said Jacob. 'Since we've drunk to the other sort of future!'

Now, *he* was an unusual man, thought Paul. This Jacob, who had neither wife nor son nor daughter and had never had a proper father, was impressive, had the sort of face he'd like to paint. Not conventionally handsome perhaps, but strong features, sharp eyes. He tried to calculate how old he was.

'Will you tell your father?' asked Jacob. 'About us all?'

'If you allow me,' said Paul, feeling rather like a sixth former in the headmaster's study.

'You may,' said Freda.

'Certainly,' said Jacob Caston.

'Will you tell yours?' Jacob pursued, turning to Rachel.

'I shall certainly tell Papa', she said. 'He will be relieved I am not going to need anything more from him. As for Mr Maynard, Paul thinks we might one day go and see him – but there is no hurry.'

It was a highly unconventional scene, thought Jacob, under this family Christmas tree. Once these unusual preliminaries were over however, Rachel turned the conversation to France, Paul saying they would have a holiday there as soon as it was feasible. 'You will be welcome in Geneva,' said Jacob. 'A honeymoon perhaps?'

Rachel had the grace to blush and began to speak of introducing Paul to her old friends in Annecy. She hadn't mentioned to Freda that her Papa's lady friend, Anais Martin, his *petite amie*, had become his second wife. Strange that she intended to follow the same profession as that stepfather who had, when all was said and done, kept her for sixteen years. But her mother had also worked, as she herself intended to do and to go on doing ...

'You are welcome here whenever you want to come over,'

Freda said when Paul had to leave, saying 'Harry will be waiting for his bedtime story. May I bring him over to see you soon?'

'Will you tell them soon all about us?' Freda asked.

'I shall do so this evening,' said Paul. 'I feel sure there will be an invitation to Laurel Bank before the holiday is over. When do you return to Geneva, sir?' he asked Jacob Caston.

'On Tuesday,' replied Jacob, liking the politeness, which he thought unusual in young Englishmen.

'There will be time then on Monday.' They shook hands and Rachel went out to Paul's car with him.

'Thank God that's over,' she said. 'What do you think they really thought?'

'They are both most interesting people. Both good subjects for portraits! You'll find my family much more conventional. Still, you won't be marrying *them*.'

He kissed her at the gate. They'd be together in London soon, before Rachel discovered whether the job in Leeds after Easter would be hers. Till then there was everything to sort out, the divorce to finalize – and the small matter of the wedding, which they had both agreed would be a simple Registry Office affair. 'Sure the old lady wouldn't like a beano up here?' he had asked her, and she had answered, 'Rather not. She'll know we're already married in all but name! And we don't want to waste money.'

When she went back into the house the two of them were nowhere to be seen. She discovered them up in the attics where Freda was commanding her son to bring down a small attaché case in which she had remembered there was something she wanted to give her granddaughter.

'We're very happy for you,' Freda said at dinner. They had obviously been talking it over.

'I feel he's the right man for you,' said Jacob. 'I'll be gaining a new nephew – I've worked it out. As well as a new nephew-by-marriage.'

'You were the real link,' said Rachel, 'between Stainton's and the rest. If it hadn't been for you I shouldn't be in London and I wouldn't have met Paul!'

'Oh,' said Jacob carelessly. 'You'd have met him in any case!'

He said to her later that he thought she was wise to put off meeting her English father. 'If you ever do, you must take that man of yours with you. Maynard'll know then that you don't want anything from him.'

'It's true – I don't need him,' said Rachel. 'Will you be a witness at our wedding? In London.'

'That reminds me,' said Jacob. 'Your grandmother has something for you.'

Freda put a small box on the table which she withdrew from her handbag. 'Open it, darling.'

Rachel did so. Nestling in a bed of cotton wool was a thin slightly tarnished ring.

'It was what James gave me when we went away together,' said Freda simply. 'I want you to have it. I expect Paul will want to buy you a proper one as well.'

Rachel looked at it and then at Freda. 'It was only a cheap ring, the sort you could buy at a chain-store,' said her grandmother. 'But it signified love.'

'I shall have it always on my finger,' said Rachel. 'May I put it on now?'

'Let me see', said Jacob. He held the small loop in his palm.

'What a lot of life came from that,' he said lightly. Then he made a curious gesture as though he were kissing it, and handed it to Rachel.

Paul Stainton got his divorce in January 1982 and his ex-wife allowed him to have custody of Harry as long as she had access. She evinced surprise at his intention to remarry, but soon afterwards left her professor and went off with a colleague in public relations. Jacob Caston 'gave away' his niece at a small ceremony in February in Chelsea Register Office and then hurried back to Switzerland. After a holiday in the mountains of Savoy and a few days at Jacob's, Paul joined Rachel in Woolsford, where they rented a small terrace house. The post she had been interviewed for was hers, but in order for little Harry to be properly looked after they had to work out a complicated schedule. Paul would be at home painting so he could collect the child from school if Rachel took him in the mornings. It was a busy life, but full of hope. Rachel wanted Paul to depend on her, and he did. Harry was integrated after a few ups and downs into a stable family. Fortunately the child liked his stepmother from the start, but she was careful to give him time to be alone with his father.

Paul had returned to landscape painting with a commission from the Arts Council for a series of mixed media northern landscapes which were to establish his reputation even if they did not make his fortune. Two years after their marriage they bought an old house near Ilkley and Rachel commuted to work, later finding another post nearer home.

In 1984, a daughter, whom they named Amanda Freda, was born to them, and three years later a son, Roland Jacob. The twelve-year-old Harry was pleased to have both a sister and a brother. Grandfather Valentine Stainton and his wife Esmé visited whenever they came to stay in Eastcliff and also took to dropping in on Freda Osborn. It turned out that he had suspected some secret of his father's when that large amount of money arrived from Caston Computers in payment for a loan, but he had had no idea of the truth. He had never understood his father. They kept away from the subject of Evangeline, for Esmé had never liked her, and liked Freda very much.

Jacob Caston went on living in that Swiss city of nuclear research, refugees and international co-operation. But he went over every Christmas to England to his mother's, and to visit Julia's daughter and her husband.

Until his mother died he always stayed at Holm Dene where his visits were looked forward to by both the old lady and her companion. On his seventieth birthday Freda was still alive but she died later that same year at the age of ninety-four.

For over a hundred years the bond between the two families had held. Now it would go on into a new century in domestic form. Perhaps the union of Staintons and Castons had always been meant to lead to that right true end of love, found in the intimacy and tenderness of equals and involving the setting up of a home, the creation of new life, and a lifetime's companionship. Paul thanked his lucky stars he had been given a second chance and was as faithful to Rachel as she was to him.

So at last Staintons and Castons have come home together.

Who knows even so whether perhaps some young Freda somewhere is meeting some older James and beginning all over again, even in these enlightened times, to live through that mixture of heady passion followed by inevitable parting that will blight or fructify the histories of their descendants?